Peter Tremayne is the fiction pseudonym of a well-known authority on the ancient Celts, who utilises his knowledge of the Brehon law system and 7th-century Irish society to create a new concept in detective fiction.

Sister Fidelma made her first appearance in October 1993 when she appeared in no less than four short stories in different detective anthologies: 'Murder in Repose' (*Great Irish Detective Stories*, ed. Peter Haining), 'The High King's Sword' (*Chronicles of Historical Crime*, ed. Mike Ashley), 'Hemlock at Vespers' (*Midwinter Mysteries 3*, ed. Hilary Hale) and 'Murder by Miracle' (*New Constable Crime*, ed. Maxim Jakobowski). The first two Sister Fidelma mysteries, ABSOLUTION BY MURDER and SHROUD FOR THE ARCHBISHOP, are also available from Headline, and have received the following praise:

'The sister Fidelma stories take us into a world that only an author steeped in Celtic history could recreate so vividly – and one which no other crime novelist has explored before. Make way for a unique lady detective going where no one has gone before' Peter Haining

'The background detail is marvellous' *Evening Standard*

'Unputdownable' *Irish Democrat*

'Sister Fidelma . . . promises to be one of the most intriguing new characters in 1990s detective fiction' *Book & Magazine Collector*

'I believe I have a *tendresse* for Sister Fidelma. Ingeniously plotted . . . subtly paced . . . written with conviction, a feel for the time, and a chill air of period authenticity. A series to cultivate' Jack Adrian

Also by Peter Tremayne from Headline

Absolution By Murder
Shroud for the Archbishop
The Subtle Serpent
The Spider's Web
Valley of the Shadow

Suffer Little Children

Peter Tremayne

HEADLINE

First published in 1995
by HEADLINE BOOK PUBLISHING

First published in paperback in 1996
by HEADLINE BOOK PUBLISHING

10 9 8 7 6 5 4 3 2

ISBN 0 7472 4849 4

Printed and bound in Great Britain

HEADLINE BOOK PUBLISHING
A division of Hodder Headline PLC
338 Euston Road
London NW1 3BH

For my old and very good friend
Christopher Lowder –
thanks to Arnold Bennett
and *The Six Towns Magazine*

Suffer the little children to come unto me, and forbid them not . . .

– *Matthew*, 10:14

Fear them not therefore: for there is nothing concealed that shall not be revealed; and nothing hidden that shall not be known.

– *Matthew*, 10:26

HISTORICAL NOTE

The previous two Fidelma mysteries have been set in the year AD 664, firstly at the Synod of Whitby in Northumbria and secondly in the city of Rome. This is the first story which has placed her entirely in her own environment. Most readers will find seventh-century Ireland a very unfamiliar place. Its constituent five principal kingdoms, its petty kingdoms and clan areas with their place-names – and even most personal names – will be strange. Little known, too, will be the ancient Irish social system and its laws, the Laws of the Fénechus, more popularly known now as the Brehon Laws (from *breitheamh* = a judge). Yet this is Fidelma's world to which I hope the reader will be painlessly introduced.

To assist readers in geographical location, I have provided a sketch map. A list of principal characters is also given.

I have generally refused to use anachronistic names for obvious reasons although I have bowed to a few modern usages, e.g. Tara, rather than *Teamhair*; and Cashel, rather than *Caiseal Muman*; and Armagh in place of *Ard Macha*. However, I have cleaved to the name of Muman rather than the prolepsis form 'Munster' when the Norse *stadr* (place) was added to the Irish name Muman in the ninth century AD and eventually anglicised. Similarly, I have maintained the original Laigin, rather than the anglicised and prochronistic form of Laigin-*stadr* which is now Leinster.

Previous stories have demonstrated some of the differences between the Irish Church, which is now generally called the Celtic Church, and Rome. It has already been made clear that the concept of celibacy among the religious was not a popular one at this time. It must be remembered that in Fidelma's era religious houses frequently contained both sexes and they often married. Even abbots and bishops could and did marry at this period. The appreciation of that fact is essential to an understanding of Fidelma's world.

This story is placed in the year AD 665.

PRINCIPAL CHARACTERS

Sister Fidelma of Kildare, a *dálaigh* or advocate of the law courts of seventh-century Ireland
Cass, a member of the King of Cashel's bodyguard
Cathal, the dying King of Cashel
Colgú, the *tánaiste* or heir-apparent of Cashel, and Fidelma's brother

At Rae na Scríne
Intat, a *bó-aire* or local magistrate of the Corco Loígde
Sister Eisten, caring for orphans
Cétach and Cosrach, young brothers
Cera and Ciar, young sisters
Tressach, an orphan boy

At the abbey of Ros Ailithir
Abbot Brocc, a cousin of Fidelma
Brother Conghus, the *aistreóir* or doorkeeper
Brother Rumann, the *fer-tighis* or steward of the abbey
Brother Midach, the chief physician
Brother Tóla, the assistant physician
Brother Martan, the apothecary
Sister Grella, the librarian
Brother Ségán, the *fer-leginn* or chief professor
Sister Necht, a novice and assistant hostel keeper

Men of the Corco Loígde
Salbach, chieftain of the Corco Loígde
Scandlán, his cousin and petty king of Osraige
Ross, captain of a coastal *barc* or sailing vessel

Men of the kingdom of Laigin
The Venerable Dacán, the deceased
Fianamail, the king of Laigin
Forbassach, his Brehon or judge
Abbot Noé, brother of the Venerable Dacán; abbot of Fearna and advisor to Fianamail
Mugrón, captain of a Laigin warship
Midnat, a Laigin sailor
Assíd of the Uí Dego, a merchant and sea captain from Laigin

At Sceilig Mhichil
Father Mel, father superior of monastery of Sceilig Mhichil
Brother Febal, a monk

At Molua's House
Brother Molua, who runs an orphanage
Sister Aíbnat, his wife

At the Great Assembly
Sechnassach, the High King of Ireland
Barrán, the Chief Brehon of Ireland
Ultan, Archbishop of Armagh, Chief Apostle of the Faith

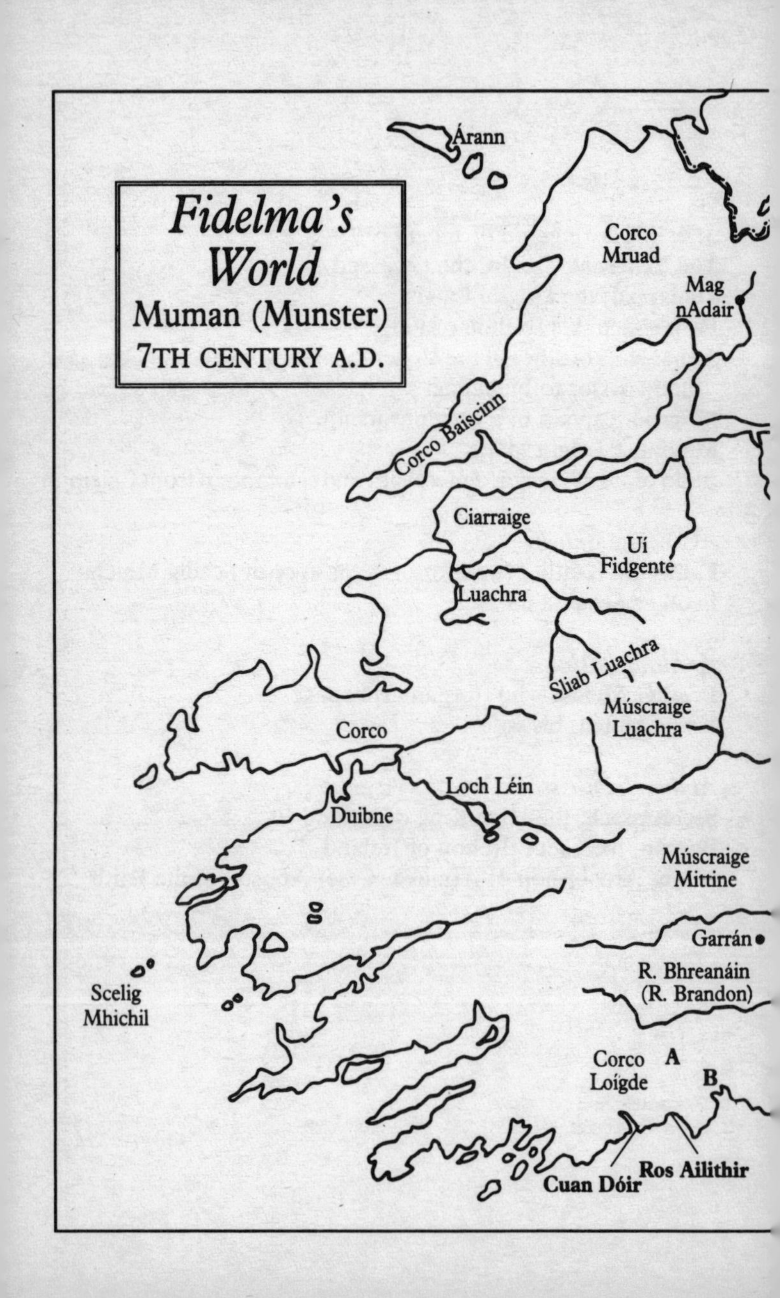

Fidelma's World
Muman (Munster)
7TH CENTURY A.D.
Árann
Corco Mruad
Mag nAdair
Corco Baiscinn
Ciarraige
Uí Fidgente
Luachra
Sliab Luachra
Múscraige Luachra
Corco
Loch Léin
Duibne
Múscraige Mittine
Garrán
R. Bhreanáin (R. Brandon)
Scelig Mhichil
Corco Loígde
A
B
Ros Ailithir
Cuan Dóir

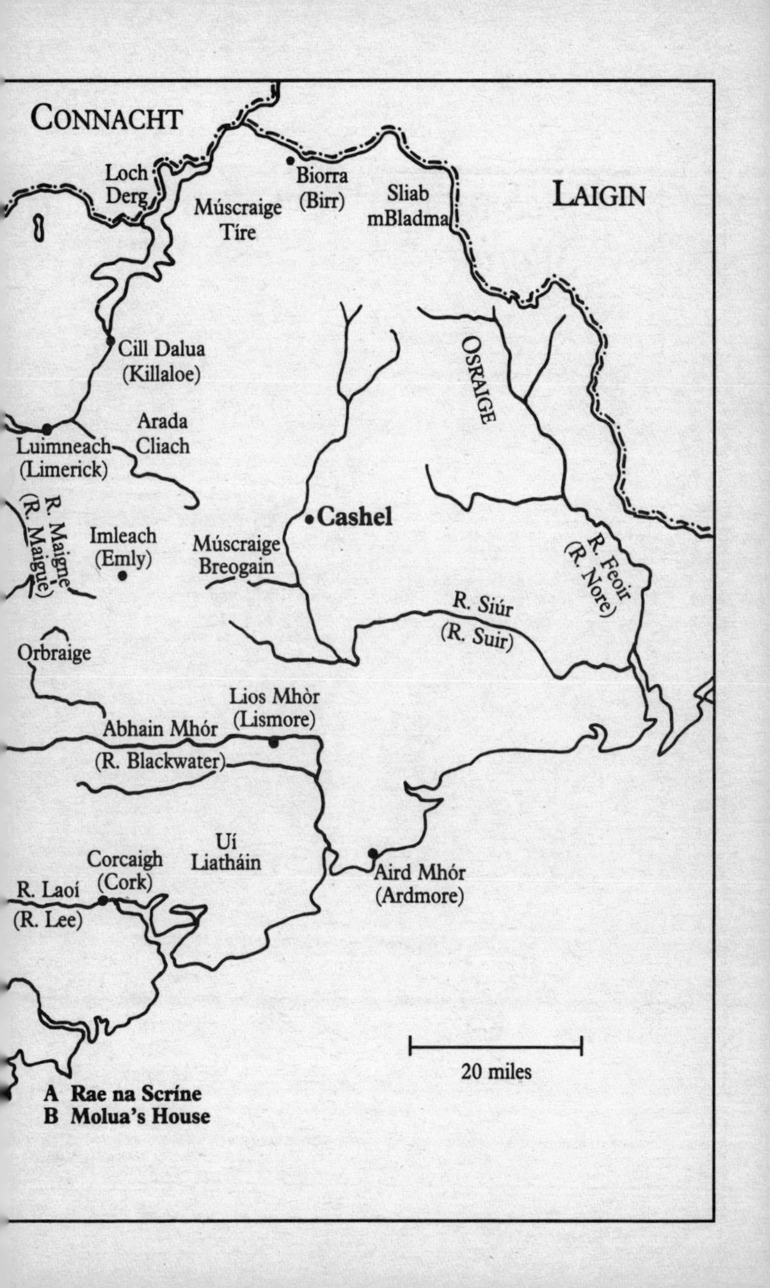
CONNACHT
LAIGIN
Loch Derg
Biorra (Birr)
Sliab mBladma
Múscraige Tíre
Cill Dalua (Killaloe)
OSRAIGE
Arada Cliach
Luimneach (Limerick)
R. Maigne (R. Maigue)
Imleach (Emly)
Múscraige Breogain
Cashel
R. Feoir (R. Nore)
R. Siúr (R. Suir)
Orbraige
Lios Mhòr (Lismore)
Abhain Mhór (R. Blackwater)
Uí Liatháin
Corcaigh (Cork)
R. Laoí (R. Lee)
Aird Mhór (Ardmore)
20 miles
A Rae na Scríne
B Molua's House

Chapter One

The storm broke with sudden violence. The white flash of lightning heralded a crash of angry thunder. A moment later the rain began to fall in heavy, icy droplets.

The horse and rider had just emerged from the shelter of a forest and halted on a ridge overlooking a broad, low level plain. The rider was a woman, clad in a long, brown woollen cloak and hood, thick and warm, wrapping her body against the late autumnal chill. She turned her gaze to the sky, unafraid of the frenzy of the tempest. The clouds were dark grey, rolling close to the ground and obscuring the distant mountain tops like a mist. Here and there, against this background, were patches of darker, scudding clouds, black and ominous, bringing the threatening thunder with them.

The woman blinked as the cold rain splattered against her face; it was chilly to the point of being painful. Her face was youthful, attractive without being pretty, and with rebellious strands of red hair streaking from under the hood of her cloak across her broad forehead. There was a faint hint of freckles on the pale skin. The eyes seemed momentarily grey, reflecting the colour of the sombre skies, yet when the lightning flashed there was a hint of green fire in them. She sat her horse with a youthful agility, her tall figure firmly in control of the restless animal. A closer examination would have revealed the silver crucifix hung around her neck and the habit of a religieuse hidden by the heavy riding cloak and hood.

Sister Fidelma, of the community of the Blessed Brigid of Kildare, had been expecting the approach of the storm for some hours now and was not surprised by its apparent sudden eruption. The signs had been there for a while. She had observed the closed pine cones on the trees, the withdrawn petals of the daisies and dandelions and the swelling stems of the meadow trefoil, as she rode along. All spoke of the coming rain to her keen, observing eye. Even the last of the swallows, preparing to disappear from the skies of Éireann for the winter months, had been keeping close to the ground; a sure indication of the tempest to come. If further indications were necessary, as she had been passing a woodsman's cabin, in the forest behind her, she had seen the smoke of the cabin fire descending instead of spiralling upwards; descending and causing small eddies around the building before dispersing into the cold air. Smoke behaving in such a manner, she knew from experience, was invariably an indication of rains to come.

She was fully prepared for the storm, though not its ferocity. As she halted a moment or two, she wondered whether to return into the forest and seek shelter there until the gusting rains had abated. But she was only a few miles from her destination and the urgency of the message she had received, to come with all speed, made her dig her heels into the sides of her horse and urge it forward down the track leading onto the great plain towards the distant hill that was just visible in spite of the driving rain and darkness of the sky.

This spectacular mound was her objective; a large outcrop of limestone rock rising over two hundred feet to dominate the plain in every direction. It rose in precipitous fashion and now and then the lightning would silhouette it. Fidelma found a constriction in her throat as she gazed on its familiar contours. She could see the fortified buildings which commanded the natural stronghold – Cashel, seat of the kings of Muman, the largest of the five kingdoms of Éireann. It was the place of her birth and her childhood.

As she rode forward, head bowed into the teeth of the wild, gusty wind, which drove the soaking rain at her, she felt a curious mixture of emotions. She felt an excited pleasure at the idea of seeing her brother, Colgú, after several years of absence but she also experienced anxiety as to why he should have sent her a message requesting her to leave her community at Kildare and hasten to Cashel as a matter of urgency.

All through her journey, questions assailed her mind, even though she could not possibly answer them. She had rebuked herself several times for wasting time and emotional energy on the matter. Fidelma had been raised in an old discipline. She found herself remembering the advice of her former master, the Brehon Morann of Tara: 'Do not place eggs on the table before you have visited the hen.' It was no use worrying about the answer to the problem before she knew the questions that she must ask.

Instead, she tried to clear her mind of such worries and sought refuge in the art of the *dercad*, the act of meditation, by which countless generations of Irish mystics had achieved the state of *sitcháin* or peace, calming extraneous thought and mental irritations. She was a regular practitioner of this ancient art in times of stress although some members of the Faith, such as Ultan, the archbishop of Armagh, denounced its usage as a pagan art because it had been practised by the Druids. Even the Blessed Patrick himself, a Briton who had been prominent in establishing the Faith in the five kingdoms two centuries before, had expressly forbade some of the meditative arts of self-enlightenment. However, the *dercad*, while frowned upon, was not yet forbidden. It was a means of relaxing and calming the riot of thoughts within a troubled mind.

In such fashion did her journey through the blustery rains, with the continuous crash of thunder and flashes of white lightning, draw Fidelma nearer to the fortress of the kings of Muman. She reached the edge of the township almost before she realised it.

Around the foot of the limestone outcrop, under the shadow of the fortress, a large market town had slowly arisen over the centuries. The day had now darkened considerably as the storm continued unabated. Fidelma reached the entrance of the town and began to guide her horse into the narrow streets. She could smell the pungent odour of turf fires and see, here and there, the dim light from numerous flickering lanterns. Suddenly, out of the dark shadows, a tall warrior, holding a lantern aloft in one hand, a spear loosely but professionally held in his shield hand, challenged her entrance.

'Who are you and what business have you here in Cashel?'

Sister Fidelma drew rein on her horse.

'I am Fidelma of Kildare,' she replied, her voice loud in order to be heard against the noise of the storm. Then she decided to correct herself. 'I am Fidelma, sister of Colgú.'

The warrior let out a low whistle and stiffened slightly.

'Pass in safety, lady. We were told to expect your coming.'

He withdrew back into the shadows to continue his uncomfortable task as a sentinel against the dangers of the night.

Fidelma guided her horse through the dark, narrow streets of the township. Her ears picked up the sound of occasional laughter and lively music coming from some of the buildings as she rode by. She crossed the town square and started towards the track which wound up to the top of the rocky hill. It had been occupied since time immemorial. Fidelma's ancestors, the Éoganachta, the sons of Eoghan, had settled there over three hundred years ago when they claimed the kingship of Muman for their own, making the rock into their political, and later ecclesiastical, centre.

Fidelma knew every inch of it for her father, Failbe Fland, had once been king of Cashel.

'Do not go further!' screeched a thin, reedy voice, rousing Fidelma abruptly from her revelry.

Fidelma halted sharply and stared down in surprise at the shapeless figure which had leapt out in front of her horse to bar the way. Only by the voice did Fidelma realise that the mess of furs and rags was a woman. The figure crouched, drenched by the rain and leaning heavily on a stick. Fidelma peered closely but could not discern the woman's features. That she was old was obvious but all was obscured save, by the lightning's illumination, the glimpse of white, rain-soaked hair, plastered to her face.

'Who are you?' demanded Fidelma.

'It matters not. Go no further, if you value life!'

Fidelma raised an eyebrow in surprise at this response.

'What threat do you make, old woman?' she commanded harshly.

'I make no threats, lady,' cackled the crone. 'I merely warn you. Death has settled in that grim palace yonder. Death will encompass all who go there. Leave this miserable place, if you value life!'

A sudden flash and roll of thunder momentarily distracted Fidelma as she tried to still her skittish mount. When she turned back, the old woman had disappeared. Fidelma compressed her lips and gave an inward shrug. Then she turned her horse along the track, up to the gates of the palace of the kings of Muman. Twice more she was challenged in her ascent and each time, at her reply, the warriors let her through with signs of respect.

A stable lad came running forward to take her horse as she finally slid from her mount in the stone-flagged courtyard, which was illuminated by oscillating lanterns, dancing with mysterious motions in the wind. Fidelma paused only to pet her horse on its muzzle and remove her leather saddle bag before striding hurriedly towards the main door of the building. It opened to receive her before she could knock upon it.

Inside she was in a large hall, warmed by a great roaring fire in a central hearth almost as big as a small room. The hall was filled with several people who turned to look at her and whisper among themselves. A servant came forward to take her bag and help her remove her travelling cloak. She shook the rain-sodden garment from her shoulders and hurried forward to warm herself at the fire. A second servant had, so the first told her, departed to inform her brother, Colgú, that she had arrived.

Of the people who stood about in the great hall of the palace, examining her drenched figure with curiosity, Fidelma saw no friendly familiar face. There was an air of studied solemnity in the hall. In fact, Fidelma caught a deeper air of melancholy about the place. Even an atmosphere of hostility. A dour-faced religious, standing with hands clasped as if in ostensive prayer, was standing to one side of the fire.

'God give you a good day, brother,' Fidelma greeted him with a smile, attempting to strike up a conversation. 'Why are there so many long faces in this place?'

The monk turned and stared hard at her, his face seeming to grow even more lugubrious.

'Surely you do not expect merry-making at such a time as this, sister?' he sniffed reprovingly and turned away before she could demand a further explanation.

Fidelma stood bewildered for a moment before glancing around in an attempt to find a more communicative soul.

She found a thin-faced man staring arrogantly at her. As she raised her eyes to meet his haughty examination, a chord of memory struck. Before she could articulate it, the man had walked across to her.

'So, Fidelma of Kildare,' his voice was brittle and without warmth, 'your brother, Colgú, has sent for you, has he?'

Fidelma was puzzled by his unfriendly tone but she responded with a smile of greeting as she identified the man.

'I recognise you as Forbassach, Brehon to the king of Laigin. What are you doing so far away from Fearna?'

The man did not return her smile.

'You have a good memory, Sister Fidelma. I have heard of your deeds at the court of Oswy of Northumbria and the service you performed in Rome. However, your talent will avail this kingdom naught. The judgment will not be impeded by your clever reputation.'

Fidelma found her smile of greeting frozen for a moment. It was as if she had been addressed in an unfamiliar language and she tried to prevent the look of incomprehension spreading on her features. Brehon Morann of Tara had warned that a good advocate should never let an adversary know what they were thinking and certainly Forbassach was indicating that, somehow, he was her adversary; though in what matter she could not begin to guess.

'I am sure, Forbassach of Fearna, that your statement is profound but I have no understanding of it,' she replied slowly, allowing her smile to relax a little.

Forbassach's face reddened.

'Are you being insolent with me, sister? You are Colgú's own sister and yet you pretend . . .'

'Your pardon, Forbassach.'

A quiet, masculine voice interrupted the tones of anger that were building in the voice of the Brehon.

Fidelma glanced up. At her side was a young man, about her own age. He was tall, nearly six feet in height, dressed in the manner of a warrior. He was cleanshaven, with dark, curly hair, and he seemed ruggedly handsome at first glance. His features were agreeable and attractive. She had no time for a more careful appraisal. She noticed that he wore a necklet of twisted gold, worked with ornate embellishments, which showed him to be a member of the Order of the Golden Collar, the élite bodyguards of the kings of Muman. He turned to her with a pleasant smile.

'Your pardon, Sister Fidelma. I am instructed to bid you welcome to Cashel and bring you to your brother at once. If you will be so good as to follow me . . . ?'

She hesitated but Forbassach had turned away scowling towards a small group who stood muttering and casting glances in her direction. Fidelma was perplexed. But she dismissed the matter and began to follow the young warrior across the paved hall, hurrying slightly to keep up with his leisurely but lengthy pace.

'I do not understand, warrior.' She gasped a little in her effort to keep level. 'What is Forbassach of Fearna doing here? What makes him so petulant?'

The warrior made a sound suspiciously like a disparaging sniff.

'Forbassach is an envoy from the new king of Laigin, young Fianamail.'

'It does not explain his disagreeable greeting nor does it explain why everyone is so mournful. Cashel used to be a palace filled with laughter.'

The warrior looked uncomfortable.

'Your brother will explain how matters stand, sister.'

He reached a door but before he could raise his hand to knock it was flung open.

'Fidelma!'

A young man came hurrying forward through the doorway. It was obvious to even the most cursory examination that he and Fidelma were related. They shared the same tallness of build, the same red hair and changeable green eyes; the same facial structure and indefinable quality of movement.

Brother and sister embraced with warmth. They broke apart breathlessly and held each other at arm's length, critically examining one another.

'The years have been good to you, Fidelma,' observed Colgú with satisfaction.

'And to you, brother. I was anxious when I received your message. It has been many years since I was last in Cashel. I feared some mishap might have befallen you. Yet you look hale and hearty. But those people in the great hall, why are they so grim and melancholy?'

Colgú mac Failbe Fland drew his sister inside the room, turning to the tall warrior: 'I will send for you later, Cass,' he said, before following Fidelma into the chamber. It was a reception room with a fire smouldering in a corner. A servant came forward bearing a tray on which were two goblets of mulled wine; the heat from them was causing little wisps of steam to rise from the hot liquid. Having placed the tray on a table, the servant unobtrusively withdrew while Colgú motioned Fidelma to a chair in front of the fire.

'Warm yourself after your long journey from Kildare,' Colgú instructed, as the thunder still rumbled outside. 'The day is still angry with itself,' he observed, taking one of the goblets of mulled wine and handing it to his sister.

Fidelma grinned mischievously as she took the goblet and raised it.

'Indeed, it is. But let us drink to better days to come.'

'An "amen" to that, little sister,' agreed Colgú.

Fidelma sipped the wine appreciatively.

'There is much to talk of, brother,' she said. 'Much has happened since we last set eyes on one another. Indeed, I have journeyed to many places: to the island of Colmcille, to the land of the Saxons and even to Rome itself.' She paused, as she suddenly noticed that there was some quality of pensiveness and anxiety in his eyes. 'But you have yet to answer my question. Why is there this air of melancholy in the palace?'

She saw a frown pass across her brother's brow and paused.

'You always did have acute observation, little sister,' he sighed.

'What is it, Colgú?'

Colgú hesitated a moment and then grimaced.

'I am afraid that it was not for a family reunion that you were asked here,' he confessed gently.

Fidelma gazed at him, waiting for her brother to elaborate. When he did not, she said quietly: 'I had not expected that it was. What is the matter?'

Colgú glanced almost surreptitiously around, as if to make sure that no one was eavesdropping.

'The king . . .' he began. 'King Cathal has succumbed to the Yellow Plague. He is lying in his chamber at death's door. The physicians do not give him long.'

Fidelma blinked; yet, deep down, she was not entirely surprised at the news. For two years now the Yellow Plague had spread itself across Europe, devastating the population. Tens of thousands had died from its virulence. It had spared neither lowly peasant, self-satisfied bishop, nor even lofty kings. Only eighteen months ago, when the plague had first arrived in Éireann, the joint High Kings of Ireland, Blathmac and Diarmuid, had both died within days of one another at Tara. A few months ago, Fáelán, the king of Laigin, had died from its ravages. Still the plague raged on unabated. Throughout the land were countless orphaned children, whose mothers and fathers had been carried off by the plague, left helpless and starving. Some members of the Faith, such as the Abbot Ultan of Ardbraccan, had responded by setting up orphanages and fighting the plague, while others, such as Colmán, the chief professor of the Blessed Finnbarr's college in Cork, had simply taken his fifty pupils and fled to some remote island in an attempt to escape it. Fidelma was well aware of the scourge of the Yellow Plague.

'Is that why you sent for me?' she asked. 'Because our cousin is dying?'

Colgú shook his head swiftly.

'King Cathal instructed me to send for you before he succumbed to the fevers of plague. Now that he cannot instruct you, it falls to me to do so.'

He reached across and took her by the elbow. 'But first you must rest from your journey. There is time enough for this later. Come, I have ordered your old room to be prepared.'

Fidelma tried to suppress her sigh of impatience.

'You know me well enough, brother. You know that I will not rest while there is a mystery to be explained. You keep goading my imagination. Come, explain what this mystery is and then I will rest.'

Colgú was about to speak when there came the sound of raised voices beyond the door. There was the noise of a scuffle and Colgú was moving towards the door to enquire what was happening when it burst open and Forbassach of Fearna stood framed in it. He was red-faced and breathing heavily with exertion.

Behind him, his handsome face scowling in anger, was the young warrior, Cass.

'Forgive me, my lord. I could not stop him.'

Colgú stood facing the envoy of the king of Laigin with displeasure on his face.

'What does this demonstration of bad manners mean, Forbassach? Surely you forget yourself?'

Forbassach thrust out his chin. His arrogant and contemptuous manner did not desert him.

'I need an answer to take back to Fianamail, the king of Laigin. Your king is on the verge on death, Colgú. Therefore it is up to you to answer the charges of Laigin.'

Fidelma set her face into an immobile expression to disguise her frustration that she did not comprehend the meaning of this confrontation.

Colgú had flushed with anger.

'Cathal of Muman still lives, Forbassach. While he lives, his is the voice to answer your charge. Now, you have breached the hospitality of this court. As *tánaiste* I demand your withdrawal from this place. When the court of Cashel needs to communicate with you then you will be summoned to hear its voice.'

Forbassach's thin lips twisted into a condescending sneer.

'I know that you merely seek to delay the answer, Colgú. As soon as I saw the arrival of your sister, Fidelma of Kildare, I realised that you will seek to delay and prevaricate. It will avail you nothing. Laigin still demands an answer. Laigin demands justice!'

Colgú's facial muscles worked in an effort to control his anger.

'Fidelma, instruct me in law.' He addressed his sister without taking his eyes from Forbassach. 'This envoy from Laigin has, I believe, overstepped the bounds of sacred hospitality. He has intruded where he should not and has been insulting. May I order him to be removed physically from this court?'

Fidelma glanced at the disdainful Brehon of Fearna.

'Do you make an apology for an unwarranted intrusion into a private chamber, Forbassach?' she asked. 'And do you make an apology for your insulting manner to the heir-apparent of Cashel?'

Forbassach's chin jerked up, his scowl deepening.

'Not I.'

'Then you, as a Brehon, should know the law. You will be thrown out of this court.'

Colgú glanced at the warrior called Cass and gave an imperceptible nod.

The tall man laid a hand on Forbassach's shoulder.

The Laigin envoy twisted in the grip and his face reddened.

'Fianamail of Laigin shall hear of this insult, Colgú. It will serve to compound your guilt when you are judged before the High King's assembly at Tara!'

The warrior had spun the Laigin envoy on his heel and propelled him through the doorway without any apparent display of undue force. Then, with an apologetic gesture to Colgú, he shut it behind them.

Fidelma, turning to her brother, who had now relaxed from his stiff posture, showed her bewilderment.

'I think that it is about time that you told me what is really happening. What is the mystery here?' she demanded with quiet authority.

Chapter Two

Colgú looked as if he were about to delay once more but seeing the light in his young sister's eyes he thought the better of it.

'Very well,' he replied. 'But let us go where we may speak more freely and without the danger of any further interruptions. There are many ears attached to heads which may harbour ill-will to the kings of Muman.'

Fidelma raised an eyebrow in surprise but made no further comment. She knew that her brother had never been one for exaggeration so she did not press him further. He would explain in his own time.

She followed him from the room without speaking and through the stone-walled palace corridors with their rich tapestries and spectacular artifacts gathered over the centuries by the Eóganacht kings. Colgú led her through a great room which she recognised as the Tech Screptra, the *scriptorium* or library, of the palace, where, as a small girl, she had learnt to read and form her first letters. As well as the impressive illustrated vellum texts, the Tech Screptra held some of the ancient books of Muman. Among them were the 'rods of the poets', wands of aspen and hazel wood on which the ancient scribes had carved their sagas, poems and histories in Ogham, the ancient alphabet, which was still used in some parts of Muman. In that Tech Screptra the little girl's imagination and thirst for knowledge had been awakened.

Fidelma paused briefly, feeling a little overwhelmed by

nostalgia, and smiling at her memories. Several brothers of the Faith were seated there poring over those same books by the light of smoking tallow candles.

She realised that Colgú was waiting impatiently for her.

'I see you still open the library to scholars of the church,' she said approvingly as she joined him and they moved on. The great library of Cashel was the personal property of the kings of Muman.

'It will not be otherwise while we are of the Faith,' Colgú replied firmly.

'Yet I have heard some stories that certain narrow-minded members of the Faith have been burning the ancient texts, the "rods of the poets", on the grounds that they were written by idolatrous pagans. In Cashel, there are many such books. Do you still preserve them from such intolerance?'

'Surely intolerance is incompatible with the Faith, little sister?' Colgú observed wryly.

'I would say so. Others might not. I am told that Colmán of Cork has suggested that all pagan books should be destroyed. Yet I say that we have a duty to ensure that the treasures of our people are not incinerated and lost because of fashionable intolerance.'

Colgú chuckled dryly.

'The matter is academic anyway. Colmán of Cork has fled this kingdom for fear of the plague. His voice no longer counts.'

Colgú continued to lead the way beyond the Tech Screptra and through the tiny family chapel. There were many stories handed down in Fidelma's family of how the Blessed Patrick himself had arrived at Cashel and had proceeded to convert their ancestor, King Conall Corc, to the new Faith. One story told how he had used the meadow trefoil, the *seamróg*, to demonstrate the idea of the Holy Trinity to Conall. Not that it was a difficult concept to understand, for all the pagan gods of ancient Ireland were triune gods, being three personalities in the one god. Fidelma had always carried a sense of time and place with her.

They passed beyond the chapel to the private chambers of the family and their immediate retinue, which were placed beyond the more generally accessible reception rooms.

A chamber had been prepared for her, with a newly lit fire blazing in the hearth. It was the very room in which she had been born and where she had spent the early years of her life. It had hardly changed.

Before the fire, a table had been set with food and wine.

Colgú waved his sister to a chair.

'Let us eat, and as we eat I will attempt to explain why King Cathal called you hither.'

Fidelma did as he bid her. She realised that her journey had been long and uncomfortable and that she was ravenous.

'Are you sure our cousin is too ill to see me?' she queried, still hesitating before the meal. 'I do not fear the Yellow Plague. These last two years I have crossed its path in safety many times. And if I do succumb, well, then surely it will be God's will.'

Colgú shook his head despondently.

'Cathal is no longer in a state to even recognise me. His physician says he may not last this night. In fact, the arrogant Forbassach of Laigin was right. It is now my duty to reply to his demands.'

Fidelma compressed her lips as she realised what that meant.

'If Cathal dies this night then you will be . . . ?'

She paused, realising that it was improper to voice the thought while their elderly cousin was alive.

Colgú, however, finished the sentence for her with a bitter laugh.

'That I shall then be king of Muman? Yes, that is exactly what it means.'

The Eóganacht kings, like all Irish kings and chieftains,

were elected into office by the *derbfhine* of their families. On the death of a king, his family, that is the living descendants of the male line of a common great-grandfather, called the *derbfhine*, would gather in assembly and vote for one among them who would next take the throne. Sons did not necessarily, therefore, inherit from fathers. Failbe Fland, the father of Colgú and Fidelma, had been king in Cashel. He had died twenty-six years before, when Fidelma and Colgú were only a few years old. Even to be considered for any office in the land, a candidate had at least to be at the 'age of choice', which was fourteen years for a girl and seventeen years for a boy. Failbe Fland's cousins had succeeded him in office until Cathal mac Cathail had been chosen as king of Muman three years before.

It was the custom and law to also elect the heir-apparent, or the *tánaiste*, during a king's lifetime. When Cathal had become king of Cashel, Fidelma's brother, Colgú, had been chosen as his *tánaiste*.

So now if Cathal died, Fidelma realised suddenly, her brother would be king of Muman, the biggest of the five kingdoms of Éireann.

'It will be a heavy responsibility, brother,' she said, reaching forward and laying a hand on his arm.

He sighed and nodded slowly.

'Yes; even in good times there would be many weighty responsibilities with this office. But these are bad times, Fidelma. There are many problems facing the kingdom. None more so than the problem that arose a few days ago and why, when he was not so ill, Cathal chose to send for you.' He paused and shrugged. 'Since you have been away from here, little sister, your reputation as a Brehon, an advocate of the courts and a solver of mysteries, has spread. We have heard how you have performed services for the High King, the King of Northumbria and even the Holy Father in Rome.'

Fidelma made a deprecating gesture.

'I was in those places at the time when my talent was

needed,' she replied. 'Anyone with a logical mind could have resolved the problems. There was nothing more to those problems than that.'

Colgú smiled quickly at her.

'You were never given to conceit, my sister.'

'Show me a conceited person and I will show you a mediocre talent. Which does not get us any nearer the reason that I was sent for. What does this have to do with Forbassach of Fearna?'

'Let me tell you in my own way. King Cathal believed that you could resolve a mystery which has threatened the safety of the kingdom. Indeed, it threatens the peace of the five kingdoms of Éireann.'

'What mystery?' prompted Fidelma as she started to help herself to some of the food that had been prepared.

'Have you heard of the Venerable Dacán?'

Fidelma allowed an eyebrow to raise slightly as she recognised the name.

'Who has not?' she replied quickly. 'He is already spoken of in some quarters as a saint. He is a teacher and theologian of no mean ability. Of course, his brother is the Abbot Noé of Fearna, the king of Laigin's personal advisor and supposedly as saintly as his brother. Both brothers are widely respected and beloved of many. Stories are told of their wisdom and charity in many corners of the five kingdoms.'

Colgú nodded his head slowly at Fidelma's glowing recital. His face assumed a weary expression as though he did not like what he was hearing but expected no less.

'You know, of course, that there has been some enmity recently between the kingdoms of Muman and Laigin?'

'I have heard that since the old king, Fáelán, died of the plague a few months ago, the new king, Fianamail, has been examining ways of enhancing his prestige by trying to pick quarrels with Muman,' she agreed.

'And what better way to enhance his prestige than to find an excuse to demand the return of the petty kingdom of Osraige from Muman?' Colgú asked bitterly.

Fidelma formed her lips in a soundless whistle of astonishment.

Osraige was a small kingdom which had long been a source of bad relationships between the two major kingdoms of Muman and Laigin. It stretched along the banks of the River Feoir from north to south. Hundreds of years before, when the kings of Muman held the High Kingship over all five kingdoms of Éireann, Osraige was under the tutelage of the kings of Laigin. When Edirsceál of Muman became High King, the men of Laigin contrived to assassinate him so that Nuada Necht of Laigin could assume the kingship. The king was murdered but the culprits discovered. Conaire Mór, the son of Edirsceál, eventually became High King and he and his Brehons met to agree what honour price the kingdom of Laigin should pay in compensation to Muman for their infamous act. It had been decided that the kingdom of Osraige should be forfeited by Laigin. Henceforth, Osraige would be part of the kingdom of Muman and its petty-kings would pay tribute to Cashel and not to Fearna, the capital of Laigin.

Now and again the kings of Laigin would raise a protest before the High Kings, requesting the return of Osraige to them. But six centuries had passed since the days of Conaire Mór when Osraige had passed to Muman. Each protest had been rejected by the Great Assembly of the Brehons of Éireann, who met every three years at the royal palace of Tara. The punishment and compensation were confirmed as being just.

Fidelma brought her gaze back to the worried face of her brother.

'Surely even Fianamail, as young and inexperienced a king as he is, would not consider attempting to wrest Osraige back by force?'

Her brother gave an affirmative gesture.

'Not by force alone, Fidelma,' he agreed. 'Do you know something of the internal politics of Osraige?'

Fidelma knew little of the kingdom and admitted as much.

'For reasons too long and complicated to explain now, nearly two hundred years ago the native kings of Osraige were replaced by a family from the Corco Loígde in the south-west of the kingdom. There has been friction in Osraige ever since. The Corco Loígde are not popular. Now and then, the Osraige have risen up to displace them. Less than a year ago, Illan, the last descendant of the native kings of Osraige with a legal claim to the kingship, was killed by the current king, Scandlán. Needless to say, Scandlán is of the Corco Loígde ruling family.'

Colgú paused a moment to gather his thoughts before proceeding.

'There is talk of an heir to Illan. Rumour has it that this heir, if he exists, would be happy to court Laigin if Laigin promised to help him dislodge the Corco Loígde as kings.'

'It would still mean a war between Laigin and Muman with Laigin having to wrest Osraige back by force,' Fidelma pointed out.

Her brother leant forward with an unhappy expression on his features.

'But what if some deed occurred, similar to the very deed that caused Osraige to be forfeited from Laigin in the first place?'

Fidelma sat straighter-backed now, her muscles suddenly tensed. Colgú's expression was grim.

'You have confirmed that you know how the Venerable Dacán of Laigin was held in the eyes of many people. He was a saintly and revered man. And you have confirmed that you know how his brother, Noé of Fearna, stands in similar regard within the sight of both his king, Fianamail, and the people of the five kingdoms.'

Fidelma caught the use of the past tense but made no reply.

She had, indeed, admitted that both men were highly respected throughout the land.

'Two months ago,' went on Colgú in a troubled voice, 'the Venerable Dacán arrived at Cashel and sought the blessing of King Cathal to work within this kingdom. Dacán had heard of the work being done at the Blessed Fachtna's abbey at Ros Ailithir and wanted to join the community there. Of course, King Cathal welcomed such a learned and esteemed scholar as Dacán to the kingdom.'

'So Dacán set off to Ros Ailithir?' intervened Fidelma when Colgú paused.

'Eight days ago we heard news that the Venerable Dacán had been murdered in his cell at the abbey.'

Fidelma realised that, even when death had become so common-place due to the ravages of the Yellow Plague, the death of the Venerable Dacán would have a resounding impact on all the five kingdoms, and more so especially due to the fact that the death was attributable to violence.

'Are you telling me that you think the new king of Laigin, Fianamail, will use this death to demand the territory of Osraige be returned to his jurisdiction as a compensation?'

Colgú's shoulders hunched momentarily.

'I not only think so, I know it to be so. It was only yesterday that Forbassach of Fearna arrived here as an envoy from Fianamail, the king of Laigin.'

Fearna was the seat of the kings of Laigin as well as the site of Noé's abbey.

'How can the news have reached them so quickly?' demanded Fidelma.

Colgú spread his hands.

'I suppose that someone rode from Ros Ailithir immediately to tell Dacán's brother, Noé, at Fearna.'

'Logical,' Fidelma agreed. 'And what does the arrogant Forbassach have to say on this matter?'

'The envoy from Fianamail was quite explicit in his demands.

Not only must the *éric* fine be paid but an honour price which entails the handing of all suzerain rights over Osraige to Laigin. If this is not done then Fianamail of Laigin will claim it by blood. You know the law better than I do, Fidelma, Are they within their rights to make such claims? I think they are, for Forbassach is no fool.'

Fidelma pursued her lips thoughtfully.

'Our law system grants the right for a killer to atone for his or her crime by payment of compensation. There is a fixed penalty, the *éric* fine, as you rightly say. This amounts to seven *cumals*, the value of twenty-one milch cows. But, often, when the victim is a man or woman of rank and influence, then the victim's kinsmen are within their rights to claim an honour price, the *lóg n-enech*. That was, in fact, the law by which Conaire Mór claimed Osraige for Muman in the first instance. If the culprit is unable to pay this honour price then their kinsmen are expected to pay it. If this is not forthcoming then the victim's kinsmen are allowed to commence a blood feud, or *dígal*, to obtain the honour price. But this does not mean that the Laigin king is entitled to do so. There are a couple of questions that need to be resolved.'

'Advise me, Fidelma,' invited Colgú, leaning forward eagerly.

'What right does Fianamail have in this matter? Only kinship allows a person to name and demand an honour price.'

'Fianamail is cousin to Dacán and speaks as kin. In this, of course, he supported by Noé, the brother of Dacán.'

Fidelma allowed herself a deep sigh.

'That certainly allows Fianamail to press his claim. But does Abbot Noé actually support him in his demands? Such demands must surely lead to an effusion of blood. Noé is a leading advocate of the Faith and beloved and respected for his conciliatory teachings, for his acts of forgiveness. How can he demand such vengeance?'

Colgú grimaced dispassionately.

'Dacán was, above all things, Noé's brother,' he pointed out.

'Even so, I find it hard to believe Noé would act in such a manner.'

'Well, he has. But you implied that there might be other reasons why Laigin could not inflict an honour-price fine on Muman. What more?'

'The most obvious question devolves on the fact that the fines can only be inflicted on the family of the person who was responsible for Dacán's death. Who killed Dacán? Only if a member of our family, the Eóganachta, as representing the kingship of Muman, is responsible, can Laigin claim an honour price from Muman.'

Colgú gestured helplessly.

'We don't know who killed Dacán, but the abbey of Ros Ailithir is governed by our cousin, Brocc. He is charged, as abbot, as being responsible for Dacán's death.'

Fidelma blinked to conceal her surprise. She had vague memories of an elder cousin who had been a distant and unfriendly figure to her brother and herself.

'What makes the king of Laigin charge our cousin with accountability for the death of Dacán? Is it simply because he is responsible for the safety of all who reside at his abbey or is something more sinister implied?'

'I don't know,' confessed her brother. 'But I do not think that even Fianamail of Laigin would make so light an accusation.'

'Have there been any steps to find out?'

'The envoy from Fianamail has simply stated that all evidence and arguments will be placed before the High King and his Chief Brehon at the great assembly at Tara. The assembly will be asked to support Laigin and hand over Osraige to Fianamail.'

Fidelma bit her lip as she thought for a moment.

'How can Fianamail be so sure that he can prove that Dacán's death is the responsibility of Muman? Forbassach, his envoy, is a vain and arrogant man, but he is an *ollamh* of the court. Even his friendship with the Laigin king, his pride in being a man of Laigin, would not blind him to the law. He must know that the evidence is strong enough to lay a claim before the High King's court. What is that evidence?'

Colgú had no answer. Instead he said quietly: 'Fidelma, the assembly of Tara is due to meet in three weeks. That does not leave us much time to resolve this matter.'

'The law also allows one month from the decision of the assembly before Fianamail can march an army into Osraige to claim the land by force if it is not handed over in peace,' observed Fidelma.

'So we have seven weeks before there is bloodshed and war in this land?'

Fidelma drew her brows together.

'Providing, that is, judgment goes to Laigin. There is much mystery here, Colgú. Unless Fianamail knows something that we do not, I cannot see how the High King and his assembly could give a judgment against Muman.'

Colgú poured another two glasses of wine and handed one across to his sister with a tired smile.

'These were the very words of Cathal, our cousin, before he succumbed to the fever. It was the reason why he asked me to send for you. The morning after the messenger had been sent to Kildare, he fell a victim to the Yellow Fever. And if the physicians are right, I shall be king before this week is out. If there is war, then it will be on my hands.'

'It will not be a good start to your rule, brother,' agreed Fidelma as she sipped at her wine and considered the matter carefully. Then she raised her eyes to examine her brother's careworn face. 'Are you giving me a commission to investigate the death of Dacán and then present the evidence to you?'

'And to the High King,' added Colgú quickly. 'You will

have the authority of Muman to carry out this investigation. I ask you to be our advocate before the High King's assembly.'

Fidelma was silent for a long while.

'Tell me this, my brother; suppose my findings are such as to support the king of Laigin? What if Dacán's death is the responsibility of the Eóganachta? What if the king of Laigin does have the right to demand Osraige as an honour price from Cashel? What if these unpalatable arguments become my findings? Will you accept that judgment under law and meet Laigin's demand?'

Her brother's face worked with complex emotions as he wrestled with the decision.

'If you want me to speak for myself, Fidelma, I shall say "yes". A king must live by the law established. But a king must pursue the commonwealth of his people. Do we not have an old saying? – what makes the people higher than a king? It is because the people ordain the king, the king does not ordain the people. A king must obey the will of his people. So do not ask me to speak for all the princes and chieftains of this kingdom nor, indeed, of Osraige. I fear they will not accept liability for such an honour price.'

Fidelma regarded him with a level gaze.

'Then it will mean bloody war,' she said softly.

Colgú attempted a grim smile.

'Yet we have three weeks before the assembly, Fidelma. And, as you say, seven weeks before the implementation of the law if the decision goes against us. Will you go to Ros Ailithir and investigate Dacán's death?'

'You do not have to ask that, Colgú. I am, above all things, still your sister.'

Colgú's shoulders sagged in relief and he gave a long, low sigh.

Fidelma laid a hand on his arm and patted it.

'But do not expect too much of me, brother. Ros Ailithir is a minimum three days' journey from here, and lies through some harsh country. You expect me to travel there, solve a mystery and travel back in time to prepare a case for the assembly at Tara? If so, you are, indeed, asking for a miracle.'

Colgú inclined his head in agreement.

'I think that King Cathal and myself both demand a miracle of you, Fidelma, for when men and women use their courage, intelligence and learning, then they are capable of inspiring a true miracle.'

'It is still a heavy responsibility you place on me,' she admitted with reluctance. She realised that she had no other decision to make. 'I will do what I can. I shall rest in Cashel tonight and hope this storm abates by tomorrow. I shall set out at first light for the abbey of Ros Ailithir.'

Colgú smiled warmly.

'And you will not set out alone, little sister. The journey to the south-west is, as you say, a harsh one, and who knows what dangers will await you at Ros Ailithir? I shall send one of my warriors with you.'

Fidelma shrugged diffidently.

'I am able to defend myself. You forget that I have studied the art of *troid-sciathagid*, battle through defence.'

'How can I forget that?' chuckled Colgú, 'for many is the time that you have bested me in our youth with your knowledge of unarmed combat. But combat in friendship is one thing, Fidelma. Combat in earnest is another.'

'You do not have to point this out, brother. Many of our religious missionaries going into the kingdoms of the Saxons, or into those of the Franks, are taught this method of self-defence in order to protect their lives. The training has already served me well.'

'Nevertheless, I must insist that you be accompanied by one of my trusted warriors.'

Fidelma was unconcerned.

'I am instructed by your commission, brother. You are *tánaiste* here and I am acting according to your wishes.'

'Then that is agreed.' Colgú was relieved. 'I already have instructed a man for the task.'

'Do I know this warrior whom you have chosen?'

'You have already met him,' her brother replied. 'He is the young warrior who earlier threw Forbassach out. His name is Cass of the king's bodyguard.'

'Ah, the young, curly-haired warrior?' asked Fidelma.

'The same. He has been a good friend and I would not only trust my life to him but yours as well.'

Fidelma gave a mischievous grin.

'That is precisely what you will be doing, brother. How much does Cass know of this problem?'

'As much as I have been able to tell you.'

'So you trust him well?' observed Fidelma.

'Do you want to speak with him on this matter?' asked her brother.

She shook her head and stifled a sudden yawn.

'Time enough to talk during the three days of our journey to Ros Ailithir. Now I would prefer a hot bath and sleep.'

Chapter Three

It had not been a pleasant journey through the great glens and across the high mountain ranges of Muman. While the storm had abated on the second day, the incessant rains had left the ground soaked with cloying mud which sucked at their horses' hooves and fetlocks like anxious, delaying hands and slowed their pace. The valley bottoms and grassy plains were turned into swampy, and often flooded, lands across which passage was almost impossible, and certainly not made with any speed. The skies continued sulky grey and threatening, with no sign of a bright autumnal sun breaking through and the moody clouds continued to hang low and dark like hill fog. Even the occasional whining wind, moaning in the tree tops, where the leaves had almost vanished, did not dispel their shroud.

Fidelma felt cold and miserable. It was not the weather for travelling. Indeed, if the matter were not so urgent, she would never have contemplated such a journey. She sat her horse stiffly, her body felt chilled to its very marrow despite the heavy woollen cloak and hood which normally helped her endure the icy fingers of inclement temperatures. In spite of her leather gloves, the hands that gripped her horse's reins were numb.

She had not spoken to her companion for at least an hour or more, not since they had left the wayside tavern where they had eaten their midday meal. Her head was bent forward into the chill air. Her concentration was devoted to keeping her horse on the narrow path as it ascended the steep hill before them.

In front of her, the young warrior, Cass, equally wrapped in a heavy woollen cloak and fur collar, sat his horse with a studied poise. Fidelma smiled grimly to herself, wondering just how much he was attempting to present a good figure to her critical gaze. It would not do for a member of the élite bodyguard of the king of Muman to show any weakness before the sister of the heir-apparent. She felt a reluctant sympathy with the young man and when, every now and then in an unguarded moment, she saw him shiver from the damp chill, she felt herself more compassionately disposed towards him.

The path twisted over the shoulder of the mountain and a blast of cold air from the south-west hit them in the face as they emerged from the sheltering outcrop of rocks. Fidelma became aware of the subtle tang of salt in the air, the unmistakable odour of the nearness of the ocean.

Cass reined in his mount and allowed Fidelma to edge her horse alongside his. Then he pointed across the tree-strewn hills and undulating plain which seemed to disappear in the direction of the southern horizon. Yet the clouds hung above the plain in such a fashion that she could not see where land ended and sky began.

'We should be at the abbey of Ros Ailithir before nightfall,' Cass announced. 'Before you are the lands of the Corco Loígde.'

Fidelma screwed her eyes against the cold wind and stared forward. She had not made the connection, when her brother had told her that the kings of Osraige came from Corco Loígde. She had not realised that the abbey of Ros Ailithir was in their clan lands. Could this be merely a coincidence? She knew little about them except that they were one of the great clans which made up the kingdom of Muman and that they were a proud people.

'What is this hill called?' she asked, suppressing a shiver.

'They call this mountain the "Long Rock",' replied Cass. 'It is the highest point before we reach the sea. Have you visited the abbey before?'

Fidelma shook her head.

'I have not been in this part of the kingdom before but I am told that the abbey stands at the head of a narrow inlet on the seashore.'

The warrior nodded in confirmation.

'Ros Ailithir is due south from here.' He indicated the direction with a wave of his hand. Then he winced as a sudden cold wind caught him full in the face. 'But let us descend out of this wind, sister.'

He urged his horse forward and Fidelma allowed him a moment to get a length ahead before she followed.

In addition to the intemperate weather, which had made their journey so unpleasant, Fidelma found that Cass was no easy travelling companion. He had only a little fund of small talk and Fidelma kept rebuking herself for the way she kept comparing him to Brother Eadulf of Seaxmund's Ham, her companion at Whitby and Rome. To her annoyance, she found that she felt a curious kind of isolation, the feeling that she had experienced when she had left Eadulf in Rome to return to her native land. She did not want to admit that she missed the company of the Saxon monk. And it was wrong of her to keep comparing Cass with Eadulf and yet . . .

She had managed to learn from the taciturn warrior that he had been in the service of Cathal of Cashel ever since he had reached the 'age of choice' and left his father's house to take service at the court of the king. Fidelma found that he had a only a slight general knowledge. He had studied at one of Muman's military academies before becoming a professional warrior or *tren-fher*. He had distinguished himself in two campaigns, becoming the commander of a *catha*, a battalion of three thousand men, in the king's army in time of war. Yet

Cass was not one to boast of his prowess in arms. At least that was a saving grace. Fidelma had made enquiries about him before they had set out from Cashel. She discovered that he had successfully fought seven single combats in Muman's service to become a member of the Order of the Golden Collar and champion of the king.

She nudged her horse down the steep path behind him, twisting and turning sometimes into the wind and sometimes in thankful shelter from it. By the time they reached the foot of the mountain, the blustery squall had begun to ease a little and Fidelma saw the bright line of light along the horizon of the western sky.

Cass smiled as he followed her glance.

'The clouds will be gone by tomorrow,' he predicted confidently. 'The wind was bringing the storm from the south-west. Now it will bring fine weather.'

Fidelma did not reply. Something had caught her attention among the foothills to the south-east. At first she had thought that it was merely a reflection from the light of the sun breaking through the heavy clouds. But what could it be reflecting against? It took her a moment or two to realise what it was.

'That's a fire over there, Cass!' she cried, indicating the direction. 'And a big one, if I am not mistaken.'

Cass followed her outstretched hand with keen eyes.

'A big fire, indeed, sister. There is a village that lies in that direction. A poor place with a single religious cell and a dozen houses. I stayed there six months ago when I was in this country. It is called Rae na Scríne, the holy shrine at the level spot. What could be causing such a fire there? Perhaps we should investigate?'

Fidelma delayed, compressing her lips a moment in thought. Her task was to get to Ros Ailithir as quickly as possible.

Cass frowned at her hesitation.

'It is on our path to Ros Ailithir, sister, and the religious cell is occupied by a young religieuse named Sister Eisten. She may be in trouble.' His tone was one of rebuke.

Fidelma flushed, for she knew her duty. Only her greater obligation to the kingdom of Muman had caused her to falter.

Instead of answering him, she dug her heels into the sides of her horse and urged it forward in annoyance at Cass's gentle tone of reproval at her indecision.

It took them some time to reach a spot in the road which was the brow of a small, thickly wooded hillock, overlooking the hamlet of Rae na Scríne. From their position on the roadway, they could see that the buildings of the village appeared to be all on fire. Great consuming flames leapt skyward and debris and smoke spiralled upwards in a black column above the buildings. Fidelma dragged her horse to a halt with Cass nearly colliding into her. The reason for her sudden concern was that there were a dozen men running among the flames with swords and burning brand torches in their hands. It was clear that they were the incendiaries. Before she could react further, a wild shout told them that they had been spotted.

Fidelma turned to warn Cass and suggest they withdraw in case the men be hostile, but she saw a movement behind them by the trees that lined the road.

Two more men had emerged onto the road with bows strung and aimed. They said nothing. There was nothing to be said. Cass exchanged a glance with Fidelma and simply shrugged. They turned and waited patiently while two or three of the men, who had obviously been putting the village to the torch, came running up the hillock to halt before them.

'Who are you?' demanded their leader, a large, red-faced individual, soot and mud staining his face. He carried a sword in his hand but no longer held the brand torch in the other. He had a steel war bonnet on his head, a woollen cloak edged in fur and wore a gold chain of office. His pale eyes were ablaze as if with a battle fever.

'Who are you?' he shouted again. 'What do you seek here?'

Fidelma gazed down at his threatening figure as if she were unperturbed. Her artificial disdain hid her fears.

'I am Fidelma of Kildare; Fidelma of the Eóganachta of Cashel,' she added. 'And who are you to halt travellers on a highway?'

The big man's eyes widened a fraction. He took a step forward and examined her closely without answering. Then he turned to examined Cass with equal attention.

'And you? Who are you?' He asked the question with a brusqueness that implied he had not been impressed to learn that Fidelma was related to the kings at Cashel.

The young warrior eased his cloak so that the man might look on his golden torc.

'I am Cass, champion of the king of Cashel,' he said, putting all the cold arrogance he could muster into his voice.

The red-faced man stood back and gestured to the others to lower their weapons.

'Then be about your business. Ride away from this place, do not look back, and you will not be harmed.'

'What is happening here?' Fidelma demanded, nodding towards the burning habitations.

'The curse of the Yellow Plague sits on this place,' snapped the man. 'We destroy it by flame, that is all. Now, ride off!'

'But what of the people?' protested Fidelma. 'On whose orders do you do this thing? I am a *dálaigh* of the Brehon Court and sister to the heir-apparent of Cashel. Speak, man, or you may have to answer before the Brehons of Cashel.'

The red-faced man blinked at the sharp tone in the young woman's voice. He swallowed for a moment, gazing up at her as if he could not believe his ears. Then he said angrily,

'The kings of Cashel have no right to give orders in the land of the Corco Loígde. Only our chieftain, Salbach, has that right.'

'And Salbach has to answer to the king at Cashel, fellow,' Cass pointed out.

'We are a long way from Cashel,' replied the man stubbornly. 'I have warned you that there is Yellow Plague here. Now begone lest I change my mind and order my men to shoot.'

He motioned with his hand to the bowmen. They raised their weapons again and extended the bowstrings. The arrow flights were firm against their cheeks.

Cass's features were taut.

'Let us do as he says, Fidelma,' he muttered. If even a finger slipped, the arrow would find a sure target. 'This man is one who does not reason except with force.'

Reluctantly Fidelma drew away and followed Cass as he urged his horse to retrace its steps back along the roadway. But as soon as they were beyond the bend in the hills, she reached forward and gripped his arm to stay him.

'We must go back and see what is happening,' she said firmly. 'Fire and sword to deal with a plague village? What manner of chieftain would sanction such a thing? We must go back and see what has happened to the people.'

Cass looked at her dubiously.

'It is dangerous, sister. If I had a couple of men or even were I on my own . . .'

Fidelma snorted in disgust.

'Don't let my sex nor holy order put fear in your heart, Cass. I am willing to share the danger. Or are you afraid of the plague?'

Cass blinked rapidly. His masculine warrior pride was stung.

'I am willing to go back,' he replied distantly. 'I was but concerned for you and your mission. However, if you demand to return, return we shall. But it would be best not to go directly back. Those warriors might be waiting in case we do. I am more concerned about them than of the plague. We will ride around the hills a little and then leave our horses to find a vantage point to observe what we can before we return to the village.'

Fidelma reluctantly agreed. The circuitous route did make sense.

It was half an hour before they found themselves hiding behind a clump of shrubs on the outskirts of the still-burning buildings. The wooden constructions were crackling in the great fire while some were crashing in on themselves in a shower of sparks and billowing smoke. It would not be long, Fidelma realised, before the village was simply a black, smouldering mess of charcoal. The red-faced man and his followers seemed to have disappeared. There were no sounds of humanity against the crack and occasional roar of the flames.

Fidelma rose slowly to her feet and eased a piece of her head-dress across her mouth to protect her lungs from the billowing smoke.

'Where are the people?' she demanded, not really expecting an answer from Cass, who was staring in incomprehension as he surveyed the flaming wreckage of what had been a dozen homesteads. She had her answer even before the question was out of her mouth. There were several bodies lying between the burning homesteads; men, women and children. Most of them had been struck down before their homes had been set ablaze. They were certainly not victims of plague.

'Sister Eisten's cabin was over that way,' pointed Cass, grimly. 'She ran a small hostel for travellers and an orphanage. I stayed when I journeyed through here six months ago.'

He led the way through the smoke and swirling debris to a corner of the village. There was a building by a rock over which water gushed from a natural well spring. The hostel had not been completely destroyed because it had been built mainly of stones, piled one upon another. But the wooden roof, the doors and what contents the building had once had, were now no more. Now it was a pile of hot, smouldering ashes.

'Destroyed,' muttered Cass, hands on hips. 'People slain and no sign of plague. There is a mystery here.'

'A feud?' hazarded Fidelma. 'Perhaps a reprisal for something this village had done?'

Cass shrugged eloquently.

'When we get to Ros Ailithir we must send a message to the chieftain of this area telling him of this deed and demanding an explanation in the name of Cashel.'

Fidelma was inclined to agree. She glanced reluctantly at the eastern sky. It would not be long before dusk. They had to be on their way to the abbey or night would fall long before they reached it.

The shrill wail of a baby, at that time and in that place, was totally unexpected.

Fidelma glanced quickly around to try to locate the origin of the noise. Cass was already ahead of her, scrambling up an incline to the edge of a wood on the fringes of the village behind the burnt-out religious hostel.

Fidelma saw no alternative but to hurry behind him.

There was a movement in the shrubbery and Cass reached forward and caught something which writhed and yelled in his clutch.

'God preserve us!' whispered Fidelma.

It was a child of no more than eight years of age, dirty and dishevelled, yelling with fright.

There was another movement further on among the trees.

A young woman emerged from behind some shrubs; her face was fleshy and white where it was not smeared with soot and dirt. Anxiety was engraved on her features. In her arms she cradled the wailing infant while around her skirts, clutching at their folds, were two little copper-haired girls who were obviously sisters. Behind her stood two dark-haired boys. They all appeared to be in a state of distress.

Fidelma saw that the woman was scarcely out of her teens though dressed in the robes of a religieuse. In spite of the baby's near concealment of it, Fidelma noticed she wore a large and unusual crucifix. It was more in the Roman style than the Irish but it was also elaborate and encrusted with semi-precious stones. In spite of her apparent youthfulness, hers was a plump, round-faced figure which, normally, would have had an air of protective motherliness. Now she seemed to be trembling uncontrollably.

'Sister Eisten!' cried Cass in surprise. 'Have no fear. It is I, Cass of Cashel. I stayed at your hostel six months ago when I was passing through this village. Do you not remember me?'

The young religieuse peered closely at him and shook her head. However, relief began to show in her features as she turned her dark eyes questioningly to Fidelma.

'You are not with Intat? You are not of his band?' she demanded, half fearfully.

'Whoever Intat is, we are not of his band,' Fidelma replied gravely. 'I am Sister Fidelma of Kildare. My companion and I are journeying to the abbey of Ros Ailithir.'

The muscles in the young sister's face, so tightly clenched before, began to relax. She tried to fight back tears of shock and relief.

'Have . . . have they . . . gone?' she finally jerked out. Her voice was vibrating in fear.

'They appear to have gone, sister,' Fidelma assured her as best she could, stepping forward and holding her hands out to take the baby. 'Come, you look all in. Give me the child, that you may rest and tell us what happened. Who were they?'

Sister Eisten lurched backward as though she was afraid to be touched. If anything, she clutched the baby tighter to her chest.

'No! Do not touch any of us.'

Fidelma paused in puzzlement.

'What do you mean? We cannot help you until we know what is happening here.'

Sister Eisten stared at her with wide, expressive eyes.

'It is the plague, sister,' she whispered. 'We had the plague in this village.'

The grip in which Cass absently held the young boy, who was still wriggling, seemed suddenly powerless. His body stiffened. The boy wrenched himself away.

'Plague?' whispered Cass, taking an involuntary step backwards. In spite of his previous attitude, faced by confirmation of the presence of the plague, Cass was clearly troubled.

'So there is plague in the village after all?' demanded Fidelma.

'Several in the village have died of it during the last few weeks. It has passed me by, thanks be to God, but others have died.'

'Is there any among you here who are sick?' pressed Cass, peering anxiously at the children.

Sister Eisten shook her head.

'Not that Intat and his men cared. We would have all died had we not hid . . .'

Fidelma was staring at her in growing horror.

'You would have been struck down whether you suffered the plague or not? Explain! Who is this Intat?'

Sister Eisten stifled another sob. She had nearly reached breaking point. With some gentle prompting, she explained.

'Three weeks ago the plague appeared in the village. First one person and then another caught it. It spared neither sex nor age. Now these children and myself are all that remains of the thirty souls who once dwelt in this place.'

Fidelma let her eyes travel from the baby, scarce more than a few months old, to the children. The two copper-haired little girls were no more than nine years old. The young boy, who had fair hair, who had removed himself from the side of Cass to stand defensively behind Sister Eisten, was also about their age. The two taller boys, scowling faces, black hair, and grey, suspicious eyes, were older. One could not be more than ten years old while the other was perhaps fourteen or fifteen. They seemed to be brothers. She returned her gaze to the plump, trembling young religieuse.

'You have not fully explained, sister,' Fidelma cajoled, knowing that the young woman might break down in a flood of tears. 'You are saying that this man Intat came and killed people, burnt your village, while there were still many healthy people here?'

Sister Eisten sniffed loudly and apparently tried to gather her thoughts together.

'We had no warriors to protect us. This was a farming settlement. At first I though the attackers were frightened that the plague would spread to neighbouring villages and were trying to drive us into the mountains so that we might not contaminate them. But they began to kill. They seemed to especially delight in slaughtering the young children.'

She gave a low moan at the memory.

'Had all the menfolk of this village succumbed to the plague, then?' demanded Cass. 'Was there no one to defend you when this attack came?'

'There were only a few men who tried to prevent the slaughter. What could a few farmers do against a dozen armed warriors? They died by the swords of Intat and his men . . .'

'Intat?' queried Fidelma. 'Again, Intat. Who is this Intat whom you keep mentioning?'

'He is a local chieftain.'

'A local chieftain?' She was scandalised. 'He dared to put a village to fire and sword?'

'I managed to get some of the children and take them to safety in the woods,' repeated Sister Eisten, sobbing as she recalled the scenes of carnage. 'We hid while Intat did his evil work. He fired the village and . . .' She stopped, unable to continue.

Fidelma gave a sharp exhalation of breath.

'What great crime has been committed here, Cass?' she asked softly, staring down to the still burning houses.

'Could someone not have gone to the *bó-aire*, the local magistrate, and demanded protection?' demanded Cass, visibly shaken by Sister Eisten's tale.

The plump sister grimaced bitterly.

'Intat *is* the *bó-aire* of this place!' she exclaimed with anger. 'He sits on the council of Salbach, chieftain of the Corco Loígde.' She seemed about to give way to exhaustion. Then she drew herself up, thrusting out her chin. 'And now you have heard the worst; now that you know that we have been exposed to the plague, leave us to perish in the mountains and go your way.'

Fidelma shook her head sympathetically.

'Our way is now your way,' she said firmly. 'You will come with us to Ros Ailithir, for I presume that these young children have no other family who will nurture them?'

'None, sister.' The young religieuse was staring at Fidelma in wonder. 'I ran a small house for the orphans of the plague and they are my charges.'

'Then Ros Ailithir it is,'

Cass was looking slightly worried.

'It is still a long way to Ros Ailithir,' he whispered. Then he added more softly: 'And the abbot may not thank you for exposing the abbey to any contact with the plague.'

Fidelma shook her head.

'We are all exposed to it. We cannot hide from it nor burn it into non-existence. We have to accept God's will whether it passes us by or not. Now, it is getting late. Perhaps we should stay here tonight? At least we will be warm.'

The suggestion drew instant protest from Sister Eisten.

'What if Intat and his men return?' she wailed.

Cass agreed: 'She is right, Fidelma. There is that likelihood. It is best not to stay here in case Intat remains close by. If he realises that there are survivors then he may wish to finish this terrible deed.'

Fidelma reluctantly gave in to their objections.

'The sooner we start out then the sooner we shall arrive. We shall ride as far as we can towards Ros Ailithir.'

'But Intat has driven off our animals,' Eisten protested again. 'Not that there were any horses but there were some asses . . .'

'We have two horses and the children can sit two or three together on them,' Fidelma assured her. 'We adults will have to walk and we may take turns carrying the baby. Poor thing. What happened to the mother?'

'She was one of those whom Intat slew.'

Fidelma's eyes were steely cold.

'He will answer before the law for this deed. As *bó-aire* he must realise the consequences of his actions. And answer he shall!' There was no vain boast in her voice; merely a cold statement of fact.

Cass watched with undisguised respect as Fidelma quietly but firmly took charge, collecting the children and placing them on the horses, taking the baby to give the exhausted young Sister Eisten a chance, so far as she was able, to recover herself. Only the younger of the two black-haired boys seemed reluctant to move from the shelter of the woods, doubtless still terrified of what he had seen. It was his elder brother who finally persuaded him with a few quiet words. The elder boy was disinclined to take the opportunity to ride on the horse but strode alongside it, insisting that as he was approaching the 'age of choice' they should regard him as an adult. Fidelma did not argue with the solemn-faced lad. They set off along the track in the direction of the abbey of Ros Ailithir with Cass silently hoping they would not encounter Intat and his band of cut-throats along the way.

Cass could understand, however, the fears that drove villagers to turn on their fellows. He had heard many a story of the Yellow Plague devastating whole communities not only among the five kingdoms of Éireann but beyond its shores from where the virulence was said to have originated. Cass realised that any genuine fear of the spread of plague did not absolve Intat and his men from their responsibilities under the law. To burn out an entire community because of fear of contagion was understandable but wrong. What he also knew, and realised that Fidelma knew it also, was that, as *bó-aire*, Intat would appreciate that if word reached Cashel of this terrible deed then he would have to face the consequences. He had only let Fidelma and Cass continue their journey unmolested in the belief they would not find out what had happened. If Intat realised that they had doubled back and come across survivors of his horrendous slaughter then their lives might be forfeit. Best to put distance between this place and themselves.

He admired the way Colgú's young sister did not seem to have any fear of the plague. He would not have associated so freely with these children had it not been for the fact that he did not wish to be shamed in front of Fidelma. So he repressed his fear and did as he was bid by her.

Fidelma chatted gaily in an attempt to keep up the spirits of the shocked and frightened children. She seized on what inconsequential topics she could, asking the young Sister Eisten where she had acquired the remarkable-looking crucifix she wore. After some prompting, Sister Eisten confessed that she had once been on a pilgrimage, which had lasted three years. Fidelma had to interrupt to say she had not thought Eisten old enough to have had such experience, but Eisten was older than her looks, being twenty-two years of age. She had journeyed with a group of religieuse to the Holy Land. She had found herself in the town of Bethlehem and made a pilgrimage to the very birthplace of the Saviour. It had been there she had purchased the ornate crucifix from local craftsmen. So Fidelma encouraged her to talk about her adventures, merely to keep the children occupied and content.

Inwardly Fidelma was far from happy. She was disconsolate, not at the idea of contact with potential plague carriers but at the fact that the conditions of her journey were even worse than they had been when, earlier that day, she had been bemoaning the weather and the cold and damp. At least she had been dryshod on horseback then. Now she was stumbling through the mud and slush of the track, trying to keep a delicate balance with the young baby in her arms. The child was constantly whimpering and trying to twist and turn, which made matters worse. Fidelma did not wish to cause alarm but even in the half light she had observed a tell-tale yellow tint to the child's skin and the fever on its little brow. Now and then, in order to keep the child from wriggling loose in her grip, Fidelma almost lost her footing in the mud which oozed around her ankles.

'How much farther is it to Ros Ailithir?' she allowed herself to ask after they had been walking two hours.

It was Sister Eisten who was specific.

'Seven miles from here, but the road does not get easier.'

Fidelma momentarily clenched her teeth and did not reply.

The gloom of dusk was rapidly spreading from the east, merging with the gloomy low-lying clouds and, almost before she realised it, a thick night fog was obscuring the roadway. The weather had not cleared yet as Cass had predicted.

Fidelma regretfully called a halt.

'We'll never make it to the abbey like this,' she told Cass. 'We'll have to find a place to stay until morning.'

As if to emphasise the dangers of night travel, a wolf pack began to yelp and bay in unison across the hills. One of the little girls began to cry, a plaintive, painful whimpering which twisted Fidelma's heart. She had learnt that the copper-haired sisters were named Cera and Ciar. The fair-haired young lad was called Tressach while the other boys, as she had guessed, were brothers – Cétach and Cosrach. This much information had she been able to extract from them during their short journey through the cold woods.

'The first thing is to light some torches,' Cass announced. 'Then we will have to find a shelter.'

He handed the reins of his horse to the elder boy, Cétach, and went to the side of the road where the woods bordered it. Fidelma listened to the snapping of twigs and a soft cursing as Cass searched for tinder dry enough to make and light a brand torch.

'Do you know if there are any dry places near here in which we can shelter?' Fidelma asked Sister Eisten.

The young religieuse shook her head.

'There is only the forest.'

Cass had succeeded in lighting a bundle of twigs, but they would not burn long.

'Best if we kindled a fire,' he muttered as he rejoined Fidelma. 'If there is nothing else, at least the trees might afford some shelter. Perhaps we can find enough bushes to create some protection. But it will be a cold night for the children.'

Fidelma sighed and nodded assent. There was little else to do. Already it was impossible to see more than a few yards. Perhaps she should have insisted that they remain in the village for the night. At least it would have been warm among the smouldering ruins. Still, there was little point in self-reproach now.

'Let's move into the wood, then, and see if we can find a dry spot. Then we'll get what sleep we can.'

'The children haven't eaten since this morning,' Sister Eisten ventured.

Fidelma groaned inwardly.

'Well, there is nothing to be done until it is light, sister. Let us concentrate on getting warm and as dry as we can. Food must be a later consideration.'

It was Cass's sharp eyes that managed to spot a small clearing among the tall trees where a large bush extended itself almost in the manner of a tent over a fairly dry area of twigs and leaves.

'Almost made for the task,' he said brightly. Fidelma could imagine him smiling in the darkness. 'I'll tether the horses out here and light a fire. I have a *croccán*, my kettle, with me and so we may have a hot drink. You and Sister Eisten can get the children under the bush.' He paused and added with a shrug: 'It's the best we can do.'

Fidelma replied: 'Yes.' There was little else to say.

Within half an hour, Cass had a reasonable fire alight and had set his *croccán*, filled with water, to boil upon it. It was Fidelma who insisted that they add herbs to the mixture, which she said would help protect them from the night chills. She wondered if Cass or Eisten would realise that an infusion of the leaves and flowers of the herb *drémire buí* was used as a protective against the scourge of the Yellow Plague. No one commented as the drink was handed around, although the children complained against the bitterness of the mixture. Soon, however, most of them were asleep – more from exhaustion than any other cause.

The cry of wolves continued to break across the strange nocturnal sounds of the wood.

Cass squatted before the fire, feeding its hungry flames with salvaged pieces of wood which hissed and spat with their unsuitability but, at least, generated enough heat to burn and send out some sort of warmth.

'We'll move on at first light,' Fidelma told him. 'If we move at a reasonable pace then we should be at the abbey by mid-morning.'

'We need to keep a watch tonight,' Cass observed. 'If not to make sure that Intat and his men are close by, then merely to ensure the fire is fed. I'll take the first watch.'

'Then I'll take the second,' Fidelma insisted, drawing her

cloak closer around her shoulders in a vain effort to create more warmth from the garment.

It was a long, cold night but apart from the baying of distant wolves and the cry of other nocturnal creatures, nothing happened to disturb their uneasy peace.

When they all awoke in the grey, listless light of the morning, with the ice chill of the new day, it was Sister Eisten who discovered that the baby had died in the night. No one mentioned the yellow hue to the waxy texture of the babe's skin.

Cass dug a shallow grave with his sword and, against the bewildered sobbing of the younger children, Sister Fidelma and Sister Eisten uttered up a quiet prayer as they buried the tiny corpse. Sister Eisten had not been able to recall its name.

By then, the clouds had rolled away and the anaemic autumnal sun was hanging low in the pallid blue sky – bright but without warmth. Cass had been right about the change in the weather.

Chapter Four

The midday Angelus bell was sounding as Fidelma and her party came within sight of the abbey at Ros Ailithir. The journey had taken longer than she had estimated for, though the day was warm and bright, the road was still sodden and muddy and the passage was difficult.

The abbey was larger than Fidelma had imagined it would be; a vast complex of grey stone buildings standing, as she had already been informed, on the hillside at the head of a narrow inlet of the sea. It was an inlet too long and narrow to be called a bay. She noticed briefly that there were several ships riding at anchor there before turning her gaze back to the diversity of grey buildings. There were several large structures all contained behind tall dark granite walls which followed a oval course around them. At their centre she could make out the imposing abbey church. It was a remarkable and unusual building. Most churches in the five kingdoms were built on circular patterns but this was built in a crucifix style with a long nave and a transept at right angles. Fidelma knew that this style was becoming more popular among the new church builders. Next to this was a lofty *cloictheach*, or bell house, from which the solemn chimes echoed across the small valley depression which led down to the sea.

One of the children, it was the younger of the two black-haired boys again, gave a low moan and started to tremble. His brother spoke sharply but quietly to him.

'What ails him?' Cass demanded. He was standing the closest to the two boys, the younger one being seated on his horse.

'My brother thinks that we may be harmed if we go where there are grown-ups,' the elder replied solemnly. 'He is scared after what happened yesterday.'

Cass smiled gently at the younger boy. 'Have no fear, son. No one down there will harm you. It is a holy abbey. They will help you.'

The elder whispered sharply to his young sibling again and then, turning, said to Cass: 'He will be all right now.'

All the children were showing signs of fatigue now; fatigue and agitation after their terrifying experience. In fact, they were all exhausted both physically as well as emotionally. The unease and restiveness of the cold night's halt had not refreshed them and they had experienced a hard trek that morning from the woods to the coast. Weariness showed on everyone's face.

'I had not realised that the abbey was so large,' Fidelma observed brightly to Cass to instil some air of normality into the depressed company. However, it was also true that she was impressed by the vastness of the buildings which dominated the inlet.

'I am told that hundreds of proselytes study here,' replied Cass indifferently.

The bell suddenly ceased its clamouring.

Fidelma motioned them forward again. She felt a passing unease because she had ignored the call to prayer. Time enough to stop and pray when she and her exhausted charges were safely under the protection of the walls of the abbey. She glanced anxiously towards Sister Eisten. The plump young woman seemed to be lost in melancholy thought. Fidelma put this down to the woman's shock at the death of the baby that morning. Soon after they had set out, she had lapsed into a malaise, a maudlin contemplation, and did not seem to be at all conscious of her surroundings. She walked automatically, her head bent downwards, eyes on the ground, and made no response when spoken to. Fidelma had noticed that she did not even bother to raise her eyes when they had come within sight of Ros Ailithir, and heard the chiming of the bell. Yes; it was better to get the party to the abbey rather than halt to indulge in ritual prayers along the roadway.

As they neared the walls of the abbey, she became aware of a few religieux at work in the surrounding fields. They seemed to be cutting kale, presumably to feed cattle. A few curious glances were cast in their direction but, generally, the men bent diligently to their work in the cold, autumnal morning.

The gates of the abbey stood open. Fidelma frowned when she saw, hanging by the side of the gate, a writhe, or bundle of twisted branches of osiers and aspen. It struck a chord in her memory but she could not identify it. She was still trying to dredge her memory about the symbolism of the writhe when she had to turn her attention to a thickset, middle-aged man in the robes of a religieux who stood in the gateway waiting for them. Where his hair grew long from his tonsure, it was speckled grey. He looked a muscular man and his grim visage seemed a warning that he was not someone to trifle with.

'*Bene vobis*,' he intoned in a deep baritone, making the ritual greeting.

'*Deus vobiscum*,' Sister Fidelma responded automatically and then decided to dispense with the rest of the usual courtesies. 'These children need food, warmth and rest,' she said without further preamble, causing the man's eyes to widen in astonishment. 'So does the Sister here. They have had a bad experience. I have to warn you that they have been exposed to the Yellow Plague so your physician needs to examine them immediately. Meanwhile, my companion and I wish to be taken to Abbot Brocc.'

The man stuttered in his surprise that a young anchoress should utter so many orders before she had been ritually admitted to the hospitality of the abbey. His brows drew together and he opened his mouth to voice his protest.

Fidelma interrupted before he could speak.

'I am Fidelma from Cashel. The abbot should be expecting me,' she added firmly.

The man stood with open mouth, gulping like a fish. Then he drew himself together as Fidelma swept by him, leading her charges through the gates. The monk turned and hurried after her, catching up with her as she entered the large, stone flagged courtyard beyond the gate.

'Sister Fidelma . . . we, that is . . .' He was clearly flustered at the abrupt manner of her entrance. 'We have been expecting you this last day or so. We were warned . . . told . . . to expect you . . . I am Brother Conghus, the *aistreóir* of the abbey. What has happened? Who are these children?'

Fidelma turned to the doorkeeper and replied tersely: 'Survivors from Rae na Scríne which has been burnt by raiders.'

The religieux stared from the pitiable children to the plump, young Sister Eisten. His eyes widened as he recognised her.

'Sister Eisten! What has happened?'

The young woman continued to stare moodily into space and did not acknowledge him.

The monk turned back to Fidelma clearly disconcerted.

'Sister Eisten is known to us in this abbey. She ran a mission at Rae na Scríne. Destroyed by raiders, you say?'

Fidelma inclined her head in brief acknowledgment.

'The village was attacked by a group of men led by someone called Intat. Only Sister Eisten and these children survived. I demand sanctuary for them.'

'You also mentioned something about plague?' Brother Conghus seemed confused.

'I am told that the reason for this horrendous attack was that there was plague in the village. This is why I ask that the physician of the abbey be summoned. Do you fear the plague here?'

Brother Conghus shook his head.

'With God's help, most of us have discovered an immunity in this abbey. We have had four outbreaks of the pestilence during this last year but it has claimed only a few lives from the young scholars. We no longer have fear of the disease. I will get someone to take poor Sister Eisten and her charges to the hostel where they will be well taken care of.'

He turned and waved a hand to a passing young novice. She was a tall girl, slightly broad in the shoulders with a carriage that seemed clumsy.

'Sister Necht, take this sister and the children to the hostel. Tell Brother Rumann to summon Brother Midach to examine them. Then see that they are fed and rested. I will speak with Midach shortly.'

His orders were issued in a series of staccato bursts. Fidelma noticed that the young girl hesitated, staring in open-mouthed surprise as she seemed to recognise Eisten and the children. Then she seemed to make a conscious effort to pull herself together and hurried forward to shepherd the children and the plaintive, plump Eisten away. Brother Conghus, assured his orders were being obeyed, turned back to Fidelma.

'Brother Midach is our chief physician while Rumann is our steward. They will take care of Sister Eisten and the children,' he explained unnecessarily. He pointed the way forward across the courtyard. 'I will bring you to the abbot. Have you come directly from Cashel?'

'We have,' confirmed Cass as they followed him. The warrior in Cass paused to draw attention to a matter Fidelma had neglected. 'Our horses need a rub down and feeding, brother.'

'I will attend to your horses just as soon as I have conducted you to the abbot,' Conghus replied.

The doorkeeper of the abbey started to hurry with somewhat unseemly haste across the paved yard, through the complex of buildings, pausing from time to time to urge them to follow with as much speed as they could. Fidelma and Cass complied, however, with a more leisurely pace which was governed by their fatigue. The walk seemed interminable but, at last, having ascended the stairs of a large building, set slightly apart from the others, the *aistreóir* halted before a dark oak door and motioned them to wait while he knocked and disappeared behind it. Only moments passed before he re-emerged and, holding wide the door, gestured for them to go inside.

They found themselves in a large vaulted chamber whose cold grey stone walls were relieved by colourful tapestries, each illustrating something of the life of Christ. A fire smouldered in the hearth and there was the smell of incense permeating through the room. The floor was carpeted with soft woollen rugs. The furniture was rich and the ornaments extravagant in their opulence. The abbot of Ros Ailithir did not appear to believe in frugality.

'Fidelma!'

A tall man rose from behind a dark, polished oak table. He was thin, with a hook nose, piercing blue eyes, and his red hair was cut in the tonsure of the Irish church, shaven at the front to a line from ear to ear and the hair hanging long at the back. There was something about his facial appearance which, to the discerning eye, suggested a relationship to Fidelma.

'I am your cousin, Brocc,' the thin man announced. His voice seemed to boom with a deep bass quality. 'I have not seen you since you were a child.'

The greeting was meant to be a warm one yet there was some false note in the abbot's voice. It was as if part of his thoughts were elsewhere while he was trying to summon a welcome.

Even when he stretched out both hands to take Fidelma's own in greeting, they were cold and flaccid and also seemed to belie the attempted tone of welcome in his voice. Fidelma had little recollection of her cousin from her exuberant childhood. Perhaps that was understandable for Abbot Brocc was at least ten or fifteen years her senior.

She returned his greeting with a degree of studied formality and then introduced Cass.

'Cass has been appointed to assist me in this matter by my brother, Colgú.'

Brocc examined Cass with an uneasy gaze, his eyes going to Cass's throat where the warrior had loosened his cloak and it had fallen away to reveal the golden necklet of his office. For his part, Cass reached out with a strong grip to take the abbot's hand. Fidelma saw Brocc's facial muscles twitch at the power of the grip.

'Come, be seated, cousin. You also, Cass. My doorkeeper, Brother Conghus, tells me that you arrived with Sister Eisten and some children from Rae na Scríne. Eisten's mission there comes under the jurisdiction of this abbey and so we are much concerned at what has happened there. Tell me the story.'

Fidelma glanced to Cass as she slumped thankfully into a chair, relaxing for the first time in twenty-four hours in some degree of comfort. The young warrior picked up the invitation that her glance implied and quickly told the story of how they had found Eisten and the children at Rae na Scríne.

Brocc's face became a mask of anger and he reached up a hand to tap absently on the bridge of his nose.

'This is an evil business. I will send a messenger at once to Salbach, the chieftain of the Corco Loígde. He will have this man Intat and his men punished for this heinous act. Leave this matter with me. I shall ensure Salbach hears of this at once.'

'And Sister Eisten and her charges?' asked Fidelma.

'Have no fears for them. We will care for them here. We have a good infirmary and our physician, Brother Midach, has dealt with ten cases of the Yellow Plague over the last year. God has been good to us. Three of the victims he has successfully cured. We have no fear of the plague here. And is it not right that we should have no fear for we are of the Faith and are in God's good hands?'

'I am delighted that you view the matter with such a perspective,' replied Fidelma gravely. 'I would expect no less.'

Cass wondered, for a moment, whether she was being ironical at Brocc's pious attitude.

'So now,' Brocc's cold eyes examined her steadily, 'let us get down to the main reason for your visit here.'

Fidelma groaned inwardly. She would prefer to have slept and recovered something of her serenity of mind before dealing with the matter. A long deep sleep was what she most desired. She would prefer to have eaten and drunk mulled wine to warm her and then fallen onto a dry bed no matter how hard. But Brocc was probably right. It would be best to get the preliminaries over with.

As she was contemplating her reply, Brocc rose from his seat and went to stand at a window which, she could see, even from her seated position, looked out across the inlet of the sea. The abbot stood, hands clasped behind his back, gazing down.

'I am aware that time is of the essence, cousin,' he said slowly. 'And I am aware that I, as abbot, am held accountable for the Venerable Dacán's death. If I was in need of reminding of the fact, then the king of Laigin has sent me a token as remembrance.'

Fidelma stared at him for a moment.

'What do you mean?' Cass articulated the question that she was about to ask.

Brocc gestured with his head through the window.

'Look down there, at the mouth of the inlet.'

Fidelma and Cass both rose and went to join the abbot, curiously peering over his shoulder towards the spot he had indicated. There were several ships at anchor in the inlet, among them two large ocean-going vessels. Brocc was specifying one of these larger vessels, riding against its sea anchor, near the exit to the sheltered bay.

'You are a warrior, Cass.' Brocc's bass voice was morose. 'Can you identify that vessel? You see the one I mean? Not the Frankish merchantman but the other one.'

Cass screwed up his eyes as he examined the lines of the ship.

'It flies the standard of Fianamail, the king of Laigin,' he replied with some surprise. 'It is a Laigin ship of war.'

'Exactly so,' sighed Brocc, turning to motion them back to their seats while resuming his own. 'It appeared a week ago. A Laigin ship of war sent to remind me that Laigin holds me accountable for Dacán's death. It sits there in the inlet, day in and day out. To emphasise the point, when it initially arrived, its captain came ashore to inform me of the intention of the king of Laigin. Since then no one from the ship has come to the abbey. It just sits at the entrance of the inlet and waits – like a cat waiting for a mouse. If they mean to destroy my peace, then they are succeeding. Doubtless they will wait there until the High King's assembly makes its decision.'

Cass flushed angrily.

'This is an outrage to justice,' he said fiercely. 'It is intimidation. It is a physical threat.'

'It is, as I have said, a reminder that Laigin demand their eye for an eye, tooth for tooth. What does the scripture say? If a man destroy the eye of another man, they shall destroy his eye?'

'That is the law of the Israelites,' Fidelma pointed out. 'It is not the law of the five kingdoms.'

'A moot point, cousin. If we are to believe that the Israelites are the chosen of God, then we should follow their law as well as their religion.'

'Time for theological debate later,' snapped Cass. 'Why do they hold you responsible, Brocc? Did you kill the Venerable Dacán?'

'No, of course not.'

'Then Laigin has no reason to threaten you.' To Cass the matter was simple.

Fidelma turned to him chidingly.

'Laigin abides by the law. Brocc is abbot here. He is the head of the family of this abbey and, in law, deemed responsible for anything that happens to his guests. If he is unable to pay the fines and compensations due, then the law says his family must do so. Because he is of the Eóganachta, the ruling family of Muman, then the whole of Muman is now held to hostage for the deed. Do you follow the logic now, Cass?'

'But that is no justice,' Cass pointed out.

'It is the law,' replied Fidelma firmly. 'You should know this.'

'And often law and justice are two things which are not synonymous,' Brocc observed bitterly. 'But you are right to state the case as Laigin sees it. There is not much time to present a defence before the High King's assembly meets at Tara.'

'Perhaps, then,' Fidelma tried to stifle a yawn, 'you had best tell me the essential facts so that I may work out some plan by which my investigation may be conducted.'

Abbot Brocc did not notice her fatigue. Instead, he spread his hands in an eloquent gesture of bewilderment.

'There is little I can say, cousin. The facts are these; the Venerable Dacán came to this abbey with permission from

King Cathal to study our collection of ancient books. We have a large number of "rods of the poets", ancient histories and sagas cut in the Ogham alphabet on wands of hazel and aspen. We pride ourselves on this collection. It is the finest in the five kingdoms. Not even at Tara is there such a collection of genealogical tracts.'

Fidelma accepted Brocc's pride, She had been instructed in a knowledge of the ancient alphabet which legend said had been given to the Irish by their pagan god of literature, Ogma. The alphabet was represented by a varying number of strokes and notches to and crossing a base line and texts were cut on wooden rods called 'rods of the poets'. The old alphabet was now falling rapidly in disuse with the adoption of the Latin alphabet due to the incoming of the Christian faith.

Brocc was continuing:

'We take exceptional pride in our Tech Screptra, our great library, and our scholars have shown that it was our kingdom of Muman which first brought the art of Ogham to the peoples of the five kingdoms. As you may know, this abbey was founded by the Blessed Fachtna Mac Mongaig, a pupil of Ita, nearly a hundred years ago. He established this place not only as a house of worship but a repository of books of knowledge, as a place of learning, a place where people from the four corners of the earth could receive their education. And they came and have been coming here ever since; a never-ending stream of pilgrims in search of knowledge. Our foundation of Ros Ailithir has become renowned throughout the five kingdoms and even beyond them.'

Fidelma could not suppress amusement at the abbot's sudden burst of enthusiasm for his foundation. Even among the religious, who were supposed to be the examples of humility, conceit was often never far from the surface.

'And that is why the abbey is named as the promontory of pilgrims,' Cass said softly, as if he wished to show that he had some knowledge to contribute.

The abbot regarded him with cold appraisal and inclined his head slightly.

'Just so, warrior. Ros Ailithir – the promontory of pilgrims. Not just pilgrims in the Faith but pilgrims of Truth and Learning.'

Fidelma gestured impatiently.

'So the Venerable Dacán, with the permission of King Cathal, came here to study. This much we know.'

'And to do some teaching as a repayment for access to our library,' added Brocc. 'His main interest was in deciphering the texts of the "rods of the poets". Most days he worked in our Tech Screptra.'

'How long was he a guest here?'

'About two months.'

'What happened? I mean, what were the details concerning the manner of his death?'

Brocc sat back, placing both hands, palm downwards, on his table.

'It happened two weeks ago. It was just before the bell sounded the hour for tierce.' He turned to Cass, to explain pedantically: 'The work of the abbey is done between tierce in the morning and vespers in the evening.'

'Tierce is the third hour of the canonical day,' explained Fidelma when she saw Cass frowning in bewilderment at the abbot's explanation.

'It is the hour when we start our studies and when some of the brothers go into the fields to work, for we have cultivated lands to tend and animals to feed and fish to harvest from the sea.'

'Go on,' instructed Fidelma, becoming irritated at the length of time the account was taking. Her eyelids were feeling scratchy and she longed for a short rest, a brief sleep.

'As I have said, it was just before the bell was due to sound for tierce when Brother Conghus, my *aistreóir*, that is the doorkeeper of the abbey, who also has the duty to ring the bell, came bursting into my chambers. Naturally, I demanded to know why he could so forget himself . . .'

'He then told you that Dacán was dead?' interrupted Fidelma, trying her best to stifle her impatience at her cousin's long-winded approach.

Brocc blinked, unused to interference when he was speaking.

'He had been to Dacán's *cubiculum* in the guests' hostel. It appears that Dacán had not been seen at *jentaculum*.' He paused and turned condescendingly to Cass. 'That is the meal by which we break our fast on rising.'

This time Fidelma did not bother to stifle the yawn. The abbot looked slightly hurt and went on hurriedly.

'Brother Conghus went to the hostel and found the body of the Venerable Dacán laying on his cot. He had been bound, hand and foot, and then, so it appeared, stabbed several times. The physician was called and made an examination. The stab wounds were straight into the heart and any one could have been fatal. My *fer-tighis*, the steward of the abbey, was given the task of making an investigation. He questioned those in the abbey but none had heard or seen anything untoward. No explanation of why or who could have done the deed came to light. Because of the fact that the Venerable Dacán was such a distinguished guest, I immediately sent word to King Cathal at Cashel.'

'Did you also send word to Laigin?'

Brocc shook his head immediately.

'There was a Laigin merchant staying at the abbey at the time. We have a busy sea route along this coast to Laigin. Doubtless this merchant took word of Dacán's death to Fearna and to Dacán's brother, the Abbot Noé.'

Fidelma leaned forward with interest.

'Did this merchant have a name?'

'I think it was Assíd. My *fer-tighis*, Brother Rumann, would know.'

'When did this merchant leave for Laigin?'

'I think it was the very day that Dacán's body was discovered. I am not exactly sure when. Brother Rumann would have such details.'

'But Brother Rumann found nothing to explain the death?' interrupted Cass.

As the abbot nodded agreement Fidelma asked: 'When did you first learn that Laigin held you responsible for the death and was demanding reparation from the King of Muman?'

Brocc looked grim.

'When that warship arrived and its captain came ashore to tell me that, as abbot, I was being held responsible. Then I received a messenger from Cashel which further informed me that reparation, in the form of the lands of Osraige, was demanded by the new king of Laigin but that King Cathal was sending for you to investigate the matter.'

Fidelma sat back in her chair, placing her hands together, fingertip to fingertip, seeking refuge for a moment in thought.

'And these are all the facts as you know them, Brocc?'

'As I know them,' affirmed Brocc solemnly.

'Well, the only clear thing is that the Venerable Dacán was murdered,' Cass summed up morosely. 'It is also clear the deed was done in this abbey. Therefore it is also clear that reparation has to be paid.'

Fidelma regarded him with a sardonic expression.

'Indeed, that is our starting point.' She smiled thinly. 'However, who is responsible for paying that reparation? That is what we must now discover.'

She rose abruptly to her feet.

Cass followed her example more reluctantly.

'What now, cousin?' asked Brocc eagerly, as he gazed up at his young relative.

'Now? Now, I think that Cass and myself will find something to eat for we have not had anything since yesterday noon and then we must rest a while. We had little sleep in the cold and damp of the forest last night. We'll begin our investigation after vespers.'

Brocc's eyes widened.

'Begin? I thought I had told you all at the abbey we know of this matter.'

Fidelma's lips thinned wryly.

'You do not appreciate how a Brehon conducts an investigation. No matter. We will begin to find out who killed Dacán and why.'

'Do you think you can?' demanded Brocc, a faint light of expectation growing in his eyes.

'That is what I am here for.' Fidelma's voice was weary.

Brocc looked uncertain. Then he reached forward to a tiny silver bell on the table and rang it.

A fleshy, middle-aged anchorite seemed to burst into the room, his every movement speaking of a frenetic activity, a scarcely concealed energy which seemed to inspire an agitation of his every limb. The nervous restlessness of the man made even Fidelma feel uncomfortable.

'This is my *fer-tighis*, the house steward of the abbey,' introduced Brocc. 'Brother Rumann will attend to all of your needs. You have but to ask. I will see you again at vespers.'

Brother Rumann seemed to physically propel them before him as he ushered them out of the abbot's chambers.

'Having heard from Brother Conghus that you had arrived, I have prepared rooms in the *tech-óiged*, sister.' His voice was as breathless as his appearance was flustered. 'You will be most comfortable in our guest hostel.'

'And food?' queried Cass. Fidelma's reference to the fact that they had eaten little in the last twenty-four hours had reminded him of that truth and created a gnawing hunger to register in his mind.

Brother Rumann's head bounced up and down, or so it seemed; a large, fleshy round ball on which the hair grew sparsely. The flesh of his moon face was so creased that it was almost impossible to see whether he was smiling or scowling.

'A meal is prepared,' he confirmed. 'I will lead you to the hostel at once.'

'The same hostel where the Venerable Dacán stayed?' queried Fidelma. When Brother Rumann nodded she made no comment.

They followed him through the grey stone aisles of the abbey buildings, across tiny courtyards and along darkened passages.

'How are Sister Eisten and the children?' she asked, after some moments of silence.

Brother Rumann made a clucking sound with his tongue, like a nervous mother hen. Fidelma suddenly smiled for that was precisely what Brother Rumann reminded her of as he waddled before them, hands flapping at his sides.

'Sister Eisten is exhausted and appears to have been greatly shocked by her experience. The children are just tired and need warmth and sleep more than anything else at this time. Brother Midach, our chief physician here, has examined them. There are no signs of any illness among them.'

Brother Rumann paused before a door of a rectangular, two-storeyed building standing by one of the main walls of the abbey, separated from the imposing central church by a square of paved stones in the middle of which stood a well.

'This is our *tech-óiged*, sister. We pride ourselves on our guests' hostel. In summer we have visitors from many places.'

He threw open the door, like a showman performing some difficult feat before a large audience, and then ushered them into the building. They immediately found themselves in a large hall which was both spacious and well decorated with tapestries and icons. A wooden staircase led them to a second floor where the steward showed them to adjoining rooms. Fidelma noticed that their saddle bags had already been placed inside.

'I trust these quarters will be comfortable enough?' asked Brother Rumann and, before they could answer, he had turned and bustled off into another room. 'For this occasion,' his calling voice beckoned them to follow him, 'I have ordered your meal to be brought here for convenience. However, from this evening, meals are taken in the refectory which is the building adjoining this one. All our guests usually eat there.'

Fidelma saw, on a table in the room, bowls of steaming broth with platters of bread, cheeses and a jug of wine with pottery goblets. It looked appetising to their hungry eyes.

Fidelma felt her mouth moistening at the sight.

'This is excellent,' she said approvingly.

'My chamber is downstairs, at the far end of the hostel,' Brother Rumann went on. 'Should you require any service then you may find me there or, by ringing the bell,' he indicated a small bronze handbell on the table, 'you can summon my assistant, Sister Necht, She is one of our young novices and serves the wants of all our guests.'

'One thing before you go,' Fidelma said, as Brother Rumann started to bustle towards the door. The plump man halted and turned back inquiringly.

'About how many people are there in the hostel?'

Brother Rumann frowned.

'Only yourselves. Oh, and we have placed Sister Eisten and the children here temporarily.'

'I was told that the abbey has hundreds of students.'

Brother Rumann chuckled wheezily.

'Do not concern yourself with them. The students' dormitories are situated on the other side of the abbey. We are a mixed community, of course, as are most houses. The male members of our order predominate. Will that be all, sister?'

'For the time being,' agreed Fidelma.

The man clucked his way out. Almost before he was beyond the door, Cass let restraint go to the winds and slid into a seat, drawing a bowl of the steaming broth towards him.

'Several hundred students and religious.' He turned a grim expression to Fidelma as she joined him at the table. 'To find a murderer amongst this number would be like trying to identify a particular grain of sand on a seashore.'

Fidelma pulled a face and then raised the wooden spoon to her mouth, savouring the warmth of the broth.

'The odds are much more in our favour,' she said, after an appreciative pause. 'That is, if the murderer is still in the abbey. From what Brocc says, people have come and gone in the interval since the killing. If I had killed the Venerable Dacán, I doubt whether I would remain here. But that would all depend on who I am and the motive for the killing.'

Cass was cleaning his bowl with satisfaction.

'The killer might be confident that he will not be caught,' he suggested.

'Or she,' corrected Fidelma. 'The curious thing about this investigation is that, in other inquiries that I have been involved with, there is always some discernible motive that comes immediately to the mind. This is not so in this case.'

'How do you mean?'

'A person is found dead. Why? Sometimes there is a robbery. Or the person is intensely disliked. Or there is some other obvious reason as a likely motive for the killing. Knowing the motive we can then start inquiries as to who is most likely to benefit from the crime. Here we have a respectable and elderly scholar who comes to a violent end but no motive immediately springs to mind.'

'Perhaps there was no motive? Perhaps he was killed by someone who was insane and . . .'

Fidelma reproved Cass gently.

'Insanity is in itself a motive.'

Cass shook his head and turned back to the bowl of broth he had been devouring and gazed sadly at the empty dish.

'I enjoyed that,' he commented almost in a tone of regret that there was no more. 'Oatmeal, milk and leeks, I think. Is it delicious or is it my ravening hunger that adds zest to the food?'

Fidelma grimaced in amusement at his enthusiastic change of conversation.

'It is said that this broth was a favourite dish of the Blessed Colmcille,' she observed. 'And you are right about its ingredients, but I think anything would taste as magnificent when one has not eaten for a while.'

Cass was already cutting a slice of cheese and Fidelma indicated that she would also like a piece. The young warrior placed the slice on her platter and cut another. Then he broke off a hunk of bread. He chewed thoughtfully, at the same time as pouring a cup of wine apiece.

'Seriously, sister, how can you hope to solve this mystery? It happened over a fortnight ago and I doubt whether the perpetrator of the deed has remained within miles of this place. Even if they have, then there appears to be no witness, no one who saw anything, nothing to lay a path to the culprit.'

Fidelma calmly took a sip of her wine.

'So, Cass, if you were me, what you would do?'

Cass paused in the act of chewing and blinked. He gave the question some thought.

'Find out as many details as one can, I suppose, in order to report back to Cashel.'

'Well,' Fidelma replied with mock seriousness, 'at least we appear to be agreed on that. Is there any further advice you would give me, Cass?'

The young warrior flushed.

Fidelma was *dálaigh*. He knew that. And she was surely mocking him for presuming to tell her how to do her job.

'I did not mean . . .' he began.

She disarmed him with a grin.

'Do not worry, Cass. If I believed that you spoke with consideration then you would find my tongue sharp and bitter. Perhaps it is good you do not flatter me. Though, truly, I know my capabilities as I also know my weaknesses, for only fools take to themselves the respect that is given to their office.'

Cass gazed uneasily into the ice-fire of those green eyes and swallowed.

'Let us agree, though,' she continued, 'that I shall not tell you how to wield your sword in combat if you do not advise me how to perform the art for which I was trained.'

The young man grimaced, a little sulkily.

'I only meant to say that the problem seems an insurmountable one.'

'In my experience, all problems start out from that viewpoint. But solving a problem means that you have to start out instead of staying still. Once your viewpoint changes then you change your view.'

'How then do you propose to start out?' he asked quickly, trying to pacify the feeling of friction which still lay below Fidelma's bantering tone.

'We will start out by questioning Brother Conghus, who found the body, then the physician who examined the body and finally our flustered house-steward, Brother Rumann, who made the initial investigation. All or any of these might have pieces of the puzzle. Then, when we have gathered all the pieces, however small, we will examine them, carefully and assiduously. Perhaps we will be able to fit them together to form a picture, who knows?'

'You make it seem rather easy.'

'Not easy,' she promptly denied. 'Remember that all information helps. Gather it and store it until you have a use for it. Now, I think I shall get some sleep before . . .'

As she began to rise a piercing shriek of terror shattered the silence of the guests' hostel.

Chapter Five

When the penetrating shriek echoed a second time, Fidelma was on her feet and moving down the corridor of the hostel with a rapidity which surprised the young warrior who followed closely on her heels. The cry had come from the first floor of the building. It had sounded high pitched, like the cry of a woman in pain.

At the foot of the stairs Fidelma almost collided with Brother Rumann. He, too, had been hurrying towards the sound of the cry and, without a word, Fidelma and Cass turned after the corpulent steward of the abbey as he made his way along the lower corridor, along which were a series of doors.

The three of them halted abruptly, astonished by the sound of a soft crooning issuing in the stillness.

Brother Rumann stood before a door and pushed it open. Fidelma and Cass peered questioningly over his shoulder.

Inside was the figure of Sister Eisten, seated on the edge of a cot with one of the black-haired lads from Rae na Scríne in her arms. Fidelma recognised him as Cosrach, the younger of the two boys. Sister Eisten was holding him and crooning a soft lullaby. The young boy lay quietly sobbing in her embrace. The sobs were now soft, gulping breaths. Sister Eisten seemed oblivious to the three of them crowding at the door.

It was the elder brother, the other black-haired lad, who, standing behind Sister Eisten, glanced up, saw them and scowled. He moved across the small chamber floor and, without appearing to do so, forced them back through the doorway into the corridor, following them and swinging the door shut behind him. He thrust out his chin; his expression seemed defiant, scowling at their intrusion.

'We heard a scream, boy,' Brother Rumann wheezed at him.

'It was my brother,' replied the boy with a surly tone. 'My brother was having a nightmare, that is all. He will be all right now. Sister Eisten heard him and came in to help.'

Fidelma bent forward, smiling reassuringly, trying to recall his name.

'Then there is nothing to be worried about, is there . . . your name is Cétach, isn't it?'

'Yes.' His tone was sullen, almost defensive.

'Very well, Cétach. Your brother and you have had a bad experience. But it is over now. There is no need to worry.'

'I am not worried,' the boy replied scornfully. 'But my brother is younger than I. He cannot help his dreams.'

Fidelma had the feeling that she was speaking to a man rather than a boy. The lad was wiser than his years.

'Of course not,' she readily agreed. 'You must persuade your brother that you are among friends now who will look after you.'

The boy waited a moment and then said: 'May I return to my brother now?'

Both boys would need time to get over the experience, thought Fidelma. She smiled again, this time a little falsely, and nodded assent.

As the door of the chamber closed behind the boy, Brother Rumann gave a distressed clucking sound before waddling back along the corridor.

Fidelma slowly retraced her steps to the stairway. Cass measured his pace to her shorter one.

'Poor little ones,' observed Cass. 'A bad thing has happened to them. I hope Salbach will find and punish Intat and his men soon.'

Fidelma nodded absently.

'At least the boy's needs seems to have stirred a response in Sister Eisten. I was more worried about her than the children. Children have a resilience. But Eisten took the death of the baby badly this morning.'

'There was nothing she could have done for it,' replied Cass logically, dismissing the emotional aspect of the event. 'Even if we had not been forced to camp in the open last night, the child would surely have died. I saw it had the plague symptoms.'

'*Deus vult*,' Fidelma replied automatically with a fatalism which she did not really believe. God wills it.

The chiming of the bell for vespers, the sixth canonical hour, brought Fidelma reluctantly from a deep sleep. Listening to the chimes, she realised that it was too late to join the brethren in the abbey church and so she dragged herself out of bed and began to intone the prayer of the hour. Most of the rituals of the church in the five kingdoms were still conducted in Greek, the language of the Faith in which the holy scriptures had been written. Many, however, were now turning to the language of Rome – Latin. Latin was replacing Greek as the one indispensable language of the church. Fidelma had little trouble switching from one language to another for she knew Latin as well as Greek, had a knowledge of Hebrew in addition to her native tongue and something of the languages of the Britons and the Saxons, too.

Having discharged her religious responsibility, Fidelma went to the bowl of water which stood on a table in her chamber and washed quickly in the near icy liquid. She towelled herself vigorously before dressing. When she was ready she went into the corridor. The door to Cass's chamber was opened and it was empty, so she proceeded down the corridor which was lit, now that dusk had fallen, with a few flickering candles in sheltered holders attached to the stone walls.

'Ah, Sister Fidelma.' It was the wheezy figure of Brother Rumann who had appeared in the gloom as she came down the stairs into the main hall on the ground floor of the hostel. 'Did you miss vespers?'

'I slept late and the bell awoke me. I made my invocations to Our Lord in my chamber.'

She bit her lip as she said it. She had not meant it to sound so defensive but she felt that there had been a tone of censure in the steward's voice.

Brother Rumann's large face creased into what she presumed was a smile, yet of disparagement or sympathy she knew not.

'The young warrior, Cass, went to the abbey church and is probably on his way directly to the *praintech*, as we call our refectory, for the evening meal. Shall I conduct you there?'

'Thank you, brother,' Fidelma solemnly replied. 'I would be grateful for your guidance.'

The pudgy religieux took a lighted lantern from its hook on the wall and proceeded to lead the way from the building along the now dark courtyard towards the adjoining building, a large construction into which many religious, both men and women, were filing in what seemed never-ending lines.

'Do not worry, sister,' Brother Rumann said. 'The abbot has given orders that you and the warrior Cass will be seated at his table at mealtimes during your stay with us.'

'At what should I worry?' queried Fidelma, glancing curiously at him.

'We have so many people at the abbey that we have to make three sittings for our meals. Those that have to wait until the third sitting often eat their meals cold, which causes complaint. This is why many of the brothers are now working on constructing a new dining hall at the eastern end of the abbey buildings. The new *praintech* is going to accommodate all of us.'

'A refectory which will contain several hundred souls under one roof?'

Fidelma could not keep the scepticism from her voice.

'Just so, sister. A great task and one which will be completed soon, *le cunamh Dé*.' He added the 'God willing' in a pious tone.

They paused in the hallway of the refectory and an attendant came forward to remove and stack their shoes or sandals, for it was the custom in most monastic communities that one sat down at the meal table in bare feet. Rumann then led the way into the crowded hall, along lines of tables packed with the religious of both sexes. The refectory hall was lit with numerous spluttering oil lamps whose pungent smell mingled with the heavy aroma of the smoky turf fire which smouldered in the great hearth at the head of the chamber. The odours were made even more piquant by the intermingling of the contents of incense burners placed at various points throughout the hall. Lamps and fire combined, however, to generate a poor heat against the cold of the autumnal evening. Only after a while, with the compactness of the two hundred bodies, did a warmth emerge.

The Abbot Brocc had already started the *Gratias* as Brother Rumann hurriedly conducted Fidelma to an empty place at the table, next to an amused looking Cass who smiled a silent greeting at her.

'*Benedic nobis, Domine Deus . . .*'

Fidelma hastily genuflected as she took her place.

'Did you oversleep?' whispered Cass cheerfully as he leant towards her.

Fidelma sniffed and ignored the question to which the answer was so obvious.

The *Gratias* ended and the room was filled with the noise of benches being scraped on the stone flags of the floor.

In spite of the fact that they had eaten only four hours before, Fidelma and Cass ate heartily of the dish of baked fish cooked with wild garlic and served with *duilesc*, a sea plant gathered from the rocks of the shore. Barley bread was served with this. Jugs of ale, stood on the table and the religious were allowed to help themselves to one pottery goblet each of the brew. The meal was finished with the serving of a dish of apples and some wheaten cakes kneaded with honey.

The meal was eaten without conversation, for this, as Fidelma realised, was the Rule of the Blessed Fachtna. However, during the course of the meal a *lector* intoned passages from the scriptures from a raised wooden lectern at the end of the room. Fidelma raised a tired smile as the *lector* chose to begin with a passage from the third chapter of *Ecclesiastes*: 'Every man should eat and drink, and enjoy the good of all his labour, it is the gift of God.'

The meal ended at the single chime of a bell and the Abbot Brocc rose to intone another *Gratias*.

Only when they were leaving the refectory, reclaiming their footwear, did Brocc approach them. At his side came the puffing figure of Brother Rumann.

'Have you rested well, cousin?' greeted the abbot.

'Well enough,' replied Fidelma. 'Now I should like your permission and authority to commence my task.'

'What can I do? You have only to ask.'

'I will need someone to act as an assistant, to find those people that I need to question and bring them to me and to run errands on my behalf. Thus they must know the abbey and be able to conduct me where I want to go.'

'Brother Rumann's assistant, Sister Necht, shall perform that task,' smiled the abbot, turning to the portly steward, who jerked his head up and down in agreement at the abbot's words. 'What else, cousin?'

'I shall need a chamber in which to conduct my inquiries. The room next to my chamber in the hostel would serve well.'

'It is yours for so long as you require it.'

'I will see this is so,' added Rumann, eager to please his abbot.

'Then there is no need to delay further. We shall start at once.'

'God's blessing on your work,' intoned the abbot solemnly. 'Keep me informed.'

He left the refectory with Brother Rumann clucking after him.

Sister Necht, Brother Rumann's assistant, was the young, heavy-looking woman whom Fidelma had seen briefly on entering the abbey. She had been asked by Conghus to take charge of Sister Eisten and the children. She was fresh-faced, with reddish, almost copper-burnished, curly hair tumbling under her head-dress. Her shoulders were too broad and her chin too square for her to be called attractive. Fidelma found that she was quick to smile but easy to upset. However, she was eager to please and obviously excited at being given a task which was not usual in the rigid sequentially ordered work that was the daily round of community.

If anything, Sister Necht showed herself to be somewhat in awe of Sister Fidelma. It was obvious that she had been told that Fidelma was sister to the heir-apparent of the kingdom, cousin to the abbot, and was, in her own right, a distinguished *dálaigh* of the law courts of the land who had stood to give judgment before the High King and even at the request of the Holy Father so far away in Rome. Young Sister Necht was clearly a hero-worshipper.

Fidelma immediately forgave her the nervousness and spaniel-like adoration. The age of innocence would soon pass. Fidelma felt that it was sad that children had so quickly to pass into adulthood. What was it that Publilius Syrus had written? If you would live innocently, do not lose the heart and mind you possessed in your childhood.

Having installed themselves in the chamber in which they

had eaten their first meal at the abbey, Fidelma sent Necht to bring the *aistreóir*, Brother Conghus, to them.

'We will start at the beginning,' she explained to Cass. 'Conghus was the first person to discover the body of the Venerable Dacán.'

Cass was unsure of his rôle now. He had no training in law and had never witnessed a *dálaigh* investigating a crime before. So he took up a seat in a corner of the chamber, in the background, and let Fidelma seat herself at the table on which a lantern had been placed to give light to the proceedings.

It was not long before a slightly breathless Sister Necht returned with the thickset doorkeeper, Brother Conghus, at her heels.

'I've brought him, sister,' gasped the girl, in a deep, husky voice which seemed her normal tone. 'Just as you said I should.'

Fidelma tried to suppress a smile and waved the young novice to take a seat by Cass.

'You may wait there, Sister Necht. You will not speak until I speak to you nor will you ever reveal anything that you may hear in this room. I must have your solemn oath on this, if you are to remain to assist me.'

The novice swore at once and assumed her place.

Fidelma then turned her sharp smile to Brother Conghus who had stood waiting in the doorway.

'Come in, shut the door and take a seat, brother,' she instructed firmly.

The doorkeeper did as he was bid.

'How may I help, sister?' he asked once he was settled.

'I must ask you some questions. I have to ask you, officially, if you know the purpose of my visit?'

Conghus shrugged: 'Who does not?'

'Very well. Let us go back to the day of the Venerable Dacán's death. I am told that you were the first to discover the body?'

Conghus grimaced as if in distaste at the memory.

'That is so.'

'Describe the circumstances, if you please.'

Conghus paused to gather his thoughts.

'Dacán was a man of regular habits. His day, so I had perceived, during the two months that he lodged at the abbey, was one of ritual observance. One could almost tell the time of day by his movements.'

He paused again as if reflecting.

'My job as doorkeeper also includes bellringer. I ring the main hours and services. The bell for matins heralds the beginning of our day which is followed by the *jentaculum*, our first meal of the day. Because we are a large community and our refectory cannot accommodate everyone, we eat in three separate sittings. Dacán invariable ate at the middle sitting as did I. This timing allows me the opportunity to pursue my duties at the ringing of the hours. After the third sitting for the *jentaculum* I ring the hour of the tierce when the work of the community starts.'

'I understand,' Fidelma said, when the doorkeeper paused and glanced at her in silent question to see if she was following.

'Well, this particular morning, two weeks ago on the day of Luan, Dacán was not at his place for the breaking of the fast. I made inquiries, for it was so unusual that he would miss a meal. You see . . .'

'You have already explained how rigid his habits were,' Fidelma interrupted quickly.

Conghus blinked and then nodded.

'Just so. Well, I ascertained that he had not been at the earlier sitting. So after I had eaten, curiosity took me to the hostel to look for him.'

'Where was his chamber?'

'On the first floor.' Conghus began to rise from his seat. 'I can show you the chamber now . . .'

Fidelma waved him back to his seat.

'You may do so in a moment. Let us continue. So, you came to search for Dacán?'

'I did. There is little more to add. I went to his chamber and called to him. There was no answer. So I opened the door . . .'

'No answer?' Fidelma interrupted. 'Surely if there was no answer, one might assume that the Venerable Dacán was not in his room? What made you decide to open the door?'

Conghus grimaced, frowning.

'Why . . . why, I saw a light flickering under the door. It is dark in the passage so any light shines out. The light attracted me. I reasoned that if Dacán had left a light burning, then I should extinguish it. Frugality is another Rule of the Blessed Fachtna,' he added sanctimoniously.

'I see. So you saw a light and then . . . ?'

'I went in.'

'What was the cause of the light?'

'There was an oil lamp lit, it was still burning.'

'Go on,' Fidelma urged, when Conghus continued to hesitate.

'Dacán was laying dead on his bed. That is all.'

Fidelma suppressed a sigh of irritation.

'Let us try to establish a few more details, Brother Conghus,' she said patiently. 'Imagine yourself back at the threshold of the door. Describe what you saw.'

Conghus frowned again and appeared to give some deep thought to the question.

'The chamber was lit by the oil lamp, which was on a small table at the side of the cot. Dacán was fully dressed. He was lying on his back. The first thing I noticed about him was that his feet and his hands were bound . . .'

'With rope?'

Conghus shook his head.

'With strips of cloth; linen cloth with parti-colours of blue and red. He also had a strip of the same cloth in his mouth. I presumed this was in the nature of a gag. Then I saw that there were bloodstains all over his chest. I realised that he had been killed.'

'Very well. Now tell me, was there any sign of a knife – the knife that inflicted the wounds?'

'None that I could see.'

'Was one found subsequently?'

'Not that I know of.'

'How were Dacán's features?'

'I do not understand,' frowned Conghus.

'Was the face calm and reposed? Were the eyes open or shut. How did he look?'

'Calm, I would say. There was no fear or pain engraved on the dead features, if that is what you mean.'

'That is precisely what I mean,' Fidelma replied grimly. 'Good. We now progress. You realised that Dacán had been killed. Did you notice anything else about the room? Had it been ransacked? Was it in order? If Dacán was so rigid in his habits it would imply that he would be scrupulously tidy.'

'The room was tidy so far as I can remember. You are right, of course, Dacán's fastidiousness was well known. But Sister Necht will tell you more about that.'

Fidelma heard a rustle and turned to frown a warning at the young novice in case she felt the need to respond.

'So.' Fidelma returned her gaze to Conghus. 'We begin to build up a picture. Go on. Having realised that Dacán had been killed, what then?'

'I made directly to see the abbot. I told him what I had discovered. He sent for our assistant physician, Brother Tóla, who examined the body and confirmed what I knew already. The abbot then placed matters in the hands of Brother Rumann. As steward of the abbey it was his job to conduct an inquiry.'

'One question here: you said that the abbot sent for the

assistant physician, Brother Tóla? Why did he not send for the chief physician? After all, the Venerable Dacán was a man of some standing.'

'That is true. But our chief physician, Brother Midach, was away from the abbey at that time.'

'You said that Dacán had been staying here two months,' observed Fidelma. 'How well had you come to know him?'

Brother Conghus raised his eyebrows.

'How well?' He grimaced wryly. 'The Venerable Dacán was not a man you came to know at all. He was reserved; austere, if you like. He came with a great reputation for piety and scholarship. But he was a man of brusque manner and testy demeanour. He was a man of regular habits . . . as I have said before . . . and never spent time merely gossiping. Whenever he went abroad from his chamber he went for a specific purpose and did not pause to exchange pleasantries or waste an hour or two in conversation.'

'You paint a very clear picture, Brother Conghus,' Fidelma said.

Conghus took it as a compliment and preened himself for a moment.

'As doorkeeper, it is my task to assess people and notice their behaviour.'

'Physically, what manner of man was he?'

'Elderly, well over three-score years. A tall man, in spite of his age. Thin, as if he were in need of a good meal. He had long white hair. Dark eyes and sallow skin. Perhaps the only real distinctive feature was a bulbous nose. His features were generally melancholy.'

'I am told that he came here to study. Do you know much about that?'

Brother Conghus pushed out his lower lip.

'On that matter you would have to consult the abbey's librarian.'

'And what is the name of this librarian?'

'Sister Grella.'

'I am told that the Venerable Dacán also taught,' Fidelma said, making a mental note. 'Do you know what he taught?'

Conghus shrugged.

'He taught some history, so I believe. But, it would probably be best if you saw Brother Ségán, our chief professor.'

'There is something else that puzzles me, though,' Fidelma said, after a moment's pause. 'You say that Dacán was austere. That was the word you used, wasn't it?'

Conghus nodded agreement.

'It is an interesting word, very descriptive,' she went on. 'Yet why did he have the reputation of one beloved by the people? Usually a man who is ascetic, compassionless and stern, for this is what austere seems to imply, would hardly be a likable person.'

'We must all speak as we find, sister,' declared Conghus. 'Perhaps the reputation, which doubtless was spread from Laigin, was unjustified?'

'That being so, why were you so worried when Dacán missed a single meal? If he were not that likable, surely human nature might react and say, why bother to go searching for such a man? Why did you go searching for the Venerable Dacán?'

Conghus looked uncomfortable.

'I am not sure that I follow your thoughts, sister,' he said stiffly.

'They are simple enough,' Fidelma pressed, her voice clear and slow. 'You seem to have been overly concerned with the fact that a man, whom you deemed unlikable, had missed the breaking of his fast to the extent that you went looking for him. Can you explain that?'

The doorkeeper compressed his lips, stared at her for a moment and then shrugged.

'A week before Dacán's death, the abbot called me to him

and told me to have a special care for Dacán. That was why I went to his chamber after he had missed his meal.'

It was Fidelma's turn to be surprised.

'Did the abbot explain why you should have this special care for Dacán?' she demanded. 'Was he afraid that something might happen to the Venerable Dacán?'

Conghus gestured with indifference.

'I am merely the *aistreóir* here, sister. I am doorkeeper and bellringer. When my abbot tells me to do something, I will do it, so long as it is not contrary to the laws of God and the Brehons. I will not question my abbot on his motives so long as those motives do not compass harm to his fellow men. It is my duty to obey and not to question.'

Fidelma gazed at him thoughtfully for a moment.

'That is an interesting philosophy, Conghus. It is one we might discuss at leisure. But let me get this clearly fixed in my mind. It was only a week before Dacán's murder that the abbot specifically asked you to keep a special watch over Dacán? He did not say why? He did not say whether he might have some reason to be fearful for Dacán's safety?'

'It is as I have already said, sister.'

Fidelma stood up with an abruptness that surprised everyone.

'Very well. Let us go downstairs so that you may show me the chamber that Dacán occupied.'

Conghus came to his feet, blinking a little at the rapid change.

He conducted them out of the room, along the corridor and down the stairs.

Cass and Sister Necht followed closely behind Fidelma. Necht's face still shone with enthusiastic excitement while Cass merely looked bewildered.

Conghus paused before a door on the ground floor of the hostel, at the far end of the corridor in which Sister Eisten and the children had their rooms.

'Does any one currently occupy the chamber?' Fidelma asked as Conghus bent to the handle in order to open the door.

Conghus hesitated and straightened up again.

'No, sister. It has been left unoccupied since the death of Dacán. In fact, his possessions have also been left untouched in the room by the order of the abbot. I believe that the representatives of Dacán's brother, Abbot Noé of Fearna, have demanded the return of these personal effects.'

'So why have they been kept?' interposed Cass, speaking for the first time since the questioning of Conghus began.

Conghus glanced at him, somewhat startled at his unexpected interruption.

'I presume that the abbot decided that nothing should be touched until the arrival of the *dálaigh* and the conclusion of the investigation.'

Conghus bent again, fumbled with the latch and then flung open the door. He was about to enter the dark room when Fidelma laid a hand on his arm and held him back.

'Get me a lantern.'

'There is an oil lamp beside the bed which I can light.'

'No,' Fidelma insisted. 'I want nothing touched or moved, if nothing has been moved so far. Sister Necht, hand me down that oil lamp behind you.'

The young novice moved with alacrity to take down the lamp from its wall fixture.

Fidelma took the lamp, holding it high, and stood on the threshold peering round.

The chamber was almost as she had envisaged it would be.

There was a bed, a wooden cot with a straw palliasse and blankets in one corner. By it was a small table on which stood an oil lamp. On the floor, just below this, was a pair of worn sandals. From a row of pegs hung three large leather satchels. There was another table at the end of the bed on which were spread some wooden writing tablets covered with a wax surface and nearby a *graib*, a stylus of pointed metal, for writing. Next to this was a small pile of vellum sheets and a cow's horn which was obviously an *adircín* used for containing *dubh* or ink made from carbon. A selection of quills taken from crows was piled next to it and a small knife ready for their sharpening. Fidelma realised that Dacán, like most scribes, would make his notes on the wax tablets and then transcribe them for permanence onto his vellum sheets, which would then be bound.

She hesitated a moment more to ensure that she had missed nothing in her initial cursory examination. Then she stepped to the table and stared at the wax writing tablets. Her lips turned down in disappointment when she saw they were empty of characters. The surface had been smoothed clean.

She turned to Conghus.

'I do not imagine that you would have noticed whether these were clean or written on at the time Dacán's body was discovered?'

Conghus shook his head negatively.

Fidelma sighed and peered at the vellum sheets. They were equally devoid of content.

She turned round. There were dark stains on the blankets still piled untidily on the bed. It needed no great intelligence to realise that the stains were dried blood. She peered along the pegs on the wall and began to examine the contents of the leather satchels ranged there. They contained a change of underwear, a cloak, some shirts and other garments. There was also some shaving equipment and toiletry articles but little else. Carefully, Fidelma repacked the items into the satchels and hung them back on their pegs.

She stood for a moment, peering round the chamber before, to the surprise of those watching, lowering herself to her knees and carefully examining the floor still holding the lantern in one hand.

It was covered in a thin layer of dust. Brother Conghus was

apparently correct when he said no one had been in the chamber since the murder. Fidelma suddenly reached forward under the bed and drew out what appeared to be a short stick. It was an eighteen-inch wand of aspen wood cut with notches. It was so inconspicuous that it might easily be overlooked.

She heard a faint gasp at the door and turned to see Sister Necht staring from the doorway.

'Do you recognise this?' she demanded quickly of the young novice, holding it up in the light.

Necht shook her head immediately.

'It was . . . no, I thought it was something else. No, I was wrong. I have not seen it before.'

Still holding her find, Fidelma's eye fell on the small table by the cot. The only thing on it was the small pottery oil lamp. She transferred the wooden stick to the hand with the lantern and reached down to lift up the lamp with her free hand. It was heavy and obviously filled with oil. She replaced it and transferred the stick back again to her other hand.

She walked back to the threshold, where the others were crowding, waiting expectantly as if she were about to make some profound announcement. She was still absently clutching the aspen wand.

Fidelma turned back into the chamber and stood holding up the lamp high in order to let its light fall on the greater part of the room. Her eyes moved slowly and carefully over the chamber trying not to miss anything.

It was a dark cell of a room. There was only a small window, high up on the wall above the bed, which would give precious little light. Not only was the window small but it was north facing. The light, she reasoned, would be a cold, grey one. A room like this, for someone to function in, would have to be permanently illuminated. She turned and examined the door. There was nothing unusual here. No lock nor bolt, just a normal latch.

'Is there anything more that you require of me, sister?'

Brother Conghus asked after they had all stood in silence a while. 'The hour approaches for me to ring the bell for the *completa*.'

The *completa* or compline was the seventh and last religious service of the day.

Fidelma dragged her gaze reluctantly from the room.

'Sister?' Conghus pressed when she appeared to be still lost deep in thought.

With a small breath of a sigh she blinked and focused on him.

'Oh? Oh yes, but one more thing, Conghus. The strips of coloured linen with which you say Dacán was bound – what happened to them?'

Conghus shrugged.

'I really cannot say. I presume that the physician would have removed them. Is that all?'

'You may go now,' she agreed. 'But I may wish to speak with you again later.'

Conghus turned and hurried away.

Fidelma glanced towards the young sister.

'Now, Sister Necht, can you find me the physician, was Brother Tóla his name?'

'The assistant physician? Of course,' the novice replied immediately, and was turning eagerly to the task before Fidelma had even told her the nature of the errand.

'Wait!' Fidelma chuckled at her enthusiasm. 'When you find him, bring him here to see me immediately. I will be waiting.'

The young sister scampered away quickly.

Fidelma began to examine the notches on the aspen wand.

'What is it?' asked Cass in curiosity. 'Can you read those ancient letters?' '

'Yes. Can you understand Ogham?'

Cass shook his head regretfully.

'I have never been taught the art of the old alphabet, sister.'

'This is one from a bundle of rods of the poets, as they are called. It appears to be a will of sorts. Yet it does not make sense. This one says "let my sweet cousin care for my sons on the rock of Michael as my honourable cousin shall dictate". Curious.'

'What does it signify?' he asked in confusion.

'Remember what I said about gathering information? It is like gathering the ingredients for a dish. You may gather something here and something there and, when all is complete, you start to construct the meal. Alas, we don't have all the ingredients yet. But at least we know more than before. We know, importantly, that this was a carefully conceived murder.'

Cass just stared at her.

'Carefully conceived? The frenzy of the attack makes it appear that the killer fell into a violent rage. That surely means that it was an act of angry impulse and not premeditated.'

'Perhaps. But it was not a violent rage that caused the old man to be bound hand and foot without a struggle. That speaks of premeditation. And what produced such a rage in the killer? A stranger, a man or women who slew at random, could surely not create the fury which caused such violence?'

She broke off and was silent as if something had just occurred to her.

'What is the matter?' Cass pressed when he saw that her mind seemed to have wandered off somewhere else. She kept looking into the chamber with a frown. Finally, she moved back into the room and placed the lantern on the writing table so that it illuminated the room to the best advantage.

'I wish I knew,' she confessed hesitantly. 'I feel that there is something not quite right about this chamber; something that I should be noticing.'

Chapter Six

Brother Tóla, the abbey's assistant physician, was a man with silvery grey hair and soft and pleasant features, continually smiling as though laughing at life. Fidelma reflected that most of the physicians whom she had encountered had been men and women with a joy for life and who regarded all its tragedies with a wry humour. Perhaps, she reasoned, this was a defence against their continual relationship with death or perhaps the very experience of death and human tragedy had conditioned them to accepting that while one had life, had reasonable health, then that life should be enjoyed as much as possible.

'There are just a few questions that I would like to ask,' Fidelma began, after the introductions were over. They were still standing outside the door of the chamber which had once been occupied by Dacán.

'Anything that I can do, sister.' Tóla smiled, his eyes twinkling with laughter as he spoke. 'I fear it will not be much, but ask your questions.'

'I am told that shortly after Brother Conghus found the dead body of the Venerable Dacán, the Abbot Brocc summoned you to examine the body?'

'This is so.'

'You are the assistant physician of the abbey?'

'That is so. Brother Midach is our chief physician.'

'Forgive me, but why did the abbot summon you and not Brother Midach?'

She had already heard the answer but Fidelma wanted to make sure.

'Brother Midach was not in the abbey. He had left the previous evening on a journey and did not return for six days. As physicians, our services are often in demand in many neighbouring villages.'

'Very well. Can you tell me the details of your findings?'

'Of course. It was just after tierce and Brother Martan, who is the apothecary, had remarked that the bell had not rung the hour . . .'

Fidelma was interested.

'The bell had not rung? How then did the apothecary know it was after tierce?'

Tóla chuckled dryly.

'No mystery there. Martan is not only the apothecary but he is interested in the measurement of time. We have, within the community, a clepsydra, a plan for which one of our brethren brought back from a pilgrimage to the Holy Land many years ago. A clepsydra is . . .'

Fidelma held up her hand in interruption.

'I know what it is. So the apothecary had checked this water-clock . . . ?'

'Actually, no. Martan frequently compares the clepsydra – or water-clock, as you call it – against a more ancient engine of measurement in his dispensary. It is old-fashioned but workable. He has a mechanism which discharges sand from one part to another, the sand is measured so that it falls in a precise time.'

'An hour glass?' smiled Cass complacently. 'I have seen them.'

'The same basis,' Brother Tóla agreed easily. 'But Martan's mechanism was constructed fifty years ago by an artisan of this abbey. The mechanism is of larger proportions than an hour glass and the sand does not complete its fall from one compartment to another for one full *cadar*.'

Fidelma raised her eyebrows in astonishment. A *cadar* was the measure of one quarter of the day.

'I would like to see this wondrous machine sometime,' she confessed. 'However, we are straying from your story.'

'Brother Martan had informed me that it was well after the time for tierce and, just then, Abbot Brocc summoned me. I went to his chambers and he told me that the Venerable Dacán had been found dead. He wanted me to examine the body.'

'And had you known Dacán?'

Tóla nodded thoughtfully.

'We are a large community here, sister, but not so large that a man of distinguished ability goes unnoticed in our midst.'

'I mean, had you personal contact with him?'

'I shared his table during meals but, apart from a few words, had little to do with him. He was not a man who encouraged friendship, he was cold and . . . well, cold and . . .'

'Austere?' supplied Fidelma grimly.

'Just so,' Tóla agreed readily.

'So you came to the hostel?' prompted Fidelma again. 'Can you describe what you found?'

'Surely. Dacán was lying on the bed. He was lying on his back. His hands were tied behind him and his feet were bound at the ankles. There was a gag in his mouth. There was blood on his chest and it was obvious, to me at least, that it was the result of several stab wounds.'

'Ah? How many stab wounds?'

'Seven, though I could not tell at first.'

'You say that he was lying on his back? Can you remember the position of the blanket? Had the blanket been thrown over him or was he lying on top of it?'

Tóla shook his head, a little bewildered by the question.

'He lay fully clad on top of the blanket.'

'Had the blood spurted from the body onto the blanket, staining it?'

'No; such wounds bleed profusely but because the man was on his back the blood had congealed mainly on his chest.'

'The blanket, then, was not used to carry the body nor wipe the blood?'

'Not to my knowledge. Why are you concerned with this blanket?'

Fidelma ignored his question and motioned him to continue.

'When I had the body removed to the mortuary and had it washed, I was able to confirm my initial findings. There were seven stab wounds in the chest, around the heart and into the heart itself. Four of them were mortal blows.'

'Does that speak to you of a frenzied attack?' mused Fidelma.

Tóla looked at her appreciatively.

'It seems to indicate an attack in hot blood. In cold blood, the attacker had only need to strike one blow into the heart. After all, the old man's hands and feet were bound.'

Fidelma pursed her lips thoughtfully and nodded.

'Continue. Was there any indication when this deed was done?'

'I can only say that, when I examined the body, the attack had not been a recent one. The body was almost cold to the touch.'

'There was no sign of the weapon?'

'None.'

'Now, can you show me exactly how the body was lying on the cot? Would you mind?'

Tóla cast a glance of curiosity at her and then shrugged. He entered the chamber while she stood at the door, holding the lamp high so that she could see everything. He placed himself in a reclining position on the cot. Fidelma noticed, with interest, that he did not lie fully on the cot but only from his waist; he hung the lower part of his body over the edge of the bed so that the feet were touching the floor. The upper part was therefore at an angle. He had placed his arms behind him to suggest them being bound. The head was well back and the eyes were shut. The position suggested that Dacán had been attacked while standing and had simply fallen back on the bed behind him.

'I am grateful, Tóla,' Fidelma said. 'You are an excellent witness.'

Tóla raised himself from the bed and his voice was dry and expressionless.

'I have worked with a *dálaigh* before, sister.'

'So, when you came in here, did you notice the state of the chamber?'

'Not specifically,' he confessed. 'My eyes were for the corpse of Dacán and what had caused his death.'

'Try to remember, if you can. Was the room tidy or was it disturbed?'

Tóla gazed around him, as if trying to recall.

'Tidy, I would say. The lamp on the table was still burning. Yes, tidy as you see the room now. I believe, from the gossip I have heard, that the venerable Dacán was an extremely fastidious man, tidy to the point of being obsessive.'

'Who told you this?' queried Fidelma.

Tóla shrugged.

'Brother Rumann, I believe. He had charge of the investigation afterwards.'

'There is now little else that I need trouble you with,' Fidelma said. 'You had the body removed and examined it. Did you touch the lamp at all? For example, did you refill it with oil?'

'The only time I touched the lamp was to extinguish it when we took Dacán's body from this chamber.'

'Presumably, Dacán was buried here in the abbey?'

To her surprise, Tóla shook his head.

'No, the body was transported to the abbey of Fearna at the request of Dacán's brother, Abbot Noé.'

Fidelma took a moment or two to gather her thoughts.

'I thought that Abbot Brocc had refused to send any of the property of Dacán back to Laigin, knowing it would be the subject of investigation?' she said sharply. 'This seems a contrary thing – that he kept the possessions of Dacán but sent the body to Laigin.'

Tóla shrugged diffidently.

'Perhaps the reason lies in the fact that one cannot preserve a corpse,' he replied with a grim smile. 'Anyway, by that time, Brother Midach, our chief physician, had arrived back at the abbey and took over the arrangements. He was the one who authorised the removal of the body.'

'You said that was almost six days later?'

'That's right. A Laigin ship had arrived to demand the body. Of course, by that time, we had already placed the body in our own crypt, a cave in the hill behind us where the abbots of this monastery are interred. We had the corpse placed aboard the vessel from Laigin and presumably the Venerable Dacán's relics will now reside in Fearna.'

Fidelma shook her head in bewilderment.

'Does it not seem curious that Laigin was so quick to learn about the death of Dacán and so quick to demand the return of his body? You say that the Laigin ship arrived here six days after the killing?'

Tóla shrugged expressively.

'We are a coastal settlement here, sister. We are constantly in touch with many parts of the country and, indeed, our ships sail to Gaul with whom we regularly trade. The wine in this abbey, for example, is imported directly from Gaul. With a good tide and wind, one of the fast *barca* could leave here and be at the mouth of the River Breacán within two days. Fearna is only a few hours' ride from the river's mouth. I have sailed there myself several times. I know the waters along this southern coast well.'

Fidelma knew the capabilities of the *barca*, the lightly built coastal vessels which traded around the shores of the five kingdoms.

'That is, as you say, with ideal conditions, Tóla,' she agreed. 'It still seems to me to show that Abbot Noé learnt very quickly of his brother's death. But, I'll grant you, it could be done. So Dacán's body was returned to Fearna?'

'It was.'

'When did the warship of Laigin arrive here? The one that still is at anchor in the inlet.'

'About three days after the other ship left for Fearna with the body of Dacán.'

'Then obviously both ships were sent by Laigin within a few days after Dacán's murder. The Laigin king must have known what he was going to do almost as soon as he received word that Dacán had been murdered.' She was speaking half to herself, as if clarifying a thought.

Tóla did not feel that he was required to make any comment.

Fidelma gave a long sigh as she pondered the difficulties of the case. Finally, she said: 'When you examined the body of Dacán, did any other matters strike your eye?'

'Such as?'

'I do not know,' Fidelma confessed. 'Was there anything unusual?'

Tóla gestured negatively.

'There were just the stab wounds that caused his death, that is all.'

'But there were no bruises, no signs of a struggle prior to his being bound? No marks of his being held down by force in order to bind him? No mark of his being knocked unconscious in order that he could be bound?'

Tóla's expression changed as he saw what she was driving at.

'You mean, how could his enemy bind him without a struggle?'

Fidelma smiled tightly.

'That is exactly what I mean, Tóla. Did he calmly let his attackers bind his hands and feet without a struggle?'

Tóla looked serious for the first time during their conversation.

'There were no bruises that I saw. It did not occur to me . . .'

He paused and grimaced in annoyance.

'What?' demanded Fidelma.

'I am incompetent,' sighed Tóla.

'Why so?'

'I should have asked this very question at the time but I did not. I am sure, however, that there were no bruises on the body and, while the bonds on the wrists and ankles were tight, there was no bruising to show how they had been administered.'

'What were the bonds made of?' Fidelma asked, wishing to check what she had learnt already.

'Torn pieces of cloth. As I recall they were pieces of linen and dyed.'

'Can you recall the dyes?'

'Blue and red, I believe.'

Fidelma nodded. The evidence concurred with that given by Brother Conghus.

'I suppose that they were thrown away?' Fidelma queried, presuming the worst.

She was surprised when Tóla shook his head.

'As a matter of fact, no. Our enterprising apothecary, Brother Martan, has a morbid taste for relics and decided that the bonds of Dacán might one day become a much-sought-after and valuable relic, especially if the Faith recognises him as a man of great sanctity.'

'So this Brother . . . ?'

'Martan,' supplied Tóla.

'So this Brother Martan has kept the material?'

'Exactly so.'

'Well,' Fidelma smiled in relief, 'that is excellent. However, I will have to take temporary charge of them as being evidence pertinent to my inquiry. You may tell Brother Martan that he will get them returned as soon as I have done.'

Tóla nodded thoughtfully.

'But how did Dacán get himself bound by his enemies without a struggle?'

Fidelma pulled a face.

'Maybe he did not suspect that they were his enemies until later. Just one more point of clarification, though, and then I think we are done. You said that the body was cold and implied that it had been a long time dead. How long?'

'It is hard to judge. Several hours at least. I do not know when Dacán was last seen but he may well have been killed around midnight. Certainly the death occurred during the night and not later.'

Fidelma found herself focusing on the oil lamp which stood on the table by the cot.

'Dacán was killed sometime about midnight,' she said reflectively. 'Yet when he was found the oil lamp was burning.'

Cass, who had been more or less a silent spectator to Fidelma's questioning of Brother Tóla, was watching her with interest.

'Why do you remark on that, sister?' he queried.

Fidelma went once more to the lamp and picked it up carefully so as not to spill any oil from it. Silently, she handed it to him with equal care. He took it, the bewilderment on his face increasing.

'I do not understand,' he said.

'Do you notice anything odd about the lamp?'

He shook his head.

'It is still filled with oil. If this is the same lamp, then it could not have been burning more than an hour from the time Brother Conghus discovered the body.'

* * *

Sister Fidelma sat on the cot in her chamber, hands linked together at the back of her head, staring upwards into the gloom. She had decided to call a halt to the investigation for that evening. She had thanked Brother Tóla for his help and reminded him once more that, on the following morning, Brother Martan must hand over to her the strips of cloth that had bound Dacán. Then she had bade the young, enthusiastic Sister Necht a 'good night's repose' and told her to report to her again with Brother Rumann the next morning.

She and Cass had retired to their respective rooms and now, instead of falling immediately to sleep, she sat, leaning back on her cot, with the lamp still burning wastefully while she considered the information she had gathered so far.

One thing she now realised was that her cousin, the Abbot Brocc, was being a little selective with the information he had given her. Why had he asked Brother Conghus to keep a watchful eye on Dacán only a week before Dacán was killed? Well, that was something which she would have to sort out with Brocc.

There was a soft tap on the door of her chamber.

Frowning, she swung off her cot and opened it.

Cass was standing outside.

'I saw your light still on. I hope I am not disturbing you, sister?'

Fidelma shook her head, bade him enter and take the only chair that there was in the chamber while she returned to her seat on the bed. For propriety's sake, she left the door open. In some communities, the new moral codes were changing the older foundations. Many leaders of the Faith, like Ultan of Armagh, were arguing against the continued existence of mixed communities and even putting forward the unpopular concept of celibacy among leading religions.

She was aware that an encyclical attributed to Patrick was being circulated giving thirty-five rules for the followers of the Faith. The ninth rule ordered that an unmarried monk or anchoress, each from a different place, should not stay in the same hostel or house, nor travel together in one chariot from house to house nor converse freely together. And according to the seventeenth rule, a woman who took a vow of chastity and then married was to be excommunicated unless she deserted her husband and did a penance. Fidelma had been enraged by the circulation of the document in the name of Patrick and his fellow bishops, Auxilius and Iserninus, because it was so contrary to the laws of the five kingdoms. Indeed, what had made her actually suspicious of the authenticity of the document was that the first rule decreed that any member of the religious who appealed to the secular laws merited excommunication. After all, two hundred years ago Patrick himself was one of the nine-man commission which had been established by the High King, Laoghaire, to put all the civil and criminal laws of the five kingdoms in the new writing.

To Fidelma, the circulation of the 'rules of the first council of Patrick', as they were being called, was another piece of propaganda from the camp of the pro-Roman faction which wished the Faith in the five kingdoms of Éireann to be governed entirely from Rome.

She caught herself as she became aware that Cass had been saying something.

'I am sorry,' she said awkwardly, 'my mind was drifting miles away. What were you saying?'

The young warrior stretched his legs in the cramped chair.

'I was saying that I had an idea about the lamp.'

'Oh?'

'It is obvious that someone refilled it when Dacán's body was discovered.'

Fidelma examined his guileless eyes solemnly.

'It is certainly obvious that the lamp could not have been

burning all through the night, if Dacán was killed at midnight or soon after . . . that is,' she gave a mischievous grin, 'unless we are witnesses to a miracle; the miracle of the self-refilling lamp.'

Cass frowned, not sure how to take her levity.

'Then it is as I say,' he insisted.

'Perhaps. Yet we are told that Brother Conghus discovered the body and found the lamp burning. He did not refill it. It was still burning when Brother Tóla went to examine the body and he swears that he did not refill it. He further told us, when I raised that very point, that he had extinguished the light when he and his assistant, Brother Martan, carried the body to his mortuary for examination. Who then refilled it?'

Cass thought for a moment.

'Then it must have been refilled just before the body was discovered or after the body was carried away,' he said triumphantly. 'After all, you judged for yourself that the lamp could only have burning no more than an hour by the amount of oil still left in it. So someone must have refilled it.'

Fidelma regarded Cass with a sudden amusement.

'You know, Cass, you are beginning to display the mind of a *dálaigh*.'

Cass returned her look with a frown, unsure whether Fidelma was mocking him or not.

'Well . . .' he began, starting to rise with a petulant expression.

She held up a hand and motioned for him to remain.

'I am not being flippant, Cass. Seriously, you have a made point which I have neglected to see. The lamp was certainly refilled just before Conghus discovered the body.'

Cass sat back with a smile of satisfaction.

'There! I hope I have contributed to solving a minor mystery.'

'Minor?' There was a sharp note of admonishment in Fidelma's voice.

'What matter whether a lamp is filled or unfilled?' Cass asked, spreading his hands in emphasis. 'The main problem is to find who killed Dacán.'

Fidelma shook her head sadly.

'There is no item too unimportant to be discarded when searching for a truth. What did I say about gathering the pieces of a puzzle? Gather each fragment, even if they do not seem to be connected. Gather and store them. This applies especially to those pieces which seem odd, which seem inexplicable.'

'But what would a lamp matter in this affair?' demanded Cass.

'We will only know that when we find out. We cannot find out unless we start to ask questions.'

'Your art seems a complicated one, sister.'

Fidelma shook her head.

'Not really. I would think that your art is even more complicated than mine in terms of making judgments.'

'My art?' Cass drew himself up. 'I am a simple warrior in the service of my king. I adhere to the code of honour that each warrior has. What judgments do I have to make?'

'The judgment of when to kill, when to maim and when not. Above all, your task is to kill while our Faith forbids us to do so. Have you ever solved that conundrum?'

Cass flushed in annoyance.

'I am a warrior. I kill only the wicked – the enemies of my people.'

Fidelma smiled thinly.

'It sounds as if you believe them to be one and the same. Yet the Faith says, do not kill. Surely if we kill, if only to stop the wicked and evil, then the very act makes us as guilty as those we kill?'

Cass sniffed disdainfully.

'You would rather that they killed you instead?' he asked cynically.

'If we believe in the teachings of our Faith, then we must believe this was the example Christ left us. As Matthew records the Saviour's words, "those who live by the sword shall die by the sword".'

'Well, you cannot believe in that example,' scoffed Cass.

Fidelma was interested by his reaction, for she had long struggled with some of the theology of the Faith and had still not found a firm enough ground to argue many of its basic tenants. She often expressed her doubts in argument by taking the part of a devil's advocate and through that means she clarified her own attitudes.

'Why so?' she demanded.

'Because you are a *dálaigh*. You believe in the law. You specialise in seeking out killers and bringing them to justice. You believe in punishing those who kill, even to the point of raising the sword against them. You do not stand aside and say this is God's will. I have heard a man of the Faith denouncing the Brehons also in the words of Matthew. "Judge not or you will be judge", he said. You advocates of the law ignore Matthew's words on that so do I ignore Matthew's words against the profession of the sword.'

Fidelma sighed contritely.

'You are right. It is hard to "turn the other cheek" in all things. We are only human.'

Somehow she had never felt comfortable with Luke's record of Jesus' teaching that if someone steals a person's cloak, then that person should give the thief his shirt also. Surely if one courted such oppression, such as turning the other cheek, it meant one was equally as guilty for it gave actual invitation to further theft and injury at the hands of the wrongdoer. Yet according to Matthew, Jesus said: "Think not that I am come to send peace on earth; I came not to send peace, but a sword. For I am come to set a man at variance against his father, and the daughter against her mother, and the daughter-in-law against her mother-in-law, and a man's foes, they shall be of his own household". It was confusing. And long had Fidelma troubled over it.

'Perhaps the Faith expects too much from us?' Cass interrupted her thoughts.

'Perhaps. But the expectation of humankind should always exceed their grasp otherwise there would be no progress in life.'

Fidelma's features suddenly dissolved into an urchin grin.

'You must forgive me, Cass, for at times I do but try to test my attitudes against the Faith.'

The young warrior was indifferent.

'I have no such need,' he replied.

'Then your faith is great.' Fidelma was unable to keep a note of sarcasm from her voice.

'Why should I doubt what the prelates preach?' inquired Cass. 'I am a simple person. They have considered these matters for centuries and if they say this is so, then so it must be.'

Fidelma shook her head, sorrowfully. It was at times like these that she missed the stormy arguments that she had experienced with Brother Eadulf of Seaxmund's Ham.

'Christ is God's son,' she said firmly. 'Therefore He would approve of the homage of reason, for if there is no doubt there can be no faith.'

'You are a philosopher, Fidelma of Kildare. But I did not expect a religieuse to question her Faith.'

'I have lived too long not to be a sceptic, Cass of Cashel. One should go through life being sceptical of all things and particularly of oneself. But now, we have exhausted the subject and should retire. We have much to do in the morning.'

She rose and Cass reluctantly followed her example.

After he had left her chamber, she lay back on her cot and this time she doused the lamp.

She tried hard to conjure what facts she had learnt about the

Venerable Dacán's death to her mind. However, she found other thoughts now dominating her senses. They concerned Eadulf of Seaxmund's Ham. As she thought of him, she had a curious feeling of loneliness again, as if of home-sickness.

She missed their debates. She missed the way she could tease Eadulf over their conflicting opinions and philosophies; the way he would always rise good-naturedly to the bait. Their arguments would rage but there was no enmity between them. They would learn together as they examined their interpretations and debated their ideas.

She missed Eadulf. She could not deny that.

Cass was a simple man. He was agreeable enough; congenial company; a man who held a good moral code. But, for her, he was without the sharp humour which she needed; without a broad perspective of knowledge with which her own knowledge could contest. Now that she considered it, Cass reminded her a little of someone responsible for an unpleasant episode in her early life. When she was seventeen she had fallen in love with a young warrior named Cian. He had been in the élite bodyguard of the High King, who was Cellach at that time. She had been young and carefree but in love. Cian had not cared for her intellectual pursuits and had eventually left her for another. His rejection of her had left her disillusioned. She felt bitter, although the years had tempered her attitude. But she had never forgotten her experience, nor really recovered from it. Perhaps she had never allowed herself to do so.

Eadulf of Seaxmund's Ham had been the only man of her own age in whose company she had felt really at ease and able to express herself.

Perhaps she had started the argument on Faith as a means of testing Cass.

Then, why should she want to test Cass? For what purpose? Because she wanted Eadulf's company and was looking for a surrogate?

She gave a hiss of breath in the darkness, scandalised by the idea. A ridiculous idea.

After all, she had spent several days in Cass's company on the journey here and there had been no problem.

Perhaps the key to the situation lay in the fact that she was, indeed, trying to recreate Eadulf and that recreation had been prompted by the fact that she was investigating a murder with Cass as her companion whereas, before, it was Eadulf who had been her comrade, the sounding board against which she could bounce her ideas.

But why should she want to recreate Eadulf?

She exhaled again sharply as if to expel the very thoughts from her mind. Then she turned over and buried her face angrily into the pillow.

Chapter Seven

The weather had changed again with the bewildering rapidity that was common to the islands and peninsulas of the south-west of Muman. While the sky remained a clear, almost translucent blue, the sun shone with a warmth which made the day more akin to the dying summer than to late autumn. The high winds had been dispelled although a sea breeze remained, blustery but not strong. Therefore, the sea was not totally calm, more choppy and brooding, causing the ships, anchored in the inlet before Ros Ailithir, to jerk now and then at their moorings. Above, in the gull-dominated sky, large, dark-coloured cormorants also wheeled and dived, fighting for a place to fish among the plaintive, protesting shrieks of their companions. Here and there, sooty, white-rumped storm petrels, driven seaward by the previous stormy weather were now returning to the coastline.

Fidelma had perched herself on the top of the thick stone wall of the monastery, where a walkway ran around it as if it were a battlement. She gazed thoughtfully down into the inlet. There were a few local fishing boats, a couple of coastal vessels or *barca* and an ocean-going vessel which traded with Britain or Gaul. She had been told that it was a Frankish merchantman. But it was the warship of the Laigin king, lying menacingly near the entrance to the harbour, with its sleek, malevolent lines, which took her interest.

Fidelma had sat for a long while, arms folded, examining the vessel with curiosity. She wondered what Fianamail, the young king of Laigin, hoped to gain by such an intimidating display. She could understand that demanding the territory of Osraige as an honour price was merely a political move to regain the lost territory, but he was certainly being blatant about it. No one would surely believe that the death of the Venerable Dacán, even though he was a cousin to the Laigin king, merited the return of a land which had held allegiance to Cashel for over five hundred years. Why would Fianamail threaten war over such a matter?

She gazed down on the fluttering silk standard of the Laigin kings, proudly streaking in the sea breeze which caught at the mast head. There were several warriors on deck practising their weaponry arts, which she felt was rather ostentatious and more for the benefit of observers on the shore than for the Laigin warriors to keep in practise.

Fidelma wished that she had paid more attention to that section of the Book of Acaill, the great law code, which dwelt specifically with the *muir-bretha* or sea laws. The law should surely say whether such intimidation was allowed. She had a vague feeling that the writhe, placed at the gates of the abbey, meant something in this connection but she was not sure what. She wondered whether the Tech Screptra, the library of the abbey, might have copies of the law books which she could consult on the subject.

The single bell announcing the tierce rang out from the bell house.

Fidelma pulled herself away from the mesmerising scene, rose and proceeded to walk back, along the wooden walkway along the monastery wall, towards the steps which led to the interior grounds of Ros Ailithir. A familiar figure was standing looking out to sea a little farther along the wall. It was the plump Sister Eisten. She did not notice Fidelma, so intent was her gaze on the inlet.

Fidelma arrived at her side unnoticed.

'A beautiful morning, sister,' she greeted.

Sister Eisten started and turned, her mouth rounded in surprise. She blinked and carefully inclined her head.

'Sister Fidelma. Yes. It is beautiful.' There was no warmth in her reply.

'How are you today?'

'I am well.'

The terse, monosyllabic tones seemed forced.

'That is good. You have come through a bad experience. And is the little boy well now?'

Sister Eisten looked confused.

'Little boy?'

'Yes. Has he recovered from his nightmare?' When she saw that Sister Eisten still did not appear to understand, she added: 'The boy whose name is Cosrach. You were nursing him yesterday afternoon.'

Sister Eisten blinked rapidly.

'Oh . . . yes.' She did not sound sure.

'Sister Fidelma!'

Fidelma turned as she heard her name called. It was young Sister Necht, hurrying up the steps to the walkway. She seemed anxious and Fidelma had a curious feeling that her anxiety was at finding Sister Eisten with Fidelma.

'Brother Rumann is ready to see you now, sister,' Sister Necht announced. 'He's waiting impatiently at the hostel.'

Fidelma paused and glanced at Eisten. 'Are you sure all is well with you?'

'All is well, thank you,' she replied without conviction.

'Well, if you have need of a soul-friend, you have but to call upon me.'

In the Irish Church, unlike the Roman custom where all were ordered to make a confession of their sins to a priest, each person had an *anamchara*, or a soul-friend. The position of the soul-friend was one of trust. He or she was not a confessor but more of a confidant, a spiritual guide who acted according to the practices of the faith of the five kingdoms. Fidelma's soul-friend, since she had reached the age of choice, had been Liadin of the Uí Dróna, her girlfriend since childhood. But it did not necessarily follow that the soul-friend had to be of the same sex. Colmcille and others who were leaders of the Faith had chosen soul-friends of the opposite sex.

Eisten was shaking her head swiftly.

'I already have a soul-friend in this abbey,' she said uncompromisingly.

Fidelma sighed as she unwillingly turned to follow Sister Necht. Of course all was not well with Eisten. There was something continuing to trouble her. She was about to descend the stairs when Sister Eisten's voice stayed her.

'Tell me, sister . . .'

Fidelma turned inquiringly back to the morose young anchoress. She was still staring glumly out to sea.

'Tell me, sister, can a soul-friend betray one's confidence?'

'If they do, then I fail to see how they can be a soul-friend,' Fidelma replied at once. 'It depends on the circumstances.'

'Sister!' It was Necht agitating from the foot of the stair.

'Let us talk about this matter later,' Fidelma suggested. There was no answer and after a moment she reluctantly went down the stairs after Necht.

In the room now designated for Fidelma to conduct her inquiries in, the portly figure of the *fer-tighis*, the steward of the abbey, was indeed waiting impatiently.

Fidelma slipped into her seat opposite Brother Rumann, noticing that Cass had already assumed his seat in the corner of the chamber. Fidelma turned to Sister Necht. She had given much thought to whether it was wise to continue to allow the young sister to sit in on all her interrogations. Perhaps she could be trusted to keep everything to herself; perhaps not. Fidelma had finally decided that it was better not to put temptation in her way.

'I will not want your services for a while,' she told the

disappointed-looking novice. 'I am sure you have other duties to fulfil in the hostel.'

Brother Rumann looked approving.

'Indeed, she has. There are chambers to be cleaned and tidied here.'

When Sister Necht had reluctantly left, Fidelma turned back to the steward.

'How long have you been house steward of the abbey, Brother Rumann?' she opened.

The pudgy features of the man creased in a frown.

'Two years, sister. Why?'

'Indulge me,' Fidelma invited pleasantly. 'I like to know as much background as possible.'

Rumann sniffed as if from boredom.

'Then know that I have served in the abbey since I came here when I reached the age of choice – and that was thirty years ago.'

He recited his background in a wooden, petulant tone as if he felt that she had no right to ask.

'So you are forty-seven years of age and steward for two years?' Fidelma's voice was sweetly dangerous as she encapsulated the facts he had given her.

'Exactly.'

'You must know everything there is to know about the foundation of Ros Ailithir?'

'Everything.' Rumann was nothing if not complacent.

'That is good.'

Rumann frowned slightly, wondering whether she was quietly mocking him.

'What do you want to know?' he asked gruffly, when Fidelma asked nothing further for several moments.

'Abbot Brocc requested that you conduct an investigation into the death of Dacán. What was its result?'

'That he was murdered by an unknown assailant. That is all,' confessed the steward.

'Let us start then from the time the abbot told you the news of Dacán's death.'

'The abbot did not tell me. I was told by Brother Conghus.'

'When was this?'

'Shortly after he had told the abbot of his discovery. I met him on the way to inform Brother Tóla, our assistant physician. Tóla examined the body.'

'What did you do?'

'I went to see the abbot to ask what I should do.'

'You didn't go to Dacán's chamber first?'

Rumann shook his head.

'What could I have done there before Tóla had examined Dacán? The abbot then asked me to take charge of the affair. It was after that when I went to Dacán's chamber. Brother Tóla was there just finishing his examination of the body. He said that Dacán had been bound and stabbed several times in the chest. He and his assistant Martan took the body away for further examination.'

'I understand that the room was not in any disarray and that a bedside oil lamp was still burning.'

Rumann gave a confirming nod of his head.

'Tóla extinguished the lamp when he left,' Fidelma said. 'That implied that you had already left the room when the corpse was carried out.'

Rumann looked at Fidelma with some respect.

'You have a sharp mind, sister. In fact, that is so. While Tóla was finishing his examination, I quickly looked around the room for a weapon or anything that might identify the assailant. I found nothing. So I left just before Tóla had the body carried out.'

'You did not examine the room again?'

'No. On the abbot's orders, I had the chamber shut up exactly as it was. I had, however, seen nothing there to help in the discovery of a culprit. But the abbot thought that further investigation might be needed.'

'You did not refill the oil in the bedside lamp at any stage?'

Ruman raised an eyebrow in surprise at the question.

'Why would I refill it?'

'No matter,' smiled Fidelma quickly. 'What then? How did you make your investigation?'

Rumann rubbed his chin thoughtfully.

'Sister Necht and myself were sleeping in the hostel that night and we slept soundly until the morning bell summoned us. There was only one other guest and he neither heard nor saw anything.'

'Who was the guest? Is he still at the monastery?'

'No. He was no one really . . . Just a traveller. His name was Assíd of the Uí Dego.'

'Ah yes.' She recalled that Brocc had mentioned the name. 'Assíd of the Uí Dego. Tell me if I am wrong, Rumann, but the Uí Dego dwell just north of Fearna in Laigin, do they not?'

Rumann stirred uncomfortably.

'I believe so,' he admitted. 'Perhaps Brother Midach could tell you more on that subject.'

'Why Brother Midach?' Fidelma thought the point curious.

'Well, he has travelled in those lands,' Rumann said a trifle defensively. 'I think he was born in or near that territory.'

Fidelma gave an exasperated sigh. Laigin seemed to loom down every gloomy path in this investigation.

'Tell me more about this traveller, Assíd.'

'Little to tell. He came off a coastal *barc*. I think he was a merchant, perhaps trading along the coast. He left with the afternoon tide on the day Dacán was killed. But only after I had questioned him thoroughly.'

Fidelma smiled cynically.

'And after he had assured you that he had heard and seen nothing?'

'Just so.'

'The fact that Assíd was from Laigin, and that Laigin now

plays a prominent role in this matter, surely is enough to suggest that he should have been detained here for questioning further?'

Rumann shook his head.

'How were we to know this then? On what grounds could we keep that man here? Are you suggesting that he is the murderer of his fellow countryman? Besides, like Midach, there are several brothers and sisters in this abbey whose birthplace was in Laigin.'

'I am not here to suggest things, Rumann,' snapped Fidelma, irritated by the steward's complacency. 'I am here to investigate.'

The portly religieux sat back abruptly and swallowed. He was unused to being snapped at.

Fidelma, for her part, immediately regretted her irritation and secretly admitted that the steward could hardly have acted otherwise. What grounds were there to have held Assíd of the Uí Dego? None. However, the identity of the person who had taken the news of Dacán's murder to Fearna was now obvious.

'This Assíd,' began Fidelma again, speaking in a more amicable tone, 'what makes you so sure that he was a merchant?'

Rumann screwed up his features in a meaningless grimace.

'Who else but merchants travel our coastline in *barca* and seek hospitality in our hostels? He was not unusual. We often get merchants like him.'

'Presumably his crew stayed on board the *barc*?'

'I believe they did. They certainly did not stay here.'

'One wonders, therefore, why he did not also stay on board but sought a night's lodging here?' mused Fidelma. 'Which chamber did he occupy?'

'The one currently occupied by Sister Eisten.'

'Did he know Dacán?'

'I think so. Yes, I do recall that they greeted one another in friendly fashion. That was on the evening that Assíd arrived. That was natural, I suppose, both men being from Laigin.'

Fidelma suppressed her annoyance. How could she solve this mystery when her principal witness had left the scene? Already she felt an overwhelming sense of frustration.

'Did you not question Assíd later about his relationship with Dacán?'

Rumann looked pained and shook his head.

'Why should his relationship to Dacán be of interest to me?'

'But you said they greeted one another in friendship, implying that they knew one another and not by reputation.'

'I saw no reason to ask whether Assíd was a friend of Dacán.'

'How else would you find the killer than by asking such questions?' Fidelma demanded sourly.

'I am not a *dálaigh*,' retorted Rumann, indignantly. 'I was asked to make an inquiry how Dacán came to be killed in our hostel, not to conduct a legal investigation.'

There was some truth to this. Rumann was not trained to investigate. Fidelma was contrite.

'I am sorry,' she apologised. 'Just tell me as much as you know with regard to this man, Assíd.'

'He arrived on the day before Dacán was killed and left as I have told you, on that day. He sought lodging for the night. His *barc* anchored in the inlet and was presumably engaged in trading. This is all I know.'

'Very well. And there was no one else in the hostel at the time?'

'No.'

'Is access to the hostel easy from any part of the abbey buildings?'

'As you have seen, sister, there are no restrictions within the abbey walls.'

'So any one of the many hundreds of students as well as the religious here could have entered and killed Dacán?'

'They could,' Rumann admitted without hesitation.

'Was anyone particularly close to Dacán during his stay here? Did he have particular friends either among the religious or students?'

'No one was really friendly to him. Not even the abbot. The Venerable Dacán was a man who kept everyone at a distance. Not friendly, at all. Ascetic and indifferent to worldly values. I like to relax some evenings with a board game, *brandubh* or *fidchell*. I invited him to engage in a game or two and was dismissed as if I had suggested indulgence in a blasphemous thing.'

This, at least, Fidelma thought, was a common point of agreement among those she had questioned about the Venerable Dacán. He was not a friendly soul.

'There was no one at all with whom he spoke more than any other person in the abbey?'

Rumann shrugged eloquently.

'Unless you count our librarian, Sister Grella. That, I presume, was because he did much research in the library.'

Fidelma nodded thoughtfully.

'Ah yes, I have heard that he was at Ros Ailithir to study certain texts. I will see this Sister Grella later.'

'Of course, he also taught,' Rumann added. 'He taught history.'

'Can you tell me who were his students?'

'No. You would have to speak to our *fer-leginn*, our chief professor, Brother Ségán. Brother Ségán has control of all matters pertaining to the studies here. That is, under Abbot Brocc, of course.'

'Presumably, in pursuit of his studies, the Venerable Dacán must have written considerably?'

'I would presume so,' Rumann replied diffidently. 'I often saw him carrying manuscripts and, of course, his wax writing tablets. He was never without the latter.'

'Then,' Fidelma paused to lend emphasis to her question,

'why are there are no manuscripts nor used tablets in his chamber?'

Brother Rumann gazed blankly at her.

'Are there not?' he asked in bewilderment.

'No. There are tablets which have been smoothed clean and vellum which has not been used.'

The house steward shrugged again. The gesture seemed to come naturally to him.

'It is of surprise to me. Perhaps he stored whatever he wrote in our library. However, I fail to see what this has to do with his death.'

'And you had no knowledge of what Dacán was studying?' Fidelma did not bother to reply to his implied question. 'Did anyone know why he had come in particular to Ros Ailithir?'

'It is not my business to pry into the affairs of others. Sufficient that Dacán came with the recommendation of the king of Cashel and his presence was approved of by my abbot. I tried, like others here, to be friendly with him but, as I have said, he was not a friendly man. In truth, sister, perhaps I should confess that there was no mourning in the abbey when Dacán passed into the Otherworld.'

Fidelma leaned forward with interest.

'I was led to believe, in spite of the fact that he was considered austere, that Dacán was widely beloved by the people and revered as a man of great sanctity.'

Brother Rumann pursed his lips cynically.

'I have heard that this is so – and perhaps it is . . . in Laigin. All I can say is that he was welcomed here at Ros Ailithir but did not reciprocate the warmth of our welcome. So he was generally left to his own devices. Why, even little Sister Necht went in fear of him.'

'She did? Why so?'

'Presumably because he was a man whose coldness inspired apprehension.'

'I thought his saintly reputation went further than Laigin. In most places, he and his brother Noé are spoken of as one would speak of Colmcille, of Brendan or of Enda.'

'One may only speak as one finds, sister. Sometimes reputations are not deserved.'

'Tell me, this dislike of Dacán . . .'

Brother Rumann shook his head in interruption.

'Indifference, sister. Indifference, not dislike, for there were no grounds to promote such a positive response as dislike.'

Fidelma bowed her head in acknowledgment of the point.

'Very well. Indifference, if you like. In your estimation you do not think it was enough to promote a feeling in someone here to kill him?'

The eyes of the steward narrowed in his fleshy face.

'Someone here? Are you suggesting that one of our brethren in Ros Ailithir killed him?'

'Perhaps even one of his students who disliked his manner? That has been known.'

'Well, I have never heard of such a thing. A student respects his master.'

'In ordinary circumstances,' she agreed. 'Yet we are investigating an extraordinary circumstance. Murder, for that is what we have established, is a most unnatural crime. Whatever path we follow we have to agree that someone in this community must have perpetrated this act. Someone in this community,' she repeated with emphasis.

Brother Rumann regarded her with a solemn face and tight mouth.

'I cannot say further than I have. All I was asked to do, all I did, was investigate the circumstance of his death. What else could I have done? I have not the skills of a *dálaigh*.'

Fidelma spread her hands in a pacifying gesture.

'I imply no criticism, Brother Rumann. You have your office and I have mine. We are faced with a delicate situation, not merely in terms of solving this crime but in seeking to prevent a war.'

Brother Rumann sniffed loudly.

'If you ask my opinion, I would not put it past Laigin to have engineered this whole matter. They have appealed time and time again to the High King's assembly at Tara for the return of Osraige. Each time, it has been ruled that Osraige was lawfully part of Muman. Now this.' He stabbed with his hand into the air.

Fidelma examined the steward with interest.

'Just when did you come to such an opinion, Brother Rumann?' she questioned gently.

'I am of the Corco Loígde, a man of Muman. When I heard of the honour price that young Fianamail of Laigin was demanding for Dacán's death, I suspected a plot. You were right in the first place.'

Fidelma raised an eyebrow at Rumann's angry features.

'Right? In what respect?'

'That I should have been suspicious of the merchant, Assíd. He was probably the assassin and I let him go!'

She gazed at him for a moment then said: 'One thing more, brother. How did you come to know what the demands of Laigin are?'

Rumann blinked. 'How? Why the abbot has spoken of nothing else for days.'

After Brother Rumann had left, Fidelma sat for a while in silence. Then she realised that Cass was still seated waiting for her to speak. She turned and gave him a tired smile.

'Call Sister Necht, Cass.'

A moment later the enthusiastic young sister entered in answer to the ringing of the handbell. It was clear that she had been in the process of scrubbing the floors of the hostel but welcomed the interruption.

'I hear that you went in apprehension of the Venerable Dacán,' Fidelma stated without preamble.

The blood seemed to drain momentarily from Necht's face. She shivered.

'I did,' she admitted.

'Why?'

'My duties as a novice in the abbey are to tend to the guests' hostel and take care of the wants of the guests. The Venerable Dacán treated me like a bond-servant. I even asked Brother Rumann if I could be removed from the duties at the hostel for the period that Dacán was staying here.'

'Then you must have disliked him intensely.'

Sister Necht hung her head.

'It is against the Faith but, the truth is, I did not like him. I did not like him at all.'

'Yet you were not removed from your duties?'

Necht shook her head.

'Brother Rumann said that I must accept it as the will of God and through this adversity I would gain in strength to do the Lord's work.'

'You say that as if you do not believe it,' remarked Fidelma gently.

'I did not gain any strength. It only intensified my dislike. It was a hateful time. The Venerable Dacán would criticise my tidying of his chamber. In the end, I did not bother tidying at all. Then he would send me on errands at all times of the day and night as his fancy took him. I was a slave.'

'So when he died, you shed no tears?'

'Not I!' declared the sister vehemently. Then, realising what she had said, she flushed. 'I meant . . .'

'I think I know what you meant,' Fidelma responded. 'Tell me, on the night Dacán was killed, were you on duty in the hostel?'

'I was on duty every night. Brother Rumann will have told you. It was my special duty.'

'Did you see Dacán that night.'

'Of course. He and the merchant Assíd were the only guests here.'

'I have been told that they knew each other?' Fidelma made the observation into a question.

Sister Necht nodded.

'I do not think that they were friends though. I heard Assíd quarrelling with Dacán after the evening meal.'

'Quarrelling?'

'Yes. Dacán had retired to his chamber. He usually took some books to study before the *completa*, the final service of the day. I was passing by his chamber door when I heard voices in argument.'

'Are you sure it was Assíd?'

'Who else could it have been?' countered the girl. 'There was no one else staying here.'

'So they were quarrelling? About what?'

'I do not know. Their voices were not raised but intense. Angry sounding.'

'And what was Dacán studying that night?' Fidelma frowned. 'I have been told that nothing has been taken from his chamber. Yet there were no books there nor any writing by Dacán in the room.'

Sister Necht shrugged and made no reply.

'When did you last see Dacán?'

'I had just returned from the service for the *completa* when Dacán summoned me and told me to fetch him a pitcher of cold water.'

'Did you visit his chamber after that?'

'No. I avoided him as much as I could. Forgive me this sin, sister, but I hated him and cannot say otherwise.'

Sister Fidelma sat back and examined the young novice carefully for a moment.

'You have other duties, Sister Necht, I shall not detain you from them. I will call you when I have further need of you.'

The young novice rose looking chagrined.

'You will not tell Brother Rumann of my sin of hatred?' she asked eagerly.

'No. You feared Dacán. Hate is merely the consequence of that fear; we have to fear something to hate it. It is the cloak of protection used by those who are intimidated. But, sister, remember this, that feelings of hate often lead to the suppression of justice. Try to forgive Dacán in death for his autocracy and understand your own fears. You may go now.'

'Are you sure there is nothing else I can do?' Necht asked, as she hesitated in the doorway. She looked eager again as if the confession of her hatred of Dacán had cheered her spirits.

Fidelma shook her head.

'I will call you when there is,' she assured her.

As she went out, Cass rose and came to sit in the chair vacated by Necht. He regarded Fidelma with sympathy.

'It is not going well, is it? I see only confusion.'

Fidelma pulled a face at the young warrior.

'Come let us walk by the seashore for a moment, Cass. I need the breeze to clear my head.'

They walked through the complex of the abbey buildings and found a gate in the wall which led onto a narrow path winding down to the sandy strand. The day was still fine, still a little blustery, with the ships rocking at anchor. Fidelma drew in a deep breath of salt sea air and exhaled it loudly with a resounding gasp of satisfaction.

Cass watched her in quiet amusement.

'That is better,' she said, and glanced quickly at him. 'It clears the head. I have to admit that this is the hardest inquiry that I have undertaken. In other investigations that I have worked on, all the witnesses remained in the one place. All the suspects were gathered. And I was at the scene of the crime within hours, if not minutes, of the deed being done so that the evidence could not evaporate into thin air.'

Cass measured his pace to match her shorter stride as they walked slowly along the sea's edge.

'I begin to see some of the difficulties of a *dálaigh* now, sister. In truth, I had little idea before. I thought that all they had to know about was the law.'

Fidelma did not bother to answer.

They passed fishermen on the shore, unloading their morning's catch from the small canoe-like vessels, locally called *naomhóg*, boats of wickerwork frames, covered in *codal*, a hide tanned in oak bark, and stitched together with thongs of leather. They were easy and light to carry and three men could manage the largest of them. They rode high in the water, dancing swiftly over the fiercest of waves.

Fidelma paused watching as two of these craft came ashore towing the carcass of a great beast of the sea behind them.

She had seen a basking shark brought ashore only once before and presumed that the beast was such an creature.

Cass had never seen anything like it and he moved eagerly forward to examine it.

'I had heard a story that the Blessed Brendan, during his great voyage, once landed on the back of such a monster thinking it was an island. Yet this beast, big as it is, does not look like an island,' he called across his shoulder to her.

Fidelma responded to his excitement.

'The fish Brendan is reported to have landed on was said to be far bigger. When Brendan and his companions sat down and made a fire to cook their meal, the fish, feeling the heat, sank into the sea and they barely escaped with their lives into their boat.'

An aged fisherman, overhearing her, nodded sagely.

'And that's a true story, sister. But did you ever hear of the great fish, Rosault, which lived in the time of Colmcille?'

Fidelma shook her head, smiling, for she knew old fishermen carried good tales which could often be retold around a fire at night.

'I used to fish up Connacht way when I was a lad,' the old man went on, hardly needing an invitation. 'The Connacht men told me that there was a holy mountain inland which they called Croagh Patrick, after the blessed saint. At the foot of the mountain was a plain which was called Muir-iasc, which means "sea-fish". Do you know how it received its name?'

'Tell us,' invited Cass, knowing there was no other answer to give.

'It was named because it was formed by the great body of Rosault when it was cast ashore there during a great storm. The dead beast, as it lay decomposing on the plain, caused a great pestilence through the malodorous vapours which rose from its body and descended on the country. It killed men and animals indiscriminately. There be many things in the sea, sister. Many threatening things.'

Fidelma cast a sudden glance towards the Laigin warship.

'Not all of them are creatures of the deep,' she observed softly.

The old fisherman caught the direction of her gaze and chuckled.

'I think that you would be right there, sister. And I am thinking that the fishermen of the Corco Loígde might one day have to go casting their spears at stranger creatures than a poor basking shark.'

He turned and sank his skinning knife into the great carcass with relish.

Fidelma began to walk along the shore again.

Cass hurried after her. For a few moments they walked on in silence and then Cass observed: 'There are signs of war in the air already, sister. It does not bode well.'

'I am not oblivious to it,' she replied shortly. 'Yet I cannot work miracles even though my brother expects it of me.'

'Perhaps we have to accept that this war is our destiny. That there will, indeed, be war.'

'Destiny!' Fidelma was angry. 'I do not believe in the

preordination of things, even if some of the Faith do. Destiny is but the tyrant's excuse for his crimes and the fool's excuse for not standing up to the tyrant.'

'How can you change what is inevitable?' demanded Cass.

'By first saying that it is not so and then by proceeding to make it otherwise!' she answered with spirit.

If there was anything she did not need at this moment in time it was someone telling her that things were inevitable. Sophocles had once written that that which the gods have brought about must be born with fortitude. Yet to make the excuse that one's self-induced limitations were simply destiny was a philosophy that was alien to Fidelma. The creed of destiny was simply an excuse to save oneself from choice.

Cass raised a hand, opened it and gestured as if in resignation.

'It is a laudable philosophy which you have, Fidelma. But sometimes . . .'

'Enough!'

There was a catch to her voice that made the young warrior stop. He realised how suddenly vulnerable was this young woman *dálaigh* of the court. Colgú of Cashel had put great responsibility on his sister's shoulders – perhaps too much? As Cass saw things, the death of Dacán was a riddle that would never be solved. Better to simply prepare for war with the Laigin than squander time in sorting out the tangled and insoluble web of this mystery.

Fidelma suddenly sat down on a rock and gazed at the sea as Cass stood restlessly by. In turning matters over in her mind she was trying to remember what her old master, the Brehon Morann of Tara, had once said to her.

'Better to ask twice than lose your way once, child,' he had intoned when she had failed some exercise of the mind by failing to grasp an answer he had given.

What question was she not asking; what answer had she failed to realise the significance of?

Cass was startled when, after a moment or two, Fidelma sprang up and uttered a snort of disgust.

'I must be dull-witted!' she announced.

'Why so?' he demanded as she started to stride swiftly back towards the abbey.

'Here I have been bemoaning to myself the impossibility of the task before I have even begun it.'

'I thought that you had already made a very good start on the matter.'

'I have but merely skimmed the surface,' she replied. 'I have asked a question or two but have not yet started to seek the truth. Come, there is much to be done!'

She walked swiftly back to the abbey, through the gate and across the flagged courtyards. Here and there little groups of scholars and some of the teaching religious turned from their huddled bands to surreptitiously examine her as she passed for the news had spread rapidly through the abbey of her purpose there. She ignored them, moving swiftly to the main gateway and there saw the object of her search – the enthusiastic young Sister Necht.

She was about to hail her when Necht looked up and saw Fidelma. She came running towards her, with an undignified gait.

'Sister Fidelma!' she gasped. 'I was about to set out to find you. Brother Tóla asked me to give you this package. It is from Brother Martan.'

She handed Fidelma a rectangular piece of sackcloth. Fidelma took it and unfolded it. Inside were several pieces of long strips of linen, as if torn from a larger piece of material. There were spots of deep brown which Fidelma presumed to be the stains of blood. The colour of the linen itself had been enhanced by dyes in parti-coloured fashion consisting of blues and reds. The pieces were frayed and looked fragile. Fidelma took one of the strips and held it, one end in each hand, giving it a sharp tug. It tore easily.

'Not very efficient as a constraint,' observed Cass.

Fidelma glanced appraisingly at him.

'No,' she replied thoughtfully as she rewrapped the cloth and placed the material in her large satchel purse. 'Now, Sister Necht, I need you to conduct us to Sister Grella's library.'

To her surprise the young girl shook her head.

'That I cannot do, sister.'

'Why, what ails you?' Fidelma demanded testily.

'Nothing. But the abbot has also sent me to seek you out and bring you to him. He says he must see you without delay.'

'Very well,' Fidelma said reluctantly. 'If Abbot Brocc wants to see me then I shall not disappoint him. But why the urgency?'

'Ten minutes ago, Salbach, chieftain of the Corco Loígde, arrived in response to a message which Brocc sent him. The chieftain appears very angry.'

Chapter Eight

Fidelma and Cass began to follow as Sister Necht led the way towards the chambers of the abbot. After a moment, the young novice noticed Cass following. She halted and looked embarrassed.

'What is it now?' demanded Fidelma.

'I was told to bring only yourself, sister,' she explained, with an awkward glance at Cass.

'Very well,' Fidelma sighed. 'You can wait for me at the hostel, Cass.'

The tall warrior made a small grimace of disappointment but took himself off while she continued to follow Necht. The broad-shouldered sister seemed agitated and hurried while Fidelma maintained a more leisurely pace. The young novice had to keep stopping in order to wait for her. Fidelma refused to be hurried and rejected the idea of arriving before the abbot and the chieftain of the Corco Loígde in a flustered and breathless fashion.

'It's all right, Necht,' Fidelma finally said, irritated by the girl's insistence on trying to get her to hurry. 'I know the way to the abbot's chambers from here, so you may leave me in safety.'

The girl paused and seemed about to protest but Fidelma drew her brows together in annoyance. The expression was enough to dissuade the novice from any arguments that might have been forming on her tongue. She bobbed her head obediently and left Fidelma.

Fidelma continued across the flagged yard into the granite building which housed the abbot's chambers. She had moved into a small, dark hallway and was crossing to the steps which led up to the second floor on which the abbot's main chamber was situated when a shadow stirred in the darkness at the foot of the steps.

'Sister!'

Fidelma halted and peered curiously into the shadows. The figure was familiar.

'Is that Cétach?'

The figure of the boy moved forward into the gloomy light. Fidelma noted the tension in his body, the way his shoulders were positioned, the poise of the head.

'I must speak with you,' whispered the young black-haired lad, as if he were scared of being overheard.

Fidelma raised an eyebrow in the gloom.

'It is inconvenient now. I am on my way to see the abbot. Let us meet later . . .'

'No, wait!' The voice almost rose to a wail of despair. Fidelma found Cétach's hand clutching imploringly at her arm.

'What is it? What are you frightened of?'

'Salbach, the chieftain of the Corco Loígde, is with the abbot.'

'This I know,' Fidelma said. 'But what is frightening you, Cétach?'

'When you speak with him do not mention me or my brother.'

Fidelma tried to examine the boy's features, annoyed that the shadows obscured his expression.

'Are you scared of Salbach?'

'It is too long a story – I cannot tell you now, sister. Please, do not mention us. Do not even say that you know us.'

'Why? What do you fear from Salbach?'

The boy's grip tightened on her arm.

'For pity's sake, sister!' His voice was filled with such fear that Fidelma patted his shoulder in reassurance.

'Very well,' she said. 'You have my promise. But when I am finished, we must talk and you must tell me what this means.'

'You promise that you will not mention us?'

'I promise,' she replied gravely.

The boy abruptly turned and scurried away into the shadows leaving a bemused Fidelma staring in the gloom.

She waited a moment or two before heaving a sigh and then she began to mount the steps.

Abbot Brocc was waiting impatiently for her. He had apparently been pacing before his table and stopped as she entered his chamber. Her eyes immediately fell on a figure sprawled indolently in a chair before the great fire in the abbot's chamber. The man was leaning back in the carved wooden chair, usually reserved for the abbot, one leg dangling over an arm, a large goblet of wine in one hand. He was a handsome man with hair the colour of jet, contrasting with a white skin and ice-blue eyes. He was in his early thirties. There was something saturnine about his slim features. His clothes told of wealth for they were fine woven silks and linens and he wore a small fortune in jewellery. The sword and dagger he wore were worth the full honour price of a *ceile*, a free clansman of the kingdom. All this Fidelma took in at a glance but one thing, of all the visual information, registered with her; the cold blue eyes of the chieftain had a close, foxy look. Here was a shrewd and cunning man.

'Ah, Fidelma!'

The abbot was clearly relieved as she entered.

'I was told that you had sent for me, Brocc,' she said, closing the door behind her.

'I have, indeed. This is Salbach, chieftain of the Corco Loígde.'

Fidelma turned towards the chieftain. Her mouth tightened as the man made no effort to rise but continued to sprawl in his chair, sipping his wine with deliberate slowness.

'Sister Fidelma from Kildare is my cousin, Salbach,' the abbot said nervously, seeing the clouds gathering around Fidelma's brows.

Salbach regarded her coldly over the rim of his goblet.

'I am told that you are a *dálaigh*,' he said. There was a tone in his voice as if he found the subject amusing.

'I am Fidelma of the Eóganacht of Cashel, sister to Colgú, heir-apparent of Muman,' she replied with a tone of steel. 'I am qualified in law to the level of *anruth*.'

Salbach returned her gaze for a moment or two without moving. Then he carefully put down his goblet and, with exaggerated slowness, he eased himself from the chair and stood before her. He bowed ungracefully with a jerky movement of his neck.

That Fidelma had to remind him of his manners in greeting her was a source of irritation to her. It was not because she had an abundance of vanity that made her demand that he recognise her as the sister of the heir-apparent to the kingdom, nor that she was so conceited that she had to draw attention to the fact that she possessed the status of *anruth*, only one degree below the highest that the colleges of the five kingdoms could bestow. It was the scorn that Salbach implied towards her, which she took as an insult to her sex, that caused her to demand the traditional hero's portion that was due to her. Yet even when she gave way to this emotion she recalled her mentor, the Brehon Morann, saying: 'Respect received from fear is not respect. The wolf may be respected but it is never liked.' Generally, Fidelma ignored social conventions provided people showed regard and consideration for one another simply as fellow humans. But when she came across individuals who showed no natural respect she felt she had to make the point as example. Salbach appeared to respect no one but himself.

'I apologise, Fidelma of Cashel,' he said in a tone which she felt gave no value to his words. 'I did not know that you were related to Colgú.'

Fidelma seated herself and her expression was bland.

'Why should my relatives dictate good manners?' she demanded softly.

Abbot Brocc coughed hastily.

'Fidelma, Salbach has come in response to the message I sent him.'

Fidelma found herself being scrutinised again by the cold blue eyes of Salbach. He returned to his sprawling position in the other chair and took up his wine again. There was something hooded about those eyes. They reminded her of the unblinking eyes of a buzzard regarding its prey before swooping to bear it away.

'That is good,' Fidelma replied. 'The sooner the crime committed at Rae na Scríne is dealt with, the better.'

'Crime? I am told that some frightened, superstitious people, afraid of the plague at Rae na Scríne, attacked the village in an effort to drive the people into the mountains and fire the place so that the plague might not spread. If there was a crime there, it was a crime of fear and panic.'

'Not so. It was a calm and deliberate attack.'

Salbach's mouth twitched and his tone was sharp. 'I have come here, Sister Fidelma, because I have heard your accusation against one of *my bó-aire*, a magistrate that I myself appointed but recently. I presumed that there was some mistake.'

'I take it that you refer to the man Intat? If so, there is no mistake.'

'I am told that you have accused Intat of leading a band of his warriors in the destruction of the entire village? My information is that a band of panic-stricken people from some neighbouring village burnt it down.'

'You have heard incorrectly.'

'That is a serious accusation.'

'It is a serious crime,' confirmed Fidelma coldly.

'I shall need evidence before I can act on such a charge,' Salbach replied stubbornly.

'The evidence will be found in the charred ruins of Rae na Scríne.'

'That proves the village was burnt and perhaps that people were killed. What evidence is there that Intat was responsible?'

'Cass, of the bodyguard of the King of Cashel, and I rode into the village while the terrible deed was being done. We spoke with the man called Intat. He turned us away with threat to our lives.'

Salbach's eyes widened a fraction with incredulity.

'He let you go? Surely, if he were engaged in such a crime, you would not be here to tell of it?'

Fidelma wondered why it seemed that Salbach was attempting to protect his *bó-aire*.

'Intat did not realise that we had seen what he was doing. We doubled back to the village after we had left him on the highway. Nor did he realise that there were survivors from the village who can give better testimony as to what happened than we can.'

Did Salbach swallow nervously? Did a look of apprehension grow over his features?

'There were survivors?'

'Yes.' It was Abbot Brocc who replied. 'There were half-a-dozen survivors. Some children . . .'

'Children cannot testify under law,' Salbach snapped. 'They have no legal obligations until they reach the age of choice.'

Fidelma noted that point of law came trotting swiftly from Salbach's tongue.

'There was also one adult with them,' she said softly. 'And if the one adult is not enough, then bring this man Intat before Cass and myself, and we will testify whether he is the man we saw leading those who held burning brand torches and swords in their hands and who threatened our lives.'

'How was Intat identified anyway?' demanded Salbach sullenly. 'How could you know the man's name?'

'He was identified by Sister Eisten,' answered the abbot.

'Ah! So she is the survivor of whom you speak?'

Salbach's eyes were hooded again. Fidelma would have given anything to hear the thoughts which appeared to be tumbling in his mind. His face was a mask but there seemed to be a frenzy of thoughts behind those hooded eyes.

'It is hard to believe this of Intat.' Salbach sighed suddenly, putting down his drained goblet of wine, as if he were finally convinced. 'I am saddened to hear of this evidence against him. Are Sister Eisten and the children staying in Ros Ailithir?'

Brocc replied again before Fidelma could speak.

'Yes. We will probably send them shortly to the orphanage run by Molua.'

'I would like to see them,' pressed Salbach.

'It may be some days before that can be,' Fidelma said hurriedly, with a meaningful glance at Brocc. The abbot stared in bewilderment at her. 'The abbot has ordered them to be placed in quarantine so that they can be cleared of any contagion from the Yellow Plague.'

'But . . .' began Brocc. Then bit his tongue.

Salbach had not appeared to notice this unfinished protest and was rising to his feet.

'I will be back to question Sister Eisten and the children when it is more convenient,' he said. 'But, since the matter contained a grave accusation against one of my magistrates, I felt I had to come immediately to test the evidence. I shall set out to find Intat and see what he has to say. If the crime is laid at his door, then he will answer for it before my own Brehon. You may rest assured of that, Sister Fidelma.'

'Cashel would expect no less,' replied Fidelma gravely.

Salbach stared hard at her, seeking some hidden meaning but Fidelma continued to return his look without expression.

'We are a proud people here, Sister Fidelma,' Salbach said. His voice, while soft, was full of hidden meaning. 'The Corco Loígde claim their descent from the family of Míl Easpain, who led the ancestors of the Gaels to this land at the beginning of time. A challenge to the honour of one of us is a challenge to the honour of all of us. And if one of us betrays his honour, he betrays us all and will be punished.'

He hesitated a moment, as if he would say something else, then he turned to the abbot.

'I will be on my way then, abbot,' he began but Fidelma interrupted.

'There are some questions on another matter which you may help me with, Salbach.'

Salbach glanced at her in astonishment for he had made clear that the meeting had ended. It was clear he was used to dictating his own way.

'I am busy now . . .'

'In this I am acting on behalf of the king of Cashel,' insisted Fidelma. 'It concerns the murder of the Venerable Dacán.'

Salbach hesitated as though he would dispute with her but then shrugged indifferently.

'It is a grave business,' he conceded. 'I know nothing of the death of the old man. So how can I help you?'

'Did you know the Venerable Dacán?'

'Who did not know him by reputation?' Salbach parried.

'I believe you met him?'

The question was merely a guess and Fidelma saw the quick flush on Salbach's face. It had only been an instinct which had made her chance the question.

'I did meet Dacán a few times,' Salbach admitted.

'Was that here, at Ros Ailithir?'

Fidelma had to conceal her surprise when Salbach shook his head.

'No. I met him at Cealla, at one of the great residences of the chieftains of Osraige.'

'In Osraige? When was this?'

'A year ago.'

'May I ask what you were doing in Osraige?'

'Visiting my cousin, Scandlán, who is king there.' Salbach could not keep the vanity out of his voice.

Fidelma was again reminded that her brother, Colgú, had told her that the kings of Osraige were related to the chieftains of the Corco Loígde.

'I see,' she said slowly. 'Yet you did not meet the Venerable Dacán when he came to Ros Ailithir?'

'No, I did not.'

Something prompted Fidelma to doubt him. Yet she could not get beyond that hooded buzzard expression. She realised that she did not like Salbach at all. Then she flushed as she remembered her homily to Sister Necht. In spite of that, Fidelma believed that there was something sinister about Salbach and that was why she disliked him. There was something evil and harsh in those pale eyes of his. He reminded her so much of a bird of prey.

'But you did meet with Assíd of Laigin?' she switched the question abruptly, still relying on her instinct.

Salbach's mouth slackened a little. There was a momentary glint in his eyes.

'Yes,' he admitted slowly. 'He came to my fortress at Cuan Dóir to trade.'

'He is a coastal trader?'

'Yes. He traded at our copper mines. He brought us Gaulish wine which had been landed in Laigin and we traded copper for the wine.'

'So you have known Assíd for a long time . . . in his rôle as a merchant, that is?'

Salbach grimaced negatively.

'I said that I have met him. That is all. He was trading here last summer and the summer before that. Why do you ask these questions?'

'It is my task to do so, chieftain of the Corco Loígde,' she replied with patient humour.

'Am I free to go now?' There was a condescending sneer in his voice.

'I trust that we shall hear soon that you have been successful in your search for Intat?'

'I will make a point of informing you,' Salbach replied stiffly.

With a brief bow in her direction and a curt nod to the abbot, Salbach left the room.

Abbot Brocc was looking unhappy.

'Salbach is not a person who likes losing face, cousin,' he commented anxiously. 'I felt I was witness to two cats meeting to dispute the same territory.'

'It is a pity then he places himself in such a position where confrontation results,' replied Fidelma coldly. 'He carries an insufferable arrogance in his demeanour.'

The midday Angelus bell struck.

Fidelma felt obliged to join the abbot in the ritual prayer for the hour.

When Brocc raised himself from his knees, he regarded Fidelma for a moment or two in awkwardness.

'There is other news,' he began, somewhat hesitantly. 'I did not want to say anything in front of Salbach before I told you.'

Fidelma waited uncertainly, for her cousin's face had grown unusually solemn.

'Just before Salbach arrived, a messenger came from Cashel. The king, Cathal mac Cathail, died three days ago. Your brother, Colgú, is now king of Muman.'

Fidelma's features did not change. As soon as Brocc had mentioned a messenger from Cashel, she knew what it must be about. She had known it was a matter of time even before she had left Cashel. Then she rose and genuflected.

'*Sic transit gloria mundi*. May our cousin rest in peace,' she said. 'And may God give Colgú strength for the hard task which he now faces.'

'We shall say a mass for the soul of Cathal tonight, sister,' Brocc said. 'It lacks a short while before the bell sounds for the midday meal. Perhaps you will join me in a cup of wine before going to the refectory?'

To his obvious disappointment, Fidelma shook her head.

'I have much to do before the midday meal, cousin,' she replied. 'But there is one question which I must now ask you. Brother Conghus told me that a week before Dacán was killed you had especially asked him to keep a close watch on Dacán. Why was that?'

'No mystery to that,' the abbot replied immediately. 'It was clear that the Venerable Dacán was an unfriendly man. In fact, I had heard that he had upset several of the students here. It was just a precaution to ask Brother Conghus to ensure that Dacán did not encounter trouble through his . . . how shall we say it? . . . through his unfortunate personality.'

'Thank you, Brocc. I will see you at the midday meal.'

Fidelma left the chamber with her thoughts abruptly returning to the young boy, Cétach. Why had the boy not wanted her to mention him and his brother Cosrach? What made him fear Salbach?

Yet this was nothing to do with the murder of the Venerable Dacán and time was swiftly running out before the matter would have to be argued before the High King's assembly at Tara.

She made her way directly back to the hostel and went to look for the boy Cétach. She also recalled that she must speak further with Sister Eisten. The children were not in their chambers; neither was Sister Eisten. Fidelma looked into the other chambers but could not see anyone. The only one of the children from Rae na Scríne she could find was one of the little copper-haired sisters, Cera by name. The girl sat playing with a rag doll and would not answer any of Fidelma's questions.

Fidelma gave up trying to coax some information from her and then searched the upstairs chambers before returning to the lower floor. She heard a noise from Brother Rumann's *officium* and hastened along to it. There she found Cass seated in the chamber with Brother Rumann. They were crouched either side of a *brandubh* board engaged in the popular game of 'black raven'. Rumann seemed to be an experienced player for he had taken two of Cass's provincial king pieces, leaving Cass with only his High King and two other provincial king defenders, while his own eight opposing pieces were all intact. Cass was trying vainly to reach the safety of the side of the board, which was divided into forty-nine squares, seven squares one way and seven squares the other. Even as Fidelma looked, Rumann by a deft move placed his pieces so that the High King was clearly opposed without any square to retreat to. Reluctantly, and with some bad grace, Cass conceded the game to the portly brother.

Brother Rumann glanced up with a satisfied smile as he saw Fidelma.

'Do you play this game, sister?'

Fidelma nodded curtly. Every child of a king or chieftain was taught *brandubh* and other board games of skill as part of their education. The game had a deep significance for the main piece represented the High King at Tara whose defenders were the four provincial kings of Ulaidh, Laigin, Muman and Connacht. The eight attacking pieces had to be checked by the four provincial kings, allowing the centre to hold steady or, if threatened, to escape to the side of the board, although this escape was only made in desperation when the player had no other options.

'Perhaps we shall get a chance to test each other's mettle?' invited Rumann eagerly.

'Perhaps we shall,' Fidelma returned politely. 'But I have little time now.'

She motioned with her eyes for Cass to follow her and once outside told him the news from Cashel. Like Fidelma, he was not surprised. The death of Cathal had been imminent when they had left the seat of the Muman kings.

'Your brother inherits a heavy burden, Fidelma,' Cass observed. 'Does it change matters here at all?'

'No. It only makes the success of our task more pressing.' Fidelma went on to ask him whether he had seen either of the young boys, Cétach or Cosrach.

Cass shook his head.

'As if I do not have enough on my hands.' Fidelma was exasperated. 'Is it not enough that I am trying to solve the mystery of the murder of Dacán without this further mystery concerning these children?'

When Cass looked bewildered, she unbent to tell him of what the boy Cétach had said and of her unfriendly discussion with Salbach.

'I have heard that Salbach is overbearing and arrogantly hot-tempered,' Cass confessed. 'Perhaps I should have warned you?'

'No. It is best that I made up my own mind.'

'Even so, from what you say it appears that he was almost trying to protect Intat from accusation.'

'Almost. Maybe he simply wanted proof of the accusations. After all, he had apparently appointed Intat as a magistrate himself.'

The bell for the midday meal began to sound.

'Let us forget these mysteries until later,' Cass suggested. 'The children will probably be at the midday meal anyway. I've never known a child to disappear from a meal. And if they are not there, well, I can look for them this afternoon while you carry on with your investigation.'

'That is an excellent suggestion, Cass,' Fidelma agreed readily. 'I need to question the librarian and the chief professor about the Venerable Dacán's rôle at Ros Ailithir.'

They passed into the refectory hall. Fidelma peered carefully around but saw no sign of the boys, Cétach or Cosrach, nor, for that matter, did she see Sister Eisten. Cass, as he had promised, left the refectory immediately after he had eaten to go in search of them.

It was while Fidelma was passing out of the hall at the end of the meal that she overheard a couple of students hailing a tall, elderly man as Brother Ségán. She halted and examined the chief professor, the *fer-leginn* of the college. His scrawny, dark, brooding appearance did not seem to match his personality for he greeted the two students with a ready smile and answered their questions with sentences punctuated by a throaty laugh.

Fidelma waited until the proselytes had departed and Brother Ségán was beginning move off before she saluted him by name.

'Ah, are you Fidelma of Kildare?' Brother Ségán gave her a warm smile and extended a firm hand in greeting. 'I had heard that you had arrived here. The Abbot Brocc told me of your coming. I have heard much praise of your judgments in matters of unlawful killing.'

'It is about the Venerable Dacán that I wish to speak.'

'I thought that it might be so,' grinned the lanky professor. 'Walk with me,' he invited, 'and we will talk.'

He led the way through an arch and into the walled abbey garden which was called the *lúbgort*, from the words *lúb*, a herb, and *gort*, a fenced-in cultivate plot. Even this late in autumn, various odours pleasantly assailed Fidelma's senses. She always felt at peace in gardens, especially herb gardens, for the scents put her into a tranquil mood. There was no sign of anyone within the enclosure and Brother Ségán led her to a stone seat in a tiny arboretum. On the other side of the arboretum was a well head. A small round stone wall protected it while a wooden beam on pillars supported a rope on which a bucket could be attached.

'They call this Fachtna's holy well,' explained Ségán, observing as Fidelma examined the well. 'It was the original well of the community when Fachtna chose this site but, alas, the community has far outgrown its supply. There are now other wells in the abbey but, for us, this well remains the sacred well of Fachtna.'

He motioned her to be seated.

'Now,' he said briskly, 'ask away with your questions.'

'Did you know Dacán before he came to Ros Ailithir?' she began.

Ségán shook his head with a smile.

'I had heard of his great reputation, of course. He was a learned man, an *ollamh* who was a *staruidhe*. But if you are asking whether I had ever met the man then I must reply that I had not.'

'So he was a professor of history?' Fidelma had no knowledge that Dacán was anything more than a master of divinity.

'Oh yes. History was his speciality,' confirmed Ségán.

'Did you know why Dacán came to Ros Ailithir?'

The chief professor grimaced.

'We do have a reputation, sister,' he replied with some amusement. 'Among our numerous students are many from the Saxon kingdoms and even from among the Franks not to mention Britons and those from the five kingdoms of Éireann.'

'I do not think Dacán came here simply because of the reputation of Ros Ailithir,' observed Fidelma candidly. 'I think he came here for a specific need.'

Ségán reflected for a moment or two.

'Yes, perhaps you are right,' he admitted. 'Forgive my vanity, for I would like to think that our reputation for learning was the only reason. The simple answer is that he undoubtedly came here to plunder our library for knowledge. For what particular purpose that was, I do not know. You will have to consult our librarian, Sister Grella.'

'Did you like Dacán?'

Ségán did not reply immediately, apparently gathering his thoughts. Then he held his head to one side and chuckled softly.

'I do not think "like" is an appropriate word, sister. I did not dislike him and, in academic terms, we seemed to get along well together.'

Fidelma pursed her lips a little.

'That in itself seems unusual,' she commented.

'Why so?'

'Because, by those I have already questioned, I have been told that Dacán was universally disliked here. Perhaps that was a motive for murder? I gather that he was austere, cold, unfriendly and an ascetic.'

Ségán now laughed openly, a rich rather comfortable laugh.

'These are hardly attributes for which to condemn a man to hell fire. If we went around killing everyone we disliked then by the time each of us were through there would be no one left to people the earth. Certainly Dacán was not a man possessed of humour, nor was he given to playing the clown. But he was a serious scholar and, as such, I respected him. Yes "like" is not an exact word but "respect" is, perhaps, a better term to describe my attitude to him.'

'I am told that he taught here as well as studied.'

'That is so.'

'Presumably he taught history?'

'What else? His interest was in the early stories concerning the coming to Éireann of our forefather Míl Easpain and the

Children of the Gael and how Mil's brother Amergin promised the goddess Éire that the land would henceforth be known by her name.'

Fidelma was patient.

'That path seems innocuous enough,' she commented.

Ségán chuckled again.

'Surely, sister, you were not seriously considering that Dacán was murdered because someone did not like his personality or his interpretation of history?'

'It has been known,' replied Fidelma solemnly. 'Scholars can be like savage animals when they disagree with one another.'

Ségán bowed his head in agreement.

'Yes, we are guilty as charged, sister. Some historians are as trapped in history as history is trapped in them. Dacán was, certainly, a man of his people . . .'

'What do you mean by that?' queried Fidelma quickly.

'He was a man who was intensely proud of Laigin, that's what I mean. I remember that he and our chief physician, Brother Midach, once . . .'

He suddenly compressed his lips and looked uneasy.

'Tell me,' prompted Fidelma. 'Anything, no matter how unimportant, is of value to my investigation.'

'I do not want to spread alarm, especially where there is no cause to spread it.'

'Truth is always a good cause, chief professor,' insisted Fidelma. 'Tell me about Brother Midach and Dacán.'

'They once had a row in which they nearly came to blows, that is all.'

Fidelma's eyes widened.

Here, at last, was something positive.

'What was this fierce argument about?'

'A simple matter of history. That's all. Dacán was boasting about Laigin, as usual. Midach apparently call the men of Laigin no more than foreigners. He claimed that they were simply Gauls who arrived in the province which was then called Galian. The Laigin came as mercenaries to help the banished Labraid Loinseach seize the throne of his uncle Cobhthach. Midach argued that the Gauls carried broad-pointed spears of blue-green iron called *laigin* and when they had set Labraid on the throne of Galian the kingdom became known by this name; Laigin – after their spears which had won the victory for him.'

'I have heard something of that story before,' Fidelma confessed. 'An innocuous argument, as you say. But I was given to believe that Midach himself was from Laigin?'

'Midach? From Laigin? Whoever told you that? No, Midach is contemptuous of Laigin. But he did come from somewhere along its border. Perhaps that accounts for his prejudice. Yes, that's it. He was from Osraige.'

'Osraige?' Fidelma groaned inwardly. Osraige and Laigin! No matter which way one turned there always seemed some connection with Osraige and Laigin. They appeared to permeate this entire mystery.

'Why don't you ask him?' countered the chief professor. 'Midach will tell you soon enough.'

'So Midach insulted Laigin to Dacán's face,' went on Fidelma, without replying to the question. 'What did Dacán say to that?'

'He called Midach an ignorant fool and knave. He said the kingdom was older than Muman and that it had taken its name from a Nemedian, the descendant of Magog and Japhet, who had come to this land from Scythia with thirty-two ships. He argued that Liath, son of Laigin, was the hero who founded the kingdom.'

'How did such an academic discussion get out of hand?' Fidelma was curious.

'Both argued their case in voluble tones and neither gave way even when the argument transferred into personal abuse. It was only when I and Brother Rumann intervened that each was persuaded to return to his own chambers and take oath not to bring the discussion up again.'

Fidelma pursed her lips thoughtfully.

'Did you have any clashes with Dacán yourself?'

Ségán shook his head.

'As I said, I respected the man. I left him to run his classes and I think most of his students appreciated his knowledge though, it is true, there were some reports of disharmony and antagonism among a few of them. Abbot Brocc apparently took the disharmony seriously. I think he even asked Brother Conghus to watch that Dacán did not cause serious dissension. But to be truthful, I spent little time with him.'

Fidelma reluctantly came to her feet.

'You have been most helpful, chief professor,' she said.

Brother Ségán smiled broadly.

'It is little enough. If you have further need of me, anyone will direct you to my college chambers.'

Fidelma returned towards the hostel and while crossing the flagged courtyard she came abruptly upon Cass. The warrior's face was tired.

'I have made inquiries and looked everywhere for the two boys, also for Sister Eisten,' he greeted Fidelma in disgust. 'Unless they are all purposely hiding from us, I would say that they have all left the abbey confines.'

Chapter Nine

Sister Grella came as a surprise to Fidelma. She was an attractive woman in her late thirties. Though short in height and inclined to fleshiness, nevertheless she was vivacious in character, with well-kept brown hair and humorous dark eyes. To Fidelma, only a pouting, voluptuous mouth marred her features. She was, at first impression, out of place among the sombreness of the abbey, let alone in a library. Yet this was the chief librarian of the abbey. And, in spite of her initial sensual appearance, Sister Grella carried herself in a straight-backed and stately manner, like a queen in the midst of her court. She sat, in an ornately carved oak chair, at the far end of the great library chamber, which was almost as big and as vaulted as the abbey church. It was an impressive building, even by the standards of the great libraries Fidelma had visited elsewhere in the five kingdoms of Éireann.

The books were not kept on shelves but each work was kept in a *taig liubhair* or book satchel, a leather case which hung on one of a row of pegs along the walls, clearly labelled as to its contents. Fidelma, looking at the impressive collection, was reminded of the story of the death of the saintly Longargán, a most eminent scholar and contemporary of Colmcille. On the night that the Blessed Longargán had died, all the book satchels of Ireland were supposed to have fallen from their pegs as a mark of respect and in symbolism of the loss to learning through his passing.

Most of the books contained in the book satchels were works of reference, frequently consulted by the scholars. But here and there were special works of great value, kept in beautifully ornamented leather covers and embossed with enamels and layers of gold and silver and even studded with precious stones. It was said that Assicos, Patrick's coppersmith, made quadrangular book covers in copper to hold the books of the saintly man. Some of these works were also kept in special cases of wood as well as metal.

Containers of carved wood were used to keep bundles of hazel and aspen wands, on which were cut letters in ancient Ogham, the rods of the poets, but these works were vanishing as the thin rods of wood rotted. Their information was often transferred to the new alphabet and sheets of vellum before they were destroyed.

There were several people in the musty and gloom-shrouded library. In spite of the daylight filtering through the high windows into the Tech Screptra, giant candles, in large wrought-iron stands, were lit. These cast a flickering illumination across the room. The choking atmosphere of the smoke from these candles, thought Fidelma, was hardly conducive to good scholarship. Here and there scribes sat at special tables crouching over sheets of vellum, quills of swan or goose in one hand and a maulstick to support the wrist in the other as they transcribed in elaborate or ornamental fashion some ancient work for posterity. Others sat reading quietly or with occasional sighs and the rustle of the turning page.

Fidelma made her way along the aisles of book satchels and by the various tables of the diligent scholars. No one raised their head as she passed by.

The reflected glint in the dark eyes of Sister Grella showed that the librarian had watched her approach closely. Fidelma came to the head of the hall, where the librarian's chair was placed behind a desk on a dais so that she might overlook the length and breadth of the Tech Screptra.

'Sister Grella? I am . . .' began Fidelma as she halted before the librarian.

Sister Grella raised a small but shapely hand to silence her. Then she placed a finger across her lips, rose from her seat and gestured towards a side door.

Fidelma interpreted this as an invitation to follow.

On the other side of the door, Fidelma found herself in a small chamber which was filled with shelves of books but with a table and several chairs. There were sheets of vellum on the table and a conical capped ink holder, an *adiricín*, with a selection of quills and a pen knife for cutting them into nibs. It was obviously a private workroom.

Sister Grella waited until Fidelma had entered and then closed the door behind her and, with another imperial gesture of her hand, pointed to a chair, indicating that Fidelma should be seated. As Fidelma did so, the librarian lowered herself in the same regal posture into a chair facing her.

'I know who you are and why you have come,' the librarian said in a soft soprano voice.

Fidelma smiled quizzically at the personable woman.

'In that case, my task will be made that much simpler,' she replied.

The librarian arched an eyebrow but she said nothing.

'Have you been librarian at Ros Ailithir a long time?'

Sister Grella was obviously not expecting this question to start with and she frowned.

'I have been *leabhar coimedach* here for eight years,' she replied after a moment's hesitation.

'And before that?' Fidelma pressed.

'I was not at this foundation.'

Fidelma had asked merely in order to obtain some background of the librarian but she detected a faint note of suspicion in the other's voice and wondered why.

'Then you must have come here highly recommended to

obtain such an important post as librarian without having been trained in this monastery, sister,' she commented.

Sister Grella made a dismissive gesture, a cutting motion of her left hand.

'I qualified to the level of *sai*.'

Fidelma knew that to achieve the degree of a *sai* one had to study at an ecclesiastical school for six years and have a knowledge of scriptures as well as a general knowledge.

'Where did you study?' Her interest was a natural curiosity.

Again, Sister Grella hesitated a little. Then she seemed to make up her mind.

'At the foundation of the Blessed Colmcille known as Cealla.'

Fidelma stared at her dumbfounded for a moment.

'Cealla in Osraige?'

'I know of no other,' said Grella reprovingly.

'Are you of Osraige then?' That borderland between Muman and Laigin seemed to confront her whatever path she took on this investigation. Fidelma was incredulous of the number of times that the kingdom of Osraige seemed to have connections with Ros Ailithir.

'I was,' admitted Sister Grella. 'I have yet to see what this has to do with your task. Abbot Brocc informs me that you are a *dálaigh* come to investigate the death of Dacán of Fearna. But my birthplace and qualifications have surely little to do with that matter?'

Fidelma gazed thoughtfully at the other.

The woman had become tense. The veins showed blue against the white skin of the forehead. The mouth was trembling slightly and her facial muscles seemed strained. One shapely hand was toying nervously with the silver crucifix which hung around her neck.

'I am told that the Venerable Dacán spent a considerable portion of his time in the library.' Fidelma did not bother to reply to Sister Grella's protest but went straight to her questions about Dacán.

'He was a scholar. The purpose of his visit to Ros Ailithir was to study. Where else should he spend his time?'

'How long was he here?'

'Surely the abbot would have told you that?'

'Two months,' Fidelma supplied, realising that the vivacious-looking librarian was not going to be helpful and that her questions would have to be phrased carefully to extract any information at all from her guarded responses. 'And in that two months,' Fidelma went on, 'he spent most of his time in this library studying. What did he study?'

'He was a scholar of history.'

'He was well respected for his knowledge, I know,' replied Fidelma patiently. 'But what books did he study here?'

'The books that are studied are a matter for the librarian and the scholar,' countered Sister Grella woodenly.

Fidelma realised it was time to establish her authority.

'Sister Grella,' she said quietly, so softly that the librarian had to bend forward in her chair to catch the words. 'I am a *dálaigh* engaged in the investigation of a murder. I am qualified to the level of *anruth*. This places certain rights and obligations on any whom I feel that I need to question. I am sure that as a *sai* you are perfectly aware of those obligations. You will now answer the questions that I put to you without further prevarication.'

Sister Grella suddenly sat stiff and upright as Fidelma's voice rose sharply. Her eyes had widened a little, staring in ill-concealed anger at the younger woman. That she was unused to being so roundly rebuked showed by the tinge of red on her cheeks. She swallowed noisily.

'What books did Dacán study here?' repeated Fidelma.

'He . . . he was interested in the volumes we have which applied to the history of . . . of Osraige.'

Osraige yet again! Fidelma gazed at the now impassive face of the librarian.

'Osraige? Why would an abbey in the land of the Corco Loígde have books on a kingdom that lies many miles from here?'

For the first time Sister Grella's lips twisted into a smile of superiority. It made her look coarse.

'Obviously, Fidelma of Kildare, in spite of your qualification in law, you have little knowledge of the history of this land.'

Fidelma shrug indifferently.

'Everyone is a beginner at another's trade. I am content with law and leave the profession of history to historians. Enlighten me if there is something I need to know of this matter.'

'Two hundred years ago there was a chieftain of the Osraige named Lugne. He visited this land of the Corco Loígde and met the chieftain's daughter named Liadán. For a while they dwelt together on an island off the coast here. A son was born to them whom they named Ciarán and he became one of the great apostles of the Faith in Ireland.'

Fidelma had followed the recital with care.

'I have read the story of the birth of the Blessed Ciarán which tells how his mother Liadán was sleeping one night and a star fell from heaven into her mouth and after this she became pregnant.'

The librarian was sharply indignant.

'Storytellers like to embellish their tales with fantasy but the truth, as I tell you, was that Ciarán's father was Lugne of Osraige.'

'I do not mean to argue,' Fidelma mollified her, 'just that the stories of the great apostles of Ireland are manifold.'

'I am telling you of the connection between Osraige and the Corco Loígde,' replied the librarian sourly. 'Do you want to know it or not?'

'Continue then.'

'When Ciarán grew to manhood, his father having died, he set off first to convert the people of his father's kingdom to the new Faith. At that time, two hundred years ago, the majority still had not heard the Word of Christ. He converted Osraige and he is known as its patron saint, even though he chose to site his community at Saighir, which is just north of its border. This is why he is known as Ciarán of Saighir.'

Fidelma knew this very well but this time held her tongue.

'I accept that Ciarán had a father from Osraige and a mother from Corco Loígde. Is this what Dacán was studying? A life of Ciarán?'

'The point is that when Ciarán went to bring the Faith to the Osraige he also took many followers from the Corco Loígde including his own widowed mother, Liadán, who founded a community of religieuse not far from Saighir. And with those followers he took his closest friend and relative, Cúcraide mac Duí, who, after Ciarán had defeated the pagan king of the Osraige, was made king in his stead.'

Fidelma was now suddenly interested in the story.

'So this is how the kings of the Osraige were chosen from the same family as the chieftains of the Corco Loígde?'

'Exactly. For two hundred years the Osraige have been ruled by the family of the chieftains of the Corco Loígde. This rule has often been considered unjust. During the last hundred years several kings of the Osraige, from Corco Loígde, have met their death from their people, such as Feradach who was slain in his bed.'

'And Salbach's cousin Scandlán is also from the Corco Loígde?'

'Just so.'

'Is there still a conflict over the kingship?'

'There will always be conflict until Osraige is able to re-establish its own line of kings.'

There was a slight vehemence in Grella's voice which did not pass unnoticed.

'Was this why Dacán was interested in studying the connections between Osraige and Corco Loígde?'

Grella was immediately on her guard once more.

'He studied our texts on the history of Osraige and its petty kings, that is all I know.'

Fidelma sighed deeply in exasperation.

'Come; it is surely logical? Dacán was of Laigin. Laigin has long held claims over Osraige. Perhaps Laigin was interested in placing the native kings of Osraige back in power if those kings turned their allegiance from Cashel to Laigin? Perhaps that is why Dacán was interested in the history of the kingship?'

Grella flushed and her mouth tightened.

Fidelma realised that she had been right and that Grella knew precisely what the old scholar had been studying.

'Dacán was sent here by Fianamail the new king of Laigin, or by his own brother Abbot Noé of Fearna, who is the advisor to the new king, to gather the background on the kingship of Osraige so that a case might be presented against the Corco Loígde before the High King's assembly. Surely that is so?'

Grella remained silent, staring defiantly at Fidelma.

Fidelma abruptly smiled at the librarian.

'You are placed in an awkward position, Grella. As a woman of Osraige, knowing this, you seem to indicate a support for the dispossessed native kings. But I think it is now clear why the Venerable Dacán had come to Ros Ailithir. So why was he killed? To prevent that knowledge being taken back to Laigin?'

Sister Grella's expression did not alter.

'Come, speak, Grella,' insisted Fidelma. 'We are all entitled to our opinions. You are a woman of Osraige. You doubtless have an opinion. If you supported the return of the native kings then it would also mean that you had no motive to kill Dacán.'

Grella's eyes suddenly flashed angrily.

'I? I, kill Dacán? How dare you suggest . . .' She bit her lip and attempted to control her anger. Then she spoke quietly. 'Yes, of course I have an opinion. Ciarán's legacy hangs like a millstone around our necks. But I am no revolutionary to change things.'

Fidelma sat back. She found that she had taken a step forward but it had produced many new mysteries and puzzles.

'So you provided Dacán with all the ancient texts he needed to help him gather this information for the new king of Laigin to lay a fresh claim for the return of Osraige before the High King?'

Sister Grella did not bother to reply but another thought struck Fidelma.

'Dacán was studying the texts and making notes to prepare a report to take back to Laigin, wasn't he?'

'I have admitted as much.'

'Then where did he keep all the notes and writings that he made?'

Sister Grella grimaced.

'In his chamber at the hostel, I presume.'

'Would it surprise you to know there were only a few plain sheets of vellum, some writing materials, and nothing else except . . .'

Fidelma drew from her robe the short hazel wand she had found discarded in Dacán's chamber.

Grella took it, turning it over and examining the lettering.

'It is part of the "Song of Mugain" who was daughter of Cúcraide mac Duí, the first Corco Loígde king of Osraige. It lists part of the genealogy of the native kings of Osraige. I did not even know it was missing.'

She rose from her chair and went to a corner of the chamber

and started to looking through containers in which bunches of rods were held. She found one and peered through, making clucking sounds with her tongue.

'Yes; it is a wand from this collection.'

'It is in a curious style, more like a will than a genealogy,' Fidelma pointed out.

Grella's eyes narrowed.

'Do you understand Ogham?' she demanded sharply.

'I do.'

'Well, it is not a will.' Grella's voice was querulous. 'The symbolism is that of a poem.'

'It would seem that Dacán had taken these wands back to his own chamber to transcribe and when he returned them he forgot one of the rods which had fallen to the floor in his room. Would that be a usual thing, his taking material to his chamber?'

Grella shook her head.

'Unusual. Dacán did not work in that way. He did not want anyone to know what he was working on and so he did not usually remove any material from the Tech Screptra. Usually he worked in this very chamber we now sit in. This is my private study as librarian. Nothing was ever removed from this room.'

'Then someone did remove at least one of the rods of this "Son of Mugain",' Fidelma pointed out. 'How else could it have been found in Dacán's chamber?'

'I can make no answer to that question.'

'And are you saying that he never left his notes or writings here in the library?'

Sister Grella sat stiffly before her.

'I can assure you that I know nothing of that matter.'

'Did you know Assíd, the merchant?'

The change of tack was so abrupt that Sister Grella asked her to repeat the question.

'I saw him at the evening meal on the night of Dacán's

death,' Sister Grella replied. 'What has this man to do with the matter?'

'Did you observe if Dacán knew Assíd?'

There was no reaction on Grella's features.

'Assíd was from Laigin. Most people knew, or at least knew of, Dacán in that kingdom.'

'I believe that it was Assíd who must have taken the news of Dacán's death directly to Fearna,' Fidelma continued. 'The news of his death travelled swiftly and only a fast sailing *barc*, taking the coastal route, could have reached Fearna in such a time.'

'I could not make a comment on that.'

'Well, could it be that Assíd might have taken Dacán's notes with him?'

'Are you saying that Assíd stole them?' demanded Grella. She did not seem surprised nor outraged.

'It is a possible explanation.'

'Possible, yes,' agreed Sister Grella. 'But you are surely implying that Assíd killed Dacán?'

'I have not reached such a conclusion yet.'

Fidelma rose from her seat.

Sister Grella regarded her impassively.

'Such an explanation would allow the king at Cashel to wriggle off the hook of responsibility.'

Fidelma looked down at her with a trace of a smile.

'How so?'

'Why, if Dacán was killed by a man of Laigin then the Laigin claim for Osraige as Dacán's honour price would become irrelevant, wouldn't it?'

'Exactly so,' agreed Fidelma solemnly.

She turned and left Sister Grella still seated in her chair and walked back through the stillness of the Tech Screptra, amid the sighing breaths, rustle of vellum leaves and scratching of quills.

A figure caught her eye among the racks bearing the book

satchels. The figure attracted attention mainly because it was obvious that it did not wish to be observed by her, Had it been examining the books she might not have taken any notice. But the figure was so ostentatiously trying to look like an earnest reader in the library that it was immediately worthy of a second glance. Well, if the figure so obviously did not want to be seen by her, Fidelma reasoned that she should not give notice that she had spotted it.

It was the young, eager Sister Necht.

Outside the gloomy, candle-lit Tech Screptra, the day had turned chill, the storm clouds suddenly bunching up from the west again, bringing a slow drizzling rain with them.

Fidelma groaned softly and began to hurry towards the hostel.

In the entrance chamber Brother Rumann had ensured that a slow burning fire had been lit in the great hearth. Fidelma was glad of its warmth, for the weather was truly disheartening. She wondered if Sister Eisten or the children had reappeared yet and made her way along to their chambers. The doors were open but the chambers stood empty.

Fidelma compressed her lower lip a moment. She realised that not only were the children's chambers empty but there was no sign that they had ever been occupied.

Frowning, Fidelma hurried along the corridor to the chamber which Brother Rumann used as his *officium*.

The plump cenobite was seated before his *brandubh* board apparently working out some moves.

He glanced up in surprise as Fidelma entered after only the briefest of knocks.

'Ah, it is you, sister.' His face wreathed in a smile and he glanced down at the board. 'Have you come to challenge me to that match we spoke of?'

Fidelma gave a quick negative shake of her head.

'Not for the moment, Brother Rumann. I am more interested in where the children are.'

'The children?'

'The children of Rae na Scríne.'

His face seemed to reshape itself as if bewildered.

'Why, the children were taken to Brother Midach after the midday meal. Did you want to see them before they left?'

'Left? For where?'

'Brother Midach was going to give them a final examination, to ensure that there were no signs of the plague, and then Sister Aíbnat was to take them to the orphanage along the coast which is cared for by the good sister and Brother Molua. I think that they must have left by now.'

'Have they all gone?'

'I think so, sister. Brother Midach would know.'

Fidelma found herself hurrying in search of the abbey's chief physician.

Brother Midach turned out to have the rounded features of an entertainer rather than those commonly associated with a physician. They were certainly in keeping with Fidelma's general prejudice that all physicians were possessed of humour, for they were creased with many laughter lines. He was balding, so it was hard to see where his tonsure began and what was natural baldness. His lips were thin, the eyes warmly brown and humorous and there was a careless stubble on his cheeks.

Fidelma entered his chambers without knocking. The physician was alone, apparently engaged in mixing some herbs. He glanced up with a frown.

'I am Fidelma of Kildare,' she began.

The physician examined her carefully before replying, but did not pause in what he was doing.

'My colleague, Brother Tóla has spoken of you. Are you seeking him?'

'No. I am told that you examined the children from Rae na Scríne this afternoon. Is that so?'

The physician raised his dark, bushy eyebrows.

'That is so. The abbot thought it was best to send them on directly to the care of Brother Molua, who has a house along the coast and cares for orphans. Sister Aíbnat was instructed to take them there. I was asked to examine them to see if they were fit.'

Fidelma showed her disappointment.

'So they have all gone?'

Midach nodded absently as he continued to pulp leaves by grinding his pestle in a mortar.

'We have no facilities for children here,' he explained in a conversational tone. 'The two little girls were very healthy,' he smiled. 'And the sooner the young boy, Tressach, is with others of his kind, the happier he will be. Yes, they will be better off in the house of Molua.'

Fidelma was about to turn for the door when she hesitated and frowned at the chief physician.

'You say nothing of the two brothers – Cétach and Cosrach?'

Midach raised his head from the mortar, his eyes suddenly dark and fathomless.

'What two brothers?' he demanded. 'There were two sisters . . .'

'The black-haired boys,' she interrupted impatiently.

Midach pulled a doleful face.

'I know nothing of any black-haired boys. I was asked to examine the two girls and a young lad of eight years old.'

'You saw nothing of a boy of fourteen and one of ten or so?'

Midach shook his head in mystification.

'Don't tell me that Brother Rumann has made some mistake and there were two other lads to be sent to Molua? I certainly have not seen them . . .'

Fidelma was already gone hurrying back to the hostel.

Brother Rumann started in surprise as Fidelma burst in on him again.

'The two black-haired boys,' she demanded. 'Cétach and Cosrach. Where are they?'

Brother Rumann regarded her with a woebegone expression then glanced down at his *brandubh* board. The pieces had been spilled from their positions, apparently by his jerk of surprise when Fidelma had burst through the door.

'Really, sister. A little patience. I had almost worked out a new ploy. A wonderful means of . . .'

He paused, observing, for the first time, her agitated expression.

'Is something the matter?'

'I am asking you where the two black-haired boys are – Cétach and Cosrach.'

Brother Rumann began to slowly gather the scattered pieces and replace them on the *brandubh* board.

'Sister Aíbnat was told to take all the children to Brother Midach and, if he said that they were healthy enough, then she was to set out for the house of Molua along the coast.'

'Brother Midach says that he saw only the two little girls, Ciar and Cera, and the boy of about eight years whose name was Tressach. What has happened to the other two boys?'

Brother Rumann climbed to his feet with an expression of annoyance, his hands clutching the *brandubh* pieces.

'Are you sure that they did not go with Sister Aíbnat?' he asked incredulously.

'Brother Midach knows nothing about them,' replied Fidelma with an air of exaggerated patience.

'Then where can they have hidden themselves? Stupid, wilful little children. They should have gone with Sister Aíbnat. Now it means that a second journey will have to be made to take them to Molua's orphanage.'

'When did you last see them?'

'I can't remember. Perhaps when Salbach arrived here. I recall that young Sister Necht was talking to them in their room. The order for the children to be sent to the orphanage came from Brocc shortly afterwards.'

'Is there anywhere obvious that they would have hidden themselves?' Fidelma asked, remembering how afraid Cétach had been of Salbach. Could he and his brother have hidden somewhere, waiting for Salbach to leave the abbey? Could they be remaining in hiding not realising that he had already left?

'There are many hiding places,' Rumann assured her. 'But don't worry, sister. It will soon be vespers and the bell and hunger will draw them out of their hiding place.'

Fidelma was unconvinced.

'It was thought the bell for the midday meal would lure them out for food. If you see Sister Eisten, tell her that I would like to see her.'

Brother Rumann nodded absently, turning his attention back to the *brandubh* game. He slowly began to reassemble the pieces on the board.

Back in her chamber Fidelma stretched exhausted on her cot. She wished she had told Brocc that she wanted the children from Rae na Scríne to remain at the abbey until she had resolved the mystery. It had not occurred to her that he would have them removed so soon. For every mystery solved there were new ones to be confronted.

Why had the young boy Cétach pleaded with her not to mention him or his brother, Cosrach, to Salbach? Why had the boys then vanished? Why was Salbach so reluctant to believe her charge against Intat? And had any of these matters a connection with the death of Dacán, which mystery was her main task to solve?

She gave a snort of frustration as she lay on her back with hands clasps behind her head.

So far, there was little that made sense in this investigation. Oh, there were a couple of theories that she could develop but the old Brehon Morann had warned against creating theories before all the evidence was in. What was his favourite saying? 'Do not make the cheese until you have first milked the cows.' Yet she was acutely aware of the rapid passing of her greatest enemy – time.

She wondered how her brother, Colgú, must be feeling now that he was king of Muman. She felt anxiety for her elder brother.

There would be little time to mourn the dead king, Cathal mac Cathail, their cousin. The main thing now was to prevent the impending war. And that great responsibility rested entirely with her.

She found herself wishing once again that Eadulf of Seaxmund's Ham was here with her so that she could discuss her ideas and suspicions with him. Then she felt somehow guilty for the thought and did not know why.

The sound of a door banging abruptly caused her to sit up. She could hear heavy footsteps running across the stone-flagged floor below and then ascending the steps to the second floor of the hostel. Such footsteps did not augur well. By the time the steps reached her door and halted she had swung off her cot and stood facing the door.

It was Cass who came pushing through the door, after a cursory knocking. He was breathing hard from his exertions.

He pulled up sharply in the middle of her chamber and stood with heaving shoulders facing her.

'Sister Fidelma!' He had to pause to recover his breath.

She stared at him, wondering what had made the young warrior so agitated. She quickly worked out that he would have to run a distance over a difficult path to arrive in such a condition. A warrior, such as he, did not loose breath so easily.

'Well, Cass?' she asked quietly. 'What is it?'

'Sister Eisten. She has been found.'

Fidelma read what was in his eyes.

'Has she been found dead?' she asked softly.

'She has!' confirmed Cass grimly.

Chapter Ten

The body lay by the water's edge on the sandy beach below the abbey walls. It was already dusk but a group of fishermen and several members of the religious community had gathered around with morbid curiosity. Several of them were holding brand torches which illuminated the scene. Fidelma followed Cass towards the group. She observed that Brother Midach was already there, bending to examine the body. There was a middle-aged brother with a nervous, consumptive cough, holding a lantern for Midach to work by. Fidelma assumed that this was the apothecary, Brother Martan. The physician had obviously been summoned by those who had found the young anchoress. Fidelma thought he looked visibly shaken in the flickering light.

'Clear some of these people back,' Fidelma instructed Cass quietly, 'excepting those who actually found the body.'

She bent down by Brother Midach and stared over his shoulder.

Sister Eisten's clothes were waterlogged. Her hair was plastered to her head by sea-water and across her pale, plump white face. Her features looked twisted in the anguish of a violent death. Her magnificent ornate cross was still fastened firmly around her bruised, fleshy neck.

'Not a pleasant sight,' Midach grunted, noticing Fidelma at his side for the first time. 'Keep the lantern high, Martan,' he added quickly, in an aside to the apothecary.

'Violent death never is,' murmured Fidelma. 'Did she commit suicide?'

Midach stared thoughtfully at Fidelma for a moment and shook his head negatively.

'What makes you ask that question?'

'She had a shock when Rae na Scríne was destroyed. I think she might have blamed herself. She went into a malaise when the young baby she had saved died soon afterwards. I saw her this morning and she did not seem truly recovered. Also, it was clearly no attack made in robbery for she still wears a valuable crucifix.'

'A good logic, but no; no, I do not think that she committed suicide.'

Fidelma examined the physician's assured features quickly and asked: 'What makes you say so?'

Brother Midach bent forward and turned the dead girl's head slightly, instructing Brother Martan to bring the lantern closer so that the area could be clearly seen.

Fidelma could see a gaping wound on the back of the skull. Even an immersion in the sea had not washed the blood from it.

'She was attacked from behind?'

'Someone hit her on the back of the head,' confirmed Midach. 'Only after that blow was her body dumped into the sea.'

'Murder then?'

Brother Midach sighed deeply.

'I can come to no other conclusion. There is not only the evidence of the blow on the back of the head. If you have a strong stomach, sister, look at her hands and arms.'

Fidelma did so. The wounds and burn marks spoke for themselves.

They were not self-inflicted.

'No. She was bound and tortured before she was killed. Look at those marks around her wrists. They are the marks of a rope. After she was killed, the killer must have untied the bonds and thrown her into the sea.'

Stunned, Fidelma stared at the body of the tragic young woman.

'With your permission, brother...' She bent forward and took the cold hands of the dead woman and examined them, looking carefully at the fingers and nails. Brother Midach regarded her with curiosity. Fidelma grimaced with disenchantment.

'I was hoping that she might have been able to fight her attacker and grasp something which might have given us some clue,' she explained.

'No. The final blow came probably without her even suspecting it,' Midach said. 'She would have been placed with her back to her attacker in order for him to deliver that blow.'

'Him?' queried Fidelma sharply.

Midach shrugged diffidently.

'Or her, if you like. Though I would not think it likely that a woman could do such a thing.'

Fidelma's lips thinned a moment but she made no comment.

Brother Midach stood up, dusting the sand from his robe. He motioned Martan and another brother forward from the shadows and instructed them to carry the body to the abbey.

'I'll have the body taken to the mortuarium and report this matter to the abbot.'

'Tell the abbot that I shall speak with him shortly,' Fidelma said, also rising and looking towards the small group of people who had been pushed a little further away by Cass.

'Do you think this has some connection with the death of the Venerable Dacán?' Midach paused and glanced back to her across his shoulder.

'That I hope to discover,' replied Fidelma.

Midach grimaced and, with Brother Martan hurrying behind him with the lantern, strode back towards the abbey gates.

Fidelma moved across to a group, some of whom now seemed reluctant to be involved for several of them began to sidle away. Cass had obtained a lantern to illuminate the proceedings.

'Who found the body?' Fidelma demanded, looking from one face to another.

She saw two elderly fishermen exchange glances of alarm by the light of their brand torches.

'There is no need to be fearful, my friends,' Fidelma reassured them. 'All I want to know is where and how you found the body.'

One of the fishermen, a ruddy-faced, middle-aged man, shuffled forward.

'My brother and I found it, sister.' He spoke in an uncertain, hesitant tone.

'Tell me how?' Fidelma invited in as gentle voice as she could.

'We were out in the bay, near the Laigin warship, and decided to give our nets one more cast before the dusk was upon us. As we trawled our nets we thought we had made a great catch but when we dragged the nets into the boat we saw . . .' he genuflected fearfully '. . . we saw the body of the sister there.'

'How close were you to the Laigin ship?' Fidelma asked.

'The Laigin ship sits at the entrance of the inlet but it's deep water there and one of the winter feeding grounds of haddock in these parts. Plenty of sea worms and shellfish there for them.' The fisherman suddenly spat in disgust. 'Then that warship comes along and sits right over the fishing ground.'

Fidelma looked sympathetic.

'I understand. So you and your brother moved as close as you could to the warship in order to fish?'

'We did that. We were a few yards off when we netted the poor sister. We brought the body straight back to the shore and raised the alarm.'

Cass, who was standing by her shoulder holding his lantern high, bent forward.

'Could it be that she was thrown from the Laigin ship?' he whispered.

Fidelma ignored him for the moment and turned back to the fishermen, who continued to watch her uneasily.

'What are the currents like in the bay?' she asked.

One of them rubbed his chin reflectively.

'At the moment we have an inshore tide. The currents are strong around the rocks though. They sweep all around that headland among the rocks.'

'What you are telling me is that the body could have been cast into the sea at any point along that headland.'

'Or even on the other side of the headland, sister, and swept around into this inlet.'

'And at this time a body would tend to get washed inshore here rather than seaward?' pressed Fidelma.

'That it would,' agreed the fisherman readily.

'Very well, you may go now,' Fidelma said. Then she raised her voice. 'You may all disperse to your homes now.'

The small group of morbid onlookers began to break up, almost unwillingly now, in obedience to her command.

Cass was standing peering suspiciously into the darkness across the bay. Fidelma followed his gaze. There were lights flickering on the warship.

'Can you row a boat, Cass?' Fidelma demanded abruptly.

The warrior swung round. She could not quite see his expression in the shadows.

'Of course,' he replied. 'But . . .'

'I think it is high time that we paid the Laigin warship a visit.'

'Is it wise? If Sister Eisten was murdered and thrown from the ship . . . ?'

'We have no proof nor any reasonable suspicion to that effect,' Fidelma replied calmly 'Come, let us find a boat.'

The tolling of the bell for vespers caused her to pause.

Cass, shifted the lantern so that the light fell momentarily on his face. He looked woebegone.

'We shall miss the evening meal,' he protested.

Fidelma chuckled grimly.

'I am sure that we will find something later to keep the great starvation at bay. Now let's find that boat.'

Fidelma sat in the stern of the small boat holding the lantern aloft as Cass leant into the oars, propelling the small craft across the dark, hissing waters of the inlet towards the great shadow and twinkling lights of the Laigin warship. As they drew nearer, she could see that there were several lanterns illuminating the deck of the sleek-looking vessel. There were signs of men moving here and there.

They were within a few yards when a voice challenged their approach.

'Respond,' muttered Fidelma, as Cass hesitated at the oars.

'Laigin ship, ahoy!' called the warrior. 'A *dálaigh* of the court of the Brehons demands to come aboard.'

There were several seconds of silence before the same voice that had hailed them responded.

'Come aboard and welcome.'

Cass brought the small craft alongside, under a rope ladder which led up to the side rail. A rope was thrown down for Cass to make the boat secure while Fidelma swung agilely up the ladder and over the rail.

She found half a dozen tough-looking men waiting on the deck and staring at her in surprise.

She heard Cass climbing up behind her. A man with indistinguishable features came forward with the rolling gait of a seaman and stared from Fidelma to Cass. Then he fixed his eyes on Cass.

'What do you want, *dálaigh*?' he demanded roughly.

Fidelma hissed in irritation.

'It is me whom you should address,' she snapped. 'I am Sister Fidelma of Kildare, *dálaigh* of the court of the Brehons.'

The man turned in astonishment which he hastily checked.

'From Kildare, eh? Do you represent Laigin?'

Fidelma was annoyed by the complication that her foundation of Kildare was actually situated in the kingdom of Laigin.

'No. I am of the community of Kildare but I represent the kingdom of Muman in this business.'

The sailor shuffled his feet a little.

'Sister, I do not wish to appear inhospitable, but this is a warship of the king of Laigin, acting under his orders. I do not see that you have any business here.'

'Then let me remind you of the Laws of the Sea,' Fidelma replied slowly, with careful emphasis. She wished she had a greater knowledge but was banking on the sailor having a lesser knowledge than her own. 'Firstly, I am a *dálaigh* investigating the crime of murder. Secondly, your ship, even though it is a ship of Laigin, lies at anchor in a bay of Muman. It has not sought the permission or hospitality of Muman.'

'You are wrong sister,' came the voice of the sailor; his triumphant tones were undisguised. 'We lie at anchor here with the full permission of Salbach, chieftain of the Corco Loígde.'

Fidelma was glad that the light of the lanterns did not fall directly on her face. She swallowed in her total astonishment. Was it true that Salbach had given permission to the Laigin ship to intimidate the abbey of Ros Ailithir? What could this mean? She would certainly not discover if she were forced to leave like a whipped cur with its tail between its legs. A bluff was worth trying. What was it the Brehon Morann had once said? 'Without a degree of deception, no great enterprise can ever be concluded.'

'The chieftain of the Corco Loígde may well have given you permission but that permission is not legal without the approval of the king at Cashel.'

'Cashel is many miles away, sister,' sneered the sailor. 'What the king of Cashel does not know, he cannot rule upon.'

'But I am here. I am the sister of Colgú, king of Cashel. And I can speak in my brother's name.'

There was a silence as the sailor digested this. She heard him exhale his breath slowly.

'Very well, lady,' replied the man, with a little more respect in his voice. 'What do you seek here?'

'I seek to talk to the captain of this vessel in private.'

'I am the captain,' the man replied. 'Come aft to my cabin.'

Fidelma glanced at Cass.

'Wait for me here, Cass. I shall not be long.'

The warrior looked unhappy in the light of the swinging deck lanterns.

The sailor led the way to the stern of the vessel and conducted her to a cabin below deck. It was small, crowded and smelt strongly of a man living in a confined space, body odours permeated together with the stench of the oil lamps and other smells which she could not place. For a moment or two she regretted not conducting her business on the deck in the fresh air but she did not want to let the eager ears of the sailors and warriors hear what she had to discuss.

'Lady,' invited the captain, indicating the only chair in the small crowded cabin while he himself sprawled on the end of a bunk.

Fidelma lowered herself gently into the cramped wooden seat.

'You have the advantage of me, captain,' Fidelma began.' You know my name, yet I do not know your name.'

The sailor grinned easily.

'Mugrón. A fitting name for a sailor.'

Fidelma found herself answering his smile. The name meant 'lad of the seals'. Then she brought her thoughts back to the matter in hand.

'Well, Mugrón, I would firstly like to know the purpose of your presence in the inlet of Ros Ailithir.'

Mugrón waved a hand as if to encompass his surroundings.

'I am here at the request of my king, Fianamail of Laigin.'

'That does not explain matters. Do you come in peace or war?'

'I came to deliver a message to Brocc, abbot of Ros Ailithir, telling him that my king holds him responsible for the death of his cousin, the Venerable Dacán.'

'You have delivered the message. What do you seek here now?'

'I am to wait to ensure that, when the time comes, Brocc answers to his responsibility. My king would not like him to vanish from Ros Ailithir until the High King's assembly meets at Tara. My king's Brehon has told us that this is within the law of distraint. As I said, we also have the permission of Salbach to anchor here.'

Fidelma realised, dredging some half-forgotten law from her memory, that under this pretext the ship of Mugrón was acting legally. In legal terms the ship was anchored outside the abbey in order to force Brocc to concede his responsibility for the death of Dacán, even though his hand did not commit the deed itself, and until proof was offered that he was not responsible the ship could sit there. The law went further and entitled the Abbot Noé, as closest relative to Dacán, to make a ritual fast against Brocc until culpability was admitted.

'You delivered a message to Brocc when you arrived here. Was that the official *apad* – the notice of this act?'

'It was,' agreed Mugrón. 'It was done according to the instruction of the Brehon of my king.'

Fidelma compressed her lips angrily.

She should have realised the situation sooner when she saw the bunch of twisted branches of osiers and aspens hanging at the gate of the abbey. This withe, as it was called, was the sign of a distraint against a monastic superior. It was a long time since she had had recourse to the text known as *Di Chetharshlicht Athgabála* setting out the complex rituals and law on distraint. What she did remember was that she was allowed to make three mistakes in the law without fine because it was so complex. She conceded that her first mistake was in her lapse of memory of the law of distraint.

The weather-beaten face of the sailor creased cynically as he saw the expression on her face.

'The king of Laigin places the law above all things, lady,' he said with gentle emphasis.

'It is the law that I shall speak to you about, now that I know your purpose here,' Fidelma replied spiritedly.

'What would a simple sailor, such as I, know about the law?' countered Mugrón. 'I do as I am told.'

'You have admitted that you are here as an instrument of the law, instructed by the Brehon of your king,' Fidelma responded quickly. 'You know enough law for that.'

Mugrón's eyes widened at the way she refused to be intimidated and then he grinned.

'Very well. Of what would you speak?'

'A sister of the Faith was pulled out of the water near your ship a short while ago. She was dead.'

'One of my men reported the incident to me,' agreed Mugrón. 'It happened just before nightfall. Two fisherman had snared the body in their nets. They rowed it to the shore.'

'You appear to keep a careful watch on this ship. Did none of your crew see anything suspicious? No sign of the body being put into the sea from the rocks on that headland?'

'Nothing was seen by us. We have little to do with the shore except, with the approval of Salbach, we trade for fresh meat and vegetables with some of the local people.'

'And the sister was never on board this ship?'

Mugrón's face coloured with annoyance.

'Sister Eisten was not on board this ship,' he snapped. 'Who claims that she was is a liar!'

Fidelma felt a sudden excitement at his response.

'And how did you know her name was Eisten? I did not mention it.' There was granite in her voice.

Mugrón blinked.

'You . . .'

She interrupted him with a gesture.

'Do not play games with me, Mugrón. How did you know her name? It is the truth that I want.'

Mugrón raised his arms in a helpless gesture.

'Very well, the entire truth it shall be. But I have no wish to place my life and ship in danger. Let us keep this matter between us for the time being.'

'There will be no danger so long as the truth is told,' affirmed Fidelma.

Mugrón rose from his seat, went to the cabin door and called out the name, 'Midnat'. He returned to his seat and an elderly, bearded man entered a moment later and raised his knuckles to his forehead. He was grizzled and tanned of face and his hair was a dirty, greying colour.

'Tell the sister here your name and the position that you hold on this vessel. Then tell her what happened to you when you went ashore today.'

The elderly man turned to Fidelma and bobbed his head, drawing back his lips from toothless gums.

'I am Midnat, lady. I am the cook for this vessel. I went ashore today to buy fresh vegetables and oats for the crew.'

'At what time was this?'

'Just as the bell for the midday meal was being struck at the abbey.'

'Tell Sister Fidelma what happened,' interrupted Mugrón. 'Exactly as you told me.'

The old man glanced at him in surprise.

'About the . . . ?

'Get on with it, man,' snapped Mugrón. 'Tell her everything.'

The old man raised a hand and wiped it over his mouth and chin.

'Well, I am returning to my boat. I've bought the vegetables, you see. So, I am going back . . . well, this sister hails me and asks me whether my captain will be prepared to take two passengers on a voyage.'

'She said *two* passengers?' queried Fidelma. 'What exactly did she say?'

'Like that: "Hey, sailor, do you come from that ocean-going ship?" she says. I nods. "How much will your captain charge for the passage for two to Britain or Gaul?" Then I realise that she has mistaken me for someone off the Frankish ship yonder. The big merchant ship. She offers, she says, two *screpall* for the passage.'

Fidelma stared at him in astonishment.

'The sister offered such valuable silver coins?'

Midnat nodded emphatically.

'I says: "Would that I could take it, sister, but I am just the cook from the Laigin warship there. For passage out of this land you need to contact a sailor from the Frankish merchantman at anchor on the other side of the inlet." No sooner have I said that, then she steps back with a hand to her mouth and eyes wide as if I am the devil incarnate. And she turns and runs away.'

The man paused and waited, watching Fidelma's face.

'Is that all?' Fidelma was disappointed.

'It was enough,' confirmed Midnat.

'She disappeared and you did not see her again?'

'She runs off along the seashore. I returns to my ship. Then a short while ago, just as dusk is about to descend there's a commotion. I goes on deck to see what it's about. Not far off there's a couple of local fishermen hauling a body out of the water. It's this same sister that offers me the money for a passage.'

Fidelma glanced up sharply.

'It was dusk, nearly dark. How could you be sure it was the same sister?'

'There's enough light,' said the old cook, 'and the body of the sister is wearing a curious cross around its neck. Distinctive enough for me to know that I have not seen another except worn by the sister who asks about the passage to Britain or Gaul.'

It was right enough, thought Fidelma. Eisten's Roman cross was fairly distinctive in these parts. But she decided to make certain.

'Curious? In what way?'

'It's a cross without a circle.'

'Ah, you mean a Roman cross?' Fidelma pressed.

'I don't know. If you say it is,' replied the other diffidently. 'But it's large and ornate and with some jewels worth a king's ransom encrusted on it.'

It was not surprising that the old sailor might mistake the semi-precious stones for jewels of great wealth. The identification, though tenuous, was enough to convince her of the accuracy of what the man had said.

'That will be all, Midnat.' Mugrón dismissed the sailor.

The old cook raised his knuckles to his forehead once more in a farewell salute and left the cabin.

'Well?' asked Mugrón, 'does this testimony satisfy you?'

'No, it doesn't,' Fidelma replied calmly. 'For you still have not explained how you knew the actual name of this unfortunate woman.'

Mugrón shrugged dismissively.

'Well, there is no great secret in that. I told you that we had the permission of Salbach to anchor here and pursue our distraint against Brocc of Ros Ailithir.'

Fidelma nodded.

'When we came here just over a week ago, on instruction of our king's Brehon we went straight to Salbach's fortress at Cuan Dóir to ask his permission.'

'And so?' prompted Fidelma, not understanding where Mugrón was leading her.

'At Cuan Dóir I was introduced to this Sister Eisten. When Midnat came to me and described this sister, with her strange crucifix, saying that it was the same sister who was seeking passage, I remembered the crucifix and her name.'

'So you are sure that Sister Eisten was at Salbach's fortress a week ago?' Fidelma felt confused by the apparent ceaseless twists the path of this investigation kept taking.

'Indeed. Cuan Dóir lies in the next bay, so not far from here. Why do you seem surprised that she would be there?'

Fidelma did not attempt an explanation.

'There is one thing I would like you to do, Mugrón,' she said to the captain of the Laigin warship. 'That is, I want you to accompany me to the abbey and make sure that the body of Sister Eisten is the same person as the sister you saw at Salbach's fortress. I want to be absolutely sure.'

Mugrón was hesitant.

'Well, I suppose a trip ashore will be better than sitting on this tub buffeted by the seas. Yet I cannot understand what relevance the death of this tragic young woman has to do with the killing of Dacán? Surely that is the more important matter with which you should be concerned?'

He saw the look in Fidelma's eye and raised a hand in placation.

'Yes, yes, Sister Fidelma. I'll come with you but you, as *dálaigh*, must ensure that no indignity will be done to me by any followers of the Abbot Brocc.'

'That I can assure you,' Fidelma confirmed.

'Then it is agreed.'

'There is another thing,' Fidelma said, reaching forward to stay him as Mugrón prepared to rise to his feet.

'Which is?'

'You said that you were introduced to Sister Eisten. Why was that?'

'It was while we were awaiting the arrival of Salbach in the feasting hall that I saw this young religieuse. I was interested in the cross she wore because it was not like the crucifixes worn by our native religious. I could get a good trade for such a cross in Laigin.'

'It is true,' confirmed Fidelma. 'The crucifix was obtained in Bethlehem, for Sister Eisten went on a three-year pilgrimage to the Holy Birthplace of the Christ'

'Exactly as she told me at the time, sister,' agreed the captain. 'I was told that everyone asks about it. I had asked Sister Eisten's companion to introduce me to assure her that I could be trusted. Alas, the sister valued her cross too much to trade it.'

'Who introduced you?' frowned Fidelma. 'You have implied that you knew this companion of Sister Eisten.'

Mugrón was without any guile.

'Oh yes. Of course I knew her. I had met her when I visited Fearna in the service of the old king. And she recognised me right enough. I was astonished that a lady of Laigin was to be found at the fortress of the chieftain of the Corco Loígde especially when the lady was none other than the former wife of Dacán.'

Of all the surprises Fidelma had heard during her investigations at Ros Ailithir this statement came as the biggest shock of all.

'The former wife of the Venerable Dacán?' she repeated slowly, scarcely believing what he said. 'Are you absolutely sure of this?'

'Of course I am sure. I had known that Dacán had been

married. It was fourteen years ago but I remembered her. An attractive young girl. They were not long together before she divorced him in order to pursue her religious career. I thought she had gone to Cealla.'

'And who was this former wife of Dacán?' Fidelma asked quietly. 'Does she have a name?'

'Why, of course. Her name is Grella.'

Chapter Eleven

After Mugrón had duly identified the body of Sister Eisten as being that of the same religieuse whom he had seen at Salbach's fortress, he had returned to his ship. Fidelma and Cass then made their way to the abbey kitchens in search of a meal for, having missed the evening meal, they were both ravenous. It took some insistence on Fidelma's part, and an emphasis of her position and relationship with the abbot, to persuade the surly sister in charge to provide them with a pitcher of ale, some barley bread and cold cuts from a *larac* or leg of beef. A bowl of apples was also provided and they ate voraciously and in silence at a small table in the corner of the now deserted refectory.

Fidelma had not really expected that Mugrón would fail to recognise the body of Sister Eisten but she wanted to be sure beyond any doubt that Eisten had been at Salbach's fortress. She was now faced with one more frustrating mystery, yet one which seemed to hold a slender link to the murder of Dacán. What caused her excitement was Mugrón's identification of Dacán's former wife. Why had Grella failed to mentioned that essential fact to Fidelma? The apparent answer was that Grella had been attempting to hide some guilt. Had her relationship provided grounds for Dacán's murder?

But there was something else that worried Fidelma. What had Grella and Eisten been doing at Salbach's fortress together? And why had Eisten attempted to book two passages on a ship leaving for Gaul? With whom had she been planning to travel? Was it Grella? And who had tortured and killed Eisten?

Fidelma ruminated on the questions while acknowledging that it was little use asking questions when there was no hope of providing answers.

She glanced across the table to Cass and felt a sense of frustration that she could not even begin to discuss her anxieties with him. She found herself still longing for the presence of Brother Eadulf, wishing that she could thrust and parry with the quick sword of his alert mind; dissecting, analysing and, perhaps, gradually arriving at a truth. Then she immediately began to feel guilty again.

She suddenly realised that Cass was regarding her with a quizzical smile.

'What next, sister?' he asked, putting down his empty mug of ale and sitting back, obviously satisfied with his meal.

'Next?'

'Your mind has been working like the water-clock in the bell tower. I could almost hear the mechanism of your mind as it worked.'

Fidelma grimaced awkwardly.

'There is one obvious person to see next – Sister Grella. We have to find out why she lied, or, rather, why she did not tell me the whole truth.'

She rose to her feet, followed by Cass.

'I shall come with you,' he said. 'From what you told me there is more than a possibility that she could be the murderess. If so, you should not take chances.'

This time Fidelma made no objection.

They made their way through the gloomy abbey buildings to the dark, deserted library. There was no sign of anyone working in its cold, murky hall. The seats were forsaken, the books were neatly packed in their satchel bags and there were no candles burning.

Fidelma led the way into the small chamber where Sister Grella had taken her to talk, the room where Dacán had studied. She was surprised to see a fire smouldering in the corner fireplace. While Cass bent to light a candle, Fidelma walked quickly across to the fireplace. Something had caught her eye. She leant down to pick it up.

'What do you make of this?' she asked.

Cass shrugged as he gazed at the short length of burnt twig which she held out to him.

'A stick. What else do you light fires with?'

She clicked her tongue in annoyance.

'Not usually with such sticks. Examine it more closely.'

Cass did so and saw that it was a piece of aspen with some notches of Ogham inscribed on it.

'What does it say?' he asked.

'Nothing that now makes sense. The extract here reads "the resolve of the honourable one determines the fosterage of my children". That's all.'

Fidelma placed the salvaged piece of Ogham wand in her *marsupium* and stared with interest at the remains of the fire.

'It means that someone has decided to burn an entire book.' She glanced at the holders that Grella had examined earlier in the day. It was as she suspected. 'This was the Ogham book that Dacán had been studying. One wand of it, which I discovered, remained in his chamber after his death. I brought it here to show Sister Grella, who identified it as a poem.'

'Didn't you think it was part of a will?'

Fidelma pursed her lips in a noncommittal gesture.

'Now why did someone think that it was so important that they needed to destroy it?' she asked as if she did not expect Cass to reply.

With a sigh, Fidelma led the way back through the library and into the corridor outside.

A passing cenobite glanced curiously at them.

'Do you seek Sister Grella?' he inquired politely.

Fidelma affirmed that they did.

'If she is not in the Tech Screptra, Sister Grella will be in her own chambers.'

'Where will we find her chambers?' Cass inquired a little impatiently.

The cenobite gave them detailed directions which were easy enough to follow.

The chamber of the librarian of Ros Ailithir, however, was deserted. Fidelma had knocked carefully on the door twice. She made sure the corridor was empty before turning the handle. As she fully expected, the door was not locked.

'Inside, quickly, Cass,' she instructed.

He followed her somewhat reluctantly and when he had passed into Sister Grella's chamber she closed the door and fumbled for a candle.

'This is surely wrong, sister,' muttered Cass. 'We should not be in this room uninvited.'

Lighting the candle and standing back, Fidelma regarded Cass scornfully.

'As a *dálaigh* of the court I can demand the right to search a person or premises where I have a reasonable suspicion of misconduct.'

'Then you do believe that Sister Grella killed her former husband and Sister Eisten?'

Fidelma motioned him to silence and began searching the room. For someone who had spent eight years in the abbey, Sister Grella's chamber was exceedingly sparse in personal objects. A book of devotions was placed by the bed and a few toilet articles, combs and such matter. She examined a large pitcher which was full of liquid. Fidelma sniffed suspiciously at it and her lips narrowed into a cynical smile. It was *cuirm*, the strong mead fermented from malted barley. It seemed Sister Grella liked to drink in the solitude of her chamber.

She turned to some clothes hanging from a line of pegs but was not really interested in them. There was little here of interest. It was only half-heartedly that she turned to a satchel she had spotted hanging on a peg under some of the clothes and rummaged through merely to complete her search. At first, she thought that it contained only a few undergarments. She drew them out and examined them by the light of the candle. Then among them she noticed a linen skirt which caused her to gasp in sudden satisfaction.

'Cass, examine this,' she whispered.

The warrior bent forward.

'A parti-coloured linen skirt,' he began, dismissively. 'What . . . ?'

He paused and suddenly realised what it was.

'Blue and red. The colour of the strips which bound Dacán.'

Fidelma turned to the hem of the skirt. A long strip of material had, indeed, been torn away. She expelled the air from her lungs with a long, low whistling sound.

'Then Grella is the murderess!' announced Cass in excitement. 'Here is the proof.'

Fidelma was equally excited but her legal mind urged caution.

'It is only proof of where the material, which bound Dacán, came from. However, this dress does not look like anything that a librarian of an abbey would wear. But, truthfully, Sister Grella does not seem typical of a librarian. Nevertheless, Cass, you may be called upon to witness where I found this skirt.'

'That I shall,' agreed the warrior willingly. 'I do not see that there is cause for any doubt. Grella lied to you about her relationship with Dacán and now we have found this! Is any more proof needed?'

Fidelma did not reply as she repacked the other materials in the satchel but bundled up the skirt into her *marsupium*. She walked back to the bed to make a final check. As she did so the toe of her shoe hit something on the floor; an obstruction which did not give but sent a sharp pain into her foot.

She bent immediately to the floor and peered at it. There was a loose flagstone on the floor. It was this that she had stubbed her toe on. It stood slightly proud from the other floor stones and rocked a little as she touched it.

'Help me with this, Cass,' she instructed.

The warrior took out his large knife and inserted it, easing the stone up. There was a cavity underneath. Fidelma held her candle high and peered in. She pulled forth a bundle of vellum.

Fidelma unrolled the vellum and peered at the careful calligraphy.

'The writings of Dacán,' she whispered. 'Grella was hiding them all along.'

'Then no other proof is needed. She must have killed Dacán!' remarked Cass with satisfaction.

Fidelma was too busy examining the contents of the writing to comment.

'It is a letter to his brother, the Abbot Noé.' Then she corrected herself. 'No, it is only a draft of a letter. He talks about searching for the heirs of the native kings of Osraige. But he has spilt ink over it and this is why the sheet is discarded. Listen to this, Cass . . . "The son of Illan, according to the record, has just reached the age of choice. He is old enough to be considered for the kingship. I have discovered my quarry to be hiding in the monastery of Fínán at Sceilig Mhichil under the protection of his cousin. Tomorrow, I shall depart from here and go there." Look when this is dated!' She thrust the vellum at Cass and indicated the date. 'This must have been written a few hours before he was killed.'

'What quarry?' demanded Cass. 'It seems an odd choice of words, as if Dacán was a hunter?'

'Do you know this monastery at Sceilig Mhichil?'

'I have never been there but I know it to be a small settlement on a rock-like island in the sea out to the west.'

'Dacán never set out to Sceilig Mhichil,' she murmured. 'He was dead a few hours after writing this.'

Fidelma did not replace the vellum in its hiding place but put it in her *marsupium* along with the skirt. She then bent to put the flagstone back in place and stood up.

'Sister Grella will have much to explain,' she observed.

She gazed round the chamber for a moment then blew out the candle and cautiously opened the door. There was no one outside and she moved quickly out, motioning Cass to follow. As she shut the door, she turned sharply on her heel and hurried along the corridor.

'Where now?' demanded Cass, a little aggrieved that he had to ask.

'To find Sister Grella,' she replied curtly.

'Where should we start?'

They started by asking Brother Rumann the steward, but when a full hour had produced no sign of the missing librarian, Cass suggested: 'Perhaps she has left the abbey?'

'Is there no *aistreóir* in this abbey?' snapped Fidelma.

'The doorkeeper is Brother Conghus,' Cass replied automatically before realising that she had asked the question rhetorically. He succeeded in receiving a crushing glance of scorn from the fiery green eyes of Fidelma.

'I am aware of that,' she said tightly. 'It seems, however, that people can pass out of this abbey and vanish as they will. Firstly, Eisten vanished; then the two boys from Rae na Scríne, and now the librarian is nowhere to be found.'

At least Brother Conghus had not vanished. He was in his small *officium* next to the gates of the abbey making notations on wax tablets. He glanced up in surprise as Fidelma entered without ceremony.

'Sister? How can I help you?' he asked, slowly rising to his feet.

'I am seeking Sister Grella,' replied Fidelma.

The doorkeeper raised a shoulder and let it fall in a negative fashion.

'Then the library . . . ?' he began, but Fidelma cut him short.

'If she had been there, we would not be here. Neither was she in her chamber. Has she left the abbey?'

Brother Conghus immediately shook his head.

'It is my task to record the comings and goings of people to and from the abbey,' he said. 'So far as my records show, Sister Grella has not left.'

'Do you keep a record every day?'

'Of course.'

'But this is not the only entrance to the abbey,' she pointed out.

'It is the main entrance,' replied Conghus. 'The rule is that everyone leaving or entering the abbey must report their movements so that we may know who is within the abbey walls.'

'But if she had left by the side entrance . . . ?'

'She would have informed me. It is the rule,' Conghus repeated.

'Earlier this evening, I left the abbey by the rear gate whose path leads to the shore. Then I returned and brought the captain of the Laigin warship with me. He stayed in the abbey a while before departing again to his ship. Do your records speak of this?'

Conghus flushed.

'I was not informed. The onus is on people to obey the rule and you should have informed me.'

Fidelma sighed deeply.

'This means that your records are not entirely reliable. They are only reliable in so far as people obey your rules.'

'If Sister Grella had left the abbey, she would know the rule,' replied Conghus stubbornly.

'Only if she wanted it to be known that she had left,' intervened Cass, finding something he could contribute to the conversation.

Conghus replied with a snort of annoyance.

'What do you know of Sister Grella?' Fidelma suddenly asked.

Conghus was bewildered by her question.

'Know of her? She is the librarian of the abbey and has been so ever since I have known her.'

'And you know nothing else?'

'I know that she came here from the abbey of Cealla. I know that she is well-qualified in her profession. What else should I know?'

'Was she ever married?' Fidelma asked.

'She has never mentioned anything of a marriage in her past.'

'How well did she know Sister Eisten?'

The question came as a sudden intuitive shot but it did not seem to register with Brother Conghus.

'She knew her, that is all I can say. Sister Eisten did some studying in the library earlier in the year and so I presume that the librarian would know her.'

'Then it was not a close liaison? They were not particular friends?'

'No more than any other member of the abbey whom Sister Grella knew.'

'About a week ago, Sister Grella visited Salbach's fortress at Cuan Dóir. Do you know why?'

'Did she? A week ago?' Conghus looked bemused. 'Then we should have a record of that.'

He rose and turned to a shelf of wax tablets and started to check their contents, shaking his head and clicking his tongue.

'You do not know offhand why she would go to Salbach's fortress?' demanded Fidelma, while the doorkeeper diligently searched for the right tablet.

'None, unless Salbach was presenting a gift to the library. Sometimes, some chieftains find they are possessed of the ancient rods of the poets. Such old Ogham books are rare now, even here in Muman. The abbey offers rewards for the gathering of them. It could be that Salbach found some and decided to present them to our library. But if Grella did go there for that, or any other purpose, she would have informed me that she was leaving the abbey. There is no record of her doing so.' He turned aside from his tablets to Fidelma. 'I cannot find any reference to Sister Grella having left to go to Cuan Dóir. She did, however, leave here to go to Rae na Scríne a week ago.'

'Rae na Scríne?' Fidelma echoed.

'It is so recorded,' replied Brother Conghus with a smirk. 'She went to collect a book from Sister Eisten and take some medicines to her.'

Fidelma fought back a feeling of utter frustration.

'She could have gone in the opposite direction to Cuan Dóir,' she suggested. 'Or she and Sister Eisten could have travelled to Cuan Dóir afterwards.'

'She would have told us if she was going to visit Cuan Dóir,' replied Conghus stoically. 'And there is no reference to any such journey.'

'If it were noted.'

'Of course it would be noted. To visit Salbach on behalf of the abbey would require the permission and blessing of the abbot.'

'Who said that it would necessarily be a journey on behalf of the abbey?' queried Fidelma.

'Why else would the librarian visit the local chieftain?'

'Why else, indeed?' Fidelma's patience was at an end. 'Thank you for your help, Conghus.'

Outside, Cass examined Fidelma's worried expression.

'Do you think that he is hiding something? He seems less than helpful.'

'Perhaps he is, perhaps not. I suspect that Brother Conghus simply lives by the rules and cannot conceive of anyone breaking them.'

Even as they stood hesitating outside, Conghus came hurrying out and, with a curt nod to the both of them, he scurried across the stone flags of the quadrangle to the tall bell tower.

'It must be nearly time for the *completa*,' muttered Cass.

A few moments later, as if in response to his spoken thought, the bell sounded its chimes to summon the brethren to the service.

The last time Fidelma had attended such a lavish mass had been in Rome in the luxuriant round basilica of St John of Lateran where the body of Wighard, the murdered archbishop-designate of Canterbury, lay. A dozen bishops and their attendants, and the Holy Father himself, had conducted the service.

The dark, high-walled abbey church was nothing compared to the splendour of the Roman basilica but, nevertheless, it was impressive. Tapestries covered the high granite walls, candles gave out heat, light and an assortment of perfumes. Fidelma sat in a pew reserved for distinguished guests with Cass seated alongside her. All around members of the abbey religious and their students crowded together to pay their respects to the passing of the soul of Cathal of Cashel. Though she examined their faces carefully, Fidelma could see no sign of Sister Grella.

The choristers were raising their voices in the Sanctus.

'*Is Naofa, Naofa, Naofa Tú, a Thiarna. Dia na Slua* . . .'

'You are Holy, Holy, Holy, oh Lord God of Hosts . . .'

Something made Fidelma glance across the aisle of the church; some sixth sense which pricked at her mind.

She saw the eyes of young Sister Necht staring intensely at her. The novice had been watching her keenly and now, startled, she dropped her head to peer at her feet. Fidelma was turning away when she realised someone else was staring, but this time the object of scrutiny was Sister Necht herself and the examiner was the pudgy-featured Brother Rumann. Next to Rumann, Brother Midach was also watching the young novice. What surprised Fidelma was that all trace of jollity had gone from the physician's face and if looks could kill, thought Fidelma, Midach would surely have been guilty of slaying the young woman. Then Midach caught her eye, forced a smile and dropped his gaze to concentrate on the holy office. When she turned her attention back to Brother Rumann, the moon-faced house steward was also concentrating on the words of the service.

Fidelma wondered what this curious digression meant. By the time she could concentrate again on the service the choristers had progressed into the *Agnus Dei*.

It was when the voices were pausing to begin *A Rí an Domhnaigh* – Great God – that there came a faint noise. The voices of the choristers hesitated and faded away. The noise therefore grew. There was a murmur of apprehension for the noise was that of a wailing child's voice. It was sobbing in heart-rending fashion.

Everyone peered about looking for the waif but no one could identify the source of the sound. It seemed to echo through the great abbey church, spreading as if through its very granite walls, echoing and re-echoing.

Several of the brethren, more superstitious than logical, genuflected.

Even Abbot Brocc exchanged worried glances with his senior clerics.

Fidelma felt Cass's hand on her arm. The warrior gestured

with his head towards the nave and, following his indication, Fidelma saw Brother Midach moving rapidly out of the building.

Before he had reached the door, however, the noise of the crying suddenly ceased. All was deathly still. The sound of the door slamming behind Midach caused the entire congregation to start nervously.

The choir master rapped on his wooden lectern and *A Rí an Domhnaigh* was started again, hesitantly at first but the voices eventually regained their confidence and strength.

The service continued without further incident. Abbot Brocc spoke eloquently of the sadness of the loss of the old king from the Yellow Plague but with joy of the inauguration of the new king, invoking the blessing of Christ, His Apostles and all the saints of the five kingdoms, for the future prosperity of the kingdom and for the wisdom in government of the new monarch, Colgú.

As the congregation began to break up, after the final blessing, Fidelma told Cass that she would speak with him later and began to push her way through the throng across the nave of the abbey church towards the seat where she had seen the young Sister Necht. By the time she reached the spot, there was no sign of her. She peered around into the dispersing assembly but the novice had vanished.

Suppressing a sigh of annoyance, Fidelma turned for the nearest door, which brought her out of the church opposite the spacious storerooms of the abbey. Although it was night, there were numerous lanterns sending out a shadowy light, obviously lit to help the assembly find their way back to their various dormitories.

Sunk in thought, Fidelma decided not to go straight back to the hostel but followed the path, which Brother Ségán had shown her, leading towards the herb garden. Fidelma wanted to be alone to meditate and the fragrant little garden seemed an ideal place.

It was the faint cry from the shrubbery garden ahead which alerted her to tread softly.

There were two shadows in the arboretum by the head of the well. A slight figure was being held by a stocky, more masculine-looking shadow. It seemed to Fidelma that there was something familiar about that slight figure.

'You arrogant young . . .'

The voice she recognised as belonging to Brother Midach. It was now sharp and angry.

Even as Fidelma watched, the chief physician raised an open hand and brought it down against the back of the head of the slighter figure.

There was a grunt of pain.

'How dare you lay hands on me!' came a husky voice which Fidelma thought she should know.

Fidelma was about to stride forward and demand to know what was happening when she heard Brother Midach's voice reprimanding the figure.

'You'll do as I tell you. Such an outburst will be the destruction of us all! The sepulchre carries echoes. If we are discovered then there is an end of our hopes for Osraige.'

The shadows moved in the darkness and she lost sight of them. There was no movement in the arboretum.

Fidelma listened and could hear nothing.

She moved forward cautiously. It was as if the ground had suddenly opened and swallowed them. She was perplexed for there was no gate out of the walled garden other than the one by which she had entered.

She examined the area as carefully as she could but could see no trace of Midach or his companion, no passage or doorway through which they might have vanished. She even peered down into the darkness of the well, the holy well of the Blessed Fachtna, but she had seen it in daylight and knew that it descended into almost bottomless darkness.

It was not for half an hour that she gave up the puzzle and

retraced her steps reluctantly back to the hostel. Cass was waiting for her with ill-concealed impatience.

'I was almost going to send out an alarm for you, sister,' he chided. 'What with all these people vanishing, I thought you might have gone the same way.'

'What was so urgent?' she replied, wondering whether to tell him that she had witnessed yet another astonishing disappearance. 'Is there alarm among the brothers because of the voice of the child during the service?'

Cass looked dour.

'Not so much alarm as fear. Even your cousin seems to think it was some ghostly echo of a lost soul.'

Fidelma raised a cynical smile.

'Surely there are more intelligent opinions among the scholars?'

'Well, the only one that I have heard is from Brother Rumann, who believes it is some distortion of the sound of water in the well beneath the abbey.'

'Ah,' sighed Fidelma. 'I think I shall leave them to their ignorance for a while yet. But, surely, this was not so urgent as to cause you alarm?'

Cass shook his head.

'After the service, I was on my way back here when I fell into conversation with Brother Martan. He is . . .'

'The same who has the passion for relics and who, thanks be to God, kept the pieces of linen which bound Dacán. We saw him on the shore earlier with Midach examining Sister Eisten's body.'

'Exactly so.'

'What then?' pressed Fidelma.

'Brother Martan and I were discussing why anyone should want to kill Dacán. Martan repeated that Dacán was not a likable character.'

'That much, at least, we can be sure of,' she said wearily.

'He told me that Midach once said that there were several

whom he would prefer dead, and named Dacán as one of them.'

Fidelma raised her head a little.

'Midach said that? Why did he say this?'

'Apparently, Martan was witness to one great argument that Midach had with Dacán.'

'The argument about Laigin? I have heard all about that. Midach insulted Laigin, that was all.'

'According to Martan, this was something else.' Cass looked embarrassed. 'Apparently, it was a row about Sister Necht.'

'Necht? What was it about?' Fidelma was suddenly interested.

'It seems that Dacán accused Midach of having a liaison . . . you know . . .'

Fidelma set her jaw firmly when he hesitated as if embarrassed.

'I am aware of what is implied,' she said tersely. 'Dacán accused Midach of having an affair with young Sister Necht? Are you sure? No,' she went on hurriedly, 'better that I make sure. I think I should speak with Brother Martan.'

Cass gave a smile of self-satisfaction.

'That is why I have detained him here. He is in the chamber upstairs awaiting you.'

Brother Martan, now that she saw him under a better light, was rather weak looking, A middle-aged man, with pale skin, bad teeth and the cough of a consumptive which caused his speech to be delivered in short, breathless pants. He rose as Fidelma entered the chamber but she waved him to be seated.

'I would firstly like to thank you, Martan, for keeping the strips of linen. They have served us well.'

The man's dull-eyed features did not change.

'You have told my colleague here,' she gestured to Cass, 'that Midach had an argument with Dacán.'

She saw a look of alarm spread across Martan's features.

'I did not mean to level any accusation . . .' he began. 'The chief physician has been kind to me and I would not want to place him in harm's way.'

Fidelma raised a hand to quell his alarm.

'So far as I know you have merely reported some facts. Did he have such an argument? The truth, Martan, is always the easiest path.' She added this because she saw that he had suddenly realised the implication of what he had said.

'I do not want Brother Midach to get into trouble,' he said sullenly.

'Did he have an argument or not?' Fidelma demanded sharply.

Martan nodded reluctantly.

'Tell me about it,' invited Fidelma.

'It was the day before Dacán was found. I happened to be walking along the corridor to the library. I was going to collect a copy of the *Aphorisms of Hippocrates*, which the abbey possesses.' He spoke with pride. 'As I passed down the corridor, I heard voices coming from a small side room, the chamber in which Sister Grella has her *officium*. It is a room off the main library hall which has an entrance leading into the corridor.'

Fidelma waited patiently while the brother paused to collect his thoughts.

'I heard Brother Midach's voice raised in anger and so I stopped outside the door. I was surprised to find him at the library. Also it was unusual that anything would cause anger to Brother Midach because he is usually a most happy and mirthful man.'

He paused, looking awkward.

'Go on,' invited Fidelma. 'You halted outside the open door? What then?'

'It was only that it was unusual to hear Midach so angry,' began Martan repetitiously, as if to exonerate himself from the guilt of eavesdropping. He halted as he saw the annoyance spread on Fidelma's face. 'I realised that the person he was arguing with was none other than the Venerable Dacán.'

'And the cause of the argument?'

'It seems that Dacán was accusing Midach of going through his writings, of reading material that he had no right to. Midach hotly denied it, of course. Dacán was so beside himself in rage that he threatened to report Midach to the abbot.

'Midach replied that he would report Dacán for treating the staff at the hostel as slaves, especially young Sister Necht. At that, Dacán was so angry that he accused Midach of having a relationship with Sister Necht. Midach seemed to take this seriously and replied that he simply had acted as foster-father to Necht. And his relationship was only paternal. Anyway, Midach added, it was none of Dacán's business.'

Fidelma was not surprised that Midach could be Necht's foster-father. It was quite common for children to be sent away from home for their education at the age of seven. The process was known as fostering and the foster-parents were required to maintain their fosterlings according to their rank and provide education for them. A girl would often complete her education by the age of fourteen, although some, such as Fidelma herself, could continue to seventeen. Yet fourteen was the age of choice and maturity for a girl. A boy would continue until he was seventeen. Fosterage was a legal contract regarded as being of benefit to both households. There were two types of fosterage in law. One was for 'affection' in which no fees were exchanged. The other was where the natural parents paid for the fosterage of their child. Fosterage was the principle method of educating children in society.

'Are you sure he said he was foster-father?'

'The term *datán* was definitely used.'

It was the legal term one used for a foster-father.

'Did you know that Midach was foster-father to Sister Necht?'

Martan shook his head.

'Just what did you think that Brother Midach's relationship was?' she prompted.

'To Necht?'

'Precisely.'

'Midach was Necht's *anamchara*, her soul-friend. That is all I know. As such they were friendly and close with one another.'

'So Midach obviously felt responsible for Necht?'

'I suppose so,' agreed Martan.

'Did it surprise you that Dacán would accuse Midach of such an affair? Dacán had a reputation of a man of aloof serenity. What made him suddenly attack Midach?'

'He was no saint. He was a strange, ill-tempered man who tested Midach's temper to the extreme,' replied Martan. 'All I know is that I overheard Midach reacting badly. He told Dacán not to interfere and if he continued to do so and insult Midach, then Midach would . . .'

He paused and his eyes rounded as he realised what he was about to say.

'Go on,' urged Fidelma. 'He obviously threatened physical violence.'

'Midach said he would kill him,' agreed Martan softly.

There was a pause.

'Do you think he meant it?'

'I do not,' protested the apothecary. 'Nor do I set myself to judge other people in their personal habits of life. If that was the way of it, that was the way of it. Midach would harm no one.'

'That's not what Midach himself threatened,' observed Fidelma dryly. 'When you learnt of Dacán's death just one day after this argument, did you not find it worrying? I presume that you made no mention of it to Brother Rumann, who had charge of the investigation?'

A tinge of colour edged Martan's cheeks.

'I did not report it as I did not believe it of relevance. Midach was not in the abbey when Dacán's body had been found. If you are asking me to say that I suspect Midach of murder, I shall not. Midach is a man who loves life and enjoys life. He would no more think of destroying another life than he would of taking his own life.'

'So you did not mention this matter to Rumann?' observed Fidelma. 'What made you mention the matter now?'

Martan coloured.

'I wish I had not. My only thought was that you should both know that Dacán was not the saintly man most people supposed. He could accuse people unjustly.'

'And all this came about because Dacán originally accused Midach of going through his notes and writings in the library?'

'Midach denied that also,' Martan reminded her.

'Then one more thing. You say that Midach had left the abbey on the evening before Dacán was killed. He returned six days later, so I am told. Do you know why he left and where he went?'

Martan shook his head.

'I know it was not a journey that was planned. He went by boat. It was probably some medical emergency in one of the villages. It often happens.'

'What makes you think it was not planned?'

'Because he told no one except Sister Necht, who came to inform Brother Tóla only after he had left the abbey.'

'When was that?'

'Just before the *completa*. He must have sailed on the evening tide or he could not have gone until mid-morning on the next day.'

Fidelma's narrowed.

'You are sure of this time?'

'Absolutely.'

'Well,' Fidelma leant back, 'I think you have been of considerable help to us, Martan. You may go but I would appreciate it if you did not mention our discussion to anyone . . . especially to Brother Midach. Do you understand?'

Martan rose uncertainly.

'I think so, sister. I just hope I have not said the wrong thing . . .'

'How can truth be the wrong thing to say?' inquired Fidelma gravely.

Chapter Twelve

The next morning, as Sister Fidelma was on her way to the library to see if Sister Grella had returned, she received a summons to Abbot Brocc's chambers.

'Cousin, I have a messenger leaving for Cashel this afternoon. I wondered whether you might like to take the opportunity to send messages to your brother?'

Fidelma was just about to make a negative reply when an idea occurred to her.

'Yes. I want my brother to contact the Chief Brehon so that he may order the attendance of the Laigin merchant, Assíd of Uí Dego, at the assembly when the matter of the death of Dacán is heard. It is essential that some questions are put to Assíd.'

'Assíd? The merchant who was staying here on the night Dacán was murdered?' A hope sprang into Brocc's eyes. 'Do you think that Assíd ... do you think that he may be responsible . . . ?'

She disappointed him by shaking her head.

'All I require is his presence at the hearing.'

Brocc's look of hope relapsed into a worried frown.

'Ah, I thought at least one mystery might now be solved.'

'One mystery?' Fidelma caught the nuance.

'I am given to understand that you were looking for Sister Grella last night?'

'That is so. What has happened to Sister Grella?' she asked with foreboding.

'I wished that I knew. Sister Grella has not been seen since shortly after vespers yesterday. The library has not been opened this morning and Brother Rumann tells me that there was no sign of her chamber being slept in. He inquired of Brother Conghus who then told him that you were making inquiries about her last night.'

Fidelma sat down in front of the abbot's table before continuing. 'Has she ever disappeared before?'

'Not to my knowledge,' replied the abbot. 'All this is most distressing, cousin. First, we have Dacán's death; then Sister Eisten is found murdered and now Sister Grella is missing. What am I to make of all this?'

Fidelma momentarily felt sorry for her pompous cousin. He looked like a lost, helpless child, needing someone to tell him what to do.

'I only wish that I could help you, Brocc. At this moment, I am equally as bewildered. But there are some things that I wish to ask you and which I want treated in absolute confidence.'

The abbot waited expectantly.

'Do you know much of Brother Midach's background?'

'Brother Midach?' Brocc sounded surprised. 'He is a good physician. He has been at Ros Ailithir for four years. Let's see . . . he came to us from the abbey at Cealla.'

'And Sister Necht?'

'She came to the abbey about six months ago.'

'Also from Cealla?'

'No. Whatever gave you that idea? I think she came from a village not far from here. Why don't you question her?'

'It was a passing thought.' Fidelma was disappointed. 'I thought that there was some connection between Midach and Necht.'

'Well, he did introduce her to the abbey, that is true. He attended her father in one of the villages and when her father died, leaving her an orphan, Midach proposed her induction as a novice here. I believe that he still acts as her soul-friend.'

Fidelma stifled a sigh of disappointment. She had been

wondering whether there was some further link with Osraige and between Midach and Necht. What exactly there might be, she was not sure. Osraige was certainly at the core of the mystery.

The abbot did not press her further.

'What am I to make of it all?' he repeated almost pathetically.

Fidelma had considered what ways forward there were and she now realised that, with Sister Grella missing, there was nothing she could do unless she could find some new path to follow. That meant revealing some of the information that she had gathered as a bait to lure other information.

'Did you know that Sister Grella had once been the wife of the Venerable Dacán?' she asked innocently.

Abbot Brocc's jaw dropped expressively.

'What are you saying? Did she tell you this?'

'I was told by someone who knew her in Laigin. So you did not know?'

'I knew only that she came from Cealla and was qualified to the level of *sai*. But as for being a former wife of the Venerable Dacán – are you absolutely sure . . . ?'

'I have a witness to answer that. I searched her chamber last night. I have that right,' she added quickly, as she saw annoyance form on Brocc's features. 'Dacán was bound before he was killed. The bindings were, thankfully, preserved by Brother Martan, your apothecary. Last night I found the skirt from which those bindings were torn. The skirt was hidden in a satchel in Sister Grella's chamber.'

Abbot Brocc's response, when he realised the implication of this, was to put both his hands to his head and actually whimpered.

Fidelma studied him with a contemptuous eye.

'The reputation of this abbey is shamed,' he moaned. 'What can I do? You are telling me that Grella is the murderess and the motive is for some sordid matter of passion?'

'You can forget about the shame to the abbey, for the moment, cousin,' Fidelma replied dryly. 'Let us solve the puzzle first.'

'But such news brings a blush to my cheeks,' moaned Brocc.

'Then remember that Diogenes once wrote "blushing is the colour of virtue",' Fidelma countered cynically. 'The only shame is to have none.'

Brocc drew himself together as she pricked his conceit.

'I do not care for myself,' he sniffed a little contritely. 'I was only thinking of the reputation of the abbey. So you believe that Grella killed Dacán?'

Fidelma did not bother to comment.

'Did you know, Brocc, that Sister Grella visited the fortress of Salbach at Cuan Dóir about a week ago? If so, did she have your permission to leave the abbey and visit Salbach?'

The abbot stared at her blankly.

'No. I gave Sister Grella permission to ride to Rae na Scríne a week ago to visit Sister Eisten who worked there. She was to use the visit to collect a book and take some herbs and medicines from Brother Martan to help fight the plague there. Why would she ride in the opposite direction to see Salbach?'

'Perhaps she first visited Sister Eisten and then they went together to Salbach's fortress?'

'But why?'

An idea abruptly occurred to Fidelma. If Eisten had been seeking passage for herself and Sister Grella then perhaps Grella had fled on board the merchant ship? Fidelma rose and went to the window to look down into the inlet.

Still anchored near to Mugrón's warship was the Frankish merchantman, with its heavy lines. The abbot had joined her and was gazing down in bewilderment.

'What do you see, cousin?'

'I was fearful that the Frankish merchantman had already weighed anchor.'

Brocc frowned.

'I believe it is due to sail on the mid-morning tide.'

'Then I want you to give authority to Cass to board and search that vessel before it sets sail.'

'Search?'

'Yes. A thorough search now, as we talk,' Fidelma insisted. 'I command it under my authority as a *dálaigh*.' She unbent a little and added, 'It is possible that Sister Grella might be on board.'

Brocc looked shocked but he did not reply. Instead he rang his bell to summon the *scriptor* and then issued the necessary orders to find Cass and give him Fidelma's instructions.

'If there is any trouble, tell Cass to inform the Frankish captain that while at anchor in the bay he has to obey the laws of this kingdom,' Fidelma instructed the *scriptor* as he hurried off to perform his task.

'You must explain, cousin,' Brocc said, reseating himself. 'You are saying that Grella realises that you have discovered her guilty secret and that she is trying to flee?'

'I wish I could explain fully, cousin,' Fidelma responded. 'But I am not in possession of all the facts. Can you tell me anything about Sister Eisten and her relationship with your librarian?'

Brocc raised his hands as if in supplication.

'Poor Eisten. There is little to tell. She trained at this very abbey and was initially trained to help the physician, Midach. She specialised in the care of children. She had been with us since the age of fourteen, apart from the three years during which she went on pilgrimage to the Holy Land.'

'Brother Conghus told me that she also studied in the library,' Fidelma interrupted.

'Eisten was no scholar but she did do some studying in the library earlier in the year.'

'And how did Eisten come to be sent to Rae na Scríne?'

'So far as I recall, Sister Eisten volunteered to go there and look after the travellers' hostel we maintain there. This was about six months ago. There were some orphans in the vicinity and Eisten took to looking after their needs as well. She did much good work at Rae na Scrı́ne.'

He paused and picked up a jug of water, raising his eyebrows in inquiring fashion towards Fidelma. She shook her head. Brocc then poured himself a drink and sipped it slowly.

'Go on,' Fidelma prompted.

'Well, we knew that the Yellow Plague had reached the village earlier this summer. There seemed no rhyme nor reason as to who its victims were. I and Brother Midach, for example, have had a touch of it but have recovered. So has Sister Grella. But Eisten had not. Yet she did not succumb to it.'

'There is no accounting for it,' Fidelma agreed solemnly. 'Go on.'

'Eisten insisted on remaining in the village but we heard that things were getting worse. Midach went to visit her there several times this last week. Finally you brought us the terrible news of Intat's destruction of the village and its surviving inhabitants.'

'You knew Intat, of course?'

'Not personally. But I knew that Intat was one of Salbach's right-hand men. You saw how angry Salbach was when he came to the abbey after I had reported what you had told me. At first he seemed to refuse to believe the story. He only accepted it when you told him who you were and he was therefore unable to challenge your authority.'

Fidelma leaned forward a little, anger showing on her features.

'It is a poor chieftain who accepts truth only when told him by an authority greater than his. Did it occur to you that Intat might, for some reason, have been acting with Salbach's approval?'

Brocc was horrified.

'Of course not. Salbach is of an ancient line of chieftains of the Corco Loígde. He traces his line back to . . .'

Fidelma was openly sarcastic.

'I know; he traces his line to Míl Easpain, the founder of the race of the children of the Gael. Yet he would not be the first distinguished chieftain to go contrary to the laws of God and man. Might I remind you that perhaps the very reason we have this situation is because we are prisoners of history? It was a king of Laigin, who was also a descendant of a line of ancient and distinguished kings, who took it upon himself to murder Edirsceál, the High King? That was when this drama began.'

'That is ancient history, almost legend.'

'As this will be a thousand years from now.'

Brocc sat back in his chair slowly shaking his head.

'I will not believe this of Salbach. Besides, what gain is there in this matter for him?'

Fidelma smiled thinly.

'Gain? Indeed, that is a good motive for all our actions. What do we gain from some action or another? Well, if I knew the answer to that, I would know the answer to many a question. I suppose you have known Salbach for a long time?'

'For eighteen years, from the day I came to this abbey. I have known him more closely for the last ten years, since I was elected abbot by the brethren here.'

'And what do you know of him?'

'Know? I know that he is regarded as a good chieftain. He has the pride of his ancestry and perhaps he is a little too autocratic at times. All in all, however, I think it may be said that his rule is fair and just.'

'I was told that he had ambition.'

'Ambition? Don't we all have ambition?'

'Perhaps. And perhaps Salbach's ambitious eyes have looked beyond Corco Loígde?'

'As is his right, cousin. If he is descended of the line of Ir, related to Míl Easpain who conquered this land at the dawn of time and peopled it with the children of the Gael . . .'

Fidelma grimaced as if in pain.

'Spare me from the boredom of genealogy. Ambition is fine

so long as the sparrow does not crave to become the falcon,' she commented dryly. 'Anyway, what else can you tell me of Salbach? Did he know Sister Eisten?'

'Not to my knowledge.'

'It would surprise you to know that Eisten was at Salbach's fortress with Sister Grella just over a week ago?'

Brocc's expression showed that it did surprise him.

'So you do think there is some connection, then, between poor Sister Eisten's death and that of the Venerable Dacán?' he demanded.

'A connection – yes. How strong, I do not know. But that I am determined to discover.'

Abbot Brocc's face had been growing longer as he surveyed the perplexities of the situation.

'It does not seem that you are closer to solving the mystery of Dacán's death, though. And time is not on our side, cousin.'

'I am well aware of this, Brocc,' replied Fidelma softly.

'Well, remember that I am held ultimately responsible, under the law, for the death of Dacán. I cannot afford to pay the compensation or fines.'

'Be at peace, Brocc,' Fidelma reassured him. 'Laigin is not interested in you nor the seven *cumals* of the *éric* fine. They are interested in the honour price and their eyes are set on the land of Osraige. They will be content with nothing else.'

'Yet their warship sits there still.' Brocc flung out at hand to the bay beyond the window.

'You can't begrudge Laigin its right under law,' Fidelma replied. 'The ship will do nothing. It is there only to remind you of your responsibility as abbot in charge of the community where Dacán met his death.'

There was a tap on the door and, in answer to Brocc's call, Cass entered.

Fidelma knew from his glum face that he had no news.

'Nothing,' he confirmed. 'No sign at all of Sister Grella. The captain was angry but he did not prevent my searching, even into the stinking hold of the vessel. I pledge my honour that she is not on board.'

Fidelma felt a heavy burden sinking on her shoulders.

She rose and went to the window again.

The sails of the Frankish merchantman were being unfurled. She could hear the sounds of the cracking and filling of the canvas sail before the morning offshore breeze; she could hear the cry of the orders rising to mingle with the scream of the gulls as they circled and wheeled around the sedately moving vessel.

'Another blank wall,' she said almost under her breath. 'Yet somewhere there is a door. Somewhere,' she added vehemently.

'What path will you follow now, cousin?' asked the abbot anxiously.

Fidelma was turning away from the window when she caught sight of a *barc* under full sail, sliding swiftly into the inlet, negotiating a course around the heavy merchantman like a dolphin around a ship. An idea formed quickly in her mind and she wondered why she had not thought of it before. She reached her decision almost immediately.

'I shall be leaving the abbey for a while, Brocc,' she said. 'The path that I must follow is not here.'

'Where will you go now?' Brocc looked astounded.

'I need the services of a good swift *barc*,' Fidelma responded, ignoring the abbot's question. 'Where can I charter one?'

'A sailor named Ross owns the swiftest *barc* on the coast,' Brocc said, without need for deliberation. 'But he knows it and his knowledge is reflected in his price. I see his ship is anchored below. Any fisherman will tell you where he may be found.'

'Excellent. While I am away there are some items which I want you to safeguard for me. They constitute evidence in my investigation and I cannot afford to take them on my journey.'

Brocc pointed to a large oak cabinet on the far side of his chamber.

'It has two locks,' he assured her, 'and is quite secure. I usually place the valuables of this abbey in it.'

Fidelma took her *marsupium*, which she had become in the habit of carrying, from her shoulder and placed it on the table. Wordlessly, the abbot took from under his table a set of keys on a ring, which she presumed had been hanging on some secret hook, and went to the cabinet and opened the door. He gestured for Fidelma to bring the *marsupium* to him and placed it inside. She watched as he secured the door and returned the keys to their resting place.

'Should Sister Grella reappear, I want her to be placed under guard, on my authority, until I return. Is that understood?' she asked Brocc.

The abbot indicated that it was.

Satisfied, Fidelma turned to Cass.

'Come, then, let us seek out this Ross and negotiate a price with him for our journey.'

Brocc was standing uncertainly.

'But where are you going? How long shall you be away? If I must imprison Sister Grella, I must have some idea.'

Fidelma paused at the door and once again felt sorry for her cousin's woebegone expression. Again she had the feeling of a little boy lost.

'Better that no one knows of where we have gone until we return. In the meantime, if you are able to detain Sister Grella, simply tell her that she is being held as a material witness to the death of her former husband, the Venerable Dacán. With God's help we shall return before a week is passed.'

Brocc's jaw dropped in anxiety.

'A full week?' His voice was full of distress but Fidelma had already left his chamber with Cass trailing behind her.

Chapter Thirteen

'That is Na Sceilig. See! There before us on the horizon.'

The speaker was Ross, standing on the stern deck of his ship. He was pointing out across the blue stretch of ocean. His deep green eyes, which reflected the changing moods of the sea, were narrowed. He was a short, stocky man, with greying, close-cropped hair; a grizzled veteran of forty years of sea-faring. His skin was tanned by the sea winds almost to the colour of nut. He was a man with a dour humour and always ready with a loud bellow when he was displeased.

His swift sailing *barc* was two days out from Ros Ailithir where Fidelma had negotiated a rather exorbitant price with the sailor to take them to the monastery of Fínán at Sceilig Mhichil and back again. The vessel had followed the coastal lanes, catching a faint wind blowing from the north-east which brought them around the southern extremes of Muman and then Ross had manoeuvred his vessel into the fast-flowing tide which sent them racing to the north.

Fidelma shaded her eyes with her hands and gasped at the spectacular rocks that thrust out of the sea before her. There were two islands – stark, fissured pyramids with castellated outcrops rising sheer and terrifying out of the dark, brooding seas – which were situated some eight miles from the mainland. Their sheer terrible magnificence caused Fidelma to catch her breath.

The name Sceilig implied rocks but she had not been prepared for such looming slatey masses.

'On which island is the monastery?' asked Fidelma.

'That bigger island,' indicated Ross, pointing to the pyramid-shaped spectacle rising over seven hundred feet out of the water.

'But I cannot see any place to land, let alone a place to construct habitations,' Fidelma protested, peering in amazement at the vertical sides of the island.

Ross knowingly tapped the side of his nose with a gnarled forefinger.

'Oh, there is a place to land, right enough and, if you have a head for heights, you may climb up to the monastery, for it rests high up there.' He pointed to the high peaks of the island. 'The monks call the place Christ's Saddle for it is so high. It is situated between those two points there.'

Fidelma became aware of a cacophony of noise from the wheeling seabirds. Great gannets, with six foot wingspans, wheeled, soared and circled. Now and then they would plummet vertically, a full sixty feet into the sea in search of fish.

The second island, particularly, seemed to be crowned by a ring of wheeling and crying birds. Fidelma thought at first that, by some miracle, it was snow capped until Ross pointed out that it was the excretions of birds built up over the long centuries.

'They nest on the Little Sceilig,' explained Ross. 'Not just gannets, but gulls, cormorants, guillemots, kittiwakes, razor-bills, shearwaters and fulmars and even other birds whose names I have forgotten.'

Cass, who had been standing silently by, suddenly remarked: 'Here is an awesome place to chasten the soul.'

Fidelma smiled at him, amazed that his usually stolid mind could be so moved.

'Here is a place to elevate the soul,' she corrected, 'for it shows just how insignificant we are in the great scheme of creation.'

'I still cannot see why you would wish to come to this isolated place,' Cass muttered, gazing at the breathtaking cliffs of the island.

Fidelma decided that it was time to relent a little and reveal what was in her mind.

'Remember the vellum we found in Grella's chamber? The letter Dacán wrote to his brother, Abbot Noé? He wrote it on the evening before he was killed and said that he had traced his quarry – remembered he used that word "quarry"? – to the monastery of Sceilig Mhichil. He was searching for the heir of the native line of kings of Osraige. I am following the belief that he was killed because of that knowledge and that the next step along the path to resolving the mysteries rests on that impregnable island which you see before you.'

Cass turned his gaze from the island to Fidelma and then back at the towering grey mass. He pursed his lips thoughtfully.

'You expect to find whoever it was that Dacán was looking for on the island?'

'Dacán certainly did.'

That Ross and his crew, like most seamen of the coastal waters, were highly skilled was demonstrated in the next few minutes as they negotiated to a landing place which had been invisible until they came within a few yards of it. The waves threatened to hurl the vessel against the crashing rocks as the water foamed around them, causing sea spray to drench everyone. It took a while to anchor close enough for anyone to land.

'It is not good that we hold ourselves against the rocks of this landing place,' cried Ross, having to shout to make himself heard above the crashing of the waves and cry of the seabirds. 'When you have landed we will pull back from the island and stand off until such time as you signal us to pick you up.'

Fidelma raised her hand in acknowledgment and prepared herself to leap from the side of the boat onto the narrow granite ledge which constituted a natural quay.

Cass jumped first so as to secure a position and ensure he could catch Fidelma in order that she might land in safety.

As they turned along the narrow strip of rock they saw a brown-robed anchorite hurriedly approaching down a perilously steep path. They saw his brows drawn together in a frown as he examined them in obvious annoyance.

'*Bene vobis*,' Fidelma greeted.

The monk halted abruptly and the look of irritation intensified on his features.

'We spotted a ship coming into land. This place is forbidden to women, sister.'

Fidelma raised her eyebrows dangerously.

'Who is the Father Superior here?'

The monk hesitated at her icy tones.

'Father Mel. But, as I have said, sister, our brothers dwell here in isolation from the company of women in accordance with the views of the Blessed Fínán.'

Fidelma knew that there were some monasteries where women were strictly excluded; for some, like Fínán of Clonard or Enda of Aran, believed that the scriptures taught that women were the creation of the Evil One and should never be looked upon. Such heretical teaching was an anathema to Fidelma, who was not at all approving of the support such an idea received from Rome, which was little less than an attempt to impose celibacy and the isolation of one sex from the other on the argument propounded by Augustine of Hippo that man was created in the image of God but women were not.

'I am Fidelma, sister to Colgú, king of Muman. I am a *dálaigh* of the court, acting on the commission of the king, my brother.'

Never would Fidelma have used this form of introduction

had she felt there was any other way of overcoming this officious reception.

'I am here to conduct an inquiry into an unlawful death. Now conduct me to Father Mel at once.'

The monk looked horrified and blinked nervously.

'I dare not, sister.'

Cass ostentatiously loosened his sword in its scabbard, gazing upwards along the path by which the monk had descended.

'I think you should dare,' he said coldly, as if speaking aloud his thoughts.

The monk cast an anxious look at him and then back at Fidelma before compressing lips to conceal his angry frustration. They could see him fighting with his thoughts. After a moment or two he gestured in resignation.

'If you can follow me, then you may reach Father Mel. If not . . .' There was a trace of a sneer in his voice and he did not finished the sentence.

He turned and started off up the path which was a comfortable climb initially but then it suddenly narrowed. Indeed, the path almost ended and they were ascending along almost sheer falls from one rocky ledge to another although here and there steps had been cut by the monks into the precipitous sides of the rock. It was a tough ascent. The wind blew and buffeted at them, threatening at times to tear them from the climb and send them tumbling down the slopes into the turbulent frothy seas below. Several times Fidelma, her hair streaming, the head-dress dislodged, found herself going down on all fours and clinging on grimly to the rocks of the path in order to steady herself.

The anchorite, used to the ascent, merely quickened his pace and Fidelma, in anger, took chances in her attempt to keep up with the man. Cass, coming behind her, had to reach out a hand to steady her on several occasions. Then, at last, they came to a strange plateau, a small green place set between peaks with two stone crosses. From this point a series of steps led through fangs of rocks to another plateau where a stone wall, running along one side, was the only barrier between the plateau and the sheer cliff falling down to the sea.

Fidelma halted at the spectacular view to the white-capped Little Sceilig and the misty outline of the mainland beyond.

On the plateau was the monastery built by Fínán just over one hundred years before. There were six *clocháns*, or beehive-shaped huts of rock, with a rectangular-shaped oratory. Beyond them were other buildings and another oratory. Fidelma was surprised to see a small cemetery behind with slabs and crosses. She wondered how this inhospitable crag of an island could hold enough earth to bury anything. It was a wild, even cruel place on which to attempt an existence.

There were several brothers tending a small garden set behind an artificial shelter of stone-slabbed walls. She noticed, also to her surprise, that there were two wells.

'This is truly an amazing place,' she whispered to Cass. 'No wonder the brothers are so obdurate about their privacy.'

The anchorite who had accompanied them had disappeared, presumably into one of the stone buildings.

They had been spotted by the gardeners who had halted their work and were muttering uneasily among themselves.

'I do not think that they are pleased to see you, Fidelma,' Cass said, his hand staying on the hilt of his sword.

The anchorite reappeared with the same abruptness as he had vanished.

'This way. Father Mel will speak with you.'

They found a wizened-faced old man seated cross-legged in one of the beehive-shaped huts. It was small so that they either had to follow the old man's example and seat themselves on some sheepskins which covered the floor or stay standing, slightly stooped. Fidelma gave the lead by lowering herself into a cross-legged position in front of the old man.

He gazed at her thoughtfully with bright blue eyes. His face seemed hewed out of the rock of his island. Stern and granite-like. The lines were many and were etched deeply into his weather-beaten brown face.

'*In hoc loco non ero, ubi enim ovis, ibi mulier . . . ubi mulier . . . ibi peccatum*,' intoned the old man dispassionately.

'I am aware that you have no wish to associate with women,' Fidelma replied. 'I would not intrude on your rule unless there was a greater purpose.'

'Greater purpose? The association of the sexes in the Faith is contrary to the discipline of the Faith,' grunted Father Mel.

'On the contrary, if both sexes forsook each other there would soon be no people, Faith or church,' returned Fidelma cynically.

'*Abneganbant mulierum administrationem separantes eas a monasteriis*,' intoned Father Mel piously.

'We can sit here and discourse in Latin, if you like,' Fidelma sighed. 'But I am come on more important matters. I do not wish to impose myself where I am unwelcome, though I find it hard to believe that there are places within the five kingdoms of Éireann where our laws and customs have been so sadly rejected. However, the sooner I can get answers to my questions then the sooner I can depart from this place.'

Father Mel allowed an eyebrow to twitch in irritation at her response.

'What is it you wish?' he demanded coldly. 'My disciple told me you were a *dálaigh* with a commission from the temporal king of this land.'

'That is so.'

'Then what must I do to help you fulfil your commission and allow you to depart swiftly?'

'Do you have anyone from the land of Osraige in this monastery?'

'We welcome everyone into our brotherhood.'

Fidelma checked her irritation at the unspecific response.

'That was not what I asked.'

'Very well, I am from Osraige myself,' replied Father Mel with diffidence. 'What would you ask of me?'

'I believe that some time ago someone from Osraige found sanctuary here. A descendant of the native kings. An heir of Illan. If that is so, then I wish to see him for I fear his life is in danger.'

Father Mel almost smiled.

'Then perhaps you wish to talk to me? Illan, of whom you speak, was my cousin, though I would not consider myself heir to any temporal glory.'

'Is this true?' Dacán had said the heir of Illan was being looked after by his cousin but she was hardly expecting the cousin to be this aging Father Superior.

'I am not in the habit of lying, woman,' snapped the old man. 'Now, do you believe me to be in danger of my life?'

Fidelma slowly shook her head. Father Mel himself was certainly no threat to the security of the current petty kings of Osraige nor a possible rallying point for any future insurrection.

'No. There is no danger for you. But I am told that there is a young heir of Illan. That his cousin, obviously yourself, was taking care of him.'

Father Mel's face was set like stone.

'There is no young heir to Illan on this island,' he said firmly, 'You may take my holy oath of office on it.'

Could this long, arduous journey have really been for nothing? Had Dacán made that same mistake? Father Mel could not take such an oath unless it were true.

'Is there anything else?' came Father Mel's curt tone.

Fidelma rose to her feet trying to hide her disappointment.

'Nothing. I accept the truth of what you say. You shelter no young heir of Illan.' She hesitated. 'Have you been visited by a merchant named Assíd of Laigin?'

Father Mel met her gaze evenly.

'There are many merchants that land here. I do not recall all their names.'

'Then does the name of the Venerable Dacán mean anything to you?'

'As a scholar of the Faith,' replied the Father Superior easily. 'Everyone has surely heard of the man.'

'Nothing else?'

'Nothing else,' affirmed the old man. 'Now, if that is all . . . ?'

Fidelma led the way from the building, bitterly disappointed. Cass followed with bewilderment on his features.

'Is that all?' he asked. 'Surely, we did not come all this way for this?'

'Father Mel would not have taken oath that there was no young heir of Illan in this monastery if there was,' Fidelma pointed out.

'Religious have been known to lie,' countered Cass darkly.

They were suddenly aware of an anchorite, a flat-faced, lugubrious-looking man of middle age, blocking their path.

'I . . .' the man hesitated. 'I overheard. You asked if there was anyone from Osraige here. Refugees.'

The monk's face mirrored some deep conflict of emotions.

'That's right,' she agreed. 'What is your name?'

'I am Brother Febal. I tend the gardens here.'

The monk abruptly took out of his robes a small object and handed it with all solemnity to Fidelma.

It was a corn doll. It was old, weather-worn, with the stuffing bursting out from broken joins where the weave had burst or torn.

'What's this?' demanded Cass.

Fidelma stared at it and turned it over in her hands. 'What can you tell us about this, brother?'

Brother Febal hesitated, throwing a look towards the hut of the Father Superior and he motioned them to follow a little way down the path, out of sight of the main complex of buildings.

'Father Mel has not told you the exact truth,' he confessed. 'The good Father is afraid, not for himself but for his charges.'

'I was sure that he was being frugal with the truth,' Fidelma replied gravely. 'But I cannot believe he would lie so blatantly if there was a young heir to Illan of Osraige on this island.'

'There is not, so he spoke the truth,' Brother Febal replied. 'However, six months ago he brought two boys to the island. He told us that their father, a cousin of his, had died and he was going to take care of them for a few months until a new home could be arranged for them. When the younger child became bored here, as young children would, the elder boy made him this corn doll to amuse him. When they left, I found that the boy had left it behind.'

Fidelma looked puzzled.

'Two boys. How old?'

'One about nine years old, the other only a few years older'

'Then there was not an older boy with them? A boy reaching the age of choice?'

To her disappointment, Brother Febal shook his head.

'There were only the two lads. They were from Osraige and cousins of Father Mel. That I know.'

'Why do you tell us this?' demanded Cass suspiciously. 'Your Father Superior did not trust us with the truth.'

'Because I recognise the emblem of the king of Cashel's bodyguard and because I overheard that you, sister, are an advocate of the courts. I do not think that you seek to harm the boys. Above all, I tell you because I fear great danger may come to them and hope that you will help them.'

'What makes you think that danger threatens?' Fidelma asked.

'Just over two weeks ago a ship arrived here with a religieux who took the two boys away with him. I heard Father Mel address the man as "honourable cousin". Yet within days another ship arrived here on the same mission as yourself. There was a man who demanded the same information as yourself.'

'Can you describe him?'

'A large, red-faced man, clad in a steel helmet and woollen cloak edged in fur. He claimed he was a chieftain and wore a gold chain of office.'

Fidelma swallowed in amazement.

'Intat!' cried Cass triumphantly.

Brother Febal blinked anxiously.

'Do you know the man?'

'We know that he is evil,' affirmed Fidelma. 'What did he learn about these boys?'

'Father Mel told him the same story as he told you. But one of the brothers, just as this man was departing, unintentionally mentioned the two lads and the fact that they had been taken away a short time before by a religieux.'

'And Intat went away?'

'He did. Mel was outraged. He demanded that each of us forget the boys. But I have faith that you act in the children's best interests. But not the man who came searching for them. If he finds the children . . .' The monk ended with an expressive shrug.

'We do seek to protect them, brother,' Fidelma assured him. 'It is true that they are in grave danger from that man, Intat. Do you know who the boys were, what their names were and where they have gone?'

'Alas, even Father Mel would not pronounce their names but called them by the Latin forms of Primus and Victor. See on the doll, that piece of rag is marked with the words "*Hic est meum. Victor*". It means, "this is mine, Victor" in Latin.'

'Can you describe them?' Fidelma did not point out that she knew well what the words meant.

'Not really. They both had burnished copper-coloured hair.'

'Copper-coloured?' Fidelma felt frustrated, hoping to hear something which she might have recognised.

'Did you learn where they were sent when they left here?'

'Only that the religieux who took them was from an abbey somewhere in the south. The young one, Victor, was a nice child. Return this doll to him and I shall pray to Michael the Archangel, guardian of our little monastery, for their safety.'

'Can you tell us about the religieux . . . what did he look like?'

'That I cannot. He kept his robes wrapped around his body and head for the weather was inclement. I did not observe his features well. He was not young but neither was he old. That is all I can say.'

'Thank you, brother. You have been most helpful.'

'I will lead you down the path and signal your ship. My conscience is easy now that I have made confession to you of this burden.'

Cass laid a restraining hand on Fidelma's arm.

'Why don't we go and confront that old goat again?' he demanded. 'Let's tell him what we know and demand to know where this cousin has taken the two boys?'

Fidelma shook her head.

'We will get nothing further from a man such as Father Mel,' she replied. 'Our path is back at Ros Ailithir.'

Once on board Ross's *barc* again, the ship close-hauled along the thin, poking figures of the southern peninsulas of the kingdom, heading swiftly southward.

'A long trip for so little,' mused Cass, as he stood watching Fidelma turning the worn doll over and over in her hands.

'Sometimes even a word or sentence might resolve the greatest puzzle and put it all into shape,' countered Fidelma.

'What did we learn from this arduous trip to Sceilig Mhichil that we did not suspect before? Had we questioned that old religieux further . . .'

'Sometimes confirmation of knowledge is as important as

the knowledge itself,' interrupted Fidelma. 'And we have linked Intat into this mystery of Dacán's killing. Dacán was looking for the son of Illan whom he thought was at the age of choice. Now we know there were two young sons, not at the age of choice at all. Intat arrives here looking for the offspring of Illan. Dacán was working for Laigin but Intat was a man of the Corco Loígde. There is a picture beginning to form here.'

'Apart from Intat's involvement in this conundrum, what else have we learnt?' demanded Cass.

'We have learnt that the monastery on Sceilig Mhichil has, as its patron, Michael the Archangel. That its very name means "rock of Michael". And we have learnt that Mel called the man who collected the boys "honourable cousin".'

Cass was not sure if Fidelma was joking.

'But what practical information have we learnt?' he demanded.

Fidelma smiled blandly.

'We have learnt several other points. There are two heirs to Illan. They left Sceilig Mhichil two weeks ago about the same time that Dacán was murdered and they are now being hunted by Intat. I believe that Intat was looking for them when he burnt Rae na Scríne. I do not think he found them and I will lay a wager that they may be found at Ros Ailithir or nearby.'

'If they are still alive.' Cass suddenly became interested. 'We don't even know who they are. Two copper-haired lads. I have encountered no copper-haired boys. We don't even know their true names. We know that Primus and Victor were not their real names. That presents no clue that we can follow.'

'Perhaps not,' Fidelma admitted thoughtfully. 'Then, again . . .' She shrugged abruptly and was silent.

Chapter Fourteen

Abbot Brocc's thin features relaxed with relief when Fidelma entered his chamber.

'I had just heard that you had landed. Was your trip fruitful, cousin?' he asked eagerly, rising to greet her.

'It has added to my knowledge,' Fidelma replied evasively.

The abbot hesitated, apparently wondering whether to press his cousin further on the point but then decided against it.

'I have news.' He indicated that she should be seated. 'However, I think it is bad news.'

Fidelma seated herself as Brocc held up a wax tablet.

'Yesterday I received this message – the High King means to arrive here within the next few days.'

Fidelma's surprise obviously gratified him. She sat up straight. Her eyes were wide.

'Sechnassach, the High King? Is he coming here?'

Brocc nodded emphatically.

'He has ruled that the court should hear Laigin's claims against Muman, in the matter of the death of Dacán, in the abbey where Dacán was killed. His words are that it was . . .' Brocc hesitated and squinted at the tablet, '. . . *appropriate* that the hearing should be in this place.'

'So?' Fidelma lingered over the word, like a long sigh. 'And the entire court is coming with him?'

'Of course. The Chief Brehon Barrán will sit in judgment with the High King and Archbishop Ultan of Armagh is coming to represent the ecclesiastical orders of the five kingdoms. Your brother Colgú and his advisors will also be arriving any day now.'

'And I suppose young Fianamail, the king of Laigin, and his advocates will be here soon?'

'Fianamail is bringing the Abbot Noé and his Brehon Forbassach.'

'Forbassach! So Forbassach will plead the case for Laigin?'

As much as she disliked the hawk-faced advocate of Laigin, Fidelma knew that he was possessed of a quick wit and was a capable counsel, one who certainly should not be underestimated. He would undoubtedly be at his sharpest for he would want to repay Fidelma for having had him ejected from Cashel.

'Exactly when are they all expected to arrive?' she asked, feeling, as Brocc had forewarned, it was not good news.

'Within a few days, by the end of the week at the latest.' Brocc was clearly nervous at being host to such an assembly where he stood in place of the accused. 'Tell me, cousin, are you any nearer to resolving this mystery?'

His voice was almost pleading but Fidelma could not allay his obvious fears.

She stood up and moved to the window, peering down into the inlet.

'I saw, as we were coming into Ros Ailithir, that Mugrón's warship still rides at anchor out there.'

Brocc's shoulders sagged a little.

'Laigin will not give up their plaint before the assembly meets.'

Fidelma turned back into the chamber towards the abbot.

'I presume the High King and his entourage will come by ship around the coast?'

'As will the king of Laigin and his retinue,' confirmed Brocc. 'I am expected to give hospitality to all of them. Brother Rumann and Brother Conghus are at their wits' end to find extra accommodation and food. Oh, and that means that the extra chamber in which you have conducted your investigations can no longer be available to you. You may still use the same chamber in the hostel for personal use, as befits your rank, but the young warrior, what's his name . . . Cass? He will have to use a bed in one of the dormitories.'

'It cannot be helped. You have much to do to prepare for the assembly.'

Brocc examined her with a pessimistic eye.

'And you also, cousin, for on you depends all our futures.'

Fidelma did not need Brocc to remind her. The words of the Gospel of Luke came suddenly into her mind: 'Unto whomsoever much is given, of them shall much be required.' Never, since she had received her qualification in law, had so much been required of her. She felt that responsibility was like a heavy weight. Despite her most strenuous efforts she was still looking into a smoked mirror where enticing shadows could be seen but nothing that was clear nor which made any sense.

Brocc saw the anxiety on her face and relented his own attitude.

'It is just that I am truly beginning to worry now, cousin. I have never attended a High King's assembly before,' he added with some morbid fascination. 'Were it not that I am charged as responsible in this matter it would have been an exhilarating experience.'

Fidelma raised a cynical eyebrow.

'Exhilarating experience? It may also be a fatal one if I cannot present a case that will clear you and prevent the claim of Laigin leading to a war between the two kingdoms.'

There was an uncomfortable silence, then Fidelma said, without expectation of a positive answer: 'You have not told me whether there is any news of Sister Grella. I presume she has not returned?'

Brocc grimaced gloomily and confirmed her expectation.

'No. She has simply vanished. From what you told me I fear that she has fled with her guilt.'

Fidelma frowned and rose.

'That we shall see. I shall need the material which I left with you.'

Brocc nodded readily, reaching under his table for the keys. She watched as he went to the cabinet and unlocked the door, swinging it open. He took out her *marsupium* and handed it to her.

She rummaged through its contents to check everything was there.

Fidelma gave a sharp intake of breath. Someone had been through the contents of the bag. The burnt piece of Ogham stick and the pieces of vellum that she had found in Sister Grella's chamber were gone. Yet the linen bonds and the skirt from which they had been taken were still there.

'What is it?' Brocc asked, moving swiftly to her side.

She stood quietly awhile. It was no use responding emotionally to the disappearance of the crucial evidence which she had gathered and placed there for safekeeping.

'Someone has removed some vital pieces of evidence from my bag.'

'I do not understand, cousin,' breathed Brocc. He looked genuinely bewildered. His face was flushed with mortification.

'When was the last time you opened this cabinet, Brocc?' she asked.

'When you asked me to deposit the bag into it for safekeeping.'

'And where have you kept the keys?'

'They are hung, as you have seen, on hooks under this table.'

'And many people knew of that?'

'I thought that I was the only one who knew exactly where the keys were kept.'

'It would not take a great deal of effort to find them. How many people knew that valuables were sometimes kept in that cabinet?'

'Only some of the senior members of the abbey.'

'And, needless to say, anyone could have access to your chamber while you were performing the duties of your office?'

Brocc exhaled softly.

'No member of the brethren of this abbey would commit such a crime as theft from their abbot, cousin. It trespasses against the boundaries of the rules of our order.'

'So does murder,' Fidelma replied dryly. 'Yet someone in this abbey killed both Dacán and Sister Eisten. You say only the senior members of the abbey knew that valuables were sometimes placed there. Such as who?'

Brocc rubbed his chin.

'Brother Rumann, of course. Brother Conghus. Our chief professor Brother Ségán. Brother Midach . . . oh, and Sister Grella, of course. But she is not here. That is all.'

'It is enough.' Fidelma was irritated. 'Did you by any chance mention that I had left some valuables with you while I was away?'

Brocc started nervously and a red glow suffused his thin cheeks.

'My senior clerics did ask me where you had gone,' he admitted reluctantly. 'I could not tell them, as I did not know. But they were all concerned that this matter be cleared up. I said that I thought you had evidence, that you left . . . well, I think I mentioned that . . . I said that Sister Grella was to be held until you returned and . . .'

He faltered under Fidelma's angry gaze.

'So, perhaps it would not take long for anyone to find the logical hiding place for these keys. You might just as well have issued instructions.'

'What can I say?' Brocc spread his hands as if to shield himself from the scorn in her voice. 'I am truly sorry.'

'No more sorry than I, Brocc,' Fidelma snapped, moving for the door, angered at Brocc's careless attitude which had led to the loss of her salient evidence. 'But the loss of that material will not prevent me from discovering the culprit, only, perhaps, from proving their involvement.'

The first person she saw as she crossed the quadrangles to the hostel was the young Sister Necht. She looked startled as she caught sight of Fidelma.

'I thought that you had left us,' she greeted in her slow, husky voice.

Fidelma shook her head.

'I cannot leave until my investigation is complete.'

'I heard that you have ordered that Sister Grella be held.'

'Sister Grella has disappeared.'

'Yes. Everyone knows and believes that she has fled. Has anyone looked for her at Cuan Dóir, Salbach's fortress?' the novice suggested.

'Why so?' demanded Fidelma, startled.

'Why?' The sister rubbed her face and considered for a moment. 'Because she has frequently visited there without telling anyone. She is a good friend to Salbach.' Necht paused and smiled. 'I know this because Sister Eisten told me.'

'What did Eisten say?'

'Oh, that Grella once invited her to Salbach's fortress because Salbach was supposed to be interested in her orphanage. She told me that they seemed very good friends.'

Fidelma looked at the guileless eyes of the novice for a minute.

'I understand that Midach is your *anamchara*, your soul-friend?'

Fidelma wondered why the question brought such a look of panic to the novice's face. Yet it was gone in a trice. Sister Necht forced a nervous smile.

'It is true.'

'Have you known Midach long?'

'Most of my life. He was a friend of my father's and introduced me to the abbey.'

Fidelma wondered how best to approach the subject on her mind and decided that the best way was the most direct.

'You do not have to put up with abuse, you know,' she said. She remembered Midach's rough handling of the young religieuse; of the slap on her head.

Sister Necht flushed.

'I am not sure what you mean,' she countered.

Fidelma grimaced in conciliatory fashion. She did not want the girl to feel humiliated by another seeing her being abused.

'It is just that I overheard Midach giving you a tongue-lashing for something and thought he might have maltreated you. It was in the herb garden a week ago just before I left.'

Fidelma realised there was something more than humiliation in the eyes of the novice. There was something akin to fear.

'It was . . . was nothing. I had failed to perform a task for Midach. He is a good man. Sometimes his temper becomes a little frayed. You will not report this to the abbot? Please?'

Fidelma smiled reassuringly.

'Not if you do not want me to, Necht. But no one, especially no woman, should put up with verbal abuse from others. The *Bretha Nemed* makes it an offence in law for a woman to be harassed and especially to be verbally assaulted. Did you know this?'

Sister Necht shook her head, gazing at the floor.

'No woman need stand by and be abused by anyone,' went on Fidelma. 'And the abuse need not be a physical assault but if a person mocks a woman, criticises their appearance, draws attention to any physical blemish or wrongfully accuses them of things that are not true, then they have redress under the law.'

'It was not so serious, sister,' Necht said, with a further

shake of her head. 'I thank you for your interest but, really, Midach meant me no harm.'

The midday Angelus was sounding and Sister Necht muttered an excuse and hurried off.

Fidelma sighed deeply. There was something more to that matter, she felt. There was definitely an aura of fear about the young girl when Fidelma had mentioned the scene in the herb garden. Well, she could do no more than advise Necht of her rights under law. Perhaps she ought to have a word with Midach himself.

She found Cass at the door of the guests' hostel.

'Have you heard the news?' His voice was excited.

'Which news?' she demanded bitterly.

'Why, about the coming here of the High King. It is all over the abbey.'

'That!' The word was almost an ejaculation.

Cass frowned. 'I thought it would be important to you. It does not leave you much time to prepare a defence of Muman against the claims of Laigin.'

Fidelma set her jaw firmly and said in measured tones: 'Truly, Cass, I do not have to be reminded of my responsibilities. There is worse news than the imminent assembly and that is that someone has stolen some of our evidence from Brocc's chamber. Apparently, the stupid man mentioned the fact that I had left it there to several people and so certain items have been taken from my *marsupium* which I left there.'

Cass raised his eyebrows.

'Certain items?' He repeated. 'Why not steal the entire bag?'

Fidelma jerked her head up as his words registered. She had overlooked the obvious. Only the Ogham stick and the vellum had been taken. Yet the bindings and Grella's skirt, from which they had been taken, were left. What did that signify? Why was the thief so selective about what evidence they had removed?

She considered matters for a moment and then gave a sigh of frustration.

'Where are you off to now?' demanded Cass as Fidelma suddenly began striding away across the courtyard that separated the hostel from the abbey church.

'There is something I should have done before we left for Sceilig Mhichil,' she called across her shoulder. 'Sister Necht had just reminded me of it.'

'Sister Necht?'

Cass trailed after her. He was beginning to be exhausted by Fidelma's abrupt changes and wished she would confide in him more readily than she did.

'It seems that we are running here and there and the more we move the less close we get to our goal,' he complained. 'I thought that the ancients taught that such excessive motion does not necessarily mean progression?'

Fidelma, engrossed in her own anxieties, was irritated by what she perceived as the warrior's bland remark.

'If you can solve this puzzle by sitting in a room, staring at the wall, then do so.'

The sourness in her tone caused Cass to wince a little.

'I am not criticising you,' he said hurriedly, 'but what good will a visit to the abbey church do?'

'Let us discover,' Fidelma replied curtly.

Brother Rumann, the steward, was coming out of the door of the abbey as they went up the steps.

'I heard that you had returned from Sceilig Mhichil,' he greeted in his wheezy tones, full of affability. 'How was your journey? Have you learnt anything?'

'The journey was fine,' she replied evenly, 'but how did you know we went to Sceilig Mhichil?'

The even tone disguised the fact that she was suddenly on guard. She had, in fact, been very careful not to tell even her cousin, the Abbot Brocc, where she was going. No one in the abbey should have known.

Rumann looked uneasy and frowned.

'I am not sure. Someone mentioned it. I think it might have been Brother Midach. Was it a secret?'

Fidelma did not reply but changed the subject.

'I am told that the tomb of the Blessed Fachtna is contained within the abbey church? Can you tell me where it is located?'

'Of course.' Rumann positively preened himself. 'It is a place of pilgrimage on the fourteenth day of the feast of Lúnasa, his feastday. Let me show you, sister.'

Rumann turned and began to move wheezily along the lengthy nave beyond the transept to the High Altar.

'Have you heard the story of how Fachtna was blind when he came to this spot and, thanks to the intercession of a great miracle here at Ros Ailithir, where there was then nothing but open lands, he received his sight back and, in gratitude, built this abbey?' asked Rumann.

'I have heard the story,' replied Fidelma, though not responding to the steward's enthusiasm for his subject.

Rumann conducted them up the steps that surrounded the slightly raised area on which the High Altar stood and then move around behind it into the apse, the vaulted curved recess behind the altar where the officiating priest or abbot usually conducted the rituals of the 'dismissal' in accordance with the rites of the Church. In the apse lay a large sandstone slab which stood three inches above the rest of the floor. Incongruously, at the head of the slab, on a small stone plinth stood a statue of a cherub. At the foot of the slab was a similar plinth with a seraph upon it.

'You will see just a simple cross,' pointed Rumann, 'and the name Fachtna in the ancient Ogham script.'

'Do you read Ogham?' she asked innocently.

'My rôle as steward of the abbey requires me to be proficient in many forms of learning.' Rumann's fleshy face was complacent.

Fidelma turned back to the stone slab.

'What lies beneath this stone?' she queried.

Rumann looked puzzled.

'Why the sepulchre of Fachtna, of course. It is the only tomb within the abbey walls.'

'I mean, what sort of tomb is it? A hole in the ground, a cave or what?'

'Well, no one has ever opened it since Fachtna was interred there over a century ago.'

'Really? Yet you described it as a sepulchre.'

'It is true that it is known as the sepulchre,' replied Rumann. 'Perhaps it is some sort of catacomb or cave. It would be sacrilege to enter to confirm that. There are several such caves hereabouts. We have other interesting tombs of that sort at Ros Ailithir but most of them lie without the walls of the abbey.'

'Then there is no entrance to this sepulchre from the walled garden at the back of the church?' she demanded abruptly.

Rumann stared down at her in bewilderment.

'No. Whatever makes you ask such a question?'

'So the only entrance to the sepulchre is by the removal of this sandstone slab. It seems too strong and heavy.'

'That it is, sister. And no one has been able to remove it in over a century.'

Cass began asking Rumann about other burial places for he could see that Fidelma wanted to be left to her own devices for a few moments. The plump-faced house steward's attention was distracted.

Fidelma went down on one knee by the great slab. She reached out a hand to touch that which had attracted her attention. It was slippery and cold. Cold candle grease spilt into a crevice by the old stone.

Someone entered the church with a noisy clatter of the great doors. Fidelma rose swiftly and saw that it was Brother Conghus who had entered and was beckoning frantically to Rumann.

The steward excused himself and hurried off down the aisle of the nave.

When he had gone Fidelma turned to Cass with lowered voice.

'There is a way into that sepulchre, I swear it.'

Cass raised an eyebrow.

'What makes you say that? And what has it to do with the investigation?'

'Look at that candle grease and tell me what you observe.'

Cass looked down.

'It's just candle grease. There are plenty of such spots in the church. You can break a leg by slipping on them unless you watch where you tread.'

She sighed impatiently.

'Yes. But they are all where they should be. Under candle holders. This spot is in a place where no candles hang. And see the way it has fallen.'

'I don't understand.'

'Really, Cass. Look. Observe. Deduce. Do you see that the edge of the stone slab is a straight line where it rests on the floor? Around it are splashes of candle grease which have grown cold. Look closer. Look at the join. It is as if the grease had been dropped before the slab was put in place, that the slab was slung back over the top of it.'

Cass rubbed the back of his neck in his bewilderment.

'I still don't understand.'

She groaned and lowered herself to both knees, pushing at the slab, trying to compel it to move, first in one direction and then another. Her efforts were without success.

Finally, and reluctantly, she rose to her feet.

'That sepulchre holds a valuable key to this business,' she said thoughtfully. 'Someone has opened it and just recently. I think I am finally beginning to see the path through the darkness of this mystery . . .'

Brother Rumann came padding swiftly back to where they

stood. They could see from his face that he was bursting with some important news.

'Sister Grella has been seen,' he blurted.

'Has she returned to the abbey?' asked Fidelma in excitement.

Rumann shook his head.

'Someone saw her riding with Salbach in the woods of Dór. It would seem that the chieftain of the Corco Loígde has found her. Excuse me, I must take this news to the abbot.'

Fidelma watched him hurry away. Cass was doing his best to conceal his excitement.

'Well.' He smiled with satisfaction. 'I think our mystery is near its end, eh?'

'How so, Cass?' she asked wearily.

'If Salbach has found Sister Grella, then we have found the culprit. You gave orders yourself to detain her. She was the person who was most implicated by the evidence,' he pointed out. 'Doubtless she stole that evidence from the abbot's chamber.'

'Yet Sister Grella has not been seen in the abbey since she disappeared.'

'Well, maybe she returned without being noticed. I say, there is your thief and if she is the thief, she is also Dacán's killer. She would surely know that the evidence in that *marsupium* proves as much. It is logical that she would wish to destroy it. She probably heard from someone in the abbey that Brocc had the evidence.'

Fidelma suddenly gazed thoughtfully at him. She had neglected to tell him that the evidence that had been left behind implicated Grella rather than the reverse. She decided to keep this information to herself for the time being.

'It is a possible explanation,' she conceded. 'Where are the woods of Dór?'

'Cuan Dóir is Salbach's fortress which is situated between the woods and the sea. It is less than a quarter of an hour's journey across the headland,' Cass replied. 'We may meet Salbach escorting Grella along the road, that is if he is bringing her back to the abbey.'

'Much power in that word "if",' muttered Fidelma but did not explain herself further. 'I think we shall discover something else about Grella and Salbach as a result of this journey. Let's get our horses from the stables.'

Cass suppressed a sigh of irritation. He found Fidelma a most exasperating woman.

Chapter Fifteen

Cuan Dóir, Dór's harbour, was a short ride across the headland from Ros Ailithir. In fact, it was little more than three miles from the gates of the abbey. The track ran within sight of the stormy sea through wild scenery of granite rocks, gorse and heather, a landscape devoid of trees because of the nearness of the expanse of ocean with its prevailing coastal winds. Almost halfway along this path they crossed the remains of an ancient stone circle. Tall, grey granite sentinels stood as silent testimony to the beliefs and practices of the ancients, forming a circle some thirty feet in diameter, while just beyond was a small stone cabin. It seemed to fit so naturally into the wild, windswept landscape and conjure images of times past.

A little further on, the path descended into an inlet which seemed as natural a harbour as the one offered by Ros Ailithir. It was an area replete in fuchsia-strewn hedgerows which laced a breathtaking scenery. There were a few ships anchored in the small harbour. Several buildings comprised the township but dominating them was the fortress of Salbach: a round, stone-walled stronghold, well appointed to control the sea approaches as well as the road to the harbour. Fidelma saw that, like many of the fortresses she had seen, its walls, which rose some twenty feet high, were of dry stone. She estimated the circular fortification was probably some hundred feet in diameter with only one entrance, a large gateway with sloping jambs big enough for only one horse and rider to pass through at a time.

Armed warriors lounged at this gate watching with ill-concealed curiosity as Fidelma and Cass rode up.

'Is Sister Grella of Ros Ailithir within the gates?' called Fidelma as they halted. She had not bothered to dismount.

'This is the fortress of Salbach, chieftain of the Corco Loígde,' came the uncompromising reply from one of the guardians of the portal. He did not bother to change his lounging posture as he leant against the wall staring at them.

Fidelma decided to change tack.

'Then we should like to see Salbach.'

'He is not here,' came the wooden response.

'Then where is he, man?' demanded Cass, moving forward so that the warrior could see his golden collar emblem and know him for one of the élite warriors of Cashel.

The man made no sign that he had observed the emblem. He gazed insolently back at Cass.

'He went riding a while ago.' As Cass was about to make a sharp retort, the warrior relented and pointed with his spear. 'He will probably be hunting in the wood of Dór, which is in that direction.'

'Was anyone with him?' demanded Fidelma.

'Salbach likes to hunt alone.'

This statement brought forth a low chuckle from the other guard as if it were some witticism.

Fidelma motioned Cass to follow and they turned in the direction of the distant woodland which the warrior had indicated.

'If Grella is not with Salbach, what need to go in search of him?' inquired Cass as he realised her intent.

'Perhaps Salbach does not hunt alone?' Fidelma suggested. 'The idea seemed to amused our taciturn friend's companion.'

They walked their horses at a quiet pace along the track as it twisted upward again from the shoreline, crossing undulating ground for a few miles before entering a thick woodland area which was, Fidelma noticed, rich in the variety of its trees although it was predominated by conifers intermixed with many birch and hazels. Heather grew everywhere in abundance. They followed the main track as it cut through the forest.

The woodland suddenly halted to make way for a river, cutting its way tempestuously down from the distant hills and heading in a broad sweep towards the sea behind them. It was wide but looked shallow enough. Fidelma was about to cross when Cass called softly to stay her.

He pointed wordlessly.

She saw, a short distance along the banks on the farthest side, a small woodsman's *bothán* or cabin. There was smoke rising from its chimney.

Outside, in front of the cabin, stood two horses. One was fairly richly accoutred while the other was in plain harness.

Fidelma exchanged a meaningful glance with Cass.

'We'll cross,' she instructed, and proceeded to urge her horse through the rapidly flowing water. The track had, in fact, come to a natural ford and the water was little more than two feet in depth at its deepest point. They eased their horses carefully across to the far bank.

'We'll leave our horses in that clearing,' Fidelma said, pointing to a small, sheltered spot a little way ahead of them. 'Then we will make our way to the *bothán*. It is my guess that we will find both Salbach and our missing librarian there.'

Cass shook his head in perplexity but did not say anything.

Fidelma choose to make her way to the cabin surreptitiously, for she had embarked upon a series of thoughts which had brought her to a conclusion that she found scarcely creditable but whose progression seemed to fit the facts she had gathered so far.

They followed a small path which kept parallel with the river bank and brought them to the small clearing in which the woodsman's cabin stood.

They halted at the edge of the trees before the open area and Fidelma raised her head to listen.

There came the sound of a woman's peal of laughter from within the cabin.

Fidelma smiled in grim satisfaction towards Cass. It seemed that she had been right in her prediction.

She had started forward towards the cabin when Cass reached forward and grabbed her arm to halt her.

It was then she heard the soft pounding of a horse at a canter.

Swiftly, she moved back into the shelter of the shrubbery and crouched down beside Cass.

A rider burst into the clearing before the woodsman's cabin from the direction of what must have been a track through the forest on the far side of the clearing. The figure was that of a thick-set man. He was clad in a woollen cloak but dishevelled and dirty.

'Salbach!' cried the warrior, reining in his horse before the cabin and sitting at ease, leaning slightly forward on the pommel.

A moment or two passed before Salbach appeared at the door of the cabin pulling on his shirt.

'What news?' he called. Salbach was carrying a fur-lined cloak over his arm and this he proceeded to slip round his shoulders.

'The hearing is to take place at Ros Ailithir within days. And Ross's *barc* is anchored in the inlet. They must have returned.'

Fidelma saw Cass glance in her direction with rounded eyes. She pulled a face and turned back to the two men.

'Does she know?' demanded Salbach.

'I doubt it. There was nothing to be learnt at Sceilig Mhichil.'

'Well, I think I know where they might be hidden,' Salbach was saying.

'That will please the *bó-aire*,' grunted the warrior.

Salbach was walking to his horse and he swung himself easily into the saddle. He did not even glance back at the cabin.

'I'll accompany you to Cuan Dóir and as we go I'll give you my instructions for Intat.'

Fidelma heard Cass draw in his breath sharply.

The two riders, Salbach and the warrior, moved down to the river, trotting their horses along the shallows until they reached the ford. Fidelma and Cass could hear the splash of their passage as they crossed it.

Cass pursed his lips in a soundless whistle.

'I thought Salbach was supposed to be sending warriors to capture Intat to try him for his crime at Rae na Scríne?' he whispered.

'Intat is obviously Salbach's man,' replied Fidelma, rising and brushing the leaves from her skirt. 'I had suspected as much. Come, I think it time we had a word with our missing librarian.'

She strode firmly across the clearing to the cabin door and pushed it open without ceremony.

Sister Grella, not yet fully dressed, swung round, her eyes staring in consternation.

Fidelma smiled humourlessly.

'Well, Sister Grella? It seems you have decided to quit the religious life.'

Sister Grella, her jaw slack, open-mouthed, her face pale, stared beyond Fidelma to where Cass was returning her gaze in equal astonishment over Fidelma's shoulder. Grella broke the spell by grabbing a garment to cover herself.

Fidelma saw her embarrassment and turned to cast a look of reproach at Cass.

The young warrior, red in the face, backed out of the cabin and took a stand beyond the door.

'Dress yourself, Grella,' instructed Fidelma, 'and then we shall talk.'

'Where is Salbach?' whispered the erstwhile librarian. 'What are you going to do?'

'Salbach has ridden off,' Fidelma replied. 'And in answer to your second question, well, that depends. Now hurry up and get your clothes on.'

Fidelma, spotting a chair, seated herself.

Grella began to dress hastily.

'Are you going to take me back to the abbey?'

Fidelma allowed a cynical smile to play at the corner of her mouth.

'You are answerable to ecclesiastical law as well as civil law for your conduct.'

'There is no sin in it. Salbach plans to make me his second wife. I have quit the abbey.'

'Without informing the abbot? But, you say, Salbach is already married?'

'His wife is old,' replied Grella, as if this explained everything.

'Just as Dacán was old?' Fidelma asked innocently.

Grella jerked her head in surprise. Then, recovering her poise, she shrugged.

'So, you have found out? Yes, like Dacán was. Shrunken, worn and weak, he was. That's why I divorced him.'

'Since the coming of the Faith to this land, the custom of taking a second wife or husband, or of taking a concubine, has been condemned by the bishops,' Fidelma commented. 'Should Salbach take you as a second wife, you will be condemned by the church anyway.'

Grella sneered.

'A few years ago Nuada of Laigin had two wives. The civil law still provides the rights of a second wife.'

'I know the law, Grella. But you are a religieuse and should know that the rules of the Faith are oft-times contrary to the civil law.'

'But your task is to uphold the civil law,' Grella snapped.

Fidelma did not press the matter further because she knew that while the Church opposed polygny, which had been widespread in ancient times, there was only limited success. Finally, one Brehon, writing the law text of the *Bretha Crólige*, had written in despair: 'there is dispute in Irish law as to which is more proper, whether many sexual unions or a single one; for the chosen people of God lived in plurality of unions, so that it is easier to praise it rather than to condemn it.' Grella was right. But it was not the morality of her liaison with Salbach of the Corco Loígde that was uppermost in Fidelma's mind.

'Did you plan never to return to the abbey? Why then did you take no personal possessions with you?'

Grella bit her lip. She finished her dressing and setting her hair to rights. She stood in front of Fidelma, hands on hips.

'I don't need to excuse myself. There is little of mine at the abbey and what I need Salbach can supply. As for returning, perhaps I would have returned after I had become Salbach's wife. None would then dare to level any accusations against me. I would have Salbach's protection.'

'Salbach is equally answerable to the law as you are, Grella. There are some questions you need to answer and at once. You knew that your former husband, Dacán, had come to Ros Ailithir for a special purpose?'

'How much do you know?' demanded Grella. In spite of her glare of anger there was some alarm in her eyes.

'I know that you were once married to Dacán.'

'Mugrón must have told you. A stupid coincidence that he saw me at Cuan Dóir.'

'He saw you there with Sister Eisten,' Fidelma said quietly. Grella did not rise to her bait.

'So what does it matter? I have told you my relationship with Salbach.'

'Why did you take Sister Eisten to Salbach's fortress?'

Grella frowned a moment.

'Salbach asked me. He had heard that Eisten was running an orphanage at Rae na Scríne. He wanted to meet her and the children. He knew that I was friendly with the young woman.'

'And did she take the children there?' Fidelma was nonplussed.

But Grella shook her head.

'She accompanied me to Cuan Dóir but refused to take the children. She did not want them to travel because of the Yellow Plague.'

'Was Salbach annoyed when she did not take them?'

Grella peered curiously at her.

'Why would he be annoyed?'

Fidelma sat back and did not reply for the moment.

'Did you know that Eisten has been murdered?'

Grella's face was suddenly a tight mask. It was clear that she had heard the news and behind the mask Fidelma saw that the librarian was clearly upset.

'I heard only a few days ago.'

'Not before?'

She shook her head and somehow Fidelma knew she was telling the truth.

'You seem upset about it. You tell me that you were friendly with her. How friendly?'

'Since Eisten studied in the library with me earlier this year we have been soul-friends.'

Soul-friends! Yes, Eisten had told Fidelma that she had a soul-friend in the abbey. What was it Eisten had asked on the last time Fidelma had seen here? Can a soul-friend betray a confidence?

'So you had few secrets from each other?'

'You know the role of the *anamchara*,' snapped Grella. Her expression told Fidelma that she was unlikely to speak further about the matter.

'You have already told me that you knew what work Dacán was engaged upon,' said Fidelma, changing tack.

'I told you so when you came to see me at the library.'

'But you did not add the specific that he was actually seeking the descendants of the native ruling house of Osraige.'

Grella shot a nervous look at Fidelma.

'How do you know that?' she countered.

'I read Dacán's writings.'

Grella's hand reached up as if to clutch at her own throat.

'You . . . you saw them?'

Fidelma examined her carefully.

'I searched your chamber, Grella. It was silly of you to think that you could hide that material. Or that you could misinterpret the Ogham wands to me.'

To her astonishment, for she thought the woman would vigorously deny any knowledge, Grella shrugged.

'I thought that no one would find them. I thought that I had hidden them safely. I meant to destroy them.'

'You did not know that I removed them a week ago?'

'I have already told you that I have not been back to the abbey since then.'

'No?' Fidelma let the matter pass for the moment. 'Well, you knew that Dacán was searching for the heir of Illan, who claimed to be the rightful aspirant for the petty kingship of Osraige?'

'I have already admitted it,' conceded Grella.

'And you told Salbach about it?'

The woman shrugged diffidently but did not reply.

'Salbach's cousin is Scandlán, the current king of Osraige, isn't he? So Salbach would have an interest in ensuring that the son of Illan was not discovered.'

'I simply thought Salbach ought to know that someone was looking for Illan's offspring,' replied Grella. 'I sought to prevent any future wars in Osraige. Illan was the cause of a great deal of bloodshed when he attempted to overthrow Scandlán.'

'So you told Salbach about Dacán. Salbach realised that Laigin wanted to reassert its power over Osraige, perhaps establish a client king who would answer to Laigin rather than to Muman.'

Grella stood indifferently.

'If you say so.'

'Dacán was therefore a danger to Salbach's family in Osraige. Was that the reason you killed your former husband?'

For a moment Grella's shock seemed genuine.

'Who accuses me of killing him?' she demanded.

'The bonds with which he was tied were strips of linen; red and blue in colour. Do you own a red and blue linen skirt?'

'Of course not.' There was no conviction in her quick denial.

'So if I tell you that, while searching your chamber, I discovered such a skirt from which part had been torn off and that the part matched the bonds with which Dacán had been tied before he was killed, would you still deny ownership?'

Grella flushed and looked less confident.

'Do you own such a dress?' pressed Fidelma. 'Better to tell the truth if you have nothing to hide.'

Grella's shoulders hunched in resignation.

'That is my dress right enough, but I have not worn it since I came to Ros Ailithir. I had meant to give it away to the poor but . . .' She stared earnestly into Fidelma's eyes. 'I may have betrayed old Dacán's confidence and told Salbach what he was doing, and I believe I was justified in doing so, but I did not kill him. After all, why kill Dacán? He would have led Salbach to Illan's heir. That was what Salbach wanted.'

Fidelma paused as she saw the logic of her argument but she continued: 'And do you deny that, within these last few days, you returned to the abbey and entered the abbot's chamber to remove some of the evidence from his personal cabinet?'

Grella simply stared in incomprehension.

Fidelma knew that the woman was telling the truth. She had banked everything on her intuition that if Grella was not the culprit, then she knew enough to reveal who it was and possibly, confronted by the accusation backed by the evidence which Fidelma had, that she would confess.

'You knew there was a bag of evidence left by me in the abbot's cabinet?' she pressed desperately.

'Certainly not,' Grella responded. 'How could I when I had not realised that you had removed anything from my chamber? I told you that I have not been back to the abbey during this last week.'

'You chose an odd time to leave the abbey. It is suspicious. Wouldn't you say so?'

'It was Salbach's suggestion that I came with him that night. For too long I have been hiding my affection for Salbach. It was time that we came into the open about our love.'

'You'll forgive me when I repeat that your timing was a matter of great coincidence.'

'I did not murder Dacán,' replied Grella firmly.

Fidelma suppressed a gentle sigh.

'Tell me then, why did you hide Dacán's papers?'

'That's not hard to tell. I did not want anyone else to know what Dacán had been engaged in. It were better that Laigin did not find the son of Illan. If they did not, then they would not be able to use Illan's heir to overthrow Salbach's cousin.'

'And Salbach would be grateful to you for this information?'

'I love Salbach.'

'And so all this you did out of your . . . love . . . for Salbach?'

Sister Grella's eyes were pools of indignant fire.

'Well now,' Fidelma said, rising, 'Laigin is doing that very thing, demanding Osraige as the honour price for the slaughter of Dacán. It seems that the very war you claim that you sought to prevent will take place.'

Grella rose with her.

'Let me appeal to you as a woman, Fidelma. I was married to Dacán when I was fifteen. It was an arranged marriage in this new custom of the Faith where I had little say. I stayed three years with that old man. He was not capable of fathering children and it was on those grounds that I asked for a divorce. Rather than be shamed by a hearing before the Brehon, in which such a matter would be discussed, Dacán gave me that divorce without contention. He taught me many things, for which I am grateful. He taught me enough to allow me to go to an ecclesiastic college, the college of Cealla, to study and attain my degree. The strange thing is that, in a way, I cared for that old man, unfriendly though he was, as if he had been my father. I did not kill him, Fidelma of Kildare. I am guilty of several things, but I did not kill him.'

'Sister Grella, some sense within me makes me want to believe you. However, the evidence is against you. The evidence of Dacán's hidden papers. The bonds with which he was tied. Your sudden disappearance from the abbey after you had not told me the truth about your former marriage to Dacán and other matters.' Fidelma compressed her lower lip in thought. 'You knew that Dacán was searching for the heir of Illan. The evening before he died, he wrote to his brother that he had discovered where Illan's heir was hiding. The evidence suggests that you killed him to prevent him finding the heir of Illan in order to please your lover, Salbach.'

'No! This is not true. You cannot claim that I am guilty of that deed!'

'No? Perhaps not. It seems that it will be for the High King's assembly to decide.'

'Yet you know, in the heart, Fidelma, that it is not true,' pressed Grella angrily.

'I am appointed by the king of Cashel. I can only follow my duty. I have a war to prevent. Cass!'

The young warrior came into the cabin. He looked from Grella's white, pinched face, to Fidelma's stern expression.

'Cass, Sister Grella will be returning with us to Ros Ailithir as our prisoner.'

'Then she has confessed?' The relief on Cass's face was obvious.

Grella hissed angrily.

'Confess to something I did not do? Take me as a prisoner to the abbey. Salbach will free me – one way or the other!'

'Don't count on it,' smiled Cass without humour.

They returned together to Ros Ailithir. Fidelma led the way while Cass rode close beside Sister Grella. Fidelma was quiet during the short ride, deep in thought. There was something nagging at her. If Sister Grella was being truthful then she was no nearer to Dacán's killer than before. She had not even proved the link between Salbach and Intat. Even if Grella had killed Dacán, betrayed her soul-friend Eisten, could she have also killed her? And where were the sons of Illan? Why had Dacán been so sure that there was an heir at the age of choice? Where were these boys called 'Primus' and 'Victor' . . . ? 'Victor' and 'Primus' . . . 'Primus' . . .

Chapter Sixteen

Victor!

That was the name which kept troubling Fidelma; it had been tumbling around in her mind since Sceilig Mhichil. The images of the two black-haired boys from Rae na Scríne were also in her mind's eye. But the sons of Illan had been described as copper-haired. Yet the name, the name Victor . . . *Hic est meum. Victor.* Didn't the name mean 'triumphant' and 'victorious' and wasn't the equivalent in Irish – Cosrach?

She suddenly gasped at the ease of the solution to the conundrum. The sons of Illan had been called Primus and Victor. Primus meant 'first' and wasn't Cétach just a pet form of *cét* which also meant 'first'? Cétach bore the name of a son of the legendary prince who founded the kingdom of Osraige. Primus – Cétach. Victor – Cosrach! Although the two boys had vanished, surely the other children from Rae na Scríne might be able to identify or describe the religieux who had brought them to Sister Eisten for safekeeping.

She halted her horse abruptly causing, a startled Cass to draw rein lest his steed collide with her. Sister Grella's mount, almost impacting with his, shied and nearly stumbled.

Fidelma cursed softly under her breath, blaming herself for a fool that she had not seen that simple solution before.

'What is it?' Cass demanded, a hand snaking to his sword hilt, looking around as if expecting an attack from an unseen enemy.

'An idea!' she replied happily. She knew now whom Dacán had been searching for and why Cétach had been so afraid of Salbach. It must have been Cétach and Cosrach whom Intat had been sent to kill when he set fire to Rae na Scríne.

'Only an idea? I thought there was danger,' Cass complained in annoyance.

'There is nothing more dangerous than an idea, Cass,' laughed Fidelma, intoxicated with the simple logic of her conclusion. 'A single idea, if it is right, saves us years of laborious experience, the harsh learning of trial and error.'

Cass glanced around nervously.

'Ideas may not threaten our lives with swords and arrows.'

Fidelma chuckled dryly, still happy with her thoughts.

'They may be more harmful than that. Come on.'

Without further explanation, she urged her horse to break into a canter along the trail leading down into Ros Ailithir.

Brother Conghus met them at the gate and, as they arrived, the abbot himself came hurrying up.

'Sister Grella!' he gasped, looking from Grella to Fidelma in astonishment. 'You have captured the culprit, cousin?'

Fidelma, to Cass's surprise, made no effort to dismount. She leant forward across the pommel of her saddle and spoke quietly to her cousin.

'Grella is to be held securely on my authority. She has much to answer for before the assembly of the High King when it meets here. What she wants to tell you as an explanation for her disappearance is entirely up to her.'

Abbot Brocc looked anxiously.

'Does this mean that you have reached a conclusion?' He glanced across his shoulder at the abbey with an almost conspiratorial air. 'The High King and his retinue have already arrived. Barrán, the Chief Brehon, has been asking about you and . . .'

Fidelma held up a hand to silence the worried abbot.

'I can say no more at this time. We will return as soon as possible.'

'Return? Where are you going?' Brocc's voice was almost a wail as Fidelma urged her horse away from the abbey gates.

'Guard Sister Grella well, if for nothing less than her own safety,' Fidelma called across her shoulder.

Cass, his face showing that he was equally as perplexed as the abbot, urged his horse after her.

'If you cannot tell the abbot, sister,' he complained, after he had caught up with her, 'perhaps you can tell me? Where are we going now?'

'I need to find the orphanage where the children from Rae na Scríne were taken,' she replied. 'I know it lies along this coast to the east.'

'You mean the place run by Brother Molua?'

'Do you know it?' She was surprised.

'I know of it,' Cass asserted. 'I spoke to Brother Martan about it. It should not be too difficult to find. It lies about ten miles to the east of here along the coast near a tidal estuary. But why do you want to go to this orphanage? What knowledge can we pick up there?'

'Oh, Cass!' muttered Fidelma, 'if I knew that, I would not need to go!'

Cass shrugged helplessly but followed as Fidelma urged her horse along the highway.

It proved, as Cass said, not more than ten miles across a broad headland. There were several stone and timber buildings which rose above the mud banks of a large tidal estuary into which a river pushed sedately from the mountains to the north. They had to cross the river at a narrow ford which led to the cluster of buildings which, Fidelma noticed as she grew nearer, were surrounded by a wooden fencing. A broad-shouldered man met them at the gates. He wore the clothes of a forest worker but Fidelma noticed the crucifix which hung around his muscular neck.

'*Bene vobis*, my friends,' he called out as they halted their horses before him. He had a loud baritone voice, full of joviality, and a smiling face to match it.

'And health to you,' replied Fidelma. 'Are you Brother Molua?'

'My given name is Lugaid being named after Lugaid Loígde, the progenitor of the Corco Loígde. But as it is such a distinguished name, sister, why, I merely answer to its more gentle diminutive. Molua suits me better. How may I serve you?'

Fidelma slid from her horse and introduced herself and Cass.

'It is not often that we have such distinguished visitors,' the big man said. 'An advocate of the court and a warrior of the king of Cashel's élite. Come, let me first stable your horses and then, perhaps, you will allow my house to offer you hospitality after your journey?'

Fidelma did not protest as the man insisted on leading off their horses to a stable. She gazed about the small complex of buildings with interest. There were several children playing around what was a chapel, in fact no bigger than an oratory. An elderly religieuse was sitting under a tree further on with half a dozen children round her. She was playing a small wooden reed pipe, a *cuisech*, and she played it well, so Fidelma thought. The sister seemed to be teaching the children short airs, happy and joyful.

Brother Molua returned smiling.

'This is a peaceful spot, brother,' Fidelma observed approvingly.

'I am content with it, sister,' agreed Molua. 'Come this way. Aíbnat!'

A round-faced, homely woman came to the door of one of the buildings. She seemed to share Molua's bluff, smiling features.

'Aíbnat, we have guests. This is my radiant wife, Aíbnat.'

Fidelma saw that Molua was possessed of a sense of humour for the meaning of the woman's name was 'radiant girl'.

'I heard that you were both at Ros Ailithir,' the woman greeted them. 'Were you not there to investigate old Dacán's death?'

Fidelma nodded affirmatively.

'Enough time to talk when our guests have eaten, Aíbnat,' chided Molua as he ushered them all into the building. They found themselves in a warm chamber in which an oven threw out heat. On it were great pots simmering with aromatic ingredients. Molua motioned them to be seated at a table and produced a pitcher and several pottery goblets.

'Let me offer you some of my special *cuirm* to keep out the chill. I distil it myself,' he added with pride.

Cass readily agreed while Fidelma gazed approvingly around at the kitchen.

'How many do you have to feed here?' she asked, interested in the large number of cooking pots.

It was Aíbnat who replied.

'At the moment we have twenty children under the age of fourteen here, sister. And there are four of us to look after them. My husband, myself and two other sisters of the Faith.'

Molua poured the drinks and they sipped the rough but pleasant-tasting spirit with relish.

'How long has this orphanage been here?' asked Cass.

'Since the first devastations of the Yellow Plague two years ago. Some communities were so badly hit that entire families were wiped out and there was no one to care for the children who remained,' explained Aíbnat. 'That was when my husband sought permission of the Abbot Brocc at Ros Ailithir to turn his small farmstead here into a place of refuge for the orphans.'

'You seem to be succeeding very well,' Fidelma approved.

'Will you eat, after your journey?' invited Molua.

'We are hungry,' acknowledged Cass, for they had not eaten since that morning.

'But it lacks several hours before your evening meal,' Fidelma pointed out, with a sharp, reproving look at the young warrior.

'That's of little consequence,' smiled Aíbnat. 'A plate of cold badger meat or . . . I know . . . I have a meat pudding, the meat of the sheep, cooked with rowan berries and wild garlic. That complemented by kale and onions and barley bread. Then a dish of sloes and honey to finish with. What would you say to that?'

Molua was smiling happily.

'My wife has a reputation as the best cook of the Corco Loígde.'

'A well-deserved one if the choice of food is anything to go by,' applauded Cass.

Aíbnat was blushing with pleasure.

'We have hives here, so the honey is our own.'

'I had noticed that you have an abundance of beeswax candles,' Fidelma observed. In many poorer homes the usual form of candlewax was often meat grease or melted tallow into which a peeled rush had been dipped.

'Now while Aíbnat prepares the food,' Molua said, sitting down and refilling their goblets from the pitcher of mead, 'you may tell me why my poor house has been so honoured by your presence.'

'A week ago Aíbnat brought some children here.'

'Yes. Two little girls, no more than nine, and a boy about eight years old,' agreed Molua.

Aíbnat turned from her culinary preparations, frowning.

'Yes. They were the children rescued from Rae na Scríne. Didn't you have something to do with that?'

Cass smiled grimly.

'Indeed. We were the ones who rescued them.'

Molua was shaking his head.

'We heard of that terrible crime. It is beyond understanding that people can be so cruel to their neighbours in time of distress. Such injustice has been condemned by everyone.'

Fidelma could not help airing her cynicism.

'It was Plato who wrote that mankind always censures injustice but only because they fear to become victims of it and not because they shrink from committing it.'

Molua's face was sad.

'I cannot believe that, sister. I do not believe that man sets out purposely to commit injustice. He always does it because he is blinded by some distorted image of a perceived morality, or of a just cause.'

'What morality or just cause, however distorted, could have been raised at Rae na Scríne?' demanded Cass.

Molua shrugged.

'I am but a simple farmer. When I cultivate a field, turning it with my plough, I destroy life. I destroy the natural grasses and growths in that field. I destroy the natural habitats of field voles, of badgers and other creatures. To them, that is injustice. To me, it is a just cause – the cause of feeding starving people.'

'Animals!' Cass muttered. 'Who is concerned about justice for animals?'

Molua looked pained.

'Are they not also God's creatures?'

'I see the point that you are making, Molua,' Fidelma intervened. 'In intellectual discourse, we would doubtless agree. There was a reason why the deed was done at Rae na Scríne but whether the reason was thought justifiable the action is not and cannot be.'

Molua inclined his head.

'I accept that.'

'Very well. There were two boys named Cétach and Cosrach, also from Rae na Scríne, who were supposed to be brought to this orphanage. But they disappeared. One was about ten and the other was older – perhaps fifteen. They had black hair.'

Aíbnat and Molua exchanged a look and both shook their heads.

'No children answering those descriptions have turned up here.'

'No. I did not think they would. But perhaps I might be allowed to question the other children?' pressed Fidelma. 'They might know some details about these boys.'

Aíbnat frowned slightly.

'I would not like the children to be upset. Remembering that terrible event may unsettle them.'

Fidelma tried to be reassuring.

'I would not ask these questions if it were not important. I cannot guarantee that they will not get upset. Nevertheless, I must insist in this matter.'

Molua nodded slowly.

'She has the right,' he explained to his wife. 'She is a *dálaigh* of the courts.'

Aíbnat looked unpersuaded.

'Then let me be with them when you ask these questions, sister.'

'Of course,' Fidelma agreed readily. 'Let us go now and speak with them, just the two of us. Then they will not be intimidated.'

'All right,' agreed Aíbnat, glancing at Molua. 'You can finish preparing the food for our guests while we do so,' she instructed.

Aíbnat led the way to the small chapel and called to the children playing there. At her call, two little girls and a sulky-looking boy detached themselves reluctantly from the throng of playing, shouting children. Fidelma could barely recognise them as the terrified children she had found among the ashes and ruins of Rae na Scríne. They came clustering round the skirts of Aíbnat and she led them towards a more isolated part of the compound where a felled tree provided a great seat by a small, gushing stream which ran through the settlement to join the bigger river beyond.

'Sit down, children,' instructed Aíbnat, as she and Fidelma seated themselves on the log.

The boy refused, continuing to stand and kick sullenly at the log. Fidelma noticed that the boy had a little wooden toy sword in his belt. The two little girls immediately sat cross-legged on the grass before them and stared up expectantly.

'Do you recognise this lady?' inquired Aíbnat.

'Yes, she is the lady who took us away so the wicked men would not find us,' replied one of the little girls solemnly.

'Where is Sister Eisten?' chimed in the other. 'When is she going to visit us?'

'Soon.' Fidelma smiled vaguely, after Aíbnat had shot her a warning glance, shaking her head slightly. The children had clearly not been told what had happened to Eisten. 'Now there are some questions I want to ask. I want you all to think carefully about them before you answer. Will you do that?'

The two girls nodded seriously but the boy said nothing, scowling at the log and not meeting Fidelma's smiling gaze.

'Do you remember the other two boys who were with you when I found you?'

'I remember the baby,' said one of the little girls gravely. Fidelma recalled that her name was Cera. 'It went asleep and no one could wake it.'

Fidelma bit her lip.

'That's right,' she said encouragingly, 'but it is the boys that I am interested in.'

'They wouldn't play with us. Mean, spiteful boys! I didn't like them.' The other little girl, Ciar, set her face sternly and sat with folded arms.

'Were they mean, those boys?' pressed Fidelma eagerly. 'Who were they?'

'Just boys,' replied Ciar petulantly. 'Boys are all the same.'

She gave a look of derision towards the little boy who ceased kicking at the log and sat down abruptly.

'Girls!' he sneered back.

'Remind me what your name is,' Fidelma encouraged with a smile. She had recalled the girls' names but she could not remember what the boy had been called.

'Shan't say!' snapped the boy.

Aíbnat clucked her tongue in disapproval.

'His name is Tressach,' she supplied.

Fidelma continued to smile at the boy.

'Tressach? That name means "fierce and war-like". Are you fierce and war-like?'

The boy scowled and said nothing.

Fidelma forced her smile to broaden.

'Ah,' she said, with a little sarcasm, 'perhaps I misheard the name. Was it Tressach or Tassach? Tassach means idle, lazy, one who can't be bothered to speak. Tassach sounds more like you, doesn't it?'

The boy flushed indignantly.

'My name is Tressach!' he grunted. 'I'm fierce and war-like. See, I already have my warrior's sword.'

He drew the carved toy sword from his belt and held it up for her inspection.

'That is a fearsome weapon, indeed,' Fidelma replied, attempting to sound solemn though her eyes were dancing with merriment. 'And if you are, indeed, a warrior then you will know that warriors have to obey a code of honour. Do you know that?'

The boy stared at her in uncertainty, replacing the sword in his belt.

'What code?' he demanded suspiciously.

'You are a warrior, aren't you?' pressed Fidelma.

The boy nodded emphatically.

'Then a warrior is sworn to tell the truth. He has to be

helpful. Now if I ask you about the boys named Cétach and Cosrach, you must tell me what you know. It is the code of honour. You were obviously named Tressach because you are a warrior and bound by that code.'

The boy sat still seeming to ponder this and at last he smiled at Fidelma.

'I will tell.'

She breathed a sigh of relief.

'Did you know Cétach and Cosrach well?'

Tressach grimaced.

'They wouldn't play with any of us.'

'Any of you?' queried Fidelma, frowning.

'Any of the children in the village,' supplied Ciar. 'Boys!'

Tressach turned on her angrily but Fidelma interrupted.

'Didn't they come from the village?'

Tressach shook his head.

'They only came to our village a few weeks ago to live with Sister Eisten.'

'Were they orphans?' demanded Fidelma eagerly.

The boy looked blankly at her.

'Did they have a mother or father?' pressed Fidelma.

'I think they had a father,' the little girl named Cera chimed in.

'Why so, darling?' prompted Fidelma.

'She means that old, old man who used to come to the village to see them,' supplied the boy.

'An old man?'

'Yes. The old man who brought those mean boys to Sister Eisten's house in the first place.'

Fidelma leant forward eagerly.

'When was this, darling?'

'Oh, weeks ago.'

'What did he look like?'

'He had a cross, like the one you're wearing, around his neck,' Cera gave a look of triumph towards Tressach.

The boy grimaced in annoyance at her.

'Who was he?' Fidelma did not really expect the children to answer the question.

'He was a great scholar from Ros Ailithir,' announced Tressach with an air of complacence.

Fidelma was astonished.

'How do you know this?' she asked.

''Cos Cosrach told me when I asked. Then his brother came up and told me to shut up and go away and if I told anyone about his *aite* he would hit me.'

'His *aite*? He used that word?'

'I'm not making it up!' sniffed the boy petulantly.

Fidelma knew that the term of endearment, *aite*, was an intimate form of address for a father. But because, for centuries, young children in the five kingdoms of Éireann had been sent away for fosterage, to gain their education, the intimate words for 'father' and 'mother' were often transferred to the foster-parents, so that the foster-mother would be addressed as '*muimme*' and the father as '*aite*'.

'No, of course you are not making it up,' Fidelma reassured him, many thoughts racing through her mind. 'I believe you. And how would you describe this man?'

'He was nice looking,' supplied Ciar. 'He would not have hit us. He was always smiling at everyone.'

'He looked like an old wizard!' declaimed Tressach, not to be outdone.

'He was not! He was a jolly old man,' chimed in Cera, evidently fed up with being left out of the conversation for more than her fair share of time. 'He used to tell us about the herbs and flowers and what they were good for.'

'And this jolly old man came to visit Cétach and Cosrach often?'

'A few times. He visited Sister Eisten,' Ciar corrected. 'And it was me he told about herbs,' she added. 'He told me about, about . . .'

'He told everybody,' replied Tressach scornfully. 'And those boys were living at Sister Eisten's house, so visiting them was the same thing as visiting Sister Eisten! There!'

He stuck out his tongue at the little girl.

'Boys!' sneered Ciar. 'Anyway, sometimes he brought another sister with him. But she was strange. She was not really like a sister!'

'Girls are so stupid!' grunted the young boy. 'She was dressed like a sister.'

Sister Aíbnat caught Fidelma's eye. She obviously felt that the questioning had continued long enough.

Fidelma held up a hand to prevent the argument developing.

'All right now. Just one more thing . . . are you sure the man came from Ros Ailithir?'

Tressach nodded vehemently.

'That's what Cosrach told me when his brother threatened to punch me.'

'And this sister who accompanied him? Can you describe her? What was she like?'

The boy shrugged disinterestedly.

'Just like a sister.'

The children seemed to lose interest now and scampered away in the direction of the sister who was playing the reed pipe.

Fidelma, deep in thought, accompanied Aíbnat back to where Molua had laid the table for their meal. Aíbnat seemed totally bewildered by the conversation but did not question Fidelma further on the matter. Fidelma welcomed the silence as she turned the facts over in her mind. As they entered, Cass looked up and examined Fidelma's perplexed expression.

'Did you get the information you want?' he asked brightly.

Fidelma laughed dryly.

'I do not know what information I wanted,' she responded. 'But I have gathered another stone to build my cairn of knowledge. Yet one which does not make sense at the moment. No sense at all.'

The meal which Aíbnat and Molua provided was comparable to the feasts that Fidelma had enjoyed in many a feasting hall of kings. She had to force herself to eat sparingly for she realised that it was a ten-mile ride back to Ros Ailithir and riding on a full stomach was not good for the body. Cass, on the other hand, gave himself unchecked to the meal and accepted more of the heady *cuirm* spirit.

Aíbnat quietly attended to their wants while her husband excused himself and disappeared to look after some mysterious errand.

When Molua brought out their horses, they found that the big farmer had watered, fed and groomed the animals.

Fidelma thanked both Aíbnat and Molua profusely for their hospitality and swung into the saddle.

Fidelma gave their erstwhile hosts a blessing and they began to turn their path back towards Ros Ailithir.

'What did you learn, Fidelma?' demanded Cass, once they were out of earshot, crossing the river's ford and ascending across the wooded hills which crowned the large headland.

'I found out, Cass, that Cétach and Cosrach were taken to Rae na Scríne just a few weeks ago to live with Sister Eisten. They are . . .' she paused to correct herself, 'They were the sons of Illan.'

'But the brother at Sceilig Mhichil said that Illan's sons had copper-coloured hair, like the little girls.'

'Anyone can dye hair,' observed Fidelma. 'Moreover, they were several times visited by someone from Ros Ailithir. Cosrach boasted to the boy Tressach that the man was a scholar. That someone Cétach and Cosrach called *aite*!'

Cass looked amazed.

'But if this person was their father then they were not the sons of Illan. Illan was killed a year ago.'

'*Aite* can also mean foster-father,' Fidelma pointed out.

'Perhaps,' Cass said reluctantly. 'But what does it mean and how does it fit the puzzle of this murder?'

'It would be no puzzle if I knew,' Fidelma reproved. 'The man was sometimes accompanied by one of the sisters. There is a path here which leads to Intat! And we know that Intat is Salbach's man. There is a circle here if only we could find a way of entering it.'

She lapsed into a thoughtful silence.

They had gone over a mile, perhaps not more than two miles, when, topping a rise, Cass glanced over his shoulder and exclaimed in surprise.

'What is it?' cried Fidelma, swinging round in her saddle to follow his gaze.

Cass did not have to reply.

A tall, black column of smoke was rising into the pale-blue, cold autumnal sky behind them.

'That's coming from the direction of Molua's place, surely?' Fidelma said, her heart beginning to beat fast.

Cass stood in his stirrups and seized the overhanging branch of a tree, hauling himself up into the topmost branches with an agility which surprised Fidelma.

'What do you see?' she cried, peering up into the dangerously swaying branches.

'It is Molua's place. It must be on fire.'

Cass scrambled down the tree and jumped to the ground, a pile of early fallen leaves breaking his drop. He brushed himself down and grabbed the reins of his horse.

'I don't understand it. It's a big fire.'

Fidelma bit her lip, almost causing blood to flow as a terrible idea grew in her mind.

'We must go back!' she shouted, turning her horse.

'But we must be careful,' warned Cass. 'Let the incident at Rae na Scríne serve us as a warning.'

'That is precisely what I fear!' cried Fidelma, and she was already racing her horse back towards the column of smoke.

Cass had to urge his horse to its utmost stride to keep place with her. Although he knew that Fidelma was of the Eóganacht and brother to Colgú, who was now his king, Cass was always surprised that a religieuse could ride so well as Fidelma did. It seemed that she had been born in the saddle; that she was at one with her horse. She nursed it with dexterity as it thundered along the trail they had only recently traversed.

It was not long before they came over the brow of the hill and saw the great muddy estuary spread before them.

'Halt!' yelled Cass, pulling rein. 'Behind those trees, quickly!'

He was thankful that for once Fidelma did not question him but obeyed his orders immediately.

They drew up behind the cover of a copse of amber-yellow leafed aspens with a surrounding dense thicket.

'What did you see?' Fidelma commanded.

Cass simply pointed down the hill.

She narrowed her eyes and saw a band of armed horsemen breaking through the fragile fences which surrounded the small community of Molua and Aíbnat. A squat man sat on his horse before the burning buildings as if surveying the handiwork of his men. There were a dozen of them. They completed their grim business and then went riding away through the trees on the far side of the river. The squat rider, who was obviously their leader, turned with a final glance at the burning buildings and galloped after them.

Fidelma suddenly gave vent to a cry of impotent rage. She had heard Salbach say, as he rode away from the cabin in the forest, 'I know where they might be . . . I'll give you my instructions for Intat.' She had heard and not understood. She should have realised. She could have prevented . . . At the back of her raging mind a voice told her it was the second major mistake she had made.

'We must get down there!' cried Fidelma in fury. 'They may be hurt.'

'Wait a moment,' snapped Cass. 'Wait for the assassins to leave.'

His face was grey, his jaw was tight set, the muscles clenched. He already knew what they were bound to find in the inferno that was the once the prosperous farm settlement.

However, Fidelma was already urging her horse from the cover and racing down the hill.

Cass gave a cry after her but, realising that she would not obey, even though there might be danger from the attackers, he drew his sword and urged his horse after her.

She galloped down the hill, splashing through the ford at speed and tore to a halt in front of the buildings.

She flung herself from the saddle and, raising an arm, to protect herself from the fierceness of the heat, she ran forward towards the burning buildings.

The first bodies that she saw, sprawled by the entrance, were those of Aíbnat and Molua. An arrow had transfixed Aíbnat's breast while Molua's head was almost severed by a sweeping sword cut. They were quite obviously beyond help.

She saw the first child's body nearby and a cry stifled in her throat. She was aware that Cass had ridden up and dismounted behind her. He still had his drawn sword in hand and he stared about him impassively but with horror mirrored in his eyes.

One of the two sisters who had been helping Sister Aíbnat to take care of the children was slumped against the chapel door. Fidelma realised in revulsion that she was held there by a spear which had been run through her body to transfix her to the wooden door. Half a dozen little bodies were clustered at her feet, some of the children's hands still clinging to her skirts. Each one of the children had been stabbed or had their tiny skulls shattered by blows.

Fidelma held an overwhelming urge to be sick. She turned aside and could not quell the bile that rose to her throat.

'I . . . I am sorry,' she mumbled as she felt Cass's comforting arm on her shoulders.

He said nothing. There was nothing one could say.

Fidelma had seen violent death many times in her life but she had seen nothing so heartrending, so poignant as these dead little bodies who, a few moments ago, she had seen happy and laughing, singing and playing together.

She attempted to quell her loathing, pull herself together and move on.

There was the body of the other sister of the Faith who had been playing the pipes, lying still under the same tree where Fidelma had seen her, the pipes now broken in two and lying near her outstretched and lifeless hand, obviously crushed by the foot of some maniacal assassin. There were more bodies of children near her.

The buildings were burning fiercely now.

'Cass.' Fidelma had to force the words, through the tears and heartache she felt. 'Cass, we must count the bodies. I want to know if the children from Rae na Scríne are among them . . . whether everyone is accounted for.'

Cass signalled his acknowledgment.

'The little boy certainly is,' he said quietly. 'He lies just over there. I'll look for the girls.'

Fidelma went forward to where Cass had indicated and found the twisted body of Tressach. His head had been cleaved with one blow. Yet he lay as if asleep, a hand carelessly flung out before him with the other still held tightly to his wooden sword.

'Poor little warrior,' muttered Fidelma, kneeling down and letting her slim hand stroke the fair hair of the child.

Cass appeared after a while. His face was even more grim than ever.

Fidelma raised her eyes to his.

His expression was enough.

'Where are they?'

The warrior jerked his thumb behind him.

Fidelma rose and went round the corner of the chapel. The two little copper-haired girls, Cera and Ciar, were clasped in one another's arms, as if trying to protect each other from the cruel fate which crushed both their skulls without any compassion.

White-faced, Fidelma stood and stared at the once idyllic farmstead which Aíbnat and Molua had given over to the purposes of an orphanage.

Tears gathered in her eyes and trickled down her cheeks.

'Twenty children, three women religieuses, including Sister Aíbnat, and Brother Molua,' reported Cass. 'All dead. This is senseless!'

'Evil,' agreed Fidelma vehemently. 'But we will find some twisted sense behind it.'

'We should get back to Ros Ailithir, Fidelma.' Cass was clearly worried. 'We dare not tarry in case that barbaric horde returns.'

Fidelma knew that he was right but she could not resist carrying the body of little Tressach over to the side of the chapel so that he could be with the two little girls from Rae na Scríne. There she said a prayer over them and then she turned and said a prayer for all who had met their deaths at Molua's farm.

At the gate she paused and gazed down at Molua's body.

'Was there a just cause in the minds of the people who perpetrated this infamy?' she whispered. 'Poor Molua. We will never discuss philosophy now. Were you just animals to be driven out from the land under some terrible plough-share working for some mysterious greater good?'

'Fidelma!' Cass's voice was fearful but his fear was for her safety alone. 'We should leave now!'

She clambered back on her horse while he mounted his and they cantered away from that place of death.

'I cannot believe that there are such barbarous people in

this land,' Cass said as they paused on the top of the hill and gazed back to the burning settlement.

'Barbarous!' Fidelma's voice was a whiplash. 'I tell you, Cass, that this is evil. There is a terrible evil at work here and I swear by those tiny, mangled remains down there that I shall not rest until I have rooted it out.'

Cass shivered at the vehemence in her voice.

Chapter Seventeen

'Where to now, sister?' Cass demanded as Fidelma, instead of turning her horse along the track that led to the abbey of Ros Ailithir, continued westward.

'Back to Salbach's fortress,' Fidelma replied, tight-mouthed. 'We shall confront him with this atrocity.'

Cass looked troubled.

'This might be a dangerous course, sister. You say that Intat is Salbach's man. If so, then Salbach himself has ordered this crime.'

'Salbach is still chieftain of the Corco Loígde. He would not dare harm a *dálaigh* of the courts and sister of his king!'

Cass did not respond. He did not point out to the angry young woman that if Salbach had sanctioned Intat's violence then that same violence proved that he had forgotten his honour and oath of chieftainship. If he was involved, and could condone the slaughter of innocent children and religious, he would not hesitate to harm anyone else who threatened him. Only after they had continued for a while along the path to Cuan Dóir did Cass venture to suggest: 'Wouldn't it be better to wait until your brother, Colgú, arrives with his bodyguard and then question Salbach from a position of strength?'

Fidelma did not bother to grace the question with an answer. At that moment, her mind was too filled with anger and a determination to track down Intat. If Salbach stood behind Intat, then he, too, must fall. She allowed anger to blind her to logic and in her anger she was not prepared to pause and reflect.

Cuan Dóir seemed as peaceful as ever as they rode directly up to the entrance of Salbach's fortress. It seemed impossible that a short ride away an entire farmstead and over twenty people, adults and children, had just been massacred.

The same disinterested warrior, still standing nonchalantly leaning against the gatepost, was keeping guard. Once more he denied that Salbach was in the fortress but this time he gave a knowing wink at Fidelma.

'He is probably out hunting in the woods again, sister.'

Fidelma restrained her bubbling anger.

'Know me, warrior, for a *dálaigh* of the courts,' she said tightly. 'Know me also for the sister of Colgú, king of Cashel.'

The warrior stirred uneasily and shifted his stance into one of respectful attention.

'That information does not change my answer, sister,' he replied defensively. 'You may dismount and explore the halls of Cuan Dóir yourself but you will not find Salbach. He was here for a while earlier but rode back towards the forest of Dór again.'

'When was this?' demanded Cass.

'No more than a few minutes ago. I presume he had an assignation in the woodsman's hut. But that is all I know.'

Fidelma dug her heels into the sides of her horse, signalling Cass to follow.

'Back to the woodsman's cabin?' called Cass as they cantered along the track.

'We will start there first,' agreed Fidelma. 'Salbach obviously went back to find Grella.'

They cantered swiftly along the path, northwards to the woods, crossing the river at the ford and turning along the bank towards the small cabin in the forest clearing. It did not take them long. Fidelma, this time, made no pretence of hiding herself. She rode straight towards the cabin and halted in front of it.

'Salbach of the Corco Loígde! Are you in there?' she cried, without dismounting. She did not think that there would be an answer for there was no sign of Salbach's horse.

A silence greeted them.

Cass swung off his horse and taking out his sword moved cautiously to the cabin. He pushed open the door and disappeared inside.

After a moment he returned, sword in hand.

'There is no sign of anyone,' Cass reported in annoyance. 'What now?'

'Let us looked around the cabin,' Fidelma replied. 'There might be something which may suggest where else we can look for Salbach.'

Fidelma dismounted. They hitched their horses to the rail and went into the cabin.

It was deserted as Cass had said. It was left exactly as it had been when they had taken Grella from it.

'I doubt that Salbach will be far away,' muttered Fidelma. 'If he has reasoned out that we have taken Grella, and he cares that much about her, he may have gone to the abbey to demand her release.'

Cass was about to reply when they heard the clatter of horses' hooves resounding outside the cabin. Cass started for the door but before he could reach it it had burst open.

A large, red-faced individual, clad in a steel helmet and woollen cloak edged in fur, wearing a gold chain of office and with his sword drawn, stood in the doorway; behind him were half a dozen warriors. His tiny eyes blazed triumphantly as they fell on Cass and Fidelma.

His image had long been burnt into Fidelma's memory. It was Intat.

'Well now,' he chuckled delightedly, 'if we do not have the mischief-makers. And where is Salbach?'

'Not here, as you can see,' replied Cass evenly.

'Not here?' Intat looked round as if to confirm his statement. 'I told him . . .' he began and then clamped his jaw shut, standing glowering at them from the threshold of the cabin.

'So there is no one here but the two of you?'

Fidelma stood quietly, regarding the man with narrowed eyes.

'As you can see, Intat. Put up your sword. I am a *dálaigh* of the courts and sister to Colgú, your king. Put up your weapons and come with us to Ros Ailithir.'

The red-faced man's eyes widened as if in astonishment. He half turned his head to the men standing behind him outside the cabin.

'Hear this woman?' He laughed sourly. 'She tells us to lay down our arms. Have a care, men, for this slip of a girl is a mighty *dálaigh* of the law as well as a woman of the Faith. Her words will wound and destroy us unless we have a heed.'

His men guffawed at the crude wit of their leader.

Intat turned back to Fidelma and gave a humorous grimace which made his face ugly.

'You have disarmed us, lady. We are your prisoners.'

He made no effort to lower his sword.

'Do you think that you are not accountable for your deeds, Intat?' she asked quietly.

'I am only accountable to my chieftain,' sneered Intat.

'There is a greater authority than your chieftain,' snapped Cass.

'None that I recognise,' returned Intat, turning to him. 'Put down your own weapon, warrior, and you shall not be harmed. That I promise.'

'I have seen how you treat those who are defenceless,' replied Cass with a sneer. 'The people of Rae na Scríne and the little children at Molua's farmstead had no weapons. I have no illusions about the value of your promises.'

Intat gave another loud chuckle, as if amused by the warrior's defiance.

'Then it seems that you have written your own destiny, whelp of Cashel. You had best consult with the good sister and reflect on your fate. Be killed now or surrender and live a while longer. I will let you discuss the matter for a moment or two.'

The red-faced man drew back to his grinning cronies crowding in the doorway.

Cass also moved back a few paces, further into the cabin, still in the ready position, sword held before him.

'Move back behind me, sister,' he instructed quietly, speaking almost out of the side of his mouth in a tone so low that she could hardly hear him. He kept his eyes, gimlet-like, on Intat and his warriors.

'There is no way out,' she whispered in reply. 'Do we surrender?'

'You saw what this man is capable of. Better to die defending ourselves than be slaughtered like sheep.'

'But there are several warriors. I should have listened to you, Cass. We have no means of escaping.'

'One has but not two,' Cass quietly replied. 'Behind me and to the left there is a stair to a loft. There is a window up there. I noticed it a moment or so ago. While I engage them, run for the stairs and get out of the window. Once outside, seize a horse and attempt to reach the sanctuary of the abbey. Intat cannot attack there.'

'I can't leave you, Cass,' Fidelma protested.

'Someone has to try to make it to Ros Ailithir,' Cass replied calmly. 'The High King is already there and you can bring his troops. If you do not do so, then we shall have both perished in vain. I can hold them off for a while. This is our only chance.'

'Hey!'

Intat took a pace forward, his red face grinning with a smile that caused Fidelma to shiver.

'You have spoken enough. Now do you surrender?'

'No, we do not,' replied Cass. Then he suddenly yelled: 'Go!'

The latter word was meant for Fidelma. She turned and leapt for the stairs. Most days she spent time practising the *troid-sciathagid*, the ancient form of unarmed combat, and this physical discipline had made her body supple and well-muscled beneath the seemingly soft exterior. She reached the top of the stairs with easy strides and launched herself, without pausing, for the window, grasping its ledge and hauling itself upwards in a frenzied motion.

Below her, in the cabin, she could hear metal clashing against metal and the terrible animal cry of men intent on killing each other.

Something struck the wall nearby. She realised it was an arrow. Another shaft grazed her forearm as she hauled herself over the bottom ledge of the window.

She paused a second, fighting an impulse to peer back. Then she hung her full length from the window ledge and dropped onto the soft, muddy ground behind the cabin. She landed almost as agilely as a cat, crouching on all fours. She was up and running in a split second; around the cabin to the front of it where the horses had been left. As well as the horses belonging to her and Cass, there were three other horses belonging to Intat and his men who were crowding in through the door of the cabin from where she could hear the sounds of combat.

She increased her pace for the nearest horse.

Out of the corner of her eye she saw one of Intat's men disengage himself from the mêlée at the door of the cabin and turn in her direction. He saw her and gave a cry of rage. Another man turned as well. Instead of a sword, like his companion, he was armed with a bow and already he was trying to fix an arrow to it. The first man came on towards her with hesitation, his sword raised.

Fidelma realised that she could not reach the horse before her attacker, so she halted, spun around to face his charge, quickly positioning her feet into a firm position.

The last time Fidelma had practised the *troid-sciathagid* in earnest had been against a giant of a woman in a Roman brothel. She hoped that she had not lost her skill. She let the man run in upon her, ducking and grabbing at his belt, using his forward momentum to pull the surprised ruffian over her shoulder.

With a cry of astonishment, the man went flailing head first and crashed into a nearby wooden barrel, splitting it with the impact of his head so that the water gushed into a spurt.

Fidelma rose quickly to her feet, ducking as she heard the twang of a bow string and felt the breath of an arrow in its flight past her cheek. Then she was hauling herself up into the saddle and thumping her heels against the horse's belly. With a startled whinny, the beast sprang forward across the clearing and into the woods.

She was aware of renewed cries behind her and she knew that at least one of Intat's men had mounted up and was in pursuit of her. Whether others had joined in, she did not know. She had only identified Intat and three men at the cabin. She did not think that the one she had thrown into the barrel would have been in condition to give chase for a while. And surely Cass was dealing with Intat in person. She had to keep in advance of her pursuer. It would not take her long to reach the abbey.

She took the road for Ros Ailithir through the woodland, praying that the High King would not delay giving the order to his men to accompany her back to the rescue of Cass. She also hoped that her escape would draw Intat away from Cass and give Cass an opportunity to make his own escape as Cass had given her that opportunity.

Now she began to bitterly regret her impetuosity born of rage. She should have taken notice of Cass's advice.

Head low along the neck of her horse, she found herself uttering sharp cries which would have brought a blush to her superior, the Abbess of Kildare, had that pious woman heard her young charge conjuring a rich variety of curses to urge her steed to further efforts.

She glanced back across her shoulder.

There were a couple of riders strung out behind her. She could see the leading pursuer was none other than Intat himself. Her heart went cold. She tried not to think what that signified. There was no question that Intat rode a stronger horse than Fidelma for he was gaining on her with ease.

In desperation, Fidelma turned her horse from the main track, hoping that it might make up across country what it was obviously loosing to its pursuers on the straight track. It was a mistake for, not knowing the crisscross forest paths, she found she was unable to keep up even the speed that she had maintained on the straight track. Intat was gaining. She could hear the pounding hooves of his horse and the deep rasping of its breath.

Suddenly a river barred her progress. It was the same river that ran by the cabin which had twisted round in its course. She had no choice but to plunge straight into it, hoping it was as shallow as it had been by the cabin; hoping that it was shallow enough to ford. It wasn't. She was halfway across when her horse stumbled, lost the bottom and plunged in panic underneath the water. Fidelma tried to cling on but found herself swept off while the animal went careering forward, found the bottom again and stumbled out of the water.

Desperately, Fidelma struck out but Intat was already urging his horse into the water.

He gave a loud shout of triumph.

She turned, saw him coming and struck out again in reckless desperation to reach the far bank. In her heart she realised it was impossible to escape. She splashed through the shallows, stumbled and slipped on the mud bank.

Intat's mount was pawing the air almost above her. The thick-set warrior leapt from the saddle and stood in the shallows above her, both hands clasping the hilt of his sword.

'So, *dálaigh*, you have created enough trouble for me. This is where it ends.'

He raised the sword.

Fidelma flinched, put her arm up in an automatic defensive response and closed her eyes.

She heard Intat grunt sharply and when nothing happened she opened her eyes.

Intat was staring, his eyes unfocused. He was still standing swaying above her. Then slowly he began to sink down. It was then she saw two arrow shafts sticking from his chest. The sword slipped from his hands and he pitched forward on his face into the river before her.

With a cry, more to release her pent-up emotion than as a call for help, she scrambled swiftly up the muddy bank.

She became aware of horses milling around her and swung to face the new threat.

'Fidelma!' cried a familiar voice.

She stared in disbelief as her brother swung down from his mount and came running towards her, arms outstretched.

'Colgú!'

He hugged her violently and then held her at arms' length, concern in his eyes and, observing that she was not harmed, he grinned wryly.

'Where is the sister who said she could take care of herself?'

She blinked back the tears of relief. Across the river some of Colgú's bodyguard had rounded up Intat's other henchman.

'You have arrived not a moment too soon,' she breathed jerkily. 'How was this done?'

Colgú grimaced and gestured towards a nearby band of about thirty mounted men, riding under his banner.

'We are on our way to Ros Ailithir to the assembly called by the High King. My scouts saw you being pursued and we came to intercept you. But where is Cass?' He frowned in annoyance. 'I gave him the charge of protecting you.'

Fidelma was anguished.

'Cass is back at the cabin in the forest there. He tried to keep our attackers at bay while I escaped to get help from Ros Ailithir. We must get back there immediately. He was fighting with Intat.' She indicated the man's body, now floating in the shallows of the river. 'We must be quick, for he may be injured.'

Colgú's face was serious.

'Very well. On the way you will have to tell me what is happening. Who is . . . *was* this man Intat?'

One of Colgú's men had gone forward to drag Intat's body out of the river and was now bending over it.

'The man still lives, my lord,' the warrior called. 'But I doubt for long.'

Fidelma turned and scrambled down on the mud bank to where the warrior was holding the head and shoulders of Intat above the water. She crouched down beside him and took his head in both her hands.

'Intat!' she called loudly. 'Intat!'

The man's eyes flickered open but there was no focusing in his dark eyes.

'You are dying, Intat. Do you wish to due in sin?'

He did not answer.

'Who told you to slaughter the children?'

There was no reply.

'Was it Salbach? Did he tell you?'

She saw his lips beginning to move and she bent forward to hear the wheezy sound of his breath.

'I . . . I'll meet – meet you in . . . *hell*!'

The body suddenly gave a spasmodic jerk and was still. Colgú's man shrugged and glanced at Fidelma.

'Dead,' he said laconically.

Fidelma rose and her brother reached forward a hand to haul her back up the river bank.

'What made you ask about Salbach?' he said with sharp curiosity. 'What is going on?'

'Intat was one of Salbach's chieftains.'

'Was Salbach responsible for this?'

Fidelma pointed to where Intat's companion was being held.

'Have your men question him. I am sure that he may incriminate Salbach in this affair. But let us hasten back now to find Cass.'

Colgú signalled one of his men for a dry cloak and placed it around Fidelma's shoulders. She was shivering with the cold and damp and not a little with the shock of what had happened to her. Colgú helped her back on her horse, giving orders to his men. Then, when they were all mounted, Colgú and his bodyguard turned to cross the ford of the river, with their prisoner. They joined the track into the forest north of Cuan Dóir. On the way, Fidelma explained as much as she could to her brother. Particularly, she spoke of the slaughter of the innocents by Intat at, so she now fully believed, Salbach's instigation.

'How does this fit in with Dacán's murder?' demanded Fidelma's brother.

'I have not worked out every detail but, believe me, there is a connection. And I will argue that connection at the High King's assembly.'

'You know that the assembly will be any day now? In fact, as soon as we arrive at Ros Ailithir. I am told that the High King is already there and Fianamail of Laigin's ships have been sighted off the coast.'

'Brocc has already warned me,' Fidelma acknowledged.

Colgú looked far from happy.

'If you are claiming that Salbach is involved and responsible for Dacán's killing then we might as well acknowledge that Laigin has a just claim to demand an honour price from this kingdom. Salbach is a chieftain of Muman, answerable to Cashel.'

'I am claiming nothing, as yet, brother,' Fidelma replied sharply. 'And it is the truth I seek, whatever that truth is.'

They halted before the now quiet cabin in the forest. The unconscious form of Intat's other henchman still lay sprawled among the fragments of the heavy barrel where Fidelma had thrown him. He was only just beginning to groan and stir into consciousness.

Her heart lurched when she saw Cass's horse still tethered and standing patiently outside the cabin.

Two of Colgú's bodyguard immediately dismounted and, with drawn swords, pushed into the interior of the cabin.

One of them returned to the doorway after a moment with a steely expression on his face.

Fidelma knew just what the interpretation of that expression was.

She slipped from her saddle and hurried inside.

Cass lay on his back. There was one arrow embedded in his heart and another in his neck. His attackers had not even allowed him the honour of a warrior's defence. All he had was his sword but they had shot him down from the doorway. Now he lay with his eyes opened, staring unseeingly upwards.

Fidelma bent down, her face cold and set, and closed the sightless eyes of his once-handsome face.

'He was a good man,' Colgú said softly as he came up behind her and gazed down.

Fidelma's shoulders heaved imperceptibly.

'Good men are so often destroyed by evil,' she muttered. 'I wish he had been alive to see this matter resolved.'

She stood up, both fists clenched tight in her anguish. She turned a sorrowful face to her brother, unable to prevent the tears. An inner voice told her that she had committed her third mistake. Her own vanity had led Cass to his death. She had made three mistakes and now she was allowed no more.

'He died defending me, Colgú,' she said quietly.

Her brother inclined his head.

'I think he would have wanted it that way, little sister. So long as his efforts were not wasted, his soul will be satisfied. His death will not cancel your investigation?' he added anxiously, as the thought occurred to him.

Fidelma's lips compressed for a moment.

'No,' she said firmly, after a moment. 'Death cancels many things but never the triumph of truth. His soul will soon rest easy for I believe that I am near to reaching that truth which has evaded me for so long.'

Chapter Eighteen

Fidelma perched on the top of the bastion, by the walkway which ran around the exterior wall of the abbey, and gazed thoughtfully down into the inlet before Ros Ailithir. The quiet bay had suddenly become a forest of masts and spars rising from countless ships. Warships and coastal *barca* had congregated in the sheltered harbour, like a shoal of fish in a spawning ground, bearing dignitaries from the High King's own royal domains of Meath as well as from Laigin itself. The annalists, who would record the proceedings, had also arrived with the Chief Brehon. There was the ornate vessel which had brought Ultan, Archbishop of Armagh, Chief Apostle of the Faith in the five kingdoms, and his advisors.

Only the representatives of Muman had arrived overland by horse. And it had been a lucky thing for Fidelma that they had. In her life Fidelma had seen and been associated with many violent deaths. Indeed, death seemed a constant companion to her in her profession. Then death was not too far removed from anyone living close to nature and attuned to the realities of life. It was as natural to die as to be born and yet many still feared death. Even that fear was natural, conceded Fidelma, for children often fear to go into the dark and death was an unknown darkness. In spite of her reflections, it did not alleviate her intense sadness at the death of Cass. He had had much to live for, much to learn. She felt a terrible guilt that it had been her stubborn will that had caused his death. Had she listened to his warning not to go rushing into Salbach's lair, he might still have been alive.

She regretted having been so harsh with him in argument and deplored her sin of vanity in that she had prided herself on intellectual superiority. Yet, even now, that small voice in the deep recesses of her mind asked her whether she was sad for Cass or sad for her own mortality. She felt uncomfortable at that insistent little voice. She remembered a line from her Greek lessons, a line from Bacchylides: 'The hardest of deaths to a mortal, is the death they see ahead of them.'

She tried not to dwell on the sadness she felt but attempted to bring her thoughts to the immediate matter in hand, seeking comfort with an axiom of her mentor, the old Brehon Morann of Tara: 'He who is remembered is not dead for to be truly dead you must be forgotten entirely'.

The sun was lowering now across the distant western mountains and tomorrow, at tierce, the bell would summon those concerned to the abbey church where the High King's court would be assembled to hear the claims of Laigin concerning the death of Dacán.

'Sister Fidelma?' She raised her head and found young Sister Necht standing a little way off, regarding her with a solemn face. 'I do not want to disturb you.'

Fidelma indicated the wall beside her.

'Seat yourself. You are not disturbing me. What is it that I can do for you?'

'Firstly, I wanted to tell you that I was sorry to hear of the death of your companion, Cass,' the novice said as she seated herself awkwardly, her voice made deeper by emotion. 'He was a good man. I would have liked to have been a warrior like him.'

Fidelma found herself unable to prevent a gentle smile of amusement on her lips at the concept.

'Surely a vain ambition for a young novice?'

The girl blushed furiously.

'I meant . . .'

'No matter,' Fidelma pacified. 'Forgive me an indelicate humour. It is but a self-defence for my own sadness. You said there was something else?'

The young girl hesitated then nodded.

'I came to bring you some news. Your brother's warriors have captured Salbach and brought him to Ros Ailithir.'

'That is good news, indeed,' confirmed Fidelma with satisfaction.

'Apparently he was found with his cousin in a secret rendezvous.'

'His cousin? Do you mean with Scandlán, the king of Osraige?'

Sister Necht nodded emphatically.

'Have they brought Scandlán here as well?'

'He came of his own accord, crying out that it was an outrage that his brother should be so treated.'

'Has Salbach admitted that Intat acted under his command?'

'That I do not know, sister. Abbot Brocc told me to find you and give you this news. I think that Salbach is refusing to answer any questions. But Brocc asks whether you wish to attempt to question Salbach before the hearing tomorrow.'

Fidelma rose immediately.

'That I do. Where are Brocc and my brother Colgú now?'

'They are in the abbot's chambers,' replied Sister Necht.

'Then I shall find my way there.'

'I am looking forward to the assembly tomorrow,' smiled Necht. 'Good night, sister.'

She turned and hurried away. For a moment or so, Fidelma stood watching her ungainly carriage as Necht made her way into the darkness of the abbey corridors. Some thoughts stirred in her mind, a confusion of ideas which she could not work out. Fidelma shrugged and turned in the direction of Brocc's chambers.

Fidelma knocked and, in reply to Brocc's summons, entered. Her brother was seated where Brocc usually sat. Colgú smiled as his sister came in. Brocc was sharing a jug of wine with him.

'Did Sister Necht find you, cousin?' asked the abbot unnecessarily.

Fidelma inclined her head in an affirmative.

'She told me that you have Salbach in a cell,' she replied. 'That is good.'

'But we also have to put up with his cousin from Osraige crying to the heavens that no such innocence was ever so scandalously defamed.' Colgú grimaced wryly. 'Yet there is now no doubt of Salbach's role in the hideous crimes at Rae na Scríne and the house of Molua. The two companions of Intat were quickly persuaded to place responsibility for their deeds on to others.'

Fidelma raised her eyebrows in anticipation. Her brother nodded his head in confirmation to her unasked question.

'They admitted that they were paid to do what they did by Intat and they further swear that they were witnesses to Intat receiving his instructions from Salbach.'

'This is so,' Brocc added with satisfaction. 'But they disclaim any culpability or knowledge about the murders of Dacán and Eisten. My *scriptor* has already written out their statements for you to read and we will hold them in the abbey ready to testify before the assembly tomorrow.'

Fidelma smiled in relief and took the wax tablets which Brocc handed her, glancing though them quickly.

'We have taken a good stride along the path to a resolution. I wonder if Salbach will admit the truth if I present him with this evidence?'

'It is worth a try,' Colgú agreed.

'Then I shall go and question him at once.'

Colgú rose and moved to the door.

'Then I'd better come with you.' He grinned at his younger sister. 'You need someone to keep an eye on you.'

Salbach stood defiantly in his cell as Sister Fidelma entered. He did not even bother to acknowledge Colgú, who entered with her and stood just inside the door.

'Ah, I thought you would come, Fidelma of Kildare.'

His voice was cold and taunting.

'I am glad that I have fulfilled your expectation, Salbach,' she replied with equal solemnity. 'The High King's assembly meets tomorrow.'

Fidelma took the solitary wooden chair in the cell for herself. Salbach frowned, hesitating at her assured manner, but continued to stand, feet apart, arms folded before him. He said nothing as Fidelma allowed her appraising gaze to wander over him. She felt repulsed by this man who could order the death of children without a qualm.

'Grella must be much besotted by you, Salbach, not to see beyond the mask which you wear for her,' she finally said.

Salbach's expression changed momentarily to one of confusion only to be replaced as quickly by anger and dislike as he returned her scrutiny.

'Are you sure that I wear a mask for her? Are you sure that she is merely intoxicated with the idea of love or can you allow, in your heart, that she can be in love with me and I with her?'

Fidelma grimaced in distaste.

'Love? The emotion is hard to see in your heart. No, I see before me the suffering of little children. There is no room for an emotion such as love in the heart of the person who could order such suffering.'

Nevertheless, Fidelma could see some perversity in the situation. Perhaps Salbach did, after all, feel an infatuation akin to love for the attractive librarian of Ros Ailithir.

'Would you hold me responsible for the deeds of Intat?' Salbach demanded sourly.

'Yes. You might as well know that if you hire men then their loyalty is not to a chieftain but to his money. Intat's own men bear witness to your leadership.'

Salbach was stony-faced.

'And if I say they lie?'

'Then you must prove it before the assembly. That may be difficult. As for myself, I know that these men do not lie just as you know they tell the truth.'

Salbach grinned bitterly.

'Then we will leave it to the decision of the High King's assembly. It will be my word as chieftain of the Corco Loígde. My word and my honour. And now I must keep silent. We will talk no more.'

Fidelma stood up and glanced quickly at her brother. She could see that there was disappointment in his eyes.

'I expected no less, Salbach. We will meet in the court when it assembles tomorrow. But before we do, think well on the matter, for you stand condemned by the men you hired. Let me leave you to meditate the words of Socrates: "false words are not only evil in themselves, but they infect the soul with evil". How infected is your soul, Salbach?'

Outside, Colgú gave vent to his disappointment.

'He does not admit anything. If he does not, what then? Even if you prove his culpability, Laigin may still hold Cashel as responsible?'

'I hope I shall have the final piece of the puzzle fitted into place by the time of the assembly,' replied Fidelma. 'In the meantime, I must get some rest. It will be a long day tomorrow and I have much to consider.'

It was well after the *completa* when Fidelma started awake, still fully dressed and lying on her cot in her darkened chamber where she had fallen asleep. She came awake with one thought clear in her mind; it concerned the uncompleted task that had been nagging at her mind for some days now. She rose and quietly left the hostel.

Fidelma entered the abbey church, which was in total darkness. All the lights had been doused after the last service of the day. She chose not to light a lamp but moved cautiously through the shadows, using the soft light of the moon, casting its pallid light through the tall windows, to illuminate her way. She moved warily towards the High Altar. Making her way around it, she stared down at the shadowy slab of the tomb of the Blessed Fachtna.

She was sure that this was the key to the last piece of the mystery which had been nagging at her mind.

She had been staring at it for several minutes before she realised that something was not quite right. The slab was slightly crooked, at an angle to the back of the altar. She remembered clearly that the slab had originally been at a perfect parallel to the back of the altar.

She dropped to her knees and pushed a little.

To her surprise, the slab moved easily as if on a slide. She stopped when it started to squeak in the darkness and cautiously looked around. She could see nothing in the long shadowy interior of the church.

She moved to the altar and took one of the tall, tallow candles, uttering a swift prayer for forgiveness for her presumption in removing it from God's holy table. Then she moved back to the slab, lit the candle, and placed it on the floor. On her knees again, she began to push at the slab. It moved again and then halted as if meeting an obstruction.

She paused frustrated for a moment but then realised that there must be some hidden mechanism.

She moved to the other side of the slab and began to push it back as though to close it.

That was when the mechanism was revealed to her, for she saw, out of the corner of her eye, the small statue of the cherub, which stood at the head of the slab, moving on its plinth.

With a suppressed exclamation, Fidelma moved quickly across to the figurine, seizing it and starting to twist it in the reverse direction.

It was a lever, a clever means of locomotion, for the more she twisted it the more she felt it pulling some mechanism which in turn propelled the slab sideways away from the entrance to the tomb below. A pair of steps stood revealed by the flickering light of her candle.

Taking up the light, she began carefully to descend the steps into the tomb.

They led into a crypt, dank and musty-smelling.

In all it was no more than twenty feet below the floor of the church. It was a single plain chamber, so far as the light from the candle showed her. It was about thirty feet long and fifteen feet wide. It was built almost as a small scale replica of the large church above, with a raised stone platform at one end which parodied the High Altar. Except, as Fidelma noticed, it was not an altar at all but a stone sarcophagus with a stone slab for a lid. On it were engraved words in Ogham and in the Latin script both in Irish and Latin. It told the reader that Fachtna, son of Mongaig, rested there.

She saw that there were candle-holders in the sepulchre and in curiosity she went to examine them. The grease was not cold although it was not pliable. The candles had certainly been in use and quite recently.

In one corner she suddenly realised that there was a pile of clothes. She went to examine them and also found a bundle of blankets, as if someone was sleeping in the vault. There was also a pitcher of water and a bowl of fruit. On one of the beds her eye caught a piece of vellum.

It took a moment for her to find the missing items from her *marsupium*: Dacán's draft letter to his brother; the burnt Ogham stick and some other items from the library which related to the family of Illan. They were just lying as if discarded.

She smiled grimly.

At last everything was coming together; all the little items of information were beginning to fit and form a pattern. It was a pity that Cass was not here to appreciate the fulfilment of her exhortation to make sure all the fragments were gathered and stored until such time as a pattern emerged.

A noise above her made her start.

Someone was at the High Altar in the church above. They were standing by the open tomb.

She realised that her way back up into the church was now blocked off if she wished to avoid discovery. Whoever it was, they were beginning to descend the stairs into the tomb. She moved quickly towards the sarcophagus, thinking to conceal herself.

Now she could hear voices above her.

'Look at this,' she heard a familiar voice say. 'I thought that I had told you to close the slab when we left?'

A younger voice, she recognised it as Cétach's, answered: 'I thought I had, brother. I was sure I had not left it as wide open as this.'

'No matter. Go down. I shall come and let you out at the usual time. But be absolutely quiet tomorrow for the court will be meeting above you. Not a sound. Remember, you nearly gave the game away during the service last week. One cry and they will find the way down to you. If they do then we shall all rue the day.'

Another child's voice began to sniffle in protest.

The voice of Cétach admonished the whining one, who was surely Cosrach.

'It will not be for long,' Fidelma heard the first voice say in a more cajoling tone. 'Father and I will be able to get you away from this place within the next day or so.'

'Will Father be coming with us?' asked Cétach's voice.

'Yes. We will soon all be home in Osraige.'

Fidelma moved behind the sarcophagus as she heard soft steps begin to descend into the vault. It was pointless confronting the sons of Illan at this time. There were some final links to be put into place before the mystery was completely resolved.

Behind the sarcophagus she was surprised to see a dark opening and instead of dousing her candle, as she had been poised to do, she moved into the darkness. It was a passageway which twisted and turned a few times until it came to a flight of stone steps. They led sharply upwards.

Curiosity led her up until the steps ended about four feet from a rocky ceiling. She thought for a moment that she had come to a dead end but she became aware of a small aperture, two feet in width and three feet high. A faint flickering light came through it. This time she did douse her candle and she saw a pale moonlight. Carefully she leaned through the aperture.

She caught her breath in surprise as she observed what was beyond it.

She was leaning out into a circular well some ten feet below its opening to the sky. She turned her head and saw nearby, in the gloomy light, iron rungs running close by the aperture; close enough for her to reach out and swing herself up onto them. In a few minutes she was clambering over the lip of the well up into the moonlit herb garden behind the back of the abbey's church.

She sat for a moment or two on the edge of the well's circular stone wall, smiling with a genuine satisfaction.

She had all the main pieces now. It was a question of sorting them and fitting them into place.

Time enough to reveal the tangled skein at the assembly in the morning.

Chapter Nineteen

The abbey church itself had been turned into the *Dál*, or court, for the purpose of the High King's great assembly. The building was bursting with people, both religious and others, who spilled through the doors. The occasion was regarded as momentous, for never in the memory of the people had a High King held an assembly outside his personal territory of royal Meath. On a specially constructed dais before the High Altar sat the Chief Brehon of the five kingdoms of Éireann. He was the one person who was so influential that even the High King was not allowed to speak at the great assemblies until he had spoken. Fidelma had never seen Barrán before and she tried to gauge his personality in spite of his ceremonial robes of office which disguised his features. All she could make out were bright, unblinking eyes, a stern, thin-lipped mouth and a prominent nose. He could have been any age at all.

Next to him on the dais, at his left hand, sat his personal *ollamh*, a learned advocate to consult with him on matters of law, then sat a *scriptor* and an assistant to keep the record. On the Chief Brehon's right hand sat the High King himself – Sechnassach, lord of Meath and High King of Ireland. He was a thin man, in his mid-thirties, with scowling features and dark hair. Fidelma knew from her own experience at Tara that Sechnassach was not the stern, authoritarian ruler that he appeared to be. He was a thoughtful man, possessed of a dry sense of humour. She wondered whether he would recall that without her aid, in solving the mystery of the theft of the High

King's ceremonial sword, Sechnassach might never have sat on the throne. Then she felt guilty for allowing such a thought to come to her mind as if some personal bias would influence the High King in her favour.

Next to the High King sat Ultan, Archbishop of Armagh, Chief Apostle of the Faith of the five kingdoms. He was a dour, elderly man, with white, untidy hair. Fidelma knew that Ultan had the reputation of being supportive to the Roman faction and had often favoured the idea that the ecclesiastical laws should displace the civil laws of the five kingdoms.

Directly in front of this impressive gathering of judges was a small lectern which had been set up in the manner of the *cos-na-dála*, the tribune from which each *dálaigh*, or advocate, would plead their case.

On the right-hand side of the High Altar, in the transept, the benches were occupied by the representatives of Laigin with their fiery young king, Fianamail, and his advisors. Fidelma had already picked out the grim, grey-visaged Abbot Noé of Fearna. And she saw that in front, seated next to his king, was the thin, cadaverous Forbassach, who would be presenting the claims of Laigin.

Fidelma's brother Colgú and his advisors filled the benches in the transept on the left-hand side of the High Altar. Fidelma, as their *dálaigh*, sat alongside her brother, awaiting her turn to be called before the *cos-na-dála* to state the case for the kingdom of Cashel.

The rest of the church, along the broad nave, was packed with spectators of every degree and station, filling it with a stuffy, airless atmosphere in spite of the grandeur and sweep of the tall building. Fidelma had noticed several warriors bearing the insignia of the High King; these were his *fianna* or bodyguard. They were stationed at strategic points around the church and were the only armed warriors allowed at the assembly. The warriors of Colgú and Fianamail were confirmed to quarters outside the abbey walls.

The proceedings opened abruptly with Barrán, the Chief Brehon, rapping on the wooden table before him with his staff of office and calling for silence.

The hubbub of the assembly slowly died away and an expectant quiet emerged.

'Be it known that there are three ways to destroy wisdom in a court of law,' intoned the Chief Brehon with the words of the ritual opening. His voice was deep and rich in tone, resounding through the church. His light-coloured eyes glinted as he glared around. 'The first way is a judge without knowledge, the second way is a pleading without understanding and the third way is a talkative court.'

Archbishop Ultan then rose slowly and asked a blessing on the court and its proceedings in his thin, reed-like monotone.

After Ultan had reseated himself, the Chief Brehon called on the advocates of either side to stand and identify themselves. Once they had done so he reminded them of the procedures of the court and of the sixteen signs of bad advocacy. For any one of the sixteen prohibitive aspects, an advocate could be fined one *séd*, a gold coin which was the value of one milch cow. The fine, Barrán reminded them, would be imposed if the advocates abused each other, incited those attending the court to violence, indulged in self-praise, spoke too harshly, refused to obey the orders of the court or shifted the grounds of their pleas without reason. Having accepted that they understood, Barrán indicated that the hearing could begin.

'Remember that there are three doors through which the truth may be recognised in this court: a patient counter-pleading; a firm case; and reliance on witnesses,' Barrán gave the ritual warning to the advocates.

Forbassach moved forward to the *cos-na-dála*, for as Laigin was demanding compensation for a death, it was his right to present the arguments first. He did so simply and without theatrics, merely stating that the Venerable Dacán, a man of Laigin, had been given hospitality by the king of Muman, in that he had been allowed into the kingdom to both study and teach at the abbey of Ros Ailithir. It was the abbot's immediate responsibility to provide for the safety of those he took into his house.

Nonetheless, Dacán had been murdered in a most horrible fashion at Ros Ailithir. No murderer had been found and so the responsibility lay with the abbot and ultimately with the king of Muman. The king was responsible for the safety of Dacán firstly because he had been welcomed into the kingdom and secondly because the abbot was a kinsman and the king was head of his family and responsible for all fines made against that family. That was the law. And that law was specific in terms of culpability. For every death the fine was seven *cumals*, the worth of twenty-one milch cows. That was the basic fine. But what of Dacán's honour price? He was a cousin to the king of Laigin. He was a man of the Faith, whose benevolence and scholarship were known throughout the five kingdoms of Éireann.

When, several centuries before, the High King, Edirsceál of Muman, had been assassinated, the Chief Brehon and his assembly had determined that the honour price of Edirsceál was such that they ordered that the kingdom of Osraige should be handed over to Muman. Now Laigin demanded that Osraige should be handed back to them as the honour price for Dacán.

Fidelma sat through Forbassach's plea with bowed head. There was nothing new in his statement and he had delivered it in a moderate, unemotional and clear fashion which the court could follow with ease.

With a glance of complacent satisfaction in Fidelma's direction, Forbassach returned to his seat. Fidelma saw the young king, Fianamail, leaning forward and smilingly patting his advocate on the shoulder in approval.

'Fidelma of Kildare,' Barrán turned to the Muman benches, 'will you now plead for Muman?'

'No,' she said in a clear voice, causing a ripple of astonishment from the court. 'I am here to plead for truth.'

There was an angry murmuring, especially from the Laigin benches, as Fidelma rose and made her way to the tribune before the Chief Brehon. Barrán was frowning in annoyance at her dramatic opening.

'I trust that you do not imply that we have heard wilful lies before this court?' There was a dangerous coldness in his voice.

'No,' replied Fidelma calmly. 'Nor have we heard the whole truth but only so small an amount that no judgment can be safely made upon its evidence.'

'What is the substance of your counter-plea?'

'It is of two elements, Barrán. Firstly, that the Venerable Dacán was not honest about his activities when he came to Muman. That lack of honesty exonerates both the king and the abbot from their responsibilities under the law of hospitality.'

There was a gasp of indignation from the Laigin benches and she could see, from the corner of her eye, that the Abbot Noé was leaning forward in his seat, white-faced in scarcely controlled anger as he stared at her.

'Secondly,' went on Fidelma unperturbed, 'that if the identity of Dacán's murderer was revealed, and it was found that the murderer was not of the family of the king of Cashel, nor holding allegiance to him, then the advocate of Laigin would have no claim to make against Cashel. That is the substance of my plea.'

Forbassach had stood up.

'I challenge this plea. The first argument is an insult to a compassionate and pious scholar. It accuses a devout man, now unable to defend himself, of lying. The second argument is mere contention and not supported by evidence.'

Barrán's expression was serious.

'You are experienced in the ways of the courts, Sister Fidelma. Therefore I would presume that you do not make these statements without some substantiation?'

'I do not. But I will ask your indulgence as this is a long and complicated story and I will need a little time to unravel it to the court.'

She paused, her expression asking a question of the Chief Brehon. Barrán indicated that she should continue.

'When I was asked to investigate the death of Dacán by my brother, Colgú, I did not realise what a long, tortuous path I had to tread. Not only had Dacán been killed but many others had to perish before I neared the end of that path. Cass, of the king of Cashel's bodyguard, sent by my brother as my companion in this quest; Sister Eisten; many other religious of the house of Molua; and twenty innocent little children. And there were others at Rae na Scríne who have not been accounted.'

Forbassach was on his feet, protesting once again.

'We are here to speak of the murder of Dacán and no others,' he angrily pointed out. 'To raise the matter of other deaths is merely some screen by which Fidelma is attempting to obscure Laigin's case.'

Barrán frowned at Laigin's advocate.

'You will reseat yourself, Forbassach, and with a warning. Did I not recite the sixteen signs of bad advocacy? Wait until the *dálaigh* of Cashel has made her submission and then argue your case. I must point out that she did not interrupt your plea once.'

Forbassach slumped back with annoyance on his features.

'I will continue,' Fidelma went on quietly. 'Truly, this was a complex affair. It has its roots centuries ago in the conflict over the kingdom of Osraige. During the last centuries Laigin have argued many times that Osraige should be returned to its jurisdiction and each time, at their assemblies, the Brehons of the five kingdoms have upheld the initial decision to cede it to Muman.

'At the same time, for the last two hundred years, the people of Osraige have been ruled by kings from the Corco Loígde. This was because the Blessed Ciaran of Saighir, the son of an Osraige father and a mother from the Corco Loígde, imposed his own family as kings there after he had begun to convert the people of Osraige to the Faith. Since then the descendants of the native chieftains have lived under this injustice. Several Osraige kings from the Corco Loígde have been slain in quarrels in that troubled land.

'It is obvious that Laigin, whose admitted ambition all these years has been to have Osraige returned to it, have watched and perhaps even encouraged the unrest there.'

There was a chorus of angry shouts from the benches on which Laigin's representatives sat. Many even stood up and shook their fists at Fidelma.

The Chief Brehon rapped his staff upon the table for order.

Forbassach had sprung to his feet again but Barrán turned and stared at him in such a way that he sank back without speaking.

'I must warn the representatives of Laigin that it will do their case little good to demonstrate in such a manner.' He turned, his eyes glinting, to Fidelma. 'And must I remind you, Sister Fidelma, that a fine of one *séd* is payable if an advocate incites a court to violence?'

Fidelma bowed her head.

'I am contrite, Barrán. I had not thought my words would provoke anger nor, in fact, did I think that they would be contested. What I have said is simply a matter of common knowledge.'

At this point the High King leant towards his Chief Brehon and whispered something. The Chief Brehon nodded swiftly and instructed Fidelma to continue her plea.

'The struggle for the kingship of Osraige developed last year into a struggle between Scandlán, the cousin of Salbach of the Corco Loígde, and Illan, a descendant of the line of native kings. Illan was killed by Scandlán over a year ago.'

There was a sound of disturbance, this time from the benches of Muman. A stocky, florid-faced man had risen with anger on his features. He had a mass of sandy hair and a bushy beard, standing like a bear at bay.

'I demand to speak!' he cried. 'I am Scandlán, king of Osraige.'

'Sit down!' The Chief Brehon's heavy bass voice quelled the whispering that was echoing through the church. 'As king you surely know the rules of procedure of this assembly?'

'My name is being sullied!' protested the muscular chieftain. 'Do I not have a chance to answer my accuser?'

'There is no accusation at the moment,' Fidelma said. 'What then is in error?'

The High King was again whispering to the Chief Brehon. Fidelma saw a smile hovering on the High King's lips.

'Very well,' agreed the Chief Brehon. 'There is one question that I will ask of Scandlán now. King of Osraige, did you kill Illan?'

'Of course I did,' snapped the sandy-haired man. 'It is my right as king to protect myself and Illan was in insurrection against me and . . .'

The Chief Brehon raised his hand for silence.

'Then it seems that Sister Fidelma has only stated the truth. She has impugned no mean motive, so far. We will hear you later if either of the learned advocates call upon you to give testimony. Until then, you will not interrupt the proceedings.'

He returned his gaze to Fidelma and indicated that she might continue again.

'The death of Illan was not the end of the contention. Illan had offspring who were not then at the age of choice when they might take their official claims to the people. The problem was that no one seemed to know who the offspring of Illan were, for it appeared that he had several children. They had all been sent out of Osraige into fosterage until the time when the eldest of them would be of age and able to present his claim to his people.

'There were two people who were interested in the heirs of Illan. Scandlán was interested because he knew that sooner or later those heirs would once more contend with him for the kingship of Osraige. And Fianamail of Laigin was interested. Fianamail felt that if the heirs could be found and supported in their fight to throw out Scandlán, then Laigin might influence the future of Osraige so that it would eventually be returned to their authority.'

She paused expectantly but this time there was no outcry.

'But the heirs of Illan had vanished. The question was how to discover who they were and where they were. One way to discover the identity of these heirs, so it was thought, was to examine the genealogies of the Osraige. Now since the Corco Loígde had ruled Osraige, it had been their scribes who had kept the detailed genealogies and histories. And where were these genealogies kept?'

Fidelma paused again and glanced around at the expectant faces in the now silent abbey church.

'They were kept here, here in Ros Ailithir.'

There was a muttering as some began to see where her arguments were leading.

'Fianamail of Laigin sent his best scholar to Ros Ailithir to examine the genealogies in order to trace the heir of Illan. That scholar was none other than Dacán, brother of Abbot Noé of Fearna, and cousin to Fianamail, the king. Now let Fianamail deny this on his sacred oath!'

'A question!' cried Forbassach. 'I have the right to ask a question!'

The Chief Brehon conceded that he had.

'If the current king of Osraige was, as Muman's advocate

suggests, so keen to track down Illan's heirs, why did he not send his own scholar to examine these records which are here, in his own family territory? That would have been easy for him to do.'

'The simply answer is that he, or rather his family, did,' Fidelma replied evenly. 'But I have asked Fianamail to deny that Dacán was sent here with that task on his behalf. I deserve an answer.'

Forbassach turned to exchange a hurried word with Fianamail and the grim-faced Abbot Noé. The Chief Brehon cleared his throat meaningfully and Forbassach smiled.

'Whatever research Dacán may have been conducting, it does not cancel out the fact that he was murdered, and responsibility for his death lies with the abbot and ultimately with the king of Muman.'

His voice was firm but less assured than he had been in his opening argument.

'Not,' replied Fidelma with emphasis, 'if Dacán's purpose for being here was not what he claimed it to be.'

This time it was the *ollamh* of the Chief Brehon who bent forward and whispered into Barrán's ear. The Chief Brehon regarded Fidelma gravely.

'If this is the basis of your counter-plea, Sister Fidelma, then I am advised to caution you that it is a tenuous defence. Dacán stated that he wanted to research and teach at Ros Ailithir and on that condition he was granted the hospitality of the king of Cashel and the abbot of Ros Ailithir. The fact that he did not stipulate the precise nature of that research does not exclude him from legal protection. He was, after all, conducting research.'

'I would have to argue this,' conceded Fidelma, 'but I made my opening plea with two points. We will leave the first for the time being. I think I can demonstrate later that it is a means of dismissing culpability. But we have more important matters to deal with first. Such as the identity of Dacán's killer.'

There was another outburst of muttering among the assembly. Barrán's eyes narrowed as he leant forward in his chair and rapped for silence.

'Are you saying that you know the identity of the murderer?' he demanded.

Fidelma smiled enigmatically.

'We will come to that in a moment. I must be allowed to explain some other matters.'

Barrán gestured impatiently for her to continue.

'As I have said, Dacán came to Ros Ailithir for a single purpose. The purpose was to trace the genealogy of the Illan. To his surprise, Dacán found that his former wife, Grella from the abbey of Cealla, was working here as librarian. He thought that he had been the recipient of good fortune for Grella was from Osraige and her relationship with Dacán had not ended in enmity. So Dacán enlisted her help to obtain the records which he required. She gave that help willingly because she was also interested in finding the heirs of Illan. Alas, her reasons for that interest were not the same as those of her former husband.'

There was another commotion from the benches behind Fidelma.

Barrán raised a tired head and called for order while his *ollamh* began hurriedly speaking in an undertone to him.

Fidelma turned and saw Sister Grella standing, her face distorted and filled with passion.

'Sister Grella, be seated!' ordered Barrán as his *ollamh* identified her.

'I will not sit and be insulted!' cried Grella hysterically, 'nor unjustly accused.'

'Has Sister Fidelma insulted you?' demanded the Chief Brehon wearily. 'I am not aware that she has. If so, please tell me in what way has the insult been made? Were you or were you not married to Dacán of Fearna?'

'Mugrón, the captain of the Laigin warship, stands ready to

give witness,' warned Fidelma quickly, pointing to where the seaman sat on the Laigin benches.

'I was married to Dacán but . . .' conceded Grella.

'And that marriage ended in divorce?' interposed the Chief Brehon.

'Yes.'

'When Dacán came to Ros Ailithir, did he know that you were librarian of the abbey?'

'No.'

'But he enlisted your help for his research?'

'Yes.'

'And you gave it willingly?'

'Yes.'

'Did you share Dacán's motives for this research?'

Grella's face reddened and she hung her head.

'Then there is no insult,' Barrán said, assuming her answer. 'Be seated, Sister Grella, lest you insult this court by your animosity.'

'But I know that this woman is trying to claim that I killed Dacán! She is playing like a cat with a mouse! Let her accuse me openly!'

'Are you accusing Sister Grella of the murder of Dacán?' asked the Chief Brehon of Fidelma.

Fidelma smiled wryly.

'I think that I may eventually clear this matter up, Barrán, but by questioning Salbach, chieftain of the Corco Loígde.'

'Whatever accusations you make, Fidelma, you must substantiate them,' Barrán warned.

'That I am prepared to do.'

Barrán motioned to one of the warriors of *fianna*, the High King's bodyguard. A few moments later Salbach was brought, his hands bound before him. He stood somewhat defiantly before the assembly.

'Salbach of the Corco Loígde,' Fidelma began, 'you already stand before this assembly denounced as responsible for the actions of your *bó-aire*, Intat. Intat was responsible for the slaughter of many innocents in your name both at Ros na Scríne and at the house of Molua.'

Salbach raised his chin belligerently but did not reply.

'You do not deny these charges?' demanded the Chief Brehon.

Salbach still did not speak.

Barrán sighed heavily.

'You do not have to answer the accusation but some inference will be placed on your silence by this court. If you do not answer then the allegations must be considered as true and punishment must follow.'

'I am ready for your punishment,' Salbach said curtly. It was apparent that Salbach had reflected on the weight of the evidence against him and saw no alternative to admitting his culpability.

'And is Sister Grella also ready to accept punishment?' Fidelma asked, hoping that she had judged Salbach's feeling for the librarian correctly. If Salbach was reconciled to his punishment, she wondered whether he was as willing to inflict it on Grella? Salbach swung round to Fidelma, his expression impassive.

'She is not guilty of any of the misdeeds attributed to me,' he said quietly. 'Let her go.'

'Yet Sister Grella was your lover, wasn't she, Salbach?'

'I have admitted that.'

'It was either your cousin, Scandlán, or you – it matters not where the idea came from – who suggested that Grella might use her position as librarian to look through the genealogical books of Osraige, which are kept at the abbey, in an attempt to find Illan's heir. Isn't that true?'

'You are bound to reply,' instructed the Chief Brehon as Salbach hesitated.

'It is true.'

'Then came a coincidence. Grella told you, probably during

your pillow talk, that her former husband, Dacán, had arrived at Ros Ailithir for exactly the same purpose. He, too, was searching for Illan's heir. Knowing him to be the better scholar, Grella persuaded him to work closely with her so that she could then inform you how he was proceeding. Isn't that so? You wanted to know who the heir of Illan was as much as Dacán did. But whereas Dacán was interested in finding them to use him to serve Laigin's purpose, you wanted to find him to destroy the last of the family of native kings. That would forever safeguard the dynasty of the Corco Loígde in Osraige.'

There was a tense silence. No one spoke. All eyes were on Salbach. It was Sister Grella who broke the silence with a wail of fear as, for the first time, she finally realised the enormity of what had been done.

'But it is not true . . . I did not know that Salbach . . . I did not know he wanted to kill them . . . I am not responsible for the death of all those innocent children . . . I am not.'

Salbach turned and snapped at her to be silent.

'When Dacán discovered the whereabouts of the heir of Illan,' Fidelma went on remorselessly, 'Grella ran to tell you. It was the day before Dacán's death. He had found that the Father Superior of Sceilig Mhichil, the monastery of Michael the Archangel, was a cousin of Illan. He had discovered that Illan's heir had been taken there for safety. He wrote of his news and announced that he was about to set out for Sceilig Mhichil. He was killed before he did so.'

'How did he discover this information? Surely the records placed here would not announce the hiding place of Illan's heirs?' demanded the Chief Brehon.

'Curiously enough, they did. Dacán found Illan's will on some rods of the poets. The irony of this tale is that when Scandlán killed Illan, he seized his fortress and goods. Illan's library was also seized. In that library was his will, which he had specifically chosen to write in Ogham on rods of the poets.

The irony was that Scandlán, unable to read it, had sent it, with other books, as a gift to this abbey, the chief abbey of the Corco Loígde.'

'Even so,' protested Barrán, 'surely any reasonable scholar could have read the Ogham of the will and ultimately deciphered the information?'

'Illan was obviously a literary man, for the will was coded. I found a wand from the will in Dacán's chamber where he had carelessly left it. It went unnoticed by his murderer. I have only an extract from one rod. The others had been destroyed.'

She turned and retrieved the small piece of burnt stick which she had taken from the sepulchre the previous night.

'Only this piece now remains. This says "the resolve of the honourable one determines the fosterage of my children".'

'That sounds gibberish,' laughed Forbassach.

'Not if you know the code and the full text. The piece that I recall from the wand I found in Dacán's chamber stated: "let my sweet cousin care for my sons on the rock of Michael as my honourable cousin shall dictate".'

'Even more gibberish!' sneered Forbassach.

'Dacán did not think so. He knew that the rock of Michael was Sceilig Mhichil. It was easy to learn that the Father Superior was named Mel. The meaning of that name is "sweet". Mel was, therefore, Illan's "sweet" cousin!'

'You make the interpretation of the puzzle sound easy,' observed the Chief Brehon.

'Then allow me to return to it later. Sufficient to know at this time that Dacán deciphered the will's puzzle and wrote a report of his finding. Sister Grella saw that report and informed Salbach. Salbach dispatched Intat immediately to "the rock of Michael". But Illan's sons were no longer there. Indeed, Intat learnt that there were two sons of Illan on that rock but they had been removed by a religieux. This religieux was a cousin of Father Mel.

'It is then that Grella entered the picture again to provide information to Salbach. Grella had become soul-friend to Sister Eisten at Rae na Scríne. Eisten, by one of those apparent coincidences which are all too common in life, was the very person to whom the young sons of Illan had been given for safekeeping after their removal from Sceilig Mhichil. They had been sent to her orphanage at Rae na Scríne. Sister Eisten made the biggest mistake of her life. She confessed the intrigue to her soul-friend, Sister Grella.

'Grella triumphantly informed Salbach. He thought he would lay a trap by inviting Eisten and her orphans to his fortress. Once he was able to identify her charges . . . well, Eisten accompanied Grella but did not take her children. There was plague in the village and she did not want to move the children unnecessarily. It was a decision which actually saved the lives of the sons of Illan but which cost the village its existence.

'In desperation, Salbach told Intat to go to Rae na Scríne and destroy the children. The trouble was that Intat had no means to identify them. He decided, brutal man that he was, to destroy the entire village. When I and Cass came along, Intat tried to disguise the true nature of this crime by claiming that there was plague in the village and presenting himself and his men as frightened neighbouring villagers burning out the plague. Sister Eisten and some of her children survived.

'Eisten was shocked. I thought she was shocked by the death of the people and especially by the death of a baby she tried to save. However, in reality she was shocked because she had worked out the real reason for the killings. She even knew who had betrayed her. She asked me if a soul-friend could betray a confidence. I should have listened to her more closely for then she might not have been killed. I might have saved her. Do you follow the events so far, Salbach?'

Salbach's mouth was pressed tight. He was clearly shocked at the extent of her awareness and knew that there was little he could say in the face of Fidelma's remorseless knowledge except to resort to truth.

'You have a brilliant mind, Fidelma. I knew that I should not underestimate you. Yes, you are right. I accept your knowledge.'

'When you came to this abbey and found that Sister Eisten had survived with several of her children, you could not dare allow that to pass. Intat, doubtless on your orders, managed to waylay Sister Eisten while she was down at the harbour. He tortured her to find out where the sons of Illan had been taken. She would not reply and so he killed her, dumping her body in the waters of the inlet.

'Grella came to your aid once more, eventually discovering that some children from Rae na Scríne had been taken to the house of Molua. The bodies of four religious and twenty children and the charred ruins of their houses are the mute testament to Intat's visit.'

'I will deny nothing. But let me take oath that my cousin, Scandlán of Osraige, did not know my plans to safeguard the kingship of Osraige for our family. Neither did Grella. She is innocent of the blood that I have spilt.'

Fidelma regarded Salbach with an expression of undisguised revulsion. She found it difficult to accept that a man could admit responsibility for such death and destruction but could seek to protect others with a twisted concept of honour and love. But then it was a strange world and humankind were the strangest creatures in it.

Grella was sobbing openly now, crying: 'I did not know any of this! I did not know!'

Fidelma glanced at her without pity.

'You were so besotted by your love for Salbach that you had not reasoned out the truth. I concede that it is possible but find it difficult to believe. You would not believe that your lover was capable of ordering the death of little children. I think the reality is that you did not want to know what was going on around you.'

There was a commotion at one of the doors. Fidelma smiled

sourly when she saw that Scandlán's seat was empty. The Chief Brehon had noticed also and waved to a member of the *fianna* and issued instructions in a low voice.

'Your cousin will not get out of this abbey,' Barrán told Salbach.

'What does it matter now?' Salbach gave an eloquent shrug. 'I have admitted my guilt in this matter. I am prepared to stand for judgment. Doubtless my wealth and chieftainship will be forfeit as compensation and I shall be sent into exile. I am prepared for it. Let us proceed with the judgment forthwith.'

Forbassach had risen from the Laigin benches amid the pandemonium that had broken out. He was smiling crookedly.

'We are grateful to Sister Fidelma for discovering the culprit. But I must point out that Salbach, as chieftain of the Corco Loígde, still owes his allegiance to Cashel. What Fidelma is proving is that responsibility for the death of Dacán still rests with Cashel. Our demand for Osraige as his honour price is still valid.'

The Chief Brehon, Barrán, looked grave.

'That appears true. Or is there more to this story you wish to tell us, Sister Fidelma?'

'Much more,' Fidelma affirmed grimly. 'For I am not accusing Salbach of the death of Dacán. He is only responsible for the slaughter of the innocents, for the death of those I have named. Neither he nor Grella killed the Venerable Dacán.'

Chapter Twenty

There was a murmur of excitement from the Muman benches as Sister Fidelma made her surprising announcement. Colgú had been wearing a long face. He had already been aware of the point which Forbassach was bound to make. Now he stared in astonishment at his sister.

'If Salbach did not kill Dacán,' the Chief Brehon demanded, with an air of exaggerated patience, 'are you going to reveal to this assembly who did?'

'We must come to that logically,' Fidelma replied. 'First let us go back to the day when, going through the genealogies here, Dacán discovered the whereabouts of the heirs of Illan. I have already said that he sat down and wrote a letter to his brother Noé.'

Noé leaned forward in his seat and spoke rapidly to Forbassach.

The fiery advocate rose again.

'There is no proof that Dacán, even if engaged in such a search, reported to the Abbot Noé; there is no evidence that he had even been asked to report to the abbot. In view of that, this assertion is an affront to the abbot and to Fianamail of Laigin.'

'I will contest that,' replied Fidelma with assurance. 'I have also requested the presence at this hearing of Assíd of the Uí Dego. Is he within the court?'

A well-built man with the rolling gait of a sailor came forward. His skin was tanned, his hair sun-bleached and therefore it was impossible to discern its colour.

'I am Assíd,' he announced in an almost defiant tone. 'I appear before this assembly by order of the Chief Brehon but I appear unwillingly for I have no intention of bringing harm to my king.'

He stood before the *cos-na-dála* with arms folded, staring in antagonism towards Fidelma.

'Let that be so recorded,' the Chief Brehon cautioned his *scriptor*.

'Let it be recorded that Assíd is, indeed, a loyal subject of Fianamail of Laigin,' added Fidelma lightly with a smile.

'I do not deny that,' affirmed Assíd suspiciously.

'Are you the captain and owner of a coastal trading *barc*?'

'I do not deny that, either.'

'For the last year or so have you traded between Laigin and the lands of the Corco Loígde?'

'Once again, I do not deny it.'

'And you were staying in the abbey on the night the Venerable Dacán died?'

'That's common knowledge.'

'You left the abbey on the same day and sailed directly for Laigin. You went to Fearna and reported Dacán's murder to Fianamail and Abbot Noé.'

Assíd hesitated and nodded slowly, trying to see where Fidelma's path was leading.

'This was why Laigin was able to act so swiftly over this matter.' Fidelma made the statement as an explanation to the assembly, rather than putting it as a question to Assíd. 'Tell us, Assíd, for I have not had time to question you before, what were the circumstances of that evening in the abbey? Tell us when you last saw the Venerable Dacán alive and when you heard of his death?'

Assíd seemed to lose his aggressive posture for a moment and he reached forward to use the rail before him as a support, leaning his weight from the shoulders upon it.

'It is true,' he began slowly, addressing himself to the Chief

Brehon, 'that I was trading along this coast and had decided to put in to Ros Ailithir and seek a night's rest at the abbey's hostel. There I saw the Venerable Dacán . . .'

'Whom you greeted as someone you knew?' interposed Fidelma.

Assíd hesitated and then shrugged.

'Who in Laigin does not know the Venerable Dacán?' he countered.

'But you knew him better than most for you greeted him as an old friend. There is a witness,' she added in case it was denied.

'Then I shall not deny it,' Assíd agreed.

'It makes me wonder why you put in to Ros Ailithir? Pure chance? No. There were other hostels along the coast. You could even have stayed at Cuan Dóir. Yet you put in here. It leads me to suspect that you had arranged to meet Dacán.'

Assíd looked uncomfortable. It was obvious that Fidelma was correct in her assumption.

'So I asked myself why you had an assignation to meet Dacán here? Will you tell us or shall I explain?'

Assíd seemed to be attempting to catch the eye of those on the Laigin benches.

Fidelma turned to the book satchel on the bench where she had been sitting and drew out some pieces of vellum.

'I present, in evidence, the draft of a letter written by Dacán to his brother, the Abbot Noé, informing him of his discovery of a surviving heir of Illan in words that leave little doubt that he had been asked to conduct this research and also that he subsequently expected some action on the part of his brother.

'Fortunately for us, in writing this draft, Dacán spilt ink on it. Being the fastidious and methodical man he was, he put it to one side and rewrote it. He either forgot to destroy his draft or, before he could do so, it was stolen from him. It was certainly in the possession of Sister Grella and this is how we can prove that Dacán acted on his brother's commission.'

Fidelma did not bother to look at the Laigin benches – they

were curiously quiet while Barrán scanned the evidence which Fidelma had handed him.

'And you say that the finished form of this letter was given to Assíd? Assíd then took the report to Noé?' asked Barrán.

Fidelma inclined her head in agreement.

The Chief Brehon turned to Forbassach as advocate for Laigin. His expression was dour.

'Forbassach, the evidence here is clear. I now have to warn you. The law text, the *Din Techtugad*, states that a person who gives false testimony loses his honour price. False testimony is one of the three falsehoods which God avenges most severely. I will not impose the penalty at this stage, giving the Abbot Noé time to reflect on this matter.' He turned back to Fidelma. 'Please, proceed, sister.'

'Do you accept or deny this, Assíd?' she demanded.

Assíd hung his head.

'I accept that I came here to pick up a message from Dacán to take to his brother Noé. After the evening meal, I met with Dacán and he gave me the letter. We exchanged some heated words when he refused to reveal what was in it and made me swear an oath not to open it. I still have no idea of what the letter contained. I went to bed. In the morning, I heard, that Dacán had been slain. Brother Rumann, who was the steward of the abbey, questioned me as to my whereabouts. Satisfied that I knew nothing, he gave me permission to leave. I left the abbey and sailed directly for Laigin, taking the letter. I reported what had happened to the Abbot Noé. That is all I have to do with this matter.'

'A few more questions. When did you last see Dacán alive?'

'Just after the *completa*, the last service of the day. A little after midnight, I should say.'

'Where did you see him?'

'In his chamber. It was when he handed over the letter to me.'

'And where was your chamber?'

'On the floor above Dacán's.'

'And so you heard nothing after you had left him? At what time was that?'

Assíd drew his brows together, trying to recall.

'After midnight. I only heard one thing more, as I went up the stairs. I heard Dacán ringing the bell for the young novice who attended to our wants in the hostel. I heard his voice demanding that she fetch him water.'

'You may stand down, unless Forbassach wishes to question you.'

Forbassach had been talking rapidly with the grim-faced Abbot Noé. He replied that he had no questions for Assíd.

Fidelma now addressed the Chief Brehon.

'We have heard that Dacán had been successful in locating Illan's heir. He told his brother Noé that he was about to set off for Sceilig Mhichil to identify him the next day.'

'Are you telling us that he was killed to prevent him doing so?' asked Barrán.

'He was killed because it was feared he would bring harm to Illan's heir.'

'But you said that the sons of Illan had already been removed from the monastery and placed in Sister Eisten's charge. Is this not correct?'

'The story grows complicated. When Illan was killed, his sons had been placed in the care of a cousin who would foster them.'

Dramatically, Fidelma swung round and pointed at the abbey benches.

'It was Brother Midach of this abbey who was the foster-father of the two boys who were known at Sceilig Mhichil as Primus and Victor.'

Midach sat unblinking. His face was fixed in a thin smile. He said nothing. Fidelma continued:

'Dacán thought that it was Illan's cousin, Father Mel of

Sceilig Mhichil who was the fosterer. In that he did not read the will carefully enough. The will of Illan states clearly "let the resolve of the honourable one determine the fosterage of my children". Is there anyone here who does not know that the meaning of the name Midach is "honourable"? Midach was appointed the *aite* or foster-father of the sons of Illan.

'Midach, either by suspicion or accident, read the notes of Dacán in the library and realised that the old scholar was searching for Illan's children. Dacán discovered Midach reading his notes and an argument ensued. Brother Martan was a witness to this. Anxious to protect his charges, on that same evening, Midach left this abbey and sailed to Sceilig Mhichil. He removed the boys and took them to Sister Eisten, who was a former pupil of his. He was able to visit them a few times afterwards on the pretext of visiting the village and helping them with medicine again the plague. He was seen and described to me. The real names of the children of Illan, known at Sceilig Mhichil as Primus and Victor, were Cétach and Cosrach. If one attempted to put Latin names on these they would translate in such a fashion.

'Midach was shocked when he heard that Intat had raided Rae na Scríne. He believed that Dacán was working for Salbach and through him for Scandlán of Osraige. Alas, he did not realise that Grella was part of the conspiracy and was Eisten's soul-friend. However, after the attack, he found that his two wards were safe. He decided to get the two boys away from this kingdom and asked Sister Eisten to arrange passage for them.

'Cétach, the elder boy, at least, had been warned that Salbach was looking for them so when Salbach came here, Cétach pleaded with me not to mention him or his brother to the chieftain. Then they both disappeared.

'While Midach now hid the children, Eisten went to book passage for them on a merchant ship in the bay. At first she chose the wrong ship – she asked a sailor who was from the Laigin warship captained by Mugrón. Unfortunately, Intat then spotted Eisten. The rest of that tale we know. In spite of torture, Eisten would not tell where the children were and finally, in anger, Intat killed her. The children had to remain in hiding until Midach could get them safely away.'

Fidelma paused for her throat was now dry.

Barrán took the opportunity to address Midach.

'Do you deny this story or any part of it?'

Midach sat, his arms folded, without expression.

'I neither confirm nor deny it.'

The Chief Brehon turned back to Fidelma.

'There is one point in your explanation that I do not follow. You have not dealt with Dacán's death, which, as important as these events are, is the main cause of this action brought by Laigin.'

'I will come to it, Barrán,' Fidelma assured him, coughing slightly as she attempted to clear her drying throat.

'Midach was hiding the boys, Cétach and Cosrach, here in the abbey where he continues to hide them. I think that we can now bring them safely forth from the sepulchre of the Blessed Fachtna, for they will be under the protection of the High King. Is this not so?'

The question was directed to Sechnassach.

The High King returned Fidelma's interrogative look with a brief smile.

'They are so protected, Fidelma of Kildare.'

'Midach, will you bring them forth?'

The physician rose unsteadily. He found difficulty speaking.

Fidelma decided to prompt him.

'If you go to the statue of the cherub behind the High Altar and twist it one half turn to the left it will release the spring which pivots a flagstone.' Midach's mouth slackened in surprise.

'How did you discover this?' he demanded in consternation.

'The steps beneath lead down to the secret sepulchre of the Blessed Fachtna, the founder of this abbey,' went on Fidelma.

'It is there, since the death of Sister Eisten, that Cétach and Cosrach have been in hiding. Is that not so, Midach?'

Midach's shoulders slumped in resignation.

'It is even as she has said,' he mumbled. 'She seems to know everything.'

A couple of the High King's guards moved at a gesture from Sechnassach and followed Fidelma's instructions. A few moments later the two young black-haired lads were brought blinking from the underground tomb to stare in fear at the mighty assembly.

The Chief Brehon immediately sought to reassure them of their safety.

Forbassach was on his feet.

'I must point out that we, of Laigin, have no wish to harm these boys . . . if they, indeed, are the sons of Illan.'

'They are the sons of Illan,' confirmed Fidelma. 'And if their hair is washed clean of that black dye you will find two thatches of copper-coloured hair. Midach dyed their hair as an extra precaution when he took them to Sister Eisten. Isn't that so?'

Midach seemed too dispirited to answer.

Forbassach was on his feet repeating himself.

'We sought the heirs of Illan simply to identify them. To discover their whereabouts. The purpose of this was to offer our support for their claims and restore them to the kingship of Osraige. There is only one power here that would oppose that purpose – Cashel. As we have claimed all along, Cashel's interest would be to destroy them. It was in Cashel's interests to kill Dacán. We repeat our original claim, that Osraige be forfeit for the honour price of Dacán.' He smiled towards the two young boys. 'But as neither boy is anywhere near the age of choice, whereby he might be affirm as king, then the right of the kingship must devolve in the gift of Fearna.'

At once Colgú, ignoring the protocol of the court, was on his feet in anger.

'Cashel is not at the centre of this claimed conspiracy to harm these boys. Salbach admits that he is the culprit. For that Cashel shall punish him. The evil of the chieftain of the Corco Loígde is not to be put on the shoulders of Cashel!'

'Yet Corco Loígde owes allegiance to Cashel,' sneered Forbassach in reply. 'What other shoulders but Cashel can the guilt rest on?'

Barrán held up both hands. His face showed dismay and there was irritation in his eyes.

'That you both forget the protocol of this court is a matter of sadness. That you both persist in a squabble before me is a matter of penalty. Colgú, you are find one *séd*, the value of one milch cow, for not allowing your *dálaigh* to present your arguments. Forbassach, you are more guilty of an offence being not only trained in law but the advocate of your king. You shall be find one *cumal*, the value of three milch cows. If this occurs again the penalties shall not be so light.'

Barrán gave everyone a moment to settle down again and instructed the two young boys be brought before the *cos-na-dála*.

'Am I to understand that these boys are both under the age of choice?' he asked, turning to Midach.

'They are,' agreed the physician, accepting his role as their foster-father.

'Then we cannot give any weight to their evidence,' sighed the Chief Brehon. 'Nevertheless, we may call upon them but what they say, if contradicted by other evidence, may be discounted. This is the law.'

'I am aware of this, Barrán,' agreed Fidelma. 'And, unless Forbassach insists, I have no wish to call them.'

'I would prefer Sister Fidelma to deal with the specific matter of the murder of Dacán,' replied Forbassach.

'Then I shall do so,' replied Fidelma. 'It should be obvious now that Dacán's death was essentially connected with the task that he had come to Ros Ailithir to perform. He was killed because it was thought he presented a threat. But let me point this out, that it is true that Dacán alive was worth more to Salbach than Dacán dead. So who, then, was Dacán a threat to? He was clearly a threat to the children of Illan, as I have said before.'

Forbassach was on his feet yet again.

'And I have said, Laigin was no threat to these children. It sought to help them.'

'But did the children know that?'

Fidelma's question was sharp and left an uneasy silence.

She turned to Midach. The once-jocular physician looked tired and exhausted before her.

'Dacán had been two months at the abbey researching before you learnt that he was looking for your foster children. When you discovered that you immediately set off to remove them from Sceilig Mhichil. You left here on the very night Dacán was killed, the night he wrote to inform his Brother Noé that he was leaving for Sceilig Mhichil.'

Barrán intervened, thinking to preempt Fidelma.

'And did you kill Dacán, Brother Midach?'

'Dacán was alive when I left the abbey,' Midach replied quietly but firmly.

'That is true,' Fidelma affirmed quickly. The Chief Brehon raised his hands in protest.

'How can you know that?'

'Simple enough. We know that Dacán was killed around midnight. Certainly not before. Midach had to be on board his ship just after vespers in order to sail with the evening tide for Sceilig Mhichil. I checked the tides with the local sailors. If he had delayed then he could not have been able to sail until the following morning.'

'Then who did kill Dacán?' Barrán was totally perplexed.

'Someone who, like Midach, believed that Dacán meant harm to the children of Illan.'

There was a silence as everyone realised, after all the proceedings, they were now on the verge of the final revelation.

Fidelma was surprised at the fact that no one had leapt to the same conclusion that she had been drawn to some time before. When no one spoke, when no one moved, Fidelma shook her head.

'Why – who else but the children of Illan would feel threatened by Dacán?' she asked. 'Who else but the eldest son of Illan, who was more threatened than his brothers?'

Everyone was looking at the young boy Cétach.

'But you have just stated that these two boys were still on Sceilig Mhichil at this time. They were at least two or three days sailing away from Ros Ailithir,' Barrán pointed out.

'I did not say it was either of these two boys,' Fidelma said loudly above the hubbub.

Again the effect of her words was like water on a fire. There was stunned silence.

'But, you said . . .' began the Chief Brehon wearily.

'I said that the eldest of Illan's sons killed Dacán.'

'Then . . . ?'

'Illan had three sons. Isn't that right, Midach? Dacán, in his letter to his brother, wrote that Illan's eldest son had just reached the age of choice. That rules out these two lads, who are a long way from the age of seventeen. That also means that Illan had a third son.'

'You seem to know everything, Fidelma,' Midach said grimly. 'Yes. My cousin Illan had three sons. They were all placed in my charge to foster when Illan was killed. The two youngest had already been sent to Sceilig Mhichil to our cousin, Mel. Indeed, everything happened just as you have explained.'

'So where did you send the eldest son?' demanded Barrán.

Midach set his jaw firmly.

'I cannot betray the trust of my family.'

'The eldest son was brought to Ros Ailithir under a false identity,' Fidelma intervened.

She turned and scanned the rows of the religious who had

crowded into the abbey church and found the white mask that was the face of Sister Necht.

'Come forward, Sister Necht, or should that be Nechtan?' Fidelma added, making the feminine name into its masculine form.

The ungainly 'sister' rose, the eyes darted from side to side as if seeking a method of escape, and then the shoulders slumped in resignation.

A tall member of the High King's guard moved across and tapped the 'sister' on the shoulder, motioning 'her' to go to the well of the court before the judges. Slowly, reluctantly, 'Sister Necht' obeyed.

Not a sound could be heard as all eyes watched the figure walk slowly to where Fidelma was waiting. There seemed no attempt now to disguise the masculine posture of the 'novice'.

'Allow me to present Nechtan, son of Illan of the Osraige. Nechtan is the eldest brother of Cétach and Cosrach.'

'Sister Necht' squared 'her' shoulders and thrust out 'her' chin in defiance as 'she' stood before Fidelma.

'Would you mind moving your head-dress?' asked Barrán.

'Sister Necht' threw back the head-dress.

'The hair is coppery, almost red,' Forbassach admitted in querulous tones. 'But this . . . this person . . . still looks like a girl.'

'Do we have to go further with this charade, Nechtan?' asked Fidelma. 'Speak the truth.'

'It is all over, my boy,' cried Midach in doleful resignation. 'Let us admit to the truth.'

The copper-haired youth stared at Fidelma almost with hatred in his eyes.

'Yes: I am Nechtan, son of Illan,' he said with an air of pride.

'It was all my idea,' Midach explained hastily. 'I did not know what else to do. I knew that Scandlán and his family were looking for Illan's heir. I had already seen Illan's will and knew the boys were left in my care and that the younger were supposed to go to Sceilig Mhichil. I thought that they would be safe on Sceilig Mhichil. But I did not know where else to hide Nechtan, but then the idea came into my mind that he could hide himself at the abbey as a novice and so I could keep a close eye on him. Those searching for the heirs of Illan were searching for his sons, not for a girl.'

'Although just seventeen, Nechtan, with his husky voice and slight figure, became a young woman,' Fidelma agreed. 'With the sprigs and berries of the elder to use as dye and create a redness to the lips and cheeks, Nechtan became Sister Necht.'

'I initially thought that Dacán was an agent for Scandlán,' went on Midach. 'When I discovered that he had deciphered Illan's will, I left the abbey immediately to bring them away before they were discovered. I brought the two boys back and arranged for Sister Eisten to take them at Rae na Scríne. It was only after I returned to the abbey that I discovered that Dacán had been killed.'

'And when did Nechtan confess that he had killed him?' demanded Fidelma.

'The next . . .' Midach bit his lip and hung his head. Nechtan stared in front of him without speaking, showing no emotion.

The Chief Brehon leant forward.

'Why did the boy kill Dacán?' demanded Barrán. 'Let us finally get this point cleared.'

Fidelma grimaced sorrowfully.

'Sister Necht, or rather Nechtan, killed Dacán out of fear. Midach, before leaving for Sceilig Mhichil, had told him that he believed Dacán was working for his enemies. Necht already hated Dacán as an autocratic, uncaring personality. It needed but a spark. A few hours after Midach left to rescue his brothers, Nechtan slew Dacán. I do not think that the act was cold-blooded. It was only after the deed was done that Nechtan sought to portray it as something premeditated.'

'What do you mean?' demanded Barrán.

'Nechtan killed Dacán and later attempted to lay a path

which would lead to another person in an effort to have that person blamed.'

'How?'

'After Midach had left the abbey, Nechtan was summoned to Dacán's chamber to fetch water. Perhaps words were exchanged. Nechtan took out a knife and, in hot temper, rained a series of blows at the old man.'

'He suspected who I was, I know it!' Nechtan protested, speaking for the first time. The previously husky voice was now slightly sharpened and more masculine. There was no emotion in it. 'It was my life or his. He would have killed me if he had known who I was.'

Forbassach was sitting shaking his head in bewilderment. Fidelma gestured towards him.

'You may believe the honourable advocate for Laigin when he argues that Dacán and Laigin meant no harm to the children of Illan,' Fidelma said. 'So you, Nechtan, killed Dacán from an unjustified fear. Dacán was seeking you in order to get Laigin to support your claim to the Osraige kingship. It can be argued that you had an understandable fear. But what made this more heinous, Nechtan, was that you then went to great pains to lay a path to Sister Grella.'

'I knew that Sister Grella was working with Dacán. I also knew that Grella was Salbach's lover,' Nechtan replied defensively. 'When Midach went to save my brothers, I decided to save us all. If Grella was accused of Dacán's murder then it would be a just retribution.'

'You tried to destroy all the material that Dacán collected which would have identified you and your brothers. You did not realise that Grella had taken a draft of the letter Dacán was sending to his brother so that she could inform Salbach. Also you neglected to retrieve an Ogham wand which had rolled under the bed in Dacán's chamber. You showed great dismay when I found it. You had to follow me when I took it to Grella in the library to check it was not incriminating. Grella recognised it and pretended that it was something else to lead me from the scent. I left it at the library and, later that night, you returned to the library and burnt it with the other Ogham sticks in order to cover your tracks.'

'But Dacán was bound before he was killed,' pointed out the Chief Brehon. 'How did this boy accomplish that?'

'He was bound after he was killed to further implicate Grella. It was obvious that he was not bound before because the strips of cloth from Grella's dress were so fragile that even an ailing child could have burst those bonds asunder. I noticed this at an early point in my investigation and knew then that I was looking for some carefully worked out plot.'

Fidelma spoke directly to Nechtan.

'You must have lain awake for the rest of the night thinking about your deed. You decided that you must not only lay a path of suspicion away from yourself but, as you have admitted, you had a brilliant idea to visit some poetic justice on the person whom you believed to be one of your enemies.'

Nechtan stood silently.

'You waited until the bell sounded for matins and you watched as Sister Grella made her way to that service. Hoping that no one had yet discovered Dacán's body, you entered Grella's chamber and found an old dress from which you tore strips of linen. It was the only distinctive piece of clothing you could find. You probably hoped that it was something she wore often so that the strips could immediately be identified. You did not realise that no religieuse would wear such a dress and that it was simply an old dress which she never wore any more.

'You took the strips to Dacán's chamber. You went in to find it in darkness. The oil in the lamp had run out. So you refilled it and lit it. It was obvious that no one had been there. You then tied Dacán's ankles and his hands. In order to tie the hands behind him you had to turn his body over chest down on the bed, leaving the bloodstains on the blanket. I found these curious because he was laying on his back on the bed with chest wounds and the blood was on the blanket under the body. The body had to have been moved for a purpose. Then you left, forgetting to extinguish the lamp. Half-an-hour later Brother Conghus arrived. Your false clue meant nothing at the time. There was no one trained to deduce its significance. It meant nothing until I arrived over a week later to pick up the trail.

'When I came back from Sceilig Mhichil and discovered that certain items had been removed from the bag which I had left with Abbot Brocc, I began to suspect what had happened. The items which had been stolen were the ones which gave information and clues to the identification of the sons of Illan. Those which were left behind were part of the evidence which implicated Sister Grella in the murder.'

Fidelma paused, waiting for the boy to respond. After a while Barrán addressed him.

'You say nothing. Do you admit to this?'

The boy shrugged.

'I have nothing to say. I acted in self defence.'

'That seems as good as a confession,' warned the Chief Brehon.

'If you say so,' replied the boy without emotion.

Midach moved forward, his face troubled as he embraced the boy.

'My son, I am your *anamchara* and your foster-father. I have guarded you in all things. I will procure the best advocate to defend you.'

Midach's face dissolved in anguish as he gazed towards Fidelma.

'It is my fault. It is my grievous fault! I put the fear of Dacán in him.' He swung round to face the Chief Brehon. 'Can you accept my guilt in place of this boy?'

Barrán shook his head.

'The boy is now beyond the age of consent. He has an adult's responsibility. As for putting the fear of Dacán in him, you merely gave it some tangible form, for apparently the boy already hated Dacán and, through hate, feared him.'

'Yes, he acted out of fear. Even Fidelma of Kildare admits that much.'

'That may be so. But to deliberately implicate an innocent person brings a worse crime.'

'A further word, Barrán,' Fidelma interrupted. 'This court will have done its duty in absolving the abbot of Ros Ailithir and the king of Muman from any culpability in the death of Dacán of Fearna. This assembly must confine itself to considering the claim by Laigin for compensation. It is now up to the court to rule on that matter. It has no further function.

'Nechtan will have to come before a further court to answer for his actions as, indeed, will Salbach, whose crimes greatly outweigh all others. Let that further court decide the degree of guilt that is on Nechtan's shoulders. And I will, if Nechtan so wishes, stand with him as his advocate, for I believe no boy, whether he has just reached the age of choice or not, should live in such fear of his life as the three sons of Illan have had to live this last year. I think that fear goes in some way to ameliorating his guilt if not absolving it.'

Midach was staring at Fidelma in astonishment, as were many others in the court.

Barrán cleared his throat impatiently.

'I thank you, Fidelma of Kildare,' he said dryly, 'for reminding me of the issues at stake here. Yet I do not think I or the assembly would have forgotten them.'

Fidelma hung her head at the Chief Brehon's gentle irony.

Barrán turned from Fidelma to Forbassach.

'Advocates of Cashel and Fearna, have you completed your pleas and counter-pleas?'

Fidelma hesitated before adding: 'I would just remind the court of what I said in my opening. Dacán, as has now been admitted by his own brother, Noé of Fearna, came to this kingdom in stealth to discover the whereabouts of the sons of

Illan to use them for the political purposes of the kingdom of Laigin. I contend this subterfuge caused Dacán to forfeit any claim he or his relations have under the laws of hospitality. Responsibility does not lay with the abbot of Ros Ailithir nor ultimately with Cashel.

'Secondly, I have revealed the real culprit to be Nechtan, son of Illan of Osraige, who killed Dacán because he believed that his life, and the lives of his younger brothers, were in danger. It is not the jurisdiction of the court to rule on his culpability but I would add that there are extenuating circumstances to Nechtan's act.'

Fidelma returned to her seat and sat down for the first time since she had risen to plead.

Barrán motioned to Forbassach to sum up his case and to rebut that which he did not agree with.

The advocate of the king of Laigin had been bent in discussion with his unhappy-looking young king and the stony-faced abbot of Fearna. He turned round and rose, speaking hesitantly,

'Laigin now accepts that Cashel is not responsible for Dacán's death. But a death has taken place and the law must find responsibility.'

Barrán turned and held a whispered conversation with the High King and then Ultan of Armagh. After a moment he turned back to address the assembly.

'The case before this court was simple. Sister Fidelma has reminded us of it. It was to adjudicate whether the responsibility for the death of Dacán lay at the door of Cashel. If so, the demand of Laigin was specific. Laigin demanded the kingdom of Osraige as the sum of the honour price of Dacán. The evidence that we have heard results in the adjudication that responsibility does not rest with Cashel. Therefore it follows that the demand for the honour price is dismissed. Osraige continues, as it has these last six centuries, to owe its allegiance to Cashel, its kings paying tribute to Cashel and not to Fearna.'

There was a ripple almost of verbal applause as the judgment was given.

Barrán held up his hand for silence.

'Nevertheless, with the agreement of the High King, there are other matters which I feel this court should consider in passing this judgment. We have heard why such a tragic path of death and destruction has been followed here. It has its roots in the fact that the people of Osraige do not find the kingship imposed by the family of Ciarán of Saighir, a kingship from the family of the chieftains of the Corco Loígde, to be a just kingship. The Blessed Ciarán had, misguidedly we feel, established the Corco Loígde in Osraige. It is now time for the descendants of the native kings of Osraige to return to their rightful role. We would admonish the king of Cashel to take steps to ensure that the people of his petty kingdom of Osraige choose freely whomsoever they wish to govern in accordance with the laws of rightful succession.'

Colgú rose, his face solemn.

'Nothing grieves me more than to hear what has transpired in my kingdom. This bloodshed of the innocent shall not go unpunished. No longer can the family of the chieftains of the Corco Loígde have any moral right to rule Osraige. The people of Osraige shall choose. It shall be so. My oath of honour, it shall. I pledge it before this court.'

The Chief Brehon acknowledged Colgú with a smile.

'Your words have gladdened your High King. Then there is one more admonishment that we feel it is in our judgment to make. It will be left to a court of Cashel to fix the degree of guilt and the amount of fine and compensation which must lay at the door of the unfortunate Nechtan. However, we have heard enough at this court to say that Dacán's honour price is tarnished by his deceptive undertaking on behalf of Laigin. The fine for the death of a scholar of Dacán's standing is fixed in law at seven *cumals*, that is the value of twenty-one milch cows. The true honour price for a man of his ecclesiastic standing is twenty *séd*, the value of twenty milch-cows. A total of forty-one *séd* would be the sum payable by whoever is found guilty of his death. However . . .'

Barrán looked towards the king of Laigin.

'It will be seen that there are other culprits in this matter. This court will direct that those who asked Dacán to proceed with his task disrupted the peace of these kingdoms and threatened a bloody war. They must share responsibility. The honour price for a king of a province is sixteen *cumals* and because that king has besmirched his honour, sixteen *cumals* has to be made payable from the king of Laigin to the High King.'

Fianamail was pale and sullen but silent.

'A further seven *cumals* shall be payable by Fianamail to the king of Cashel for the casting of a shadow on his honour. That is the judgment of the court. Does Fianamail of Laigin have anything to say?'

The young king rose hesitantly, seemed about to speak and then shook his head and sat down. He whispered to his *dálaigh*.

Forbassach, as advocate, rose.

'Laigin accepts the admonition of the court,' he said quietly. '*Cedant arma togae* . . . let arms yield to the gown of the law.'

'That is as it must be,' agreed the Chief Brehon, solemnly. 'The business of this assembly is now ended.'

Epilogue

Fidelma was sitting with her brother on the bastion of the walkway of the abbey's high walls overlooking the inlet. The small bay was quiet and deserted now, apart from a few local coastal *barca* and fishermen's boats. The great assembly of ships bearing the High King and his entourage, the Archbishop of Armagh and Fianamail of Laigin and his retinue, had all departed. Even the threatening warship of Mugrón, which had seemed an immovable part of the scenery of the inlet, had weighed anchor and followed the Laigin fleet away from the coasts of Muman. What was left was a quiet, tranquil scene.

'Truly, Fidelma,' Colgú was more boisterous and no longer looking tense or weary, 'you have shown that your reputation is well founded.'

Fidelma gave an indifferent shrug.

'There is nothing to be satisfied about,' she replied. 'If I were not the instrument of the downfall of these evil people, then it would have been someone else. Didn't Euripides say that evil people by their own nature can never prosper?'

Colgú looked suddenly solemn.

'I believe that you are thinking more of Salbach than of young Nechtan, aren't you? If you had not brought about Salbach's downfall at this stage then I think that many people would have lost their lives in the resolution of that evil. At least the Corco Loígde can appoint a new chieftain and one, I trust, with more honour and humanity in him. And, perhaps, Osraige will be more content with the freedom to choose their native rulers again. So far as I am concerned, Salbach's dishonour is equally shared by Scandlán.'

Fidelma look at him approvingly.

'That is good. Although I cannot prove it, I believe that Scandlán of Osraige was involved in this plot to destroy all opposition to his dynasty. As for young Nechtan, if he accepts me as his advocate, I shall defend him,' Fidelma said firmly. 'He was the prisoner of his circumstance and his fear was great.'

'But his hand did strike those blows into Dacán's chest,' Colgú pointed out.

'And terror guided his thoughts and lent him the strength. There are degrees of culpability in all things.'

'Well, the spectre of war has diminished thanks to you, Fidelma.'

'For this time, at least,' Fidelma smiled wryly. 'My mentor, the Brehon Morann of Tara, used to say that the path of mankind through history was preceded by forests and followed by deserts and wastelands.'

'He was no optimist,' grinned Colgú.

Fidelma grimaced.

'If you can divorce yourself from people then you are bound to make the observation that mankind has very little to commend it,' she said. 'Great art and philosophy does not come out of the human condition. It arrives in spite of the human condition.'

The chimes of the vesper bell caused them to glance up simultaneously at the abbey's bell tower. Colgú grinned at his younger sister and placed a brotherly arm around her shoulders.

'Come, let us go and eat heartily. There is time to be gloomy later. I think it ill behoves you to be the pessimist, little sister.'

Fidelma allowed herself to be led towards the refectory by her brother.

'Well, the reverse is in pretending that everything is well in